Jesse Craig read the interviewer's first question and stopped. It was a simple one. "Why are you in Cannes?" Well, he thought, that's a good beginning. And a good end. He went over to the desk and sat down and pulled out a sheet of paper and a pen. "Why am I in Cannes?" He wrote slowly. He hesitated. Then, without really thinking of what he was doing or writing, he wrote, almost automatically, "I am in Cannes to save my life."

Jesse Craig is the unforgettable hero of Irwin Shaw's magnificent new novel. A film producer of great quality, Craig is at the crossroads of his life. With Craig, and his dazzling, tumultuous world, Shaw has created his finest novel.

"Stunning!"—*Minneapolis Tribune*

IRWIN SHAW

Evening in Byzantium

A DELL BOOK

Published by
DELL PUBLISHING CO., INC.
1 Dag Hammarskjold Plaza
New York, New York 10017
Copyright © 1973 by Irwin Shaw

Dell ® TM 681510, Dell Publishing Co., Inc.

ISBN: 0-440-13150-2

Reprinted by arrangement with
Delacorte Press
New York, New York 10017
Printed in the United States of America
First Dell printing—June 1974
Second Dell printing—July 1976
Third Dell printing—September 1976
Fourth Dell printing—November 1976
Fifth Dell printing—November 1976
Sixth Dell printing—March 1977
Seventh Dell printing—May 1978

TO SALKA VIERTEL

Evening in Byzantium

• OVERTURE •

Dinosauric, obsolete, functions and powers atrophied, dressed in sports shirts from Sulka and Cardin, they sat across from each other at small tables in airy rooms overlooking the changing sea and dealt and received cards just as they had done in the lush years in the rainfall forest of the West Coast when in all seasons they had announced the law in the banks, the board rooms, the Moorish mansions, the chateaux, the English castles, the Georgian town houses of Southern California.

From time to time phones rang, and hearty, deferential voices spoke from Oslo, New Delhi, Paris, Berlin, New York, and the card players barked into the instruments and gave orders that at another time would have had meaning and no doubt been obeyed.

Exiled kings on annual pilgrimage, unwitting Lears permitted small bands of faithful retainers, living in pomp without circumstance, they said, "Gin," and, "You're on the schneider," and passed checks for thousands of dollars back and forth. Sometimes they talked of the preglacial era. "I gave her her first job. Seventy-five a week. She was laying a dialogue coach in the Valley at the time."

And, "He brought it two and a half million over the budget, and we had to yank it in Chicago after three days, and now look at him, the pricks in New York say he's a genius. Shit."

And they said, "The future is in cassettes" and the

youngest of them in the room, who was fifty-eight, said, *"What future?"*

And they said, *"Spades. Double."*

Below, on the terrace seven feet above sea level, open to the sun and wind, leaner and hungrier men spoke their minds. Signaling the hurrying waiters for black coffee and aspirin, they said, "It isn't like the old days."

They also said, "The Russians aren't coming this year. Or the Japanese," and, "Venice is finished."

Under shifting clouds, in sporadic sunlight, the shifty young men carrying lion cubs and Polaroid cameras wound among them, with hustlers' international smiles, soliciting trade. But after the first day the cubs were ignored except by the tourists, and the conversation flowed on, and they said, "Fox is in trouble. Big trouble," and, "So is everybody else."

"A prize here is worth a million," they said.

"In Europe," they said.

And, "What's wrong with Europe?" they said.

"It's a Festival-type picture," they said, "but it won't draw flies in release."

And they said, "What are you drinking?" and, "Are you coming to the party tonight?"

They spoke in English, French, Spanish, German, Hebrew, Arabic, Portuguese, Rumanian, Polish, Dutch, Swedish, on the subject of sex, money, success, failure, promises kept and promises broken. They were honest men and thieves, pimps and panderers, and men of virtue. Some were talented, or more than that, some shrewd, or less than that. There were beautiful women and delicious girls, handsome men and men with the faces of swine. Cameras were busy, and everybody pretended he didn't know that photographs were being taken.

There were people who had been famous and were no longer, people who would be famous next week or next year, and people who would die unknown.

There were people going up and people going down, people who had won their victories easily and people unjustly flung aside.

They were all gamblers in a game with no rules, placing their bets debonairly or in the sweat of fear.

At other places, in other meetings, men of science were predicting that within fifty years the sea that lapped on the beach in front of the terrace would be a dead body of water and there was a strong probability that this was the last generation to dine on lobster or be able to sow an uncontaminated seed.

In still other places bombs were being dropped, targets chosen, hills lost and taken; there were floods and volcanic eruptions, wars and the preparation for wars, governments shaken, funerals and marches. But on the terrace for two weeks in springtime France, all the world was printed on sprocketed strips of acetate that passed through a projector at the rate of 90 feet per minute, and hope and despair and beauty and death were carried around the city in flat, round, shining tin cans.

• ONE •

THE plane bucked as it climbed through black pillars of cloud. To the west there were streaks of lightning. The seat-belt sign, in English and French, remained lit. The stewardesses served no drinks. The pitch of the engines changed. The passengers did not speak.

The tall man, cramped in next to the window, opened a magazine, closed it. Drops of rain made pale, transparent traces, like ghostly fingers, along the Plexiglas portholes.

There was a muffled explosion, a ripping noise. A ball of lightning rolled down the aisle, incredibly slow, then flashed out over the wing. The plane shuddered. The pitch of the engines changed again.

How comfortable it would be, the man thought, if we crashed, how definitive.

But the plane steadied, broke out of the clouds into sunlight. The lady across the aisle said, "That's the second time that's happened to me. I'm beginning to feel I'm being followed." The seat-light signs went off. The stewardesses started to push the drink cart down the aisle. The man asked for a Scotch and Perrier. He drank appreciatively as the plane whispered south, high across the clouded heart of France.

Craig took a cold shower to wake himself up. While he didn't exactly have a hangover, he had the impression that his eyes were fractionally slow in keeping up with the movements of his head. As usual on such mornings he decided to go on the wagon that day.

He dried himself without bothering to towel his hair. The cool wetness against his scalp was soothing. He wrapped himself in one of the big rough white terrycloth bathrobes the hotel supplied and went into the living room of the suite and rang for breakfast. He had flung his clothes around the room while having a last whisky before going to bed, and his dinner jacket and dress shirt and tie lay crumpled on a chair. The whisky glass, still half-full, was beaded with drops of moisture. He had left the bottle of Scotch next to it open.

He looked for mail in the box on the inside of the door. There was a copy of *Nice-Matin* and a packet of letters forwarded from New York by his secretary. There was a letter from his accountant and another from his lawyer in the packet. He recognized the monthly statement from his brokers among the other envelopes. He dropped the letters unopened on a table. With the way the market was going, his brokers' statement could only be a cry from the abyss. The accountant would be sending him unpleasant bulletins about his running battle with the Internal Revenue Service. And his lawyer's letter would remind him of his wife. They could all wait. It was too early in the morning for his broker, his accountant, his lawyer, and his wife.

He glanced at the front page of *Nice-Matin*. An agency dispatch told of more troops moving into Cambodia. *Cambodge,* in French. Next to the Cambodian story there was a picture of an Italian actress smiling on the Carlton terrace. She had won a prize at Cannes some years before, but her smile revealed that she had no illusions about this year. There was also a photograph of the president of France, M. Pompidou, in Auvergne. M. Pompidou was quoted as addressing the silent majority of the French people and assuring them that France was not on the brink of revolution.

Craig dropped *Nice-Matin* on the floor. Barefooted, he crossed the carpeted, high-ceilinged white room, furnished for liquidated Russian nobility. He went out on the balcony and regarded the Mediterranean below him on the other side of the Croisette. The three American assault ships that had been in the bay had departed during the night. There was a wind, and the sea was gray and ruffled, and there were white-caps. The beach boys had already raked the sand and put out the mattresses and umbrellas. The umbrellas trembled unopened because of the wind. A choppy surf beat at the beach. One brave fat woman was swimming in front of the hotel. The weather has changed since I was last here, he thought.

The last time had been in the autumn, past the season. Indian summer, on a coast that had never known Indians. Golden mist, muted fall flowers. He remembered Cannes when pink and amber mansions stood in gardens along the sea front. Now the garish apartment buildings, orange and bright blue balconies flying, disfigured the littoral. Cities rushed to destroy themselves.

There was a knock at the door.

"Entrez," he called without turning, still judging the Mediterranean. There was no need to tell the waiter where to put the table. Craig had been there three days already, and the waiter knew his habits.

But when he went back into the room, it was not the waiter standing there but a girl. She was small, five feet three, four, he guessed automatically. She was wearing a gray sweat shirt, too long and many sizes too large for her. The sleeves, which seemed to have been made for a basketball player, were pushed up from her narrow tan wrists. The sweat shirt hung almost halfway to her knees over wrinkled and faded blue jeans, stained with bleach. She wore sandals. Her brown hair was long and careless, streaked with sun and salt and hanging down in a mat below her shoul-

ders. She had a narrow triangular face cut into a
curious owl-like puzzle by huge, dark sunglasses behind which he could not see her eyes. An Italian
leather pouch hung, brass-buckled and incongruously
chic, from a shoulder. She slouched as she faced him.
He had the feeling that if he looked down at her bare
feet, he would discover that she had not bathed for
some time, at least not with soap.

American, he thought. It was the reverse of chauvin-
ism.

He pulled the robe around him. It had no sash, and
it was not designed for social occasions. At the slightest movement everything dangled out.

"I thought it was the waiter," he said.

"I wanted to be sure to get you in," the girl said.
The voice was American. From anywhere.

He was annoyed that the room was so sloppy.
Then annoyed at the girl for breaking in like that
when he was expecting the waiter.

"Most people call," he said, "before they come up."

"I was afraid you wouldn't see me if I called first,"
she said.

Oh, Christ, he thought, one of those. "Why don't
you start all over again, miss?" he said. "Why don't
you go downstairs and give the concierge your name
and let him announce you and . . ."

"I'm here now." She wasn't one of those smiling,
oh-you-great-man type of girls. "I'll announce myself.
My name is McKinnon, Gail McKinnon."

"Am I supposed to know you?" You never could tell
at a place like Cannes.

"No," she said.

"Do you always barge in on people when they're
undressed and waiting for breakfast?" He felt at a
disadvantage, gripping the robe to hide his private
parts and with his hair still dripping and the graying
hair on his chest visible and the room a mess.

"I have a purpose," the girl said. She didn't move

any closer to him, but she didn't retreat. She just stood there wriggling her bare toes in her sandals.

"I have a purpose, too, young lady," he said, conscious of water dripping down from his wet hair over his forehead. "I propose to eat my breakfast and read my paper and silently and singularly prepare for the terrors of the day."

"Don't be a drear, Mr. Craig," she said. "I mean you no permanent harm. You *are* alone?" She looked meaningfully at the door to the bedroom, which was ajar.

"My dear young lady . . ." I sound ninety years old, he thought, irritated.

"I mean I've been watching you," she said, "for three days, and you haven't been with anybody. Any female body, I mean." While she spoke, the dark glasses swept the room. He was conscious that her glance held for an extra fraction of a second when she saw the script on the desk.

"What are you?" he asked. "A detective?"

The girl smiled. At least her teeth smiled. There was no way of telling what her eyes were doing. "Have no fear," she said. "I'm a kind of a journalist."

"There's no news in Jesse Craig this season, miss. I bid you good morning." He took a step toward the door, but she did not move.

There was a knock, and the waiter came in carrying the tray with the orange juice and coffee, croissants and toast, and the little folding table.

"*Bonjour, m'sieur et 'dame,*" the waiter said with one swift look at the girl. The French, Craig thought, can leer instantaneously and without the slightest change of expression. He was conscious of the girl's costume, fought down an impulse to correct the leer. Shamelessly, he wanted to say to the waiter, "I can do better than *that,* for God's sake."

"I sought zere eez on'y wan breakfast," the waiter said.

"There is only one breakfast," Craig said.

"Why don't you break down, Mr. Craig," the girl said, "and ask for another cup?"

Craig sighed. "Another cup, please," he said. He had been ruled all his life by his mother's instructions about manners.

The waiter set up the table and arranged two chairs. "Eeen wan moment," he said, and left to get the second cup.

"Please be seated, Miss McKinnon," Craig said, hoping that the girl would realize that the formality was ironic. He held the chair for her with one hand while he clutched the robe closed with the other. She looked amused. At least from the nose down she looked amused. She dropped into the chair, placing her bag on the floor beside her. "And now, if you'll forgive me," he said, "I'll go in and put on some clothes more suitable for the occasion."

He picked up the script and tossed it into the desk drawer, refused to collect his jacket and shirt, and went into the bedroom, closing the door firmly behind him. He dried his hair and brushed it back, ran his hand over his jaw, thought of shaving and shook his head. He put on a white tennis shirt and blue cotton slacks and stepped into a pair of moccasins. He looked at himself briefly in the mirror, not liking the opaque ivory of the whites of his eyes.

When he went back into the living room, the girl was pouring coffee for both of them.

He drank his orange juice in silence. The girl seemed in no hurry. How many women, he thought, have I sat at a breakfast table with in my life not wanting them to talk. "Croissant?" he asked.

"No, thank you," she said. "I've eaten."

He was glad he had all his teeth as he bit into a piece of toast.

"Well, now," the girl said, "isn't this friendly? Gail McKinnon and Mr. Jesse Craig at a relaxed moment in the wild whirl of Cannes."

"Well . . ." he said.

"Does that mean I am to begin asking you questions?"

"No," he said, "it means I am going to begin asking you questions. What sort of journalist are you?"

"I'm a radio journalist. Part of the time," she said, holding her cup poised below her mouth. "I do five minute spots of people," she said, "on tape, for a syndicate that sells them to independent stations in America."

"What sort of people?"

"Interesting people. At least the syndicate hopes so." Her voice was flat and slurred, as though she was impatient with questions. "Movie stars, directors, artists, politicians, criminals, athletes, racing-car drivers, diplomats, deserters, people who believe that homosexuality should be legalized or marijuana, detectives, college presidents . . . Want any more?"

"No." Craig watched while she poured him more coffee, the lady of the house. "You said part of the time. What do you do the rest of the time?"

"I try to write interviews in depth for magazines. You're making a face. Why?"

"In depth," he said.

"You're right," she said. "Deadly jargon. You fall into it. It shall never pass my lips again."

"The morning has not been wasted," Craig said.

"Interviews like the ones in *Playboy*. Or that Falacci woman," she said. "The one who got shot by the soldiers in Mexico."

"I read a couple of hers. She cut up Fellini. And Hitchcock."

"Maybe they cut themselves up."

"Should I take that as a warning?"

"If you want."

There was something disturbing about the girl. He had the impression that she wanted something more than she was asking for.

"This town," he said, "is overrun at the moment by

hordes of publicity-hungry folk who are dying to be interviewed. People your readers, whoever they are, drool for information about. I'm somebody nobody has heard from for years. Why pick on me?"

"I'll tell you some other time, Mr. Craig," she said. "When we get to know each other better."

"Five years ago," he said, "I would have kicked you out of this room ten minutes ago."

"That's why I wouldn't have interviewed you five years ago." She smiled again, owl-like.

"I'll tell you what," he said. "You show me some of the magazine pieces that you've done on other people, and I'll read them and decide if I want to take a chance on you."

"Oh, I couldn't do that," she said.

"Why not?"

"I haven't published any." She chuckled briefly, as though what she had said had delighted her. "You'll be my first."

"Good God, Miss," he said, "stop wasting my time." He stood up.

She remained seated. "I will ask fascinating questions," she said, "and you will give such fascinating answers that editors will tumble madly over themselves to publish the article."

"The interview is closed, Miss McKinnon. I hope you enjoy your stay on the Côte d'Azur."

Still she didn't move. "It can only do you good, Mr. Craig," the girl said. "I can help you."

"What makes you think I need help?" Craig said.

"In all these years you never came to Cannes for the Festival," the girl said. "All the years you were turning out one picture after another. Now, when you haven't had your name on a movie since 1965, you arrive, you install yourself in a big plush suite, you're seen every day in the Hall, on the terrace, at the official parties. You want something this year. And whatever it is, a big splashy piece about you might just be the thing to help you get it."

"How do you know this is the first time I came for the Festival?"

"I know a lot about you, Mr. Craig," she said. "I've done my homework."

"You're wasting your time, miss," he said. "I'm afraid I'll have to ask you to leave. I have a busy day ahead of me."

"What are you going to do today?" Infuriatingly, she picked up a croissant and took a small bite out of it.

"I am going to lie on the beach," he said, "and listen to the waves roll in from Africa. There's an example of the fascinating answers I'm likely to give you."

The girl sighed like a mother humoring a recalcitrant infant. "All right," she said. "It's against my principles, but I'll let you read something." She reached down into her bag and pulled out a batch of yellow paper covered with typescript. "Here," she said, offering him the pages.

He kept his hands behind his back.

"Don't be childish, Mr. Craig," she said sharply. "Read it. It's about you."

"I detest reading anything about myself."

"Don't lie, Mr. Craig," she said, impatient again.

"You have a remarkable way of ingratiating yourself with potential interviewees, miss," he said. But he took the pages and went over to the window where the light was better because he'd have had to put on his glasses to read in the shadowed room.

"If I do it for *Playboy*," the girl said, "what you have there will be in the form of an introduction, before the actual questions and answers begin."

At least, he thought, the girls in *Playboy* have their hair done before they present themselves.

"Do you mind if I pour myself another cup of coffee?" she asked.

"By all means." He heard the china clink of the spout against the cup rim as he began to read.

"To the general public," he read, "the word 'producer' usually has pejorative connotations. The cliché about a movie producer is that he is likely to be a portly Jewish gentleman with a cigar in his mouth, a peculiar vocabulary, and a distasteful penchant for starlets. Or for that small group who have been influenced by F. Scott Fitzgerald's romantic idealization of the late Irving Thalberg in his unfinished novel *The Last Tycoon,* he is a mysteriously gifted dark figure, a benevolent Svengali, half-magician, half-master politician, who strangely resembles F. Scott Fitzgerald himself in his more attractive moments.

"The popular image of the theatrical producer is somewhat less colorful. He is less likely to be thought of as Jewish or fundamentally gross, although the admiration with which he is regarded is limited. If he is successful, he is envied as a lucky man who by chance one day picks up a script that happens to be lying on his desk, scrambles around for other people's money to back the production, and then coasts happily forward to fame and fortune on the talents of artists whose work he most often tries to corrupt in an attempt to please the Broadway market.

"Curiously enough, in a related field, that of the ballet, honor is given where honor is due. Diaghilev, who as far as is known never danced a step or choreographed a *pas de deux* or painted a décor, is recognized everywhere as a giant innovator of the modern ballet. While Goldwyn (Jewish, whip-thin, no cigar) and Zanuck (non-Jewish, with cigar, wiry) and Selznick (Jewish, portly, cigarettes) and Ponti (Italian, plump, no cigar) are not perhaps what magazines like *Commentary* and the *Partisan Review* call seminal figures in the art that they served, the films that they have produced and that plainly bear their individual marks have influenced the thinking and attitudes of populations all over the world and certainly prove that they came to their tasks equipped with something more than luck and money or an influential family devoted to nepotism."

Well, he thought grudgingly, you can't fault her grammar. She's been to school *someplace*. But he was still irritated by the offhand manner in which Gail McKinnon had broken into his morning. And irritated even more by her cool assumption that he would perform obediently. Craig would have liked to put the yellow pages down and order her from the room. But his vanity was aroused, and he wondered how she would place the name of Jesse Craig in her roster of heroes. He had to make an effort not to glance in her direction and examine her more closely. He read on.

"In the American theatre," he read, "the case is even clearer. In the 1920s Lawrence Langner and Terry Helburn, with their Theatre Guild, opened new horizons of drama, and as late as the 1940s, still functioning not as directors or writers but solely as producers, they transformed that most American of theatrical forms, the musical comedy, with *Oklahoma*. Clurman, Strasberg, and Crawford, the ruling trio of the Group Theater, while sometimes directors in their own right, made their chief contribution in their choice of controversial plays and the method of training actors in ensemble playing."

She wasn't lying, Craig thought. She had done her homework. She wasn't even born when any of this was going on. He looked up. "May I ask you a question?"

"Of course."

"How old are you?"

"Twenty-two," she said. "Does it make any difference?"

"It always makes a difference," he said. He read on with ungenerous respect. "More recent names are not hard to find, but there is no need to belabor the point. There was almost certainly someone, whatever he was called, who took on the task of assembling the talents for the festivals in which Aeschylus and Sophocles competed, and Burbage saw to it that the Globe Theatre was a running concern when Shakespeare brought in *Hamlet* for him to read.

"In this long and honorable list we now come to Jesse Craig."

Brace yourself, he thought. This is where the brick drops.

"In 1946," he read, "Jesse Craig, then aged twenty-four, first commanded attention when he presented *The Foot Soldier,* still one of the few viable dramatic works about World War Two. Between 1946 and 1965 Craig produced 10 more plays and 12 movies, a high proportion of them both critical and commercial successes. Since 1965 no production bearing his name has been seen either on the stage or screen."

The phone rang. "Excuse me," he said, picking it up.

"Craig speaking," he said.

"Did I wake you?"

"No." He glanced guardedly at the girl. She slouched in her chair, absurd in the oversized sweat shirt.

"Did you dream lascivious dreams of me all the terrible night?"

"Not that I remember."

"Brute. Are you having a good time?"

"Yes."

"Double brute," Constance said. "Are you alone?"

"No."

"Ah."

"You know better than that."

"Anyway, you can't talk at the moment?"

"Not exactly. How is Paris?"

"Sweltering. And the French as usual intolerable."

"Where are you calling from?"

"The office."

He could picture her in her office—a small, cramped

room on the rue Marbeuf, usually crowded with a dozen young men and women who looked as though they had rowed across the Atlantic instead of arriving on the freighters and steamships and aircraft for student tours that her business was to arrange for them. Anyone under the age of thirty, in whatever state, seemed to be welcome there, and it was only when Constance got a whiff of marijuana that she would rise dramatically from the desk, point fiercely at the door, and clear the room.

"Aren't you afraid someone's listening?" he asked.

Constance was intermittently suspicious that her telephone was tapped—by the French tax people, by the American narcotics people, by ex-lovers highly placed in various embassies.

"I'm not saying anything the French don't know. They glory in being intolerable."

"How're the kids?"

"As usual. Well-balanced. One angelic. One devilish."

Constance had been married twice, once to an Italian, once to an Englishman. The boy was the result of the Italian and had been thrown out of four schools by the age of eleven.

"Gianni was sent home again yesterday," Constance said matter-of-factly. "He was organizing a gang-bang in his art class."

"Come on, Constance." She was given to exaggeration.

"Actually, I think he tried to throw a little girl with glasses out of the window. He says she was looking at him. Anyway, something perfectly normal. He can go back in two days. I think they're going to give Philippa a copy of *The Critique of Pure Reason* as a term prize. They took her IQ, and they say she could be president of IBM."

"Tell her I'll bring her a navy blue sailor's jersey from here."

"Bring her a man to put inside it," Constance said. She was certain that her children, like herself, were swamped in sexuality. Philippa was nine. To Craig the girl didn't seem much different from his own daughters at that age. Except that she didn't stand up when grownups came into the room and that she sometimes used words from her mother's vocabulary that he would have preferred not to hear.

"How're things down there?" Constance asked.

"Okay."

Gail McKinnon got up politely and went out to the balcony, but he was sure she could still hear what he was saying.

"Oh," Constance said, "I put in a good word for you last night with an old friend of yours."

"Thanks. Who was it?"

"I had dinner with David Teichman. He always calls me when he comes through Paris."

"Along with ten thousand other people who always call you when they come through Paris."

"You wouldn't want a girl to have dinner alone, would you?"

"Never."

"Anyway, he's a hundred years old. He's coming down to Cannes. He says he's thinking of starting a new company. I told him you might have something for him. He's going to call you. Do you mind? At the worst, he's harmless."

"He'd die if he heard you say that." David Teichman had terrorized Hollywood for more than twenty years.

"Well, I did my bit." She sighed into the phone. "I had a bad morning. I woke up and reached out and said, 'Damn him.' "

"Why?"

"Because you weren't there. Do you miss me?"

"Yes."

"You sound as though you're speaking from a police station."

"Something like that."

"Don't hang up. I'm bored. Did you have bouilla-baisse for dinner last night?"

"No."

"Do you miss me?"

"I've already answered that."

"That's what a girl might call a very cool reply."

"It wasn't meant to be."

"Do you wish I was there?"

"Yes."

"Say my name."

"I'd rather not at the moment."

"When I hang up, I'm going to be prey to dark suspicions."

"Put your mind at rest."

"This call has been an almost total waste of money. I dread tomorrow morning."

"Why?"

"Because I'm going to wake up and reach out and you won't be there again."

"Don't be gluttonous."

"I'm a gluttonous lady. Well, get whoever it is out of the room and call me back."

"Will do."

"Say my name."

"Pest."

There was a laugh at the other end of the wire. Then the click as Constance hung up.

He put the phone down. The girl came back into the room. "I hope I didn't cramp your style," she said.

"Not at all," he said.

"You look happier than before the call," the girl said.

"Do I? I wasn't aware of it."

"Do you always answer the phone that way?"

"What way?"

"Craig speaking."

He thought for a moment. "I suppose so. Why?"

"It sounds so—institutional," the girl said. "Don't your friends object?"

"If they do," he said, "they don't tell me about it."

"I hate institutions," she said. "If I had to work in an office, I'd—" She shrugged and sat down in the chair at the breakfast table. "How do you like what you've read so far?"

"Early in my career I resolved never to make a judgment on unfinished work," he said.

"Do you still want to go on reading?"

"Yes," he said.

"I'll be still as the starry night." She slumped in the chair, leaning back, crossing her legs. Her sandalled feet were actually clean, he noticed. He remembered how many times over the years he had ordered his daughters to sit up straight. They still didn't sit up straight. The nonerect generation. He picked up the yellow pages that he had put down when he answered the telephone and began reading again.

"At the time of this interview," he read, "Craig received McK in the living room of his hundred-dollar-a-day suite in the Hotel Carlton, the pinkish ginger-bread headquarters for the VIPs of the Cannes Film Festival. He is a tall, slim, slow-moving, bony man with thick graying hair worn long and carelessly brushed back from a forehead deeply ridged by wrinkles. His eyes are a cold pale gray, deeply set in their sockets. He is forty-eight now, and he looks it. His glance is hooded, the eyelids characteristically almost half-shut. One gets the impression of a sentinel scanning the field below him through an aperture in a fortress wall. His voice, from which not all traces of his native New York have disappeared, is slow and husky. His manner is old-fashioned, distant, polite. His style of dress, in this town of peacock adornment for men and women alike, is conservative. He might be a Harvard professor of literature on a summer holiday in Maine. He is not handsome. The lines of his face are too flat and hard for that and his mouth too thin and disciplined. In Cannes, where a number of the assembled notables had either worked for him or with him and where he was greeted warmly at every appearance, he seemed to have many acquaintances and no friends. On two of his first three evenings at the festival he dined alone. On each occasion he drank three martinis before and a full bottle of wine with his meal, with no noticeable effect."

Craig shook his head and put the yellow pages down on the bookcase near the window. There were still three or four that he hadn't read.

"What's the matter?" the girl asked. She had been watching him closely. He had been conscious of her stare through the dark glasses and had carefully remained expressionless while he read. "You find a bubu?"

"No," he said. "I find the character unsympathetic."

"Read on," the girl said. "He improves." She stood up, slouching. "I'll leave it with you. I know what a strain it is reading something with the author watching you."

"Better take this stuff with you." Craig gestured toward the small pile of pages. "I am a notorious loser of manuscripts."

"Not to worry," the girl said. "I have a carbon."

The phone rang again. He picked it up. "Craig speaking," he said. Then he looked across at the girl and wished he hadn't said it.

"My boy," the voice said.

"Hello, Murph," he said. "Where are you?"

"London."

"How is it there?"

"Expiring," Murphy said. "Inside of six months they'll be turning the studios into feeding lots for Black Angus bulls. How's it down there?"

"Cold and windy."

"It's got to be better than here," Murphy said. As

usual, he spoke so loudly that everybody in the room could hear him. "We're changing our plans. We're flying down tonight instead of next week. We're booked in at the Hotel du Cap. Can you have lunch with us tomorrow there?"

"Of course."

"Perfect," Murphy said. "Sonia says give him my love."

"Give her my love," Craig said.

"Don't tell anyone I'm coming," Murphy said. "I want a few days rest. I don't want to have to run into Cannes to talk to spitballing Italians three times a day."

"Your secret is safe with me," Craig said.

"I'll call the hotel," Murphy said, "and tell them to put the wine on ice."

"I was thinking of going on the wagon today," Craig said.

"Not on my time, my boy," Murphy said. "See you tomorrow."

"Tomorrow," Craig said, and hung up.

"I couldn't help overhearing," the girl said. "That was your agent, wasn't it? Bryan Murphy?"

"How do you know so much?" Craig asked. His tone was sharper than he intended it to be.

"Everybody knows who Bryan Murphy is," the girl said. "Do you think he'd talk to me?"

"You'll have to ask him yourself, Miss," Craig said. "I'm not his agent, he's mine."

"I imagine he will. He's talked to everybody else," she said. "Anyway, there's no rush. We'll see how things work out. It'd be nice if I could listen in on you two talking for an hour or two. In fact, the best way to do the whole job," she went on, "would be to let me hang around with you for a few days. An admiring silent presence. You can introduce me as your niece or your secretary or your mistress. I'd put on a dress. I have a wonderful memory, and I won't embarrass you by taking notes. I'll just watch and listen."

"Please don't be so insistent, Miss McKinnon," Craig said. "I had a bad night."

"All right, I won't bother you anymore this morning," she said. "I'll just flee and let you read the rest of what I wrote about you and let you think it over." She slung her bag over her shoulder. Her movements were brusque, not girlish. She was not slouching now. "I'll be around. Everywhere. Wherever you turn, you'll see Gail McKinnon. Thanks for the coffee. Don't bother to see me out."

Before he could protest any further, she was gone.

• TWO •

HE paced slowly around the room. Its appearance displeased him. It was a room for frivolous transients whose only decision each morning would be whether or not to go swimming and what restaurant to choose for lunch. He tapped in the top of the Scotch bottle and put the bottle away in a cabinet, then picked up his clothes and the sweating half-filled whisky glass. He took it all into the bedroom, dumped the clothes on the bed in which he had slept. The sheets and blankets were tangled. Uneasy sleeper. The second bed was neatly turned down. Whatever lady the maid had prepared it for had slept elsewhere. It made the room seem lonely. He went into the bathroom and emptied the whisky glass into the basin and rinsed it. The counterfeit of order.

He returned to the living room and carried the little folding table with the breakfast tray out into the hall. He locked the door behind him as he went back into the apartment.

There was an untidy pile of brochures and advertising throwaways for various films on the desk. He swept them all into the wastebasket. Other people's hopes, lies, talents, greed.

The letters he had tossed on the table lay next to Miss McKinnon's manuscript. He decided on the letters. Finally, they would have to be read and answered, anyway. He tore open the letter from his accountant. First things first. That primal concern—the income tax.

"Dear Jesse," his accountant wrote, "I'm afraid the 1966 audit is going to be a tough one. The agent on your case has been in and out of the office five times, and he's a bastard. I'm writing this from my home myself, on my own typewriter, so there won't be a copy, and I advise you to burn it when you've read it.

"As you know, we've had to waive the three-year limit of review on your 1966 return; 1966 was the last time you made any real money, and Bryan Murphy set up this deal with a European company because you shot most of the picture in France and the deal looked good to everybody because it seemed that the money your company borrowed against potential profits would be treated as capital gains rather than ordinary income. Well, the IRS is challenging the basis of the deal, and this agent is a real bloodhound.

"Also—and this is for your eyes only—this particular agent looks like a crook to me. He as much as intimated to me that if you did business with him, he'd O.K. the return as filed. For a price. He intimated that eight thousand dollars would do it.

"Now you know that I never touch anything like that. I know, too, that you've never gone in for any such shenanigans, either. But I felt that you had to know what the score was. If you want to do anything about it, you'd better come out here soonest and talk to the bastard himself. And don't tell me what you say to him.

"We could go to court and almost certainly win, as the deal is on the up and up and should stand scrutiny in any court of law. But I have to warn you that the legal costs would probably run you about $100,000. And considering who you are and your reputation, the papers would have a field day with a tax-avoidance case in which you were involved.

"I think we can settle with the bastard for between sixty and seventy-five thousand. My advice is to settle and get a job quick and make it up in a year or two.

"When you answer this, send your letter to my home address. I've got a big office, and you never know whom you can trust there. Aside from the fact that the Government is not averse to opening mail these days. Best regards, Lester."

Make it up in a year or two, Craig thought. It must have been sunny in California.

He tore the letter into small pieces and threw them into the wastebasket. Burning it, as the accountant had suggested, would have been too melodramatic. And he doubted that the Internal Revenue Service went as far as bribing the chambermaids of the Côte d'Azur to piece together the shreds of letters they found in wastebaskets.

Patriot, veteran, law-abider, taxpayer, he refused to think about how his sixty or seventy thousand dollars would be spent by Mr. Nixon, by the Pentagon, by the FBI, by Congress. There was a limit to the amount of moral agony a man could be expected to inflict upon himself when he was, theoretically at least, on holiday. Maybe I ought to let Gail McKinnon read my mail, he thought. The readers of *Playboy* would be fascinated. Diaghilev at the mercy of a postage stamp.

He reached for the letter from his lawyer, then thought better of it. He picked up the batch of yellow sheets, weighed them, held them indecisively over the wastebasket. He shuffled through the pages at random. *He is forty-eight now and looks it,* he read. What does a forty-eight-year-old man look like to a twenty-two-year-old girl? Ruins. The walls of Pompeii. The trenches of Verdun. Hiroshima.

He sat down at the desk, started reading from where he had left off when the girl had gone out of the room. See yourself as the world sees you.

"He does not seem like a self-indulgent man," he read, "and according to all reports he does not indulge in others.

"Because of this, in some quarters he has a reputation for ruthlessness. He has made many enemies, and among his former collaborators there are some who speak of what they call his disloyalty. In support of this it is cited that only once has he ever done more than one play by the same author and unlike other producers has never developed a favorite roster of actors. It must be admitted that when his last two films failed, for a total loss that is estimated at more than eight million dollars, there was little sympathy shown him in the movie colony."

The bitch, he thought, where did she get that? Unlike most other journalists who had interviewed him and who had rarely read anything more about him than they had gleaned from studio publicity handouts, the girl had arrived well prepared. Malevolently well prepared. He skipped two pages, dropping them on the floor, and read on.

"It is common knowledge that at least on one occasion he was offered the top position at one of the most prestigious studios in the industry. It is said he turned the offer down in a brief telegram: 'Have already deserted sinking ship. Craig.'

"His behavior might be explained by the fact that he is a rich man, or should be a rich man if he has handled the money he has earned in a responsible manner. A director he has worked with has put it differently. 'He's just a contrary son of a bitch,' is the way the director explained it. The actress Monica Browning has been quoted in an interview as saying, 'There is no mystery there. Jesse Craig is a simple, charming, homemade megalomaniac.'"

I need something to drink, he thought. He looked at his watch. It was ten twenty-five. So, it's only ten twenty-five, he thought. He got the bottle and went into the bathroom and poured a slug of whisky and ran a little water into the glass from the tap. He took a sip and carried the glass with him back into the living room.

Glass in hand, he continued reading. "Twice Craig has been invited to serve as a member of the jury in Cannes. Twice he refused the invitation. When it became known that he had made reservations for the entire festival this year, many eyebrows were raised. For five years, after the failure of his last film, he has kept away from Hollywood and was only intermittently seen in New York. He has kept his office open but has announced no new projects. He seems to have taken to wandering restlessly for good parts of the recent years around the Continent. The reasons for his retreat are obscure. Disgust? Disillusionment? Weariness? A feeling that his work was done and the time had come to enjoy its fruits in peace in places where he had neither friends nor enemies? Or was it a failure of nerve? Is the visitor to Cannes a spent man on a nostalgic voyage to a place where he can be reminded at every turn of his earlier vigor? Or is it the sallying forth of a man who has regrouped his forces and is intent once more on conquest?

"Does Jesse Craig, in his hundred-dollar-a-day suite overlooking the Mediterranean know the answers himself?"

The typing stopped in the middle of the page. He put the pages face down on the bookcase, sipped once more from his drink. Christ, he thought, twenty-two years old.

He went out on the balcony. The sun had come out, although the wind was as strong as ever. Nobody was swimming. The fat lady had disappeared. Having her hair done or drifted out to sea. Down below, on the terrace, there was already a sprinkling of customers around the tables. He saw the careless brown hair of Gail McKinnon, the oversized sweat shirt, the blue jeans. She was reading a newspaper, a bottle of Coca-Cola in front of her.

While he was watching, a man came up to her table and sat down across from her. She put away her newspaper. Craig was too high up to hear what she was saying.

"I saw him," she was saying to the man. "He'll bite. I've got the old bastard."

• THREE •

HE took a seat. The auditorium was filling rapidly. It was a young crowd, long-haired bearded boys with Indian bands around their heads and their accompanying barefooted girls dressed in fringed leather blouses and long multicolored skirts. They would have been at home in Constance's office. The movie that morning was going to be *Woodstock*, the American documentary about a rock festival, and the devotees, appropriately clad for revolt, had taken over the town. Craig wondered how they all would dress when they were his age. When he was *their* age, he had been happy just to shed his uniform and get into a gray suit.

He put on his glasses and spread his copy of *Nice-Matin*. He had awakened late, and since the movie was three and a half hours long, it had been scheduled to start at nine in the morning, and he hadn't had time for breakfast or the paper in the hotel.

In the warm, dull pinkish light he glanced at the front page of the newspaper. Four students had been shot and killed by the National Guard in Kent, Ohio. Murder continued, as usual, along the Suez Canal. The situation in Cambodia was confused. A French naval missile had gotten out of control and turned inland and burst near Lavandou, some miles along the coast, destroying several villas. The mayors of the adjacent towns were protesting, pointing out, reasonably enough, that this military waywardness was detrimental to *le tourisme*. A French movie director explained, in an interview, why he would never submit a film of his to the Festival.

Somebody said, *"Pardon,"* and Craig stood up, still trying to read his newspaper. There was a rustle of a long skirt as somebody slid past him and sank into the seat beside him. He was conscious of a light scent of soap that was somehow childish.

"Welcome to the morning," the girl said.

He recognized the dark glasses masking most of the face. The girl's head was wrapped in a figured silk scarf. He was sorry that he hadn't taken the time to shave.

"Isn't it wonderful," the girl said, "how we are constantly thrown together?"

"Wonderful," he said. The voice, as well as the costume, was different today. Softer, without pressure.

"I was there last night, too," she said.

"I didn't see you."

"That's what they all say." The girl looked down at her program. "Were you ever tempted to do a documentary?"

"Like everybody else."

"People say this one is *wild.*"

"Which people?"

"Just people." She let the program drop to the floor. "Did you cast an eye on the stuff I sent over?"

"I didn't even have time to order breakfast," he said.

"I like movies at nine in the morning," she said. "There's something perverse in it. It's in a big manila envelope. Further reflections on Jesse Craig. Cast an eye when you have time." She began to applaud. A tall young man with a beard was standing at the bottom of the aisle in front of the stage holding up his hand for silence. "That's the director," she confided.

"Do you know anything else he's done?"

"No." She applauded vigorously. "I'm a director buff."

The director was wearing a black armband, and he

began his speech by inviting the members of the audience to do the same as a sign of mourning for the four students who had been killed at Kent State. In his final sentence he said that he was dedicating his film to their memory.

Although Craig did not doubt the young man's sincerity, the speech and the somber decoration made him vaguely uncomfortable. In another place, perhaps, he would have been touched. He certainly was as saddened by the death of the four youths as anybody there. After all, he himself had two children of his own who might be brought down in a similar massacre. But he was in an auditorium that was gilded and luxurious, seated among an audience that was festive and there to be amused. He could not rid himself of the feeling that the whole thing smacked of showmanship, not grief.

"Are you going to wear black?" the girl asked him, whispering.

"I don't think so."

"Nor I," she said. "I don't dignify death." She sat up, straight and alert, enjoying herself He tried to pretend he didn't know she was sitting beside him.

As the house lights went down and the film began, Craig made a conscious effort to rid himself of all preconceptions. He knew that his distaste for beards and long hair was foolish and arose only because he had grown to manhood at a different time, accustomed to different styles. The manner of dress of the young people around him was at worst merely unsanitary. Fashions in clothes came and went, and a single glance at an old family album sufficed to show how ridiculous once thoroughly conservative garb could seem to later eyes. His father had worn plus fours on a holiday at the beach. He still remembered the photograph.

"*Woodstock*," he had been told, spoke for the young. If it actually did, he was ready to listen.

He watched with interest. It was immediately clear that the man who had made the picture had consider-

able talent. A professional himself, Craig appreciated the quality in others, and there was no hint of
amateurism or idle playfulness in the way the film was
shot and put together. The evidence of hard thought
and painstaking labor was everywhere. But the spec-
tacle of four hundred thousand human beings gathered together in one place, no matter who they were
or in what place they had congregated, or for what
purpose, was distasteful to him. There was a mani-
acal promiscuity reflected on the screen that depressed
him more and more as the film went on. And the music and the performances, with the exception of two
songs sung by Joan Baez, seemed coarse and repetitive to him and inhumanly loud, as though the whisper or even the ordinary tone of daily conversation
had dropped from the vocal range of young Americans. For Craig the film was a succession of orgiastic
howls without the release of orgasm. When the camera
discovered a boy and a girl making love, undisturbed
by the fact that their act was being recorded, he averted his eyes.

He watched in disbelief as one of the performers,
like a cheerleader before a crowd at a football game,
shouted out, "Give me an F!" Four hundred thousand
voices gave him an F. "Give me a U!" Four hundred
thousand voices gave him a U. "Give me a C!" Four
hundred thousand voices responded with a C. "Give
me a K!" Four hundred thousand voices gave him a K.
"What's that spell?" the cheerleader shouted, his voice
limitlessly magnified by the public address system.

"FUCK!" came the response in a hoarse, Nuremberg-
rally tidal wave of sound. Then a wild cheering. The
audience in the theatre applauded. The girl beside
him, Craig noticed, sat with her hands primly clasped
in her lap. He liked her the better for it.

He sat quietly in his seat but paid little attention to
the film after that. Who could say what that gigantic
many-throated FUCK! meant? It was a word like any
other, and he used it himself, although not often. It

was neither ugly nor beautiful in itself, and its use was now so widespread that it had almost no meaning or so many different meanings that it was no longer valid linguistic coin. In the voices of the giant choir of the young in the film it had a primitive derision, it was a slogan, a weapon, a banner under which huge destructive battalions could march. He hoped that the fathers of the four students who had been shot at Kent State would never see *Woodstock* and know that a work of art that had been dedicated to their dead children contained a passage in which nearly half a million of their children's contemporaries had mourned their death by shouting FUCK! in unison.

The film had more than an hour yet to run when he left the theatre. The girl didn't seem to notice that he was going.

The sun was shining over the blue sea, and the flags of the nations represented in the festival snapped brightly at their poles on the theater's façade. Even with the continuous traffic of cars along the waterfront and the passage of the crowds on the sidewalk and promenade, it was blessedly quiet. For this morning, at least, Cannes remembered that it was supposed to look like a Dufy.

Craig went down to the beach and walked by the water's edge, unaccompanied, a private man.

He went up to his room to shave. In the mailbox there was the large manila envelope with his name scrawled on it in a slanting, bold woman's hand and a letter post-marked San Francisco from his daughter Anne.

He tossed the envelopes onto a table in the salon and went into the bathroom and shaved carefully. Then, his face pleasingly smarting from lotion, he went back into the salon and slit open Gail McKinnon's envelope.

There was a hand-written note on top of a pile of typed yellow pages.

"Dear Mr. Craig," he read, "I'm writing this late at night in my hotel room, wondering what's wrong with me. All my life people have been glad to see me, but this afternoon and evening, every time I as much as looked in your direction, on the beach and at lunch, in the lobby of the Festival Hall, at the bar, at the party, you made me feel as though I were Hurricane Gail on her way to lay waste the city. In your career you must have given hundreds of interviews. To people who were a lot more stupid than I am, I bet, and quite a few who were downright hostile. Why not to me?

"Well, if you won't talk to me about yourself, there are a lot of people who will, and I haven't been wasting my time. If I can't get the man whole, I'll get him refracted through a hundred different pairs of eyes. If he comes out not terribly happy about himself, that's his fault and not mine."

He recognized the reporter's usual gambit. If you won't tell me the truth, I will get your enemy to tell me lies. It was probably taught in the first year a all schools of journalism.

"Maybe," he read, "I'll do the piece in an entirely different way. Like a scientist observing the wild animal in his natural state. From afar, using stealth and a telescopic lens. *The animal has a well-developed sense of territory, is wary of man, drinks strong waters, has an inefficient instinct for survival, mates often, with the most attractive females in the herd.*"

He chuckled. She would be difficult to defeat.

"I lie in wait," the note finished. "I do not despair. I enclose some more drivel on the subject, neatly typed. It is now four A.M., and I will carry my pages through the dangerous dark streets of Gomorrah-by-the-sea to your hotel and cross your concierge's palm with silver so that the first thing you will see when you wake in the morning is the name of Gail McKinnon."

He put the note down and, without glancing at the typewritten yellow pages, picked up his daughter's letter. Every time he got a letter from either one of his daughters, he remembered the dreadful confession Scott Fitzgerald's daughter had written somewhere that whenever she got a letter from her father while she was in college, she would tear it open and shake it to see if a check would fall out and then toss the letter, unread, into a desk drawer.

He opened the letter. A father could do no less.

"Dear Dad," he read, in Anne's cramped, schoolgirlish handwriting, "San Francisco is Gloomstown. The college is just about closed down, and it might just as well be a war. The Huns are everywhere. On both sides. Springtime is for Mace. Everybody is so boringly convinced he's right. As far as I can tell, our black friends want me to learn about African tribal dances and ritual circumcision of young ladies rather than the Romantic poets. The Romantic poets are irrelevant, see. The professors are as bad as everybody else. On both sides. Education is square, chick. I don't even bother hanging around the campus anymore. If you do go there, twenty people ask you to lay your pure white body down in front of the Juggernaut for twenty different reasons. No matter what you do, you are a traitor to your generation. If you don't think Jerry Rubin is the finest fruit of young American manhood, your father is a bank president or a secret agent for the CIA or, God forbid, Richard Nixon. Maybe I'll take up simultaneous membership in the Black Panthers and the John Birch Society and show everybody. To paraphrase a well-known writer: Neither a student nor a policeman be.

"I know I was the one who wanted to go to college in San Francisco because after the years of school in Switzerland some insane superpatriot convinced me I was losing my American-ness, whatever that is, and that San Francisco was the town where the real action was. And I was planning to get a job as a waitress at Lake Tahoe this summer to see how the other half lives. I no longer give a damn how the other half lives. This may be temporary, I realize. I'm abashed how temporary so many of my ideas are. Most of them don't last till lunch. And I couldn't help being American, God help me, if I lived to be a hundred. What I'd like, if it wouldn't be too much of a burden on you, would be to get on a plane and come over to Europe for the summer and let them sort things out at the college without me before the fall term begins.

"If I do come to Europe, I'd like to avoid Mother as much as I can. I suppose you know she's in Geneva this month. She writes me dire letters about how impossible you are and that you are out to destroy her and that you're a libertine and suffering from the male menopause and I don't know what all. And ever since she found out I take the Pill, she treats me as though I'm Fanny Hill or a character out of the Marquis de Sade, and the evenings will be long on the banks of Lac Léman if I visit her.

"Your favorite daughter Marcia writes from time to time from Arizona. She is very happy there, she says, except for her weight. Obviously, no news gets through to the University of Arizona, and it is still like those old college musicals with panty raids and pillow fights you see on the Late Late Show. She is putting on weight, she says, because she eats compulsively because our happy home has been broken up. Freud, Freud, in the ice cream parlor.

"I've made a lot of jokes in this letter, I see, but Daddy, I don't feel funny. Love, Anne."

He sighed as he put his daughter's letter down. I will go someplace without an address, he thought, without a post office, without a telephone. He wondered what his letters home to his mother and father, written during the war, would sound like to him if he read them now. He had burned them all when he had found them in a trunk, neatly bound, after his mother's death.

He picked up Gail McKinnon's yellow pages. Might as well get all the day's reading done at one time before facing the day.

He carried the pages out to the balcony and sat down on one of the chairs in the sun. Even if he gained nothing else from the expedition to Cannes, he would have a suntan.

"Item," he read, "he is a formal man, a keeper of distances. Dressed in a slightly old-fashioned dinner jacket at a party in the ballroom off the Winter Casino, given after the evening showing, he seemed ambassadorial, remote. In the hothouse atmosphere of this place, where effusive camaraderie is the rule of the game, where men embrace and women kiss people they barely know, his politeness can be chilling. He spoke to no one for more than five minutes at a time but moved constantly around the room, not restlessly but with cool detachment. There were many beautiful women present, and there were two at least with whom his name had been linked. The two ladies, magnificently gowned and coiffed, seemed, to this observer, at least, to be eager to keep him at their side, but he allotted them only his ceremonial five minutes and moved on."

Linked, he thought angrily. *With whom his name has been linked.* Someone has been feeding her information. Someone who knows me well and who is not my friend. He had seen Gail McKinnon at the party across the room and had nodded to her. But he had not noticed that she had followed him around.

"It was not the economic condition of the Craig family that prevented Craig from going to college, as the family was comparatively well-off. Craig's father, Philip, was the treasurer of several Broadway theatres until his death in 1946, and while he was undoubtedly under some financial strain during the Depression, he certainly could have afforded to send his only child to college when he reached the age to apply. But Craig chose instead to enlist in the army shortly after Pearl Harbor. Although he served for nearly five years and rose to the rank of technical sergeant, he won no decorations aside from theatre and campaign ribbons."

There was an asterisk after this, indicating a footnote.

On the bottom of the page, under another asterisk, he read the footnote. "Dear Mr. C., this is all desperately dull stuff, but until you unbutton, all I can do is amass facts. When the time comes to put everything together, I shall mercilessly trim so as to keep the reader from dying of boredom."

He went back to the paragraph above the footnote. "He was lucky enough to come out of the war unscathed and even luckier to have in his duffel bag the script of a play by a young fellow enlisted man, Edward Brenner, which, a year after Craig's discharge from the army, he presented under the title *The Foot Soldier*. The elder Craig's theatrical connections undoubtedly aided considerably in allowing a very young and completely unknown beginner to manage so difficult a coup.

"Brenner had two more plays on Broadway in later years, both disastrous flops. One of them was produced by Craig. Brenner has since completely dropped out of sight."

Maybe out of your sight, young lady, Craig thought, but not out of his or out of mine. If he ever reads this, I will hear from my young fellow enlisted man.

"On the subject of his rarely working with creative people more than once, he is reputed to have said, not for quotation, 'It is generally believed in literary circles that everybody has at least one novel in him. I doubt that. I have found a few men and women who do have one novel in them, but the greatest

number of people I have met have perhaps a sentence
in them or at the very most a short story."

Where the hell did she get it? he thought angrily.
He remembered having said something like that once
as an abrasive joke to brush off a bore, although he
couldn't remember where or when. And even if in a
rough way he half-believed it, having it in print was
not going to enhance his reputation as a lover of man-
kind.

She's goading me, he thought, the little bitch is goading me into talking to her, trading with her, bribing
her to leave the antipersonnel mines unexploded.

"It would be interesting," the article continued, "to
get Jesse Craig to make a list of the people he has
worked with, categorizing them by the above stan-
dards. Worth a novel. Worth a short story. Worth a
sentence. Worth a phrase. Worth a comma. If ever I
get to speak to him again, I shall attempt to induce
him to supply me with such a list."

She is out for blood, he thought. My blood.

The rest of the page was covered in handwriting.
"Dear Mr. C., It's late now, and I'm getting groggy.
I have tomes more to go but not tonight. If you wish
to comment on anything you've read, I'm madly avail-
able. To be continued in the next installment. Yours,
G. McK."

His instinct was to crumple the pages and toss them
over the edge of the balcony. But he held onto them,
reasonably. After all, as the girl had said, she had a
carbon. And would have a carbon of the next installment. And the next.

A liner was swinging at anchor out in the bay,
and for a moment he thought of packing his bag
and getting on it, no matter where it was going. But
it wouldn't do any good. She'd probably turn up at
the next port, typewriter in hand.

He went into the living room and tossed the yellow
sheets onto the desk.

He looked at his watch. It was still too early for the Murphy's lunch. He remembered that yesterday he had promised Constance he'd phone her. She had said she wanted a blow-by-blow report. It had been partly due to her that he had come to Cannes. "Go on down there," she had said. "See if you can hack the action. You might as well find out now as later." She was not a woman who temporized.

He went into the bedroom and put in a call for Paris. Then he lay on the unmade bed and tried to doze while waiting. He had drunk too much the night before and had slept badly.

He closed his eyes but couldn't sleep. The thousand-fold amplified electric guitars of the movie he had just seen echoed in his ears, the orgiastic bodies writhed behind his hooded eyelids. If she's in, he thought, I'm going to tell her I'm taking the plane back to Paris this afternoon.

He had met her at a fund-raising party for Bobby Kennedy when he was on a visit to Paris in '68. He, himself, was registered to vote in New York, but a friend in Paris had taken him along. The people at the party had been attractive and had asked intelligent questions of the two eloquent and distinguished gentlemen who had flown from the United States to ask for money and emotional support for their man from Americans abroad, most of whom were not permitted to vote. Craig was not as enthusiastic as the others in the room, but he had signed a check for five hundred dollars, feeling that there was something mildly comic in his offering money to anybody in the Kennedy family. While the intense political discussion was still going on in the large handsome salon whose walls were splattered with dark, nonobjective paintings that he suspected would soon be sold at prices considerably lower than his hosts had paid for them, he went into the empty dining room where a bar had been set up.

He was pouring himself a drink when Constance followed him in. He had been conscious of her staring at him from time to time during the speeches. She was a striking-looking woman, dead pale, with wide greenish eyes and jet hair cut unfashionably short. At least it would have been unfashionable on anyone else. She was wearing a short lime-green dress and had dazzling legs.

"Are you going to give me a drink? I'm Constance Dobson. I know who you are," she said. "Gin and tonic. Plenty of ice." Her voice was husky, and she spoke quickly, in bursts.

He made the drink for her.

"What're you doing here?" she asked, sipping at her drink. "You look like a Republican."

"I always try to look like a Republican when I'm abroad," he said. "It reassures the natives."

She laughed. She had a rumbling laugh, almost vulgarly robust, unexpected in a woman as slender and as carefully put together as she was. She played with a long gold chain that hung down to her waist. Her bosom was youthful and high, he noticed. He had no idea how old she was. "You didn't seem as crazy as the others about the candidate," she said.

"I detect a streak of ferocity in him," Craig said. "I'm not partial to ferocious leaders."

"I saw you write out a check."

"Politics, as they say, is the art of the possible. I saw *you* write out a check."

"Bravado," she said. "I live from hand to mouth. It's because the young like him. Maybe they know something."

"That's as good a reason as any, I suppose," he said.

"You don't live in Paris."

"New York," he said, "if anyplace. I'm just passing through."

"For long?" She looked at him thoughtfully over the raised glass.

He shrugged. "My plans are indefinite."

"I followed you out here, you know."

"Did you?"

"You know I did."

"Yes." Surprised, he felt the trace of a blush.

"You have a brooding face. Banked fires." She chuckled, the disturbing, incongruous low sound. "And nice wide skinny shoulders. I know everybody else in the place. Do you ever come into a room and look around and say to yourself, 'My God, I know everybody here!' Know what I mean?"

"I think so," he said. She was standing close to him now. She had doused herself with perfume, but it was a fresh, tart smell.

"Are you going to kiss me now?" she said, "or are you going to wait for later?"

He kissed her. He hadn't kissed a woman for more than two years, and he enjoyed it.

"Sam has my phone number," she said. Sam was the friend who had brought him along. "Use it the next time you come through. If you want to. I'm busy this time. I'm shedding a fella. I have to go now. I have a sick child at home." The green dress flowed toward the hall where the coats were piled.

He stood alone at the bar and poured himself another drink, remembering the touch of her lips on his, the tart aroma of her perfume.

On the way home he had gotten her telephone number from his friend Sam, probed delicately for information, had not reported the full scene in the dining room.

"She's a man-killer," Sam had said. "A benevolent man-killer. She's the best American girl in Paris. She has some weird job with kids. Did you ever see such legs?" Sam was a lawyer, a solid man not given to hyperbole in his conversation.

The next time he came through Paris, after Bobby

Kennedy had been killed and the election over, he had called the number Sam had given him.

"I remember you," she said. "I shed the fella."

He took her to dinner that night. Every night thereafter while he stayed in Paris.

She had been a great beauty out of Texas, had conquered New York, then Paris, a tall, slender, willful girl with a tilted, narrow dark head. Dear men, her presence demanded when she entered a room, what are you doing here, are you worth the time?

With her he saw Paris in its best light. It was her town, and she walked through it with joy and pride and mischief, lovely legs making a carnival of its pavements. She had small teeth, a dangerous temper. She was not to be taken lightly. She was a Puritan about work, her own and that of others. Fiercely independent, she scorned inaction, parasitism. She had come to Paris as a model, during, as she put it, the second half of the rule of Charlemagne. Unschooled, she was surprisingly bookish. Her age was anybody's guess. She had been married twice. Vaguely, she said. Both men, and others, had made off with money. She bore them no ill-will, neither the husbands nor the others. She had tired of modeling, gone with a partner, male, an ex-university professor from Maine, into the exchange-student business. "The kids have to know about each other," she said. "Maybe they finally won't be able to be talked into killing each other." A much older, beloved brother had been lost at Aachen, and she was furious against war. When she read the news from Vietnam, and it was particularly bad, she cursed in barracks language, threatened to move to the South Seas with her son.

As she had said the first night, she lived from hand to mouth, but dressed extravagantly. The couturiers of Paris loaned her clothes, knowing that in the places to which she was invited neither she nor their confections would go unnoticed. She left whatever bed she was in promptly at seven each morning to make breakfast for her children and send them off to school. Regardless of the night she had spent, she was at her desk promptly at nine A.M. Although Craig kept a suite in a hotel, the wide bed in her room overlooking a garden on the Left Bank became his true Paris address. Her children grew fond of him. "They're used to men," she explained. She had outgrown whatever morality she had been exposed to in Texas and ignored whatever conventions were in practice in the society or societies she adorned in Paris.

She was straightforward, funny, demanding, unpredictable, gloriously formed for lovemaking, affectionate, eager and enterprising, only serious at those moments that demanded seriousness. He had been dormant. He was dormant no longer.

He had fallen into the dull habit of not noticing or appreciating women as women. Now he was immediately conscious of beauty, a sensual smile, a way of walking; his eye had been re-educated, was youthful again, was quick and innocently lascivious for the flick of a skirt, the curve of a throat, womanly movements. Faithful to one, once more he enjoyed the entire sex. It was not the least of the gifts Constance had brought him.

She talked candidly of the men who had come before him, and he knew there would be others after him. He contained his jealousy. Now he knew that he had been suffering from deep wounds when he had met her. The wounds were healing.

In the quiet room, suffused only with the mild sound of the sea outside the window, he waited anxiously for the ring of the telephone, the darting, husky tones of her voice. He was prepared to say, "I am taking the first plane back to Paris," sure that if she had any other engagement that evening she would break it for him.

Finally the phone rang. "Oh, you," she said. The tone was not affectionate.

"Darling," he began.

"Don't darling me, Producer. I'm no little starlet wriggling her hot little ass for two weeks on a couch." He heard voices in the background—her office, as usual, was probably full, but she was not one to postpone rage because of an audience.

"Now, Connie . . ."

"Now, Connie balls," she said. "You said you were going to call me yesterday. And don't tell me you tried. I've heard that before."

"I didn't try."

"You haven't even got the grace to lie, you son of a bitch."

"Connie." He was pleading now.

"The only honest man in Cannes. Just my goddamn luck. Why didn't you try?"

"I was . . ."

"Save your goddamn excuses. And you can save your telephone calls, too. I don't have to hang around waiting for any goddamn phone to ring. I hope you've found somebody to hold your hand in Cannes because sure as Christ your franchise has run out in Paris."

"Connie, will you for God's sake be reasonable?"

"As of now. As of this minute I am purely, coldly, *glacially* reasonable. The phone's off the hook, laddie boy. Don't bother trying to get the number. Ever."

There was the angry sound as she slammed the instrument down six hundred miles away. He shook his head ruefully as he put the phone down in its cradle. He smiled a little, thinking of the dumb quiet that must have fallen among the young at her office and the frantic, professorial eruption from the adjoining room of her partner, galvanized out of his usual somnolence by her tirade. It was not the first time she had yelled at him. It would not be the last. From now on he would call her when he promised if it took hanging on the phone all day.

He went down to the terrace, had his photograph taken with a lion cub, wrote on it, "I have found a mate for you," and put it in an envelope and mailed it to her. *Express.*

It was time for his lunch with the Murphys, and he went out under the porte-cochère and asked for his car. The doorman was occupied with a peeling bald man in a Bentley and ignored Craig. The parking space in front of the hotel was crowded, with the best places reserved for the Ferraris, the Maseratis, and the Rolls-Royces. Craig's rented Simca was shunted around by the doorman to spots less exposed to public view, and sometimes, when the spate of expensive hardware was intense, Craig would find his car parked a block away on a side street. There had been a time in his life when he had gone in for Alfas and Lancias, but he had given all that up many years ago, and now, as long as a car carried him where he wanted to go, he was satisfied. But today, when the doorman finally told him that his car was parked behind the hotel and he trudged on the hunt for it past the tennis courts toward the corner where the whores loitered in the afternoon, he felt vaguely humiliated. It was as though the employees of the hotel had a subtle knowledge of him, that they were letting him know, in their scornful treatment of his humble rented car, that they did not believe he really belonged in the palace whose walls they guarded.

They will be surprised at the size of their tip when the time comes, he thought grimly as he turned the key in the ignition and started toward the Cap d'Antibes and his luncheon date with Bryan Murphy.

• FOUR •

MR. and Mrs. Murphy were down at their cabana, the concierge told him, and were expecting him.

He walked through the fragrant piney park toward the sea, the only sound that of his own footsteps on the shaded path and the crackle of cicadas among the trees.

He stopped before he reached Murphy's cabana. The Murphys were not alone. Seated in the small patio in front of the cabana was a young woman. She wore a scanty pink bathing suit, and her long hair hung straight down her back, glistening in the sunlight. When she half-turned, he recognized the dark glasses.

Murphy, in flowered swimming trunks, was talking to her. Lying on a deck chair was Sonia Murphy.

Craig was about to go back to the hotel to call Murphy on the telephone and tell him to come up because he didn't like the company at the cabana when Murphy spotted him. "Hey, Jess," Murphy called, standing up. "We're over here."

Gail McKinnon did not turn around. She stood up, though, when he approached.

"Hi, Murph," he said, and went over and shook Murphy's hand.

"My boy," Murphy said.

Craig leaned over and kissed Sonia Murphy's cheek. She was fifty but looked about thirty-five, with a trim figure and a gentle, unlined, non-Hollywood face. She was covered with a beach towel and was wearing a wide-brimmed straw hat to keep from being sunburned. "It's been too long, Jesse," she said.

"It certainly has," Craig said.

"This young lady," Murphy said, gesturing toward Gail McKinnon, "tells me she knows you."

"We've met," Craig said. "Hello, Miss McKinnon."

"Hello." The girl took off her glasses. The gesture was deliberate, like the lowering of a disguise at a masquerade ball. Her eyes were wide, jewel-blue, but somehow evasive and uncertain, prepared for pain. Face grave and open, body not quite ripe, flesh satiny, she could have been sixteen, seventeen. He had a peculiar feeling that the rays of the sun were concentrated on her, a downfall of light, that he was looking at her from a distance, himself shadowed by a cloud with a dark promise of rain. She was perfect for the moment, poised quietly against the sea, the dazzle of the reflections from the water celebrating her youth, the richness of her skin, her almost-angular shapeliness.

He had the troubling sense of having already been a witness at the scene—a girl perfect for a moment in bright sun with the sea behind her. He could not tell whether he was oppressed or exhilarated.

She reached down, not completely graceful, her long hair swinging, and he saw that there was a tape recorder at her feet. As she bent to the machine, he couldn't help but notice the soft roundness of her belly over the pink cloth of the tiny bikini, the adolescent jut of bones on generous hips. He wondered why she had disfigured herself the morning before with the absurd oversized sweat shirt, the affectation of the blank expanse of dark glass.

"She's been interviewing me," Murphy said. "Against my will."

"I bet," Craig said. Murphy was famous for giving interviews to anybody on any subject. He was a big, heavyset, squarely built man of sixty, with a shock of dyed black hair, a whisky complexion, shrewd, quick eyes, and an easy, bluff Irish manner. He was known as one of the toughest negotiators in the business and had done very well for himself while enriching his clients. He had no written contract with Craig, just a handshake, although he had represented Craig for more than twenty years. Since Craig had stopped making movies, they had only seen each other infrequently. They were friends. But, thought Craig meanly, not as close friends as when I was riding high.

"How're your girls, Jesse?" Sonia asked.

"When last heard from, they seemed okay," Craig said. "Or as okay as girls can be at that age. Marcia, I hear, has put on weight."

"If they're not up on a possession or pushing charge," Murphy said, "consider yourself a happy parent."

"I consider myself a happy parent," Craig said.

"You look pale," said Murphy. "Put on a suit and get some sun."

Craig glanced at the slender tan body of Gail McKinnon. "No, thanks," he said. "My season hasn't started yet. Sonia, why don't you and I take a walk and let them finish their interview in peace?"

"The interview is over," Gail McKinnon said. "He's been talking for a half hour."

"Did you give her anything she can use?" Craig asked Murphy.

"If you mean did I use any dirty words," Murphy said, "I didn't."

"Mr. Murphy was most informative," Gail McKinnon said. "He said the movie industry was bankrupt. No money, no talent, and no guts."

"That'll help a lot the next time you go in to make a deal," Craig said.

"Screw 'em," Murphy said. "I got my pile. What do I care? Might as well enjoy telling the truth while the mood is on me. Hell, there's a picture going into production that's been financed by a tribe of Apache Indians. What the hell sort of business are you in when you have to get script approval from Apache Indians? We ordered lobster for lunch. You got any objection to lobster?"

"No."

"How about you?" Murphy asked the girl.

"I love it," she said.

Oh, Craig thought, she's here for lunch. He sat down on one of the folding canvas chairs facing her.

"She's asked me a lot about you." Murphy jabbed a blunt finger in the direction of the girl. "You know what I told her? I told her one of the things wrong with the business is it's driven people like you out of it."

"I didn't know I had been driven out," Craig said.

"You know what I mean, Jess," Murphy said. "So it became unattractive to you. What's the difference?"

"He was most complimentary about you," Gail McKinnon said. "You would blush with pleasure."

"He's my agent," Craig said. "What do you expect he would say about me? Maybe you'd like to hear what my mother used to say about me when she was alive."

"I certainly would." The girl reached down toward the tape recorder. "Should I turn it on?"

"Not for the moment." He was conscious of the girl's small smile. She put the dark glasses on again. Once more she was an antagonist.

"Gail says you're being stony-hearted," Murphy said. It didn't take him long to call girls by their first names. "Why don't you give her a break?"

"When I have something to say," Craig said, "she'll be the first to hear it."

"I take that as a promise, Mr. Craig," the girl said.

"From what I heard my husband spouting for the last half hour," Sonia said, "you're wise to keep your thoughts to yourself, Jesse. If it was up to me, I'd put a cork in his mouth."

"Wives," Murphy said. But he said it fondly. They had been married twelve years. If they ever fought, they fought in private. The advantage, Craig thought, of late marriages.

"People ask too many questions," Sonia said. She had a quiet, motherly voice. "And other people give too many answers. I wouldn't even tell that nice young lady where I bought my lipstick if she asked me."

"Where do you buy your lipstick, Mrs. Murphy?" Gail McKinnon asked.

They all laughed.

"Jess," Murphy said, "why don't you and I wander down to the bar and leave the girls alone for a cozy little preluncheon slander session?" He stood up, and Craig stood, too.

"I'd like a drink, too," Sonia said.

"I'll tell the waiter to bring one for you," Murphy said. "How about you, Gail? What do you want?"

"I don't drink before nightfall," she said.

"Journalists were different in my day," Murphy said. "They also looked different in bathing suits."

"Stop flirting, Murphy," Sonia said.

"The green-eyed monster," Murphy said. He kissed his wife's forehead. "Come on, Jess. Apéritif time."

"No more than two," Sonia said. "Remember you're in the tropics."

"When it comes to my drinking," Murphy said, "the tropics begin just below Labrador for my wife." He took Craig's arm, and they started off together on the flagstone path toward the bar.

A plump woman was lying face down on a mattress in front of one of the cabanas, her legs spread voluptuously for the sun. "Ah," Murphy murmured, staring, "it's a dangerous coast, my boy."

"The thought has occurred to me," Craig said.

"That girl's after you," Murphy said. "Oh, to be forty-eight again."

"She's not after me for that."

"Have you tried?"

"No."

"Take an old man's advice. Try."

"How the hell did she get to see you?" Craig said. He had never liked Murphy's hearty approach toward sex.

"She just called this morning, and I said come along. I'm not like some people I know. I don't believe in hiding my light under a bushel. Then when I saw what she looked like, I asked if she had brought her bathing suit with her."

"And she had."

"By some strange chance," Murphy said. He laughed. "I don't fool around, and Sonia knows it, but I do like to have pretty young girls in attendance. The innocent joys of old age."

They were at the little service hut by now, and the uniformed waiter there stood up as they approached and said, *"Bonjour, messieurs."*

"Une gin fizz per la donna cabana numero quarantedue, per favore," Murphy said to the waiter. Murphy had been in Italy during the war and had picked up a little Italian. It was the only language besides English that he knew, and as soon as he left the shores of America, he inflicted his Italian on the natives, no matter what country he was in. Craig admired the bland self-assurance with which Murphy imposed his own habits on any environment he entered.

"Si, si, signore," the waiter said, smiling either at Murphy's accent or with pleasure at the thought of the eventual tip Murphy would leave him.

On the way to the bar they passed the swimming pool set in the rocks above the sea. A young woman with pale blonde hair was standing on the side of the pool watching a little girl learning how to swim. The little girl had hair the same color as the woman's, and they were obviously mother and daughter. The mother was calling out instructions in a language that Craig could not identify. Her tone was soft and encouraging, with a hint of laughter in it. Her skin was just beginning to turn rosy from the sun.

"They're Danes," Murphy said. "I heard at breakfast. I must visit Denmark some day."

On inflated mattresses set back from the ladder leading to the sea two girls were lying face down, enjoying the sun. Their halters were discarded so that there would be no telltale strips of city-white skin across the tanned, beautiful young backs. Their brown rumps and long legs were smoothly shaped, appetizingly tinted. The bikini bottoms were merely a symbolic gesture toward public decorum. They were like two loaves of newly baked bread, warm, edible, and nourishing. Between them sat a young man, an actor Craig recognized from two or three Italian films. The actor was equally tanned, in swimming trunks that were hardly more than a jockstrap. He had a lean, muscular, hairless body, and a religious medal hung on a gold chain down his chest. He was darkly handsome, a superb animal with black hair and very white teeth, which he showed in a pantherish smile.

Craig was conscious of Murphy beside him staring down at the trio next to the sea.

"If I looked like that," Craig said, "I'd smile, too."

Murphy sighed loudly as they continued walking.

At the bar Murphy ordered a martini. He made no concessions to what his wife called the tropics. Craig ordered a beer.

"Well," Murphy said, raising his glass, "here's to my boy." He gulped down a third of his drink. "It's wonderful finally catching up with you. In person. You don't hand out much information in your letters, do you?"

"There's not much to say these days. Do you want me to bore you with the details of my divorce?"

"After all these years." Murphy shook his head. "I never would have thought it. Well, people have to do what they have to do, I suppose. I hear you've got a new girl in Paris."

"Not so new."

"Happy?"

"You're too old to ask a question like that, Murphy."

"The funny thing is I don't feel a day older than the day I got out of the army. Stupider but not older. Hell, let's get off that subject. It depresses me. How about you? What're you doing down here?"

"Nothing much. Lazying around."

"That kid, that Gail McKinnon, must have asked me in a dozen different ways what I thought you were after in Cannes. You want to work again?" Murphy glanced speculatively at him.

"Might be," Craig said. "If something good showed up. And if anybody was crazy enough to finance me."

"It's not only you," Murphy said. "Anybody'd have to be crazy to finance almost any movie these days."

"People haven't been knocking your door down asking you to get me to work for them, have they?"

"Well," Murphy said defensively, "you've got to admit you've sort of dropped out of things. If you really want to work, there's a picture I'm putting together . . . I might be able to swing it. I thought of you, but I didn't bother writing you until it was more definite. And there wouldn't be much money in it. And it's a lousy script. And it's got to be shot in Greece, and I know about you and your politics . . ."

Craig laughed at the torrent of Murphy's excuses. "It sounds just dandy," he said. "All round."

"Well," Murphy said, "I remember the first time you came to Europe, you wouldn't go to Spain because you didn't approve of the political situation there, and I . . ."

"I was younger then," Craig said. He poured some more beer into his glass from the bottle on the bar in front of him. "Nowadays, if you wouldn't shoot a picture in a country whose politics you didn't approve of, you wouldn't expose much film. You certainly wouldn't shoot a picture in America, would you?"

"I don't know," Murphy said. "My politics is take

the money and run for the hills." He motioned to the bartender for another drink. "Well, then, if the Greek thing develops, do you want me to call you?"

Craig swished the beer around in his glass. "No," he said.

"This is no time to be proud, Jess," Murphy said somberly. "You've been out of it, so maybe you don't realize. The movie business is a disaster area. People who were getting seven hundred and fifty thousand a picture are offering to work for fifty. And getting turned down."

"I realize."

"If you're over thirty, it's don't call us, we'll call you." Murphy gulped at his drink. "Everybody is looking for some longhaired kid that nobody even heard of who'll make another *Easy Rider* for them for under a hundred thousand. It's like a sudden blight has fallen from the sky."

"It's only movies, Murph," Craig said. "Your best entertainment. Don't take it so hard."

"Some entertainment," Murphy said darkly. "Still, I worry about you. Listen, I don't like to bring up unpleasant matters, especially on a holiday, but I know you must be worrying about dough just about now . . ."

"Just about now," Craig said.

"Your wife's got lawyers all over the country, practically, and a pair of them have been in with a court order to look at my books to make sure I haven't smuggled any funds out to you that she can't get her hands on, and I know she's taking you for half, plus the house. And what you've got in the market . . ." Murphy shrugged. "You know what the market's like. And you've been living for five years with almost nothing coming in. Goddamn it, Jess, if I can swing the Greek thing, I'm going to make you do it. Just for walking around money until something breaks. Are you listening to me?"

"Of course."

"I'm making as much of an impression on you as on a stone wall," Murphy said gloomily. "You took it too hard, Jess. So you had a couple of flops. So what? Who hasn't? When I heard you were coming to Cannes, I was delighted. Finally, I thought, he's coming out of it. You can ask Sonia if I didn't say just that. But you just stand there giving me the fish eye when I try to talk sense." He drained his martini and motioned for another. "In the old days, if you had a flop, you'd come up with five new ideas that next morning."

"The old days," Craig said.

"I'll tell you what you have to do *these* days," Murphy said. "No matter how much talent you have or how much experience you have or how nice you are to your mother, you can't just sit back and wait for people to come to you begging you to take their ten million dollars to do a picture for them. You've got to get out and hustle up an idea. And develop it. Get a screenplay. And a damn good screenplay. And a director. And an actor. An actor somebody still wants to see. There're about two left. And a budget this side of a million dollars. Then I can go in and talk business for you. Not before. Those're the facts, Jess. They're not nice, but they're the facts. And you might as well face up to them."

"Okay, Murph," Craig said. "Maybe I'm ready to do just that."

"That's better. That girl says she saw a script on the desk in your room."

"At this very moment," Craig said, "there are probably scripts on the desks of a hundred rooms in the Carlton Hotel."

"Let's talk about the one on yours," Murphy persisted. "What is it—a screenplay?"

"Uhuh. A screenplay."

"She asked me if I knew anything about it."

"What did you tell her?"

"What the hell could I tell her?" Murphy asked irritably. "I don't know anything. Are you interested in a screenplay?"

"I suppose you might say that," Craig said. "Yes."

"Whose?" Murphy asked suspiciously. "If it's been turned down by one studio, forget it. You're just wasting your time. The grapevine these days is run on laser beams."

"It hasn't been turned down yet," Craig said. "Nobody's seen it but me."

"Who wrote it?"

"A kid," Craig said. "You never heard of him. Nobody ever heard of him."

"What's his name?"

"I'd rather not say at the moment."

"Even to me?"

"Especially to you. You talk your head off. You know that. I don't want anybody getting to him."

"Well," Murphy said grudgingly, "that makes sense. Do you own it? The screenplay?"

"I have an option. For six months."

"What did it cost?"

"Peanuts."

"Is it about somebody under thirty years old with plenty of nude scenes?"

"No."

Murphy groaned. "Christ," he said. "Two strikes against you from the beginning. Well, let me read it, and then we'll see what we can do."

"Hold off for a few days," Craig said. "I want to go over it again and be sure it's ready."

Murphy stared hard at him without speaking, and Craig was almost sure that Murphy knew he was lying. Not just how he was lying, or where, or for what purpose, but lying.

"Okay," Murphy said, "When you want me, I'm here. In the meantime, if you're smart, you'll talk to that girl. At length. And talk to every newspaperman you can get hold of. Let people know you're alive, for Christ's sake." He drained his glass. "Now, let's go back for lunch."

They had lunch at the cabana. The cold langouste was very good, and Murphy ordered two bottles of Blanc-de-Blanc. He drank most of the wine and did most of the talking. He quizzed Gail McKinnon roughly but good-naturedly, at least at first. "I want to find out what the goddamn younger generation is about," he said, "before they come and slit my throat."

Gail McKinnon answered his questions forthrightly. Whatever she was, she was not shy. She had grown up in Philadelphia. Her father still lived there. She was an only child. Her parents were divorced. Her father had remarried. Her father was a lawyer. She had gone to Bryn Mawr but had quit in her sophomore year. She had gotten a job with a Philadephia radio station and had been in Europe for a year and a half. Her base was London, but her job allowed her to travel a good deal. She enjoyed Europe, but she intended to go back and live in the United States. Preferably in New York.

She sounded like a thousand other American girls Craig had met in Europe, hopeful, enthusiastic, and obscurely doomed.

"You got a boy friend?" Murphy asked.

"Not really," she said.

"Lovers?"

The girl laughed.

"Murph," Sonia Murphy said reproachfully.

"I'm not the one who invented the permissive society," Murphy said. "*They* did. The goddamn young." He turned again to the girl. "Do all the guys you interview make a pass at you?"

"Not all," she said, smiling. "The most interesting one was an old rabbi from Cleveland who was passing through London on his way to Jerusalem. I had to fight for my life in the Hotel Berkeley. Luckily, his plane left in an hour. He had a silky beard."

The conversation made Craig uncomfortable. The girl reminded him too much of his daughter Anne. He did not want to think of how his daughter talked to older men when he wasn't there.

Murphy rambled on about the decline of the movie industry.

"Take Warner's, for example," he said. "You know who bought Warner's? A cemetery business. How do you like that for crappy symbolism? And the age thing. They talk about revolutions devouring their young. We've had a revolution out there, only it's devouring its old. I suppose you approve, Miss Smart-Face." He was becoming belligerent with the wine.

"Partially," Gail McKinnon said calmly.

"You're eating my lobster," Murphy said, "and you say partially."

"Look where the old have got us," Gail McKinnon said. "The young can't do any worse."

"I know that song and dance," Murphy said. "I don't have any children, thank God, but I listen to my friends' kids. The young can't do any worse. Let me tell you something, Gail Smart-Face, they can. They can do a lot worse. Put your tape recorder on again. I'll put that in the interview."

"Finish your lunch, Murph," Sonia said. "The poor girl's taken enough guff from you already."

"Seen and not heard," Murphy grumbled. "That's my motto. And now they're giving them the vote. The foundations're tottering."

Craig was relieved when the lunch was over. "Well," he said, standing, "thanks for the grub. I've got to be getting back."

"Jesse," Sonia said, "could you drive Miss McKinnon to Cannes with you? If she stays on and Murph talks to her anymore, the Immigration people will turn him back when he tries to get into the United States again."

Gail McKinnon looked at him soberly. He was reminded of his own daughters waiting for him to pick them up after a children's party.

"How did you get here this morning?" he asked ungraciously.

"A friend of mine drove me over. If you mind, I'll get a taxi."

"They charge outrageous prices," Sonia said. "It's sinful if you can get a ride with Jesse. Go in and get dressed, child," she said firmly. "Jesse will wait."

Gail McKinnon looked questioningly up at Craig. "Of course," he said.

She stood. "I won't be a minute," she said, and went into the cabana to change.

"Smart little girl," Murphy said, pouring the last drops of the wine from the bottle into his glass. "I like her. I don't trust her. But I like her."

"Don't talk so loud, Murph," Sonia whispered.

"Let 'em know my sentiments," Murphy said. "Let 'em know where I stand." He drained the wine. "Let me read that script, Jess. The sooner the better. If it's any good, I'll get it set up for you with two telephone calls."

Two telephone calls, Craig thought. No matter what he says, after lunch and two bottles of wine he thinks it's still 1960 when Bryan Murphy was still Bryan Murphy and Jesse Craig still Jesse Craig. He glanced worriedly toward the rear of the cabana where the girl was dressing behind a flimsy wooden wall. Murphy's voice carried. "Maybe in a couple of days, Murph," he said. "Don't broadcast until then, please."

"Still as a grave, my boy," Murphy said. "Grave as Warner's." He chuckled at the aptness of his simile. "I did have a good time today," he said. "Old friends and new girls and lobster for lunch and the Blue Mediterranean. Do you think the rich live better than we do, Jess?"

"Yes," Craig said.

Gail McKinnon came out, her bag swinging on its long strap from her shoulder. She had on white hip-hugger jeans and a short-sleeved navy blue polo shirt. She wasn't wearing a brassiere, and Craig noted the small, round breasts jutting firmly out against the blue cotton cloth. She had put away the dark glasses for the moment. She looked nautical, sea-fresh, pure, and undangerous. She made her thanks to her hosts demurely and politely and bent to pick up the tape recorder, but Craig reached for it first and said, "I'll carry that."

Murphy was stretching out for his siesta as they started climbing the path toward the pool and the parking lot. The plump woman Craig and Murphy had passed on the way to the bar was still lying on her stomach absorbing the sun, her legs still wide-spread and inviting. With a sigh, as though she were suffering, the woman turned over. She stared pee-vishly at Craig and the girl, her privacy destroyed. Her face was thick and heavily made up. Dark blue mascara had run in the sweat of the sun. She was no longer young, and the features were marked by self-love, lust, greed, a sly and corrupt worldliness. The face made a shocking contrast with the healthy peas-ant fullness of the body. Craig found her hideous and averted his eyes. He couldn't have borne it if she had spoken aloud.

He let Gail McKinnon walk in front of him and followed her, protecting her. In her sandals she drift-ed noiselessly over the scoured stones. Her long hair blew cleanly in the sea wind. Suddenly he remem-bered what had troubled him when he first saw her in the Murphys' patio standing in sunlight with the sea behind her. She had reminded him of his wife Penelope on a June day on the Long Island shore, girlish and rosy, poised on a dune, outlined against the incoming tide.

The Danish mother was propped up against the rocks beside the pool reading, her child sitting with her blonde head on her mother's shoulder.

A dangerous coast.

Take an old man's advice. Try.

Walking to the car, Gail McKinnon put on the ridiculous dark glasses again.

• FIVE •

WHEN he drove the car out of the gate of the hotel grounds, he turned, out of an old memory, in the wrong direction, toward Antibes, instead of toward Juan-les-Pins and Cannes. The year after his marriage he had rented a villa for a summer on the coast between the Cap and Antibes, and the habit of turning toward it, he realized a little ruefully, had remained with him all this time.

"I hope you're not in a hurry," he said to the girl beside him. "I'm going the long way round."

"I have nothing better to do today," Gail McKinnon said, "than to go the long way round with Jesse Craig."

"I used to live down this road," he said. "It was nicer then."

"It's nice now."

"I suppose so. There're just more houses." He drove slowly. The road wound along the sea. A regatta of small sails glittered far out on the blue water. An old man in a striped shirt was fishing off the rocks. Above them a Caravelle was losing altitude, coming in to land at Nice.

"When were you here before?" Gail McKinnon asked.

"Quite a few times," he said. "In 1944, for the first time, when the war was still on . . ."

"What were you doing then?" She sounded surprised.

"You said you did your homework," he teased her.

"I thought my past was an open book to you."

"Not that open."

"I was in a jeep," he said, "in an army camera unit. The Seventh Army had landed in the South of France, and we were sent down from Paris to make some film of the action down here. Our line was based near Menton, just a few miles from here. You could hear the artillery on the other side of Nice . . ."

Old soldier's maundering, he thought, and stopped. Ancient history. *Caesar ordered the camp to be set up on the hills overlooking the river. The Helvetii were in line of battle on the other bank of the river.* For the girl beside him Caesar's line and the line of young Americans before Menton were equally lost in the gulf of time. Did they even teach Latin anymore?

He looked sidelong at her. The glasses, which protected her and revealed him, annoyed him. Her youth annoyed him. Her ignorance, which was the innocent function of her youth, annoyed him. There were too many advantages on her side. "Why do you wear those damn things?" he asked.

"You mean my shades?"

"The glasses. Yes."

"You don't like them?"

"No."

With a single gesture she took them off and tossed them out of the car. She smiled at him. "That better?"

"Much."

They both laughed. He was no longer sorry Sonia Murphy had forced him into taking the girl along with him to Cannes.

"And what about that ghastly sweat shirt yesterday?" he asked.

"I experiment with different personalities," she said.

"What was today's personality?" He was amused now.

"Nice, scrubbed, virginally coquettish, in an up-to-date Women's Lib kind of way," she said. "For Mr. Murphy and his wife." She raised her arms as though to embrace the sea, the rocks, the pines shadowing the road, the entire Mediterranean afternoon. "I've never been here before, but I feel I've known this coast since I was a little girl." She pulled her legs up and turned in her seat to face him. "I'm going to come back here. Again and again and again. Until I'm an old lady with a big wide sun hat and a cane. When you were here during the war, did you ever think *you'd* come back?"

"When I was here during the war," he said, "all I thought about was getting home alive."

"Did you know then that you were going into the theatre and the movies?"

"I don't really remember." He tried to recall exactly that September afternoon long ago, the jeep moving toward the sound of the guns, the four helmeted soldiers with their cameras and carbines bumping along the lovely wild coast none of them had ever seen before, past the blown pillboxes and the camouflaged villas facing the sea. What were the names of the other three men in the jeep? The driver's name was Harte. He remembered that. Malcolm Harte. He had been killed in Luxembourg a few months later. He couldn't remember the names of the other two men. They had not been killed.

"I guess," he said, "I must have thought it was possible I'd have something to do with the movies after the war. After all, I had a movie camera in my hands. The army had taught me how to be a cameraman, and the Signal Corps was full of men who had worked in Hollywood. But I wasn't much of a cameraman. Just manufactured for the war. I knew I couldn't do *that* once the war was over." There was a melancholy pleasure in having an occasion to remember that distant time when he was a young man in the uniform of his country, in no danger, for that afternoon at least, of being shot at. "Actually," he went on, "my going into the theatre was an accident. On the troop-ship going back to the States from Le Havre I met Edward Brenner in a poker game. We became friend-ly, and he told me he'd written a play while he had been waiting in the redeployment depot at Reims to be shipped home. I knew a little about the theatre, of course, because of my father—he'd been taking me to see plays since I was nine years old—and I asked Brenner if I could read it."

"That was a lucky poker game," the girl said.

"I suppose so," Craig said.

Actually, it had not been during the poker game that they had come together but on deck, on a sunny day when Craig had been able to find a corner out of the wind and was reading a collection of the ten best American plays of 1944 that his father had sent him. (What was the APO number? It was an address he had thought he would never forget.) Brenner had passed him twice, had eyed the book in his hand, had finally crouched down, farmer-style, on his heels be-side him, and had said, "How are they? The plays, I mean."

"Medium," Craig said.

They had begun to talk then. It turned out that Brenner was from Pittsburgh and had gone to Car-negie Tech and had taken the drama course there before he was drafted—he was older than he looked —and was interested in the theatre. The next day he had shown Craig his play.

Brenner was unprepossessing to look at—a gaunt, sallow boy with sad, dark eyes and a hesitant and guarded way of talking. Among the horde of jubi-lant, loud men sailing home from the war, he had been uncomfortable and unsoldierly in his ill-fitting uniform, his manner tentative, as though a little sur-prised that he had survived three campaigns and knew he could never survive a fourth. Craig had agreed to read his play with misgivings, trying in advance to

compose anodyne comments that would not hurt
Brenner's feelings. He was unprepared for the fierce-
ness of the emotion, the harsh unsentimentality, the
rigor of the construction of the infantry private's first
dramatic work. While he himself had never done anything in the theatre, he had seen enough plays to be
convinced, with youthful egotism, of the accuracy of
his own taste. He had not measured his enthusiasm
when he had discussed Brenner's play with him, and
by the time they had passed the Statue of Liberty, the
two men were firm friends and Craig had promised
Brenner that through his father he would get the play
into the hands of producers.

Brenner had to go to Pennsylvania to be discharged
and then to resume at Carnegie Tech. Craig, who
stayed in New York pretending to be looking for
work, communicated with him only through the
mails. There wasn't much to communicate. Craig's
father had loyally approached the producers he knew,
but the play had been turned down by all of them.

"Nobody, they say," Craig had written Pittsburgh,
"wants to hear about the war. They are all idiots.
Do not despair. One way or another this play will
go on."

It went on, finally, because Craig's father died and
left twenty-five thousand dollars. "I know it's a wild
idea," Craig had written Brenner. "I don't know anything about producing, but I think I know more than
the horse's asses who turned down your play. And by
now I know an awful lot about your play. If you're
willing to bet your talent, I'm willing to bet my
dough."

Brenner was in New York two days later and never
saw Pittsburgh again. Because he was practically penniless, he moved into the room in the Hotel Lincoln
where Craig was living, and in the five months that
it took to put the play on, they were together twenty-
four hours a day. The year-long examination of the
manuscript through the mails, with the testing and

weighing of every line, had made the play their common property, and they were surprised when very occasionally their reactions to the people and ideas they had to deal with in the course of the production differed at all.

The director, a young man by the name of Baranis, who had had some experience in the theatre and who had thought he would be treated respectfully by the two neophytes, had complained one day when a pet notion of his had been calmly voted down, almost without discussion, by them. "Christ," Baranis had said, "I bet when you two guys go to sleep, you have the same dreams."

Curiously, the one time they had had a serious disagreement, it had been about Penelope Gregory, later to be Penelope Craig. She had been sent up to the office by an agent to read for a small part, and both Baranis and Craig had been favorably impressed by her beauty and by the soft, deep voice. But Brenner had been adamant. "Sure," he said, "she's beautiful. Sure, she has a great voice. But there's something I don't believe about her. Don't ask me why."

They had had Penelope up to read again, but Brenner refused to change his mind, and in the end they had compromised on a plainer girl.

During rehearsals Brenner became so nervous that he could not eat. It became part of Craig's duties, along with arguing with the scene designer, negotiating with the stagehands' union, and keeping the leading man from drinking, to lure Brenner into restaurants and get a minimum of nourishment into him to keep him alive until the curtain went up.

The day the signs were put in place outside the theatre, Craig found Brenner standing on the sidewalk in his dirty raincoat, the only coat he owned, looking wonderingly at the legend *"The Foot Soldier,* by Edward Brenner," and shaking as though he were suffering from a malarial attack. He laughed wildly when he saw Craig. "It's weird, Brother," he said, "just weird. I have the feeling somebody's going to tap me on the shoulder and I'm going to wake up and it's going to be Pittsburgh all over again."

Still shaking, he had allowed Craig to lead him to a drugstore and order a milk shake for him. "I've got a crazy double feeling," he confided over the milk shake. "I can't wait for the thing to open, and at the same time I hate to see it open. It's not only because I'm afraid it's going to flop. It's just that I don't want it all to end." He had gestured vaguely over the furniture of the soda fountain. "The rehearsals. The goddamn room in the Hotel Lincoln. Baranis. Listening to you snore at four o'clock in the morning. I know I'll never have anything like this again. Do you know what I mean?"

"Sort of," Craig said. "Finish your milk shake."

When the first reviews came in over the phone the night of the opening, Brenner had thrown up all over the floor of the hotel room, had apologized, had said, "I will love you until the day I die," had had eight Scotches, and passed out until Craig had awakened him the next day with the evening newspapers.

"What was he like then?" Gail McKinnon was saying. "Edward Brenner? When you first saw him?"

"Just another GI who had had a hard war," Craig said. He slowed the car down and pointed up the bluff to his left at a white villa set among the pine trees. "That's where I lived. The summer of 1949."

The girl stared at the broad, low building set behind a terrace on which an orange awning shaded some garden furniture from the intense sunlight. "How old were you then?"

"Twenty-seven."

"Not bad for twenty-seven," she said. "A house like that."

"No," Craig said. "Not bad."

What did he remember about that summer?

Scattered images.

Penelope water-skiing on the bay of La Garoupe, slim and tan, her hair flying, determinedly graceful in a one-piece black bathing suit as she broke through the wake of the speedboat. Brenner beside him in the boat taking home movies of Penelope clowning precarious ballet positions against the pull of the line and waving for the camera.

Brenner, himself, attempting to learn how to water-ski, trying doggedly again and again to stand up and never making it, a skinny, clumsy figure, all bones and knuckles, long, sad nose and starved shoulders burned painfully red from the sun, having to be fished out of the water finally, almost drowned from all the water he had swallowed, saying, "I am a goddamn useless intellectual," as Penelope, now aiming the camera at him like a weapon, laughed in the rocking boat.

Dancing in the open square on a velvety night in the walled town of Haut-de-Cagnes, moving to tinny French music in and out of the light of the lanterns hung along the old stone walls, Penelope, small, neat, and weightless in his arms, kissing him under the ear, smelling of sea and jasmine, whispering, "Let's not go back anywhere. *Ever.*" And Brenner sitting at a table, too self-conscious to dance, pouring wine and trying to communicate with a hard-faced French lady he had picked up the night before in the casino at Juan-les-Pins, saying, with effort, one of the ten French phrases he had learned since his arrival, *"Je suis un fameux écrivain à New York."*

Driving home in the green dawn from Monte Carlo where among them they had won 100,000 francs (at 650 francs to the dollar), Craig at the wheel of the small open car, Penelope between the two men, her head on Craig's shoulder, and Brenner shouting in his croaking voice into the wind, "Here we are, Scott, on the Grande Corniche," and all of them trying to sing "Les Feuilles Mortes," which they had heard for the first time the night before.

Lunch on the terrace of the white villa under a

huge orange awning, all three of them fresh from the morning's swim, Penelope, trim in white cotton slacks and a sailor's blue jersey, her wet hair piled up on top of her head, softly and insistently sensual, rearranging the flowers in the vase on the white iron luncheon table with brown soft hands, touching the bottle of wine in the ice bucket to make sure it was cold enough, as the old lady who served as cook and who had come with the house shuffled out with the cold soup and salad on a big clay platter from Vallauris just down the coast. What was the old lady's name? Hélène? Perpetually in black, in mourning for ten generations of her family who had died within the walls of Antibes, and who fussed lovingly over the three of them whom she called, *"Mes trois beaux jeunes Américains,"* none of whom had ever had a servant before then, and putting red, white, and blue flowers on the breakfast table for the Fourth of July and Bastille Day.

The piercing, sharp odor of the pine forest behind them in the noonday sun.

The siestas in the afternoons, Penelope in his arms in the great bed in the high-ceilinged, shadowed room, traversed here and there by light broken into thin lances by the shutters that were closed against the heat. The daily love-making, complete, potent, accepting, tender, the two locked, grateful, familiar youthful bodies, cleansed and salty, the joys of double possession, equal surrender, the fruit smell of wine on their lips as they kissed, the low chuckles as they whispered in the fragrant gloom, the insidious, arousing touch of Penelope's long nails as they moved capriciously over the hard ridges of his belly.

The night in August, Penelope and he seated after dinner on the terrace, the sea smooth in the moonlight below them, the forest quiet, Brenner off somewhere with one of his girls, when Penelope had told him she was pregnant. "Glad or sorry?" she had asked, her low voice tremulous. He leaned over and kissed her. "I guess that answers it," she said.

He went into the kitchen and brought out a bottle of champagne from the icebox, and they toasted themselves in the moonlight and decided to buy a house in New York when they went back because now that they would be a family the apartment in the Village would not be big enough for them. "Don't tell Ed," Penelope said.

"Why not?"

"He'll be jealous. Don't tell anybody. They'll all be jealous."

The routine of the mornings. After breakfast, he and Brenner sprawled in swimming trunks in the sun, the manuscript of Brenner's new play open on the table between them and Brenner saying, "What about as the curtain comes up on the second act, the stage is dark, and she comes in, goes over to the bar, you only see her in silhouette, she pours herself a drink, sobs, then knocks the whole drink down in one gulp . . . ?"

Both of them squinting against the Mediterranean light, envisaging the dark stage, the actress moving in the hushed, full theatre on a cold winter's night in the welcoming city across the ocean as they worked on the revisions of Brenner's second play, which Craig had already announced for production in November.

Craig had produced two other plays since *The Foot Soldier,* and they had both been successes. One was still running, and he had rewarded himself with the season in France as a belated honeymoon for himself and Penelope. Brenner had spent most of the royalties he had made on *The Foot Soldier,* which had not turned out to be all that much finally, and he was practically penniless again, but they had high hopes for the new play. Anyway, that year Craig had enough for everybody and was learning how to live luxuriously.

Behind them in the house there was the murmur of

Penelope's voice working on her French with the cook and the occasional ringing of the telephone as friends called, or one of Brenner's girls, to be told by Penelope that the men could not be disturbed, they were working. It was surprising how many friends had found out where they were spending the summer and how many girls knew Brenner's telephone number.

At noon, Penelope coming out in her bathing suit, announcing, "Swim call." They swam off the rocks in front of the house in deep, cold, clear water, splashing each other, Penelope and Craig, who were good swimmers, hovering close to Brenner, who once had alarmingly begun to sink, thrashing his arms and blowing desperately, in need of rescue, the performance half-real, half-play-acting. "Oh," he had said when they had hauled him out, and he was lying, pink and slippery, beached on the rocks, "oh, you aristocrats who know how to do *everything*, who will never drown."

Images of pleasure.

Memory, of course, if given the opportunity, plays false. No time, even the month or the week that you remember later as the happiest of your life, is all of one piece, all pleasure.

There was the argument with Penelope that broke out late one night two or three weeks after they had moved into the villa. About Brenner. In the shuttered bedroom, so that they had to talk in whispers to keep Brenner from overhearing, although he was at the other end of the hall and the walls were thick. "Isn't that man ever going to leave?" Penelope demanded. "I'm getting tired of never being able to make a move without seeing that sad long face hanging over your shoulder."

"Keep it low, please," Craig said.

"I'm getting tired of having to keep everything low, too," Penelope said. She was sitting up on the edge of the bed naked, brushing her blonde hair.

"As though I'm in somebody else's house."

"I thought you liked him," Craig said, surprised. He had been half-asleep, waiting for her to finish with her hair and turn out the lamp and get in beside him. "I thought you were friends."

"I like him." Penelope brushed savagely at her hair. "I'm his friend. But not twenty-four hours a day. When I married, I wasn't told I was marrying a team."

"It's not twenty-four hours a day," Craig said, knowing he sounded foolish. "Anyway, he'll probably leave when we finish getting the script ready."

"That script won't be ready until the day the lease runs out," Penelope said bitterly. "I know that man."

"That doesn't sound completely friendly, Penny."

"Maybe *he's* not so completely friendly," she said. "Don't think I don't know who it was that turned me down for the part in his play."

"He didn't even know you then."

"Well, he knows me now." Ten harsh strokes of the brush. "Don't tell me he thinks I'm the greatest actress to come to New York since Ethel Barrymore."

"We haven't discussed it," Craig said lamely. "Keep your voice down."

"I'll bet you haven't discussed it. I'll bet there're a lot of things you haven't discussed. Like the way whenever you're talking about anything seriously you ignore me. Just ignore me."

"That isn't true, Penny."

"You know it's true. The two great minds working as one, deciding the fate of the world, the Marshall Plan, the next elections, the atomic bomb, Stanislavsky . . ." The brush was going like a piston now. "Listening to me indulgently, as though I'm an idiot child . . ."

"You're absolutely irrational, Penny."

"I'm irrationally rational, Jesse Craig, and you know it."

He had to laugh then, and she laughed, too, and he

said, "Throw that damned brush away and come to bed."

And a moment later she threw the brush away and turned out the light and came to bed. "Don't make me jealous, Jesse," she whispered, holding onto him. "Don't ever leave me out. Of anything."

And then days went by just as they had before, as though there had never been the midnight conversation on the edge of the bed, Penelope being sisterly and fond with Brenner, forcing him to eat, to put some meat on his poor bones, as she said, and being demure and quiet while the men talked and unostentatiously emptying ashtrays, bringing fresh drinks, teasing Brenner gently about the girls who called and the girls who sometimes stayed overnight and came down to breakfast the next morning asking if they could borrow a bathing suit for a dip before getting back to town.

"I'm a desirable sex object on the Côte d'Azur," Brenner said, embarrassed but pleased at the teasing. "It was never thus in Pennsylvania or Fort Bragg."

Then the bad evening at the end of August when Craig was packing to catch the night train up to Paris because he had to meet the head of a movie studio there to negotiate the terms for the sale of the play that was still running in New York. Penelope came in pulling a robe around her after a bath, her eyes, usually a soft brown, now harsh and dangerous. She watched him throw some shirts into his bag.

"How long're you going to be?" she asked.

"Three days. At the most."

"Take that son of a bitch with you."

"What are you talking about?"

"You know what I'm talking about. *Whom* I'm talking about."

"Sssh."

"Don't sssh me in my own house. I'm not going to

play nursemaid to that one-play genius, that . . . that steel-town Don Juan, for three days while you go gallivanting around the nightspots of Paris . . ."

"I'm not going gallivanting anywhere, Penny," Craig said, trying to be patient. "You know that. And he's in the middle of the third act. I don't want him to interrupt . . ."

"I wish you'd be as thoughtful about your wife as you are about your holy scrounging friend. Has he bought us a dinner since he's been here? One single dinner?"

"What difference does that make? He's busted. You know that."

"I certainly do. He sure as hell makes that clear. Where does he get all the money to take those tarts out five times a week? What do you do—finance him for that, too? What is it, are you getting a vicarious kick out of his scrubby little conquests?"

"I have a great idea," Craig said quietly. "Why don't you pack and come along with me to Paris?"

"I'm not going to be driven out of my own house by any oversexed superior leech like Edward Brenner," Penelope said loudly, ignoring Craig's shushing gestures, "and let him turn this place into a whorehouse, with his cheap tarts running in and out just as near naked as the law allows. You better warn him—from now on he's got to behave himself. I'm through with behaving like the madame of a private bordello for him, taking down telephone numbers for him, saying, 'Mr. Brenner is busy now, Yvette or Odile or Miss Big Tits, can he call you back?' "

She's jealous, Craig thought, wonderingly. Go figure women out. But all he said was, "Don't turn bourgeoise on me, Penny. That went out with World War One."

"I'm bourgeoise. That's it." She began to cry. "Now you know it. Go complain to your elegant friend. He'll sympathize with you. The Great Bohemian Art-

ist who never pays for anything will offer his con-
dolences." She ran into the bathroom and locked the
door and stayed in there so long that he was sure he
was going to miss his train. But just when he heard
Brenner toot warningly on the horn of the car outside, the bathroom door opened and Penelope came
out, dry-eyed and smiling, fully dressed. She squeezed
Craig's arm and said, "Forgive the tantrum. I'm a little jittery these days," and they went out to the car
together.

As the train pulled out of the Antibes station, with
Craig leaning out the window of the wagon-lit, Penelope and Brenner were standing side by side on the
platform in the dusk waving to him.

When Craig got back from Paris, Brenner gave him
the finished copy of the play and said he had to leave
for New York. They made plans to meet in New York
at the end of September and had a farewell party,
and when Craig and Penelope put him on the train,
he said that he had never had a better time in his
whole life.

With Brenner gone, Craig read the final version
of the play Brenner had left him. As he read the
familiar pages, he was conscious of a growing unease
and at the end a vast, echoing emptiness. What
had seemed, as he worked with Brenner, to be funny
and alive and touching now was dead on the page
before him, hopeless. He realized that until then he
had been deceived by the beauty of the summer, his
appreciation of his friend's real talent, the engulfing,
optimistic joy of work. Now he was reading coldly
and saw that the play was stillborn, irretrievable. It
wasn't merely that he was sure the play would fail
commercially but with the chance that it might perhaps find a small, perceptive audience that would
give him some satisfaction in being connected with it.
It was doomed, he was sure, to general oblivion. If

it had been anybody else's play, he would have rejected it immediately. But with Brenner . . . Friend or no friend, he knew that if the play went on, Brenner would suffer. Badly.

Without telling Penelope his reaction, he gave her the script to read. She had heard them talking about it, of course, and knew what it was about, but she hadn't read a word of it. A mediocre actress, Penelope was a shrewd judge in the theatre, intuitive and tough-minded. When she had finished reading, Penelope said, "It won't go, will it?"

"No."

"They'll murder him. And you."

"I'll survive."

"What're you going to do?" she asked.

He sighed. "I'm going to put it on," he said.

She didn't mention it again. He was grateful for her tact. He didn't tell her, though, that he wasn't going to risk anybody else's money in it, that he was going to back it completely himself.

The rehearsals were disastrous. He couldn't get any of the actors he wanted or the director he wanted or even the scene designer he wanted because the play appealed to no one. He had to make do with worn-out hacks and inexperienced beginners, and he spent tortured nights trying to make up lies about the stream of refusals to protect Brenner's ego. So-and-so loved the play but had signed for Hollywood, so-and-so had promised to wait for the new Williams play, so-and-so was involved in television. Brenner remained serenely certain of success. His one triumph had made him feel inviolate. In the middle of rehearsals he even got married. To a plain, quiet woman by the name of Susan Lockridge who wore her straight black hair in a severe schoolteacherly bun and who knew nothing about the theatre and who sat entranced through the rehearsals, thinking that was the way all rehearsals looked. Craig acted as best man at the wedding and gave the party and sweated as he acted the jolly, confident host, raising his glass again and again to toast the newlyweds and the success of the play. Penelope didn't appear for the party. She was in the fourth month of her pregnancy and was sick a good deal of the time and had a plausible excuse.

A week before the opening night Craig took Susan Brenner aside and told her they were heading for disaster and that the only sensible thing was to call the whole thing off. "How do you think Eddie will take it if I tell him this?" Craig asked her.

"He'll die," the woman said flatly.

"Oh, come on," Craig said.

"You heard what I said."

"Okay," Craig said wearily, "we'll open. Maybe there'll be a miracle."

But there wasn't any miracle. Only half the audience was left when the curtain came down on opening night. In Sardi's, where they went to wait for the reviews, Brenner said to Craig, "You son of a bitch. You sabotaged it. Susan told me what you told her. You never had any faith in it, and you did the whole thing on a shoestring, and it looks it . . ."

"Why would I want to sabotage it?" Craig asked.

"You know as well as I do, Brother," Brenner said, standing up. "Come on, Sue, let's get out of here."

It was only many years later, long after the birth of Anne and Marcia, that Craig had an inkling of what Brenner had been talking about that night. It was in the middle of an argument with Penelope, when things had been going badly between them for more than a year, after a party at which, Penelope said, he had been hanging all over a pretty and notorious young actress, that Penelope supplied the missing clue. In the three days he had been in Paris, the summer at Antibes, she had slept with Edward Brenner. She meant to hurt him, and she managed it.

He was at the wheel in the bright afternoon sunshine with the sea below him to his right and the
white villa falling out of sight behind him. He turned
and took a last look at the house.

Not bad for twenty-seven. Anne had been conceived there, in the great bed in the cool, high room
overlooking the sea, the room that had been the haunt
of pleasure for three dreamlike months. He didn't
tell Gail McKinnon about Anne or Brenner or the
three months or the death of friendship or the secret
undermining of love.

What had happened to all the home movies they
had taken that summer? He had no idea where the
spools of aging, brittle film might be. Somewhere
among the old theatre programs, old magazines, brok-
en tennis racquets in the cellar of the house of Seventy-
eighth Street he had bought so as to have room for the
arrival of Anne, the house he had not visited since he
had told Penelope he wanted a divorce, the house
he would be able to walk through unerringly in total
darkness until the day he died.

He stepped on the accelerator, and the villa disappeared beyond a bend of the road. *Lesson—Stay
away from the places where you have been happy.*

The girl was silent for a moment. When she spoke,
it was as though she knew exactly what he had
been thinking of. "Murphy says your wife is a very
beautiful woman."

"Was," Craig said. "Is, perhaps. Yes."

"Is it a friendly divorce?"

"As divorces go."

"The divorce in my family was silent and polite,"
Gail McKinnon said. "Obscene. My mother just wandered away. When I was sixteen. She had wandered
away before. Only this time she didn't come back.
When I was eighteen, I asked my father why. He

said, 'She is searching for something. And it isn't me.' " The girl sighed. "She sends me a card at Christmas. From various parts of the world. I must look her up some day."

She was momentarily silent, leaning back now against the seat. Then she said, "Mr. Murphy's not what you expect a Hollywood agent to be like, is he?"

"You mean he's not small and fat and Jewish, with a funny way of talking?"

The girl laughed. "I'm glad to see you read me so carefully. Did you read what I left for you this morning?"

"Yes."

"Any comments?"

"No."

Again, she was quiet for a little while. "He's an intelligent man, Mr. Murphy," she said. "Before you came, he told me if your last picture were to come out today, it would be a hit. It was before its time, he said."

Craig paid attention to his driving, slowed down to avoid a family group in bathing suits crossing the road.

"I agreed with him," the girl said. "Maybe it wouldn't have been a hit, at least in Mr. Murphy's terms, but people would've recognized how original it was."

"You saw it?" Craig couldn't help sounding surprised.

"Yes. Mr. Murphy said the big mistake you made was not becoming a director. He says it's a director's business now."

"Maybe he's right."

"Mr. Murphy said it would have been easy any time until 1965 to get you a picture to direct . . ."

"That's probably true."

"Weren't you tempted?"

"No."

"Why not?"

"Laziness, maybe."

"You know that's not true." The girl sounded aggrieved at his evasiveness.

"Well, if you must know," Craig said, "I felt I didn't have the talent for it. At best, I would have just been pretty good. There would have been fifty better men than I at the job."

"Weren't there fifty better men working as producers?" Now her tone was challenging.

"Maybe five," he said. "And maybe if I was lucky, they would die off or go on the booze or lose their touch."

"If you had it to do all over again," the girl said, "would you do something else?"

"Nobody has it to do all over again," Craig said. "Now enjoy the scenery, please."

"Well, anyway," the girl said placidly, "it was a nice lunch."

After that, she asked no more questions, and they drove in silence along the sea and through the town of Antibes, sleepy in the sun, and on the busy highway back to Cannes.

He offered to drive her to her hotel, but she said it wasn't necessary, it was only two minutes from the Carlton, and she enjoyed walking.

There was a parking place open in front of the Carlton between a Jaguar and an Alfa. He swung the Simca into it and turned off the motor. He was sure it wouldn't be there when next he needed it.

"Thank you for the ride," the girl said, getting out of the car. "I like your friends the Murphys. And I'm sure I'd like you if I ever got the chance."

He smiled, rewarding her manners. "I'll be around," he said vaguely.

He watched her stride off along the Croisette carrying her tape recorder, Murphy isolated in a capsule. Her long brown hair shone over the blue polo

shirt. Standing there in the bright sunshine, he felt
deserted. He didn't want to be alone that afternoon,
remembering what it had been like when he was
twenty-seven. He had the impulse to hurry after her,
touch her arm, walk beside her. But he fought the
impulse down. He went into the bar, drank a pastis,
then wandered fretfully over to the rue d'Antibes
and saw half a dirty movie. It had been made in Germany and featured bosomy lesbian ladies in high
leather boots in rural settings, glades and waterfalls.
The theatre was crowded. He left and went back
toward his hotel.

Two hard-faced whores on the corner near the
tennis courts stared at him aggressively. Maybe I
should do it, he thought. Maybe it would solve something.

But he merely smiled gently at the two women and
walked on. There was applause coming from the
tennis courts, and he went in. A tournament was
being played, for juniors. The boys were wild but
moved with dazzling speed. He watched for a few
minutes, trying to remember the time when he had
moved that fast.

He left the courts and went around the corner to
the hotel, avoiding the terrace, which already had the
beginning of the evening assembly of drinkers.

When he picked up his key, the concierge gave
him some messages that had come in for him in his
absence. He had to sign for a registered letter from
his wife that had been forwarded from his hotel in
Paris. He stuffed the messages and the letter into his
pocket without reading them.

In the elevator a short man with a paunch wearing
an orange shirt was saying to a pretty young girl,
"This is the worst festival of all times." The girl
could have been a secretary or a starlet or a whore or
the man's daughter.

When he reached his apartment, he went out onto

the balcony and sat down and regarded the sea for a while. Then he took the messages out of his pocket and read them at random. He kept his wife's letter for last. Dessert.

Mr. B. Thomas and his wife would like to dine with Mr. Craig tonight. Would Mr. Craig be good enough to call back? They were at the Hotel Martinez and would be in until seven.

Bruce Thomas was a man whom he didn't know well but liked. He was a director and had had three hits in a row. He was about forty years old. He was one of the men Craig had been thinking about when he had told Gail McKinnon why he had never been tempted to direct. Tomorrow he would tell Thomas that he had returned to the hotel too late to call him back. He didn't want to dine that night with a man who had had three hits in a row.

Sidney Green had called and wanted to know if he could have a drink with Mr. Craig before dinner tonight. He would be in the bar at eight. Sidney Green was a man who had directed three or four movies and who had been hired by an independent company to prepare a series of pictures. The independent company had stopped operations a month before, and Green was in Cannes looking for a job, beseeching everyone he met to put in a good word for him. He would drink alone at the bar tonight.

Miss Natalie Sorel had called and would Mr. Craig please call back. Natalie Sorel had been one of the two magnificently gowned and coiffed ladies at the party the night before whom Gail McKinnon had noticed and celebrated. She was a fairly well-known movie actress, originally from Hungary, who played in three or four languages. She had been his mistress for a few months, five or six years ago, when he had been doing the picture in Paris, but he had lost sight of her. She was going on forty now, still lush and beautiful, and when he had seen her at the party, he had wondered why he had ever broken with her. They had spent a weekend together, he remembered, at Beaulieu, out of season, and it was one of the most satisfactory memories of his life. At the party she had told him she was getting married. Miss Natalie Sorel represented too many complicatons at the moment, he decided. Her phone would not ring.

There was a hand-written note from Ian Wadleigh. He and Wadleigh had had some drunken evenings together in New York and Hollywood. Wadleigh had written a novel that had been widely acclaimed in the early 1950s. At that time he had been a boisterous, witty man who argued loudly in bars with strangers. Since then he had written several disappointing novels and had worked on a lot of screenplays and had gone through three wives and become a drunk. Craig hadn't seen Wadleigh's name in print or on the screen for years, and he was surprised to see Wadleigh's signature on the envelope.

"Dear Jess," Wadleigh wrote in a loose scrawl, "I heard you were here and thought maybe it would be heart-warming to tie one on together, for old time's sake. I'm in a flea bag near the old port where the poor folk lead their short, nasty, brutish lives, but they're pretty good at taking messages. Call when you have the time. Ian."

Craig wondered what Wadleigh was doing in Cannes. But he wasn't curious enough to call the number Wadleigh had noted at the bottom of the page.

He opened his wife's registered letter. She had typed it herself. She was two days late in getting her monthly check, she wrote, and she was notifying her lawyer and his lawyer. If she did not receive the check within one day, she would instruct her lawyer to take the appropriate steps.

He stuffed all the loose bits of paper into his pocket and sat back and watched the darkening sea as the sun set.

The sky clouded over, and the sea turned a stony gray, and a light rain began to fall. The wind rose, and the fronds of the palm trees along the waterfront clashed with a mechanical dry noise. A white yacht, pitching in the swell, its running lights on, made for the old harbor.

He went in off the balcony and flicked the switch on the living-room wall. The lights came on, pale and watery. In the yellowish glow the room looked shabby and unwelcoming. He got out his checkbook and sat down at the desk and wrote out a check for his wife. He hadn't added up his balance in the checkbook for weeks, and he didn't do it now. He put the check in an envelope and wrote the address. Now a stranger's house, although still full of his books and papers and the furniture of half a lifetime.

He pulled open the drawer of the desk and took out the script, one of six copies that were lying there. It had no cover, and the title was on the top page— *The Three Horizons.* There was no author's name under the title. Craig took out a pen and leaned over the desk. He hesitated for a moment and then wrote, "by Malcolm Harte." It was as good a name as any. Let the work be judged entirely on its own merits, with an unknown name on its cover. The reactions would be purer. His friends would not be tempted to be lenient, his foes unaware of a new opportunity for derision. He recognized the cowardice there, but the good sense, too, the search for accuracy.

Methodically, he repeated the inscription, writing it neatly on the remaining five copies. He put a copy of the script in a manila envelope and wrote Bryan Murphy's name on it.

He thought of calling Constance. She should be home by now. And cooled down after the outburst of the morning. But if she weren't home, he knew it would sadden him, so he didn't pick up the telephone.

He went down to the crowded lobby, smiled without warmth at two people he knew but did not wish to talk to. At the concierge's desk he mailed the check to his wife and asked to have the script delivered immediately by messenger to Bryan Murphy at the Hotel du Cap. Then he wrote out a cable to Anne telling her to get on the next plane to Nice. If he was going to be unsettled by the young, it might as well be his own flesh and blood.

SIX

HE went to a small restaurant on the old port for dinner. Alone. He had spoken to enough people that day. The restaurant was one of the best in town, expensive and usually crowded. But tonight, except for himself and two loud parties of English, the men florid and excessively barbered, the women overdressed and bejeweled, the room was empty. The English groups were not connected with the Festival but were vacationing in Cannes. He had seen them all the night before at the casino, men and women alike playing for high stakes. The women were sopranoing about other holiday places, Sardinia, Monte, as they called it, Capri, St. Moritz, the compulsory stations of the rich. The men were complaining about the Labor government, currency restrictions, the bank rate, devaluation, their voices booming over the high trill of their wives.

There will always be an England, Craig thought as he ate his salade niçoise.

Pablo Picasso came in with a party of five, and the handsome woman who owned the restaurant fussed him into a table along the opposite wall. Craig looked at him once, admired the bull-like vitality radiating from the small stocky figure, the great naked head, the dark eyes that were somehow gentle and fierce at the same time. Then he averted his glance. Picasso, he was sure, enjoyed his fame, but he had the right to spoon his soup without having his every gesture noted by a middle-aged, prying American whose only claim to the artist's attention was that he had once hung a lithograph of a dove on the wall of a house he no longer owned.

The two English groups had stared briefly and incuriously at Picasso and his party as they entered the restaurant, then went back to their steaks and their champagne.

Later, the proprietress came over to his table. "You know who that is, don't you?" she said in a low voice.

"Of course."

"They . . ." There was a little sardonic gesture of her head for her British customers. "They don't recognize him," she said.

"Art is long," Craig said, "and recognition is fleeting."

"*Comment?*" The proprietress looked puzzled.

"An American joke," Craig said.

When he had finished his dinner, the proprietress gave him a brandy on the house with his coffee. If the English had recognized Picasso, he would have had to pay for his own brandy.

As he went out of the restaurant, he passed Picasso's table. Their eyes met briefly. He wondered what the old man's eyes really saw. An abstraction, an angular, ugly product of the American machine? A murderer standing over a slain Asian peasant counting bodies? A mournful, displaced clown at an alien, sad carnival? A lonely fellow human being moving painfully across an empty canvas? He deplored the conventions that ruled his conduct. How satisfactory it would be to go over to the old man and say, "You have enriched my life."

He went out of the restaurant and crossed the street to the quay to walk past the moored yachts bobbing gently in the quiet, black water. Why are you not all at sea? he wondered.

As he neared the turn of the harbor, he saw a familiar figure approaching under the lamplights. It was Ian Wadleigh, walking, shambling loosely and wearily, his head down. At the last moment Wadleigh saw him and straightened up sprucely and smiled at him. Wadleigh had grown fat and bulged out of his unpressed clothes. His collar was open to accommodate the thick, flabby throat, and a tie hung, carelessly low and askew, down the rumpled shirt. He needed a haircut, and the uncombed thick hair, going in all directions over the high, bulging forehead, gave him a wild, prophetic air.

"Just the man I wanted to see," Wadleigh said loudly. "My friend, the boy wonder." Wadleigh had met Craig when he had just turned thirty. The phrase was now meant to hurt, and it did.

"Hello, Ian," Craig said. They shook hands. Wadleigh's palm was sweaty.

"I left a note for you," Wadleigh said accusingly.

"I was going to call you tomorrow."

"Who knows where I'm going to be tomorrow?" Wadleigh's voice was a little thick. He had been drinking. As usual. He had started to drink when his books had begun to go badly. Or his books had started to go badly when he had begun to drink. The cause and effect of Ian Wadleigh.

"Aren't you here for the whole festival?" Craig asked.

"I am nowhere for nothing," Wadleigh said. He was drunker than Craig had first thought. "What are you doing?"

"When?"

"Now."

"Just taking a walk."

"Alone?" Wadleigh peered around him suspiciously, as though Craig were hiding some dubious companion among the upturned dories and the fishing equipment on the dark quay.

"Alone," Craig said.

"The loneliness of the long-distance producer," Wadleigh said. "I'll walk with you. Two comrades, veterans of the retreat from Sunset Boulevard."

"Do you always talk in movie titles, Ian?" Craig asked. He was annoyed by the writer's assumption that they were linked in disaster.

"The Art of Now," Wadleigh said. "Print is dead. Read any Canadian philosopher. Lead me to the nearest bar, boy wonder."

"I've had enough to drink for tonight."

"Lucky man," Wadleigh said. "Anyway, I'll walk with you. You've got to be going in a better direction than I am."

They walked side by side, Wadleigh self-consciously straight-backed and springy. He had been a handsome man, with bold, lean features, but his face had been destroyed by drink and fat and self-pity. "Tell me all about yourself, boy wonder," he said. "What are you doing in this shit hole?"

"I thought it was time to see a couple of movies," Craig said.

"I live in London," Wadleigh said. "Did you know that?" He asked the question harshly, daring Craig to admit that he had lost interest in his one-time friend's activities.

"Yes," Craig said. "How is London?"

"The city of Shakespeare and Marlowe," Wadleigh said, "of Queen Elizabeth and Dickens, of Twiggy and Ian Wadleigh. Another shit hole. I'm supposed to be down here doing a piece on the Festival for an English fag magazine. On spec. They pay my hotel bill. If they take the piece, they throw me another couple of pounds. They want that old magic name Ian Wadleigh on their fag cover. When they read the piece, they'll probably puke. All I've seen here is shit. And I'm going to say so. There'll be a twitter in the dovecote. The fag entertainment editor never learned how to read, so he thinks movies are today's music of the spheres. The Art of Now. He thinks Jean-Luc Godard turns out a new Sistine Chapel four times a year. Christ, he thought *Blow-up* was a masterpiece!

What do *you* think of the crap they're showing here?"

"Some good, some bad," Craig said. "I figure by the time the thing's over, we'll have seen at least six good pictures."

"Six!" Wadleigh snorted. "When you make up the list, send it to me. I'll include it in my piece. Freedom of the press. The half-dozen selections of a once-great mind."

"You'd better go back to your hotel, Ian," Craig said. "You're being a pain in the ass."

"I'm sorry." Wadleigh was genuinely contrite. "My manners have deteriorated the last few years. Along with everything else. I don't want to go back to my hotel. There's nothing there for me but a collection of fleas and half the manuscript of a book I'll probably never finish. I know I'm a bitter son of a bitch these days, but I shouldn't take it out on an old pal like you. Forgive me. You do forgive me, don't you, Jess?" He was pleading now.

"Of course."

"We were friends, weren't we?" He was still pleading. "We had some good times together, didn't we? We put down a lot of bottles together. There's still something left, isn't there, Jess?"

"Yes, there is, Ian," Craig said, although there wasn't.

"What kills me," Wadleigh said, "is what passes for writing these days. Especially in the movies. Everybody grunting and saying, Yeah, and, Like, you know, I dig you, baby, and, Let's fuck, and that's supposed to be dialogue, that's supposed to be how the noble human animal communicates with his fellow man under the eye of God. And the people who write like that get a hundred thousand a picture and win Oscars and all the girls they can handle, and I'm down to writing a crappy two-thousand-word piece on spec for a fag English magazine."

"Come on, Ian," Craig said. "Every artist has his

ups and downs. Just about everybody goes in and out of fashion in his lifetime. If he lasts long enough."

"I will be back in fashion fifty years after I die," Wadleigh said. "Posterity's darling, Ian Wadleigh. And how about you? I haven't seen many articles in the Sunday papers recently saying how wonderful *you* are."

"I'm on sabbatical leave," Craig said, "from admiration."

"It's one hell of a long sabbatical leave," Wadleigh said.

"So it is."

"That reminds me," Wadleigh said. "There's a girl here by the name of McKinnon—she's some kind of reporter—who keeps trying to pump me about you. All sorts of questions. About women. Girls. Your friends. Your enemies. She seems to know more about you than I do. Have you been talking to her?"

"A bit."

"Be careful," Wadleigh said. "She has a funny light in her eye."

"I'll be careful."

A Fiat with two girls in it slowed down along the curb, and the girl nearest them leaned out the open window and said, *"Bonsoir."*

"Get the hell out of here," Wadleigh said.

"Sal juif," the girl said. The car spurted ahead.

"Dirty Jew," Wadleigh said. "Do I look *that* bad?"

Craig laughed. "You must learn to be more polite with French ladies," he said. "They've all been brought up in convents."

"Whores," Wadleigh said. "Whores everywhere. In the audience, on the screen, on the streets, in the jury room. I tell you, Jess, this is the living and eternal capital of whoredom for two weeks each year. Spread your legs and take your money. That ought to be printed on every letterhead under the seal of the city of Cannes. And look at that. Over there." He pointed across the boulevard where there were four young men smiling professionally at passing males. "How do you like that?"

"Not very much," Craig admitted.

"You can't tell the players without a program anymore," Wadleigh said. "Wait till you read my piece."

"I can't wait," Craig said.

"I'd better send you a copy of the manuscript," Wadleigh said. "Those fags'll never print it. Or maybe I'll turn whore, too, and write just what that fag entertainment editor wants to hear. If I don't get that dough, I don't know what I'll do."

"Maybe that's just what those girls in the car and those boys over there on the corner say to themselves every night," Craig said. "If I don't get that dough, I don't know what I'll do."

"You're just too fucking Christian tolerant, Jess," Wadleigh said. "And don't think it's a virtue. The world is going to the dogs on a sickening wave of tolerance. Dirty movies, dirty business, dirty politics. Anything goes. Everything's excused. There's always a half-dozen something that isn't bad."

"What you need, Ian," Craig said, "is a good night's sleep."

"What I need," Wadleigh said, stopping on the sidewalk, "is five thousand dollars. Have you got five thousand dollars for me?"

"No," Craig said. "What do you need five thousand dollars for?"

"There're some people making a movie in Madrid," Wadleigh said. "They have a lousy script, naturally, and they need a quick rewrite. If I can get there, it's almost sure the job's mine."

"It only costs about a hundred bucks to fly from here to Madrid, Ian."

"What'll I use for the hotel?" Wadleigh demanded. "And food? And for the time it takes to sign the contract? And before the first payment? And for my lousy third wife? At this moment she's attaching the books and typewriter I left in storage in New York for nonpayment of alimony."

"You've struck a responsive chord there, Brother," Craig said.

"If you go in to make a deal and the bastards know you haven't got a dime, they grind you to powder," Wadleigh said. "You've got to be able to get up and walk out and say, Up yours, friends. You know that. I figure five thousand is a minimum."

"Sorry, Ian," Craig said.

"Okay, can you give me three hundred? I can get to Madrid and give myself a couple of days on three hundred." The fat on his throat over his loose collar was quivering.

Craig hesitated. Unconsciously, he patted his coat over his wallet. He knew he had five hundred dollars in American money and about 2000 francs in the wallet. Superstitiously, in memory of the time he had been poor, he always carried a lot of money with him. Turning down requests for loans, even from people who were strangers, was invariably painful, almost impossible, for him. He regarded this trait, rightly, as a weakness in his character. He always remembered that in *War and Peace* Tolstoy had used Pierre Bezouchov's new-found ability to turn down supplicants for money as a sign of maturity and ripening intelligence. "All right, Ian," he said, "I can give you three hundred."

"Five thousand would do better," Wadleigh said.

"I said three hundred." Craig took out his wallet and extracted three one hundred dollar bills and gave them to Wadleigh.

Wadleigh stuffed the bills roughly into his pocket. "You know I'll never pay you back," he said.

"I know."

"I won't apologize," Wadleigh said fiercely.

"I'm not asking you to apologize."

"You know why I won't apologize? Because you owe it to me. You know why you owe it to me? Because once we were equals. And now you're something, and I'm nothing. Less than nothing."

"Have a good time in Madrid, Ian," Craig said wearily. "I'm going to bed. Good night."

He left Wadleigh standing there under the lamppost, with the whores cruising by him as he stared at Craig's retreating back.

By the time he had reached his hotel, Craig had caught a chill and was shivering a little. He went into the bar, which was nearly empty at this hour between dinner and the end of the showing in the Festival Hall. He sat at the bar and ordered a hot grog for his health's sake. While he was drinking it, the bartender showed him a photograph of his son. T'' son was dressed in the archaic uniform of the Esc_ Noir of the French cavalry school at Saumur. In the photograph the young man was taking a fine black horse over a jump, his seat perfect, his hands secure. Craig admired the picture for the father's pleasure, thinking the meanwhile how wonderful it must be to devote your life to something as pretty and useless as a French cavalry squadron in 1970.

Still shivering a little and beginning to feel the advent of fever, he paid for his drink, said good night to the father of the cavalryman, and went to the lobby to get the key for his room. There was an envelope in his box, and he recognized Gail McKinnon's handwriting. Now he regretted not having asked her to have dinner with him. Wadleigh would not have spoken as he had if the girl had been at his side. Wadleigh had shaken him more than he cared to admit to himself. And he would have been three hundred dollars richer because Wadleigh wouldn't have brought himself to ask for money in front of a witness. Irrationally, too, he felt that the chill he was suffering from, and the mounting fever, could be traced to his encounter with the writer. The cold wind from the depths of Cannes.

In his room he put on a sweater and poured himself a whisky, again for his health's sake. It was too

early to go to sleep, fever or no fever. He opened
Gail McKinnon's envelope and in the yellowish glow
of the glass chandelier read what she had written to
him.

"Dear Mr. Craig," he read, "I persist. With opti-
mism. This afternoon, at lunch and in the car, I
sensed that you were becoming more friendly. You
are not really as remote a man as you try to appear.
As we passed the house where you told me you spent
a summer on the Cap d'Antibes, I felt that you wanted to say more than you allowed yourself to say. Perhaps it was out of caution, not wanting to reveal
something on the spur of the moment that you would
regret later seeing in print. So what I'm doing here
is writing out some questions that you can read at
your leisure and then write out your replies to the
ones you choose to answer in exactly the terms that
please you. You can edit as you will, free of any fear
of slips of the tongue that an unscrupulous newspaperman or newspaperwoman might take advantage
of.

"Here goes—"

He read the first question and stopped. It was a
simple one. "Why are you in Cannes?" Well, he
thought, that's a good beginning. And a good end. Intelligent girl. The all-inclusive, everlasting inquiry.
Why are you anyplace? *The answer to this question
is to determine your general knowledge of the subject. You have thirty minutes, or twenty-four hours,
or forty-eight years in which to complete the examination.*

Why are you in this city and not in another? Why
are you in this bed with this woman and not another? Why are you alone here or in a crowd there?
How have you come to be kneeling before this altar
at this time? What has driven you to say no to that
journey and yes to the one on which you find yourself? What has possessed you to cross that river yesterday, board this plane this morning, kiss this child

this evening? What has driven you to this latitude? What friends, enemies, successes, failures, lies, truths, calculations of time and geography, what reading of maps, what detours and highways have deposited you in this room at this evening hour?

A fair question deserved a fair answer.

He went over to the desk and sat down and pulled out a sheet of paper and a pen. "Why am I in Cannes?" he wrote slowly. He hesitated. Then, without really thinking of what he was doing or writing, he wrote, almost automatically, "I am in Cannes to save my life."

• SEVEN •

He stared at the sentence that he had written. That is not my handwriting, he thought. He put the pen down. He knew he was not going to write anything more that night. *Anything you say may be used against you.* He leaned back in his chair and closed his eyes.

There was a brilliant, painful light shining, a wild, loud howling somewhere. He opened his eyes. Through the wet smear of the windshield wipers two damp moons were hurtling straight at him. His hands were still loosely on the wheel. He yanked at the wheel, slid past the other car by inches on the gleaming black road. The wail of the other car's horn faded like a funeral cry behind him. He felt calm, drove alertly, not stopping, peering carefully through the streaked glass at the curves ahead of him.

A few miles farther on his hands began to shake, his body to shiver uncontrollably. He pulled over to the side of the road, stopped the car, waited for the spasm to pass. He had no idea of how long it was before his hands stopped shaking. He was conscious of cold sweat on his forehead, icicles dripping down inside his clothing from his armpits. He took out his handkerchief, wiped his forehead, breathed deeply, four profound inhalations. The air in the car smelled sour. Where was he? The rows of black trees alongside the road told him nothing. He had crossed the French border not so long ago, he remembered. He was somewhere between the Bidassosa River and Saint Sebastian. He had started from Paris that morning, had not stopped except for gasoline and a cup of coffee all day. *I have nearly died in sunny Spain.* He had intended to drive without a halt until Madrid, sleep over, go farther south—to Malaga—the next day. A man he knew, something of a friend, a matador, really the friend of a friend, was fighting in Malaga the next afternoon. He had met the man in Alicante the year before. There was a three-day *feria.* Mediterranean sunshine, parading bands, fireworks, the costumes of the Spanish south, much drinking, long, crowded hangovers, the amused irresponsibility of other people's celebrations, companions, men and women he knew well enough to enjoy on a short holiday but who meant nothing much to him, whom he only saw the four or five times in the year when he happened to go to a bullfight.

The matador was too old for the bulls. He knew it. He was a rich man. There was no sensible reason for him to go into an arena with animals who were devoted to killing him. "What can I do?" the matador had said. "It is the only thing that deeply amuses me. It is my only playground. I am lucky. I *have* a playground. Most people do not have one. So—I cannot permit them to drive me from it."

There were many ways of dying in Spain. Horns, falling asleep at the wheel.

It was the third time that year he had fallen asleep driving at night. Once outside Salzburg. Once on the *autostrada* near Florence. Tonight. He had been lucky. Or had he been? Anyway, he had opened his eyes in time. In the last years he had taken to driving nine hundred, a thousand miles at a stretch. What had he wanted to do in Salzburg, what had he planned to see in Florence? His friend the matador would be fighting in thirty different places all season. Why had he felt it was necessary to go to Malaga? He no longer remembered. He liked driving at night, the solitude, the numbing, hypnotic onrush of lights, the satisfaction of leaving a place he felt he had been in too long, the pleasure of moving through the deserted, dark streets of a new city, the accomplishment of distance.

Suicide was in every garage. He was sane enough to understand that.

He started the car, drove slowly into Saint Sebastian, found a hotel. He would not reach Madrid that night.

A bar was open near the hotel. He ordered a brandy, then another. He wasn't hungry. There were some men arguing at a table in Spanish. He listened. Their heads were bent together over the table, their voices fell to a conspiratorial hush. They might have been planning to murder Franco, free a priest, bomb the prefecture of police, take a chance on a lottery. He did not understand the language. He was soothed by his ignorance.

He called Paris from the hotel. It took a long time, and he undressed and got into bed waiting for the call to be put through. Constance answered. He had left her early in the morning. They had made love in the dawn. She had been sleepy and warm. Her lovemaking was robust as usual, generous and easy. She gave freely, took without stint, there were no favors exchanged, no debts to be paid off in bed. She never said, "Why do you have to go?" when he announced without warning that he was off to Zurich or the Côte Basque or New York. He would not have been able to answer her truthfully if she had asked.

Every once in a while they went on trips together, but that was different. They were holidays when she had time off from work. When he drove off by himself, it was not a holiday. If she was in the car with him, he drove slowly, chatting with her, playing word games, enjoying the scenery, stopping often for brandies. She liked to drive, too. She was an erratic driver, but lucky. She had never had an accident, she boasted. She should have had twenty. He had laughed once as they teetered around a curve on the wrong side of the road. She hated being laughed at. She had stopped the car and got out and said she wouldn't drive with him anymore and started walking back toward Paris. He had waited, and she had come back a half hour later, trying unsuccessfully to look imperious, and gotten into the car, and he had let her drive, and she'd stopped the car at the first café, and they'd had a brandy.

That morning, when he had left her, he had gone back to his hotel and packed his bag and sped through the early-morning traffic toward the auto route south. Once she had asked him why he bothered keeping a hotel room since almost every night he was in Paris he stayed at her place. He had said, "I'm used to hotels." She hadn't asked again.

The phone rang on the table beside the bed. The room was an immense one, with dark, high furniture. He always went to the best hotel in town, avoiding the other guests. He didn't like the ordinary run of guests in the best hotel in any town.

"Are you in Madrid already?" she asked. He might have just awakened her, but you never could tell with Constance. Five seconds after she was roused, she sounded as though she had just come, bubbling and fresh, from a cold shower.

"No," he said, "I stopped in Saint Sebastian for the night."

"How is it in Saint Sebastian?"

"They're speaking Spanish," he said.

"What a surprise." She laughed. "What made you change your mind?"

If he had been honest, he would have said, "I didn't want to die tonight." Instead, he said, "It was raining."

Another year. Five years ago. He was standing in the lobby of a movie theatre in Pasadena. There had been a sneak preview of the last picture he had made. The movie had been shot in France, its hero a young lieutenant in the American army in Germany who had deserted and had a disastrous affair with a French woman before turning himself in. The director, Frank Baranis, was in the lobby with him, sunk in a large polo coat, depressed because the audience had coughed and been inattentive throughout the film. They had been friends ever since Baranis had directed Edward Brenner's play nearly twenty years before. Baranis had been the best man at Craig's wedding. During the shooting of the film, Craig had received an anonymous letter in a woman's handwriting saying that Baranis had been sleeping with Penelope before the marriage, the very day before, the letter had said, and probably for a long time after. Craig had ignored the letter, had said nothing about it either to Penelope or Baranis. On the strength of an anonymous letter, probably from a jilted and vengeful woman, you did not ask the man who was your friend and was working day and night for you on a complicated and demanding task whether or not he had slept with your wife the day before your wedding seventeen years ago.

Craig was suddenly aware of how old Baranis looked, like a fearful, wizened monkey. He was lightly pockmarked, but he had large liquid dark eyes and a disdainful, offhand way with women that was, Craig heard, effective.

"Well," Baranis said, "we bombed. What do we do now?"

"Nothing," Craig said. "That was the picture we wanted to make, and we made it."

A man and his wife, in the crowd coming out of the auditorium through the lobby, passed nearby. The woman was short and dowdy. If she had been on sale, you would have been able to find her in gross lots on the shelves of a supermarket at clearance prices. The man was burly, bursting out of his clothes, and looked like a football coach whose team had just lost a game and was furious with his players. His face was red and flushed, his eyes glared behind rimless glasses. "What a load of shit," he was saying as he passed the spot where Craig and Baranis were standing. "They think they can get away with anything these days."

"Harry," the woman said in her supermarket voice. "Your language."

"I repeat," the man said. "A load of shit."

Craig and Baranis looked silently at each other. They had worked for nearly two years on the picture.

After a while Baranis said, "Maybe it isn't a picture for Pasadena. Maybe it'll be different in New York."

"Maybe," Craig said. Then, since it was that kind of night, anyway, he said, "Frank, a couple of months ago I got an anonymous letter that said you'd had an affair with Penelope before we were married. That you'd gone to bed with her the day before, even. Is that true?"

"Yes," Baranis said. It was still that kind of night.

"Why didn't you say something?"

"You never asked," Baranis said. "How the hell was I to know when it started you wanted to marry her?" He pulled the collar of the polo coat up around him, half-buried his face in it. He looked like a small, trapped, dying animal. "Anyway, if I had told you, you'd have married her just the same. You'd have forgiven her and hated me. You'd never have talked to me again."

"I suppose so," Craig said.

"Look at you and Ed Brenner," Baranis said. He sounded angry. "You never see *him* anymore, do you?"

"No."

"See?"

"You knew about Brenner and Penny?" Craig asked flatly.

"Everybody knew." Baranis shrugged impatiently. "So what good would it have done if I'd opened my big mouth?" Baranis sank deeper in his coat.

"No good." Craig nodded reasonably. "Come on, let's get out of here. I'll drive you home."

The picture didn't do much better in New York. It was before the time when movies about soldiers who were disillusioned with the American army were to the public taste.

He was sitting in his office signing checks on the scarred, fake mahogany desk. The office was small and shabby, two rooms, one for him and one for his secretary. Belinda Ewen had been with him since his first play. The furniture of the office also was the same he had started with back in 1946. Neither Belinda nor the furniture had improved with the passage of time. Belinda had been a small, dark, furiously energetic, almost pretty young woman when he had hired her. She was still small, dark, and energetic, but now was no longer almost pretty. Her face seemed to have been honed into severe angular lines by the abrasion of the years, her lips chipped out by a blunt knife. The desk had been fake mahogany in 1946. It just looked a little more fake now.

Penelope had campaigned to be allowed to choose a larger office for him and to decorate it herself. He had refused. He didn't like the offices of men whose wives had chosen the furniture, the thick rugs, the tasteful paintings on the walls. Penelope had also tried, at least once a year throughout their marriage, to get him to fire Belinda. "She runs the office as though it's hers, not yours," Penelope had said over and over again. "And besides, she's disrespectful to me." Among Penelope's complaints about Belinda Ewen was Belinda's style of dress. "It's grotesque,"

Penelope had said. "She looks as though she's gotten herself up to go to Coney Island with a sailor. What do you imagine people think about you when they come into the office for the first time and they see that woman decked out in all the colors of the rainbow?" He hadn't replied, as he might have, that people came to his office to work with Jesse Craig, not to pass judgment on the choice of his secretary's clothes. But he contented himself with saying, "When she marries, I'll get someone who dresses all in black."

"Married!" Penelope had sniffed. "While you're alive, that woman will never marry."

"I hope you're right," he had said. The discussion had taken place on one of the less pleasant evenings at home.

Even so, there were times when the clashing greens and purples of some new outfit that Belinda had put together made him shake his head in wonderment. Safely behind the closed door of his own office, of course.

Penelope had also suggested, in moments of anger, that he had had an affair—was still having an affair—with the secretary. He had never touched Belinda and believed that she would run screaming through the halls if he as much as brushed her cheek. And he saw no reason, if a woman did her work as efficiently as Belinda did hers, why she had to be respectful to her employer's wife.

And finally, he was superstitious. He had done well in the shabby little office with the unprepossessing, ludicrously dressed secretary; he had done better than he had ever hoped or dreamed he might do since the day when he had signed the first lease for eighty dollars a month. There was no sense in tempting fate with unnecessary signs of luxury. Although now, sitting at the old desk, in the late afternoon of an autumnal New York day, signing away at a torrent of checks after the disastrous preview in Pasadena and the neglected opening in New York, he could hardly argue that luck had made a permanent base in the bare room in which he had worked so long.

The checks he was signing were from his personal, not from his business account. For the most part they were for household bills, food, liquor, fuel, telephone, the salaries of the two maids, flowers, a bill for two thousand dollars for a sofa that Penelope had found at an antique dealer's on Madison Avenue, bills from Saks Fifth Avenue and Bergdorf Goodman for clothes that Penelope had bought, a two-hundred-dollar bill that came in monthly from Charles of the Ritz where Penelope had her hair done. There were other bills, too—tuition for Anne's school in Lausanne, tuition for Marcia's school in Maryland, insurance and garage rent for Penelope's car, a hundred-and-eighty-dollar bill for the masseuse who visited Penelope three times weekly, a savage bill from a doctor in Hollywood for treatment of Penelope's mother, who had come out to visit her daughter soon after the marriage when Craig had been making his first movie on the Coast and had immediately fallen mysteriously ill and was taking a long time to die in the most expensive place for dying in the world.

Craig had tried setting up a household account for Penelope to handle, but she was always overdrawn or neglected to pay the telephone bill so that suddenly it would be cut off, or she would pay bills twice or be too busy to bother for months on end, and there would eventually be dunning letters on his desk to annoy him. So now he had Belinda type up the checks, and once a month, in silent fury, he signed them himself. He wondered what Belinda thought as she typed out the checks for clothes that more than equaled her entire year's salary. She must also speculate, he thought, what anybody could do to a woman's hair that was worth two hundred dollars a month.

When he had finished with the last check, he threw down his pen and leaned back in his chair and looked out the streaked, dirty window of his office at the lighted windows across the street, behind which clerks and secretaries were working in the glare of neon tubes. If they had known what he had been doing at his desk for the last hour or so, they would have every right, he thought, to come storming out of their cubicles and into his office to tear his checkbook to bits. At the very least, the checkbook.

From time to time he had tried to remonstrate with Penelope about the bills she ran up, but Penelope invariably broke into tears at the mention of money. Quarreling about money was debasing. She had not dreamt when she married him that she was linking herself for life with a man who thought only in dollars and cents. In all her childhood and youth in Chicago she had never heard a word in her home about money. Listening to her, one would think that she came from a long line of landed aristocrats whose wealth was based in some illustrious, monarchal past in which plebeian matters such as debts and assets were handled only in backstairs obscurity by discreet underlings in frock coats. Actually, her father had been a traveling salesman in silks and ribbons who had died in want. Craig had had to pay for the old man's funeral.

As the discussions grew more heated, Penelope swore that she watched every cent, called on the names of wives of their friends who spent more on their clothes in one month than she did in a year, which was true, brought heaven to witness that all her efforts and expenditures were designed to make him a decent home, give him a wife he would not be ashamed to be seen with in public, bring up his children decently. He hated scenes, especially about money. Deep down he had the feeling that the large sums that had come his way in his career were not rightly his but the work of accident, luck, for doing only the things he would have happily done, anyway, for a pittance. He could not argue about money. Even in business he never dealt directly with contracts but allowed Bryan Murphy in Hollywood and his business manager on Broadway to handle that side of his affairs at all times. Not being able to dicker with a recalcitrant actor about a percentage of the profits of a play or movie, he certainly couldn't stand up to his wife's tears when it was a question of a six-hundred-dollar telephone bill or the cost of a new coat. Still, remembering his early days living in cheap hotels, he wondered by what insidious magic he found himself signing salary checks for two maids who worked in a house in which he rarely ate more than two meals a week and from which he was absent, more often than not, five or six months a year.

Although each time Belinda brought in the checks to sign she put on what Craig had come to recognize as her steadfastly noncommittal face, he found it difficult to meet her gaze and always pretended to be busy and said gruffly, keeping his head down, "Thank you, Belinda. Just put them on the desk. I'll sign them when I have the time."

When he had first met Penelope, she had been a charming young actress of moderate talent who dressed attractively and lived in a pleasant little apartment in the Village on ninety dollars a week. He wondered where that girl had gone. From a frugal young woman who washed her own stockings and underwear each night, she had turned almost immediately into someone who ransacked galleries and antique shops, who patrolled Fifth Avenue like the advance guard of a looting army, who had to have nurses for her children, who could not conceive of living anywhere in New York City except between Sixtieth and Eighty-sixth Street on the East Side. American women, he thought, take to extravagance with all the natural talent of a dolphin to the waves of the sea.

That it was as much his fault as his wife's and that he recognized this did not make the check-signing sessions any the easier for him.

He added up the amounts of the checks he had signed, entered them neatly in the checkbook. The total came to nine thousand, three hundred and twenty-six dollars and forty-seven cents. Not bad, he thought, for a man with two flops behind him.

When he had been working with Brenner on his first play, Brenner had once said to him, "I cannot take the problems of a man who makes more than fifty dollars a week seriously." Brenner had been youthfully extreme then, but he wondered what his old friend would think about him if somehow he had wandered into the office that afternoon and happened to glance down at the repeated signatures on the scraps of paper scattered across the littered desk.

On an impulse he made out one last check, in his own hand, for nine thousand, three hundred and twenty-six dollars and forty-seven cents. He left the space for the payee blank for a moment. Then he filled in the name of a hospital. It was the hospital in which his two daughters had been born.

He wrote a short note to the fund-raising committee of the hospital to go along with the contribution, put the note and the check into an envelope, and addressed it and sealed it.

He had balanced his accounts for the day.

He called through the door to Belinda. He had tried, briefly, installing a buzzer, but its implications had made him uneasy.

When Belinda came in, he gave her the checks and the one sealed envelope and said, "That'll do it for this afternoon, thank you."

Then he went downstairs to the bar next door and had enough to drink so that the evening ahead of him would be a blur.

When he got home, Penelope said, "Do you think

I'll ever live to see the day that you'll show up for dinner sober?"

The last guests had just gone. There were empty glasses all around the living room. Penelope was in the kitchen emptying ashtrays. He looked at his watch. One-thirty. Everybody had stayed too long. He sank into an easy chair, kicked off his shoes. There had been fourteen at dinner. The dinner had been very good. The company dull. He had drunk too much wine.

Theoretically, his twelve guests were his friends. Of them all, there were only two, Robert and Alice Paine, whom he considered true friends. Robert Paine was a vice-president of a publishing house, on the business side, a portly, solid, highly educated man who spoke slowly, weighing his words, ignoring small talk. Craig had met him when he had been asked to select an anthology of plays for Paine's publishing house, and he had taken an immediate liking to the man. His wife Alice was a child psychiatrist, a large, squarish, handsome woman with mannishly clipped graying hair framing a quiet oval face. Penelope thought they were heavy going, and Craig knew that they had been invited for his sake, so that he wouldn't complain too bitterly about the rest of the list.

There had been nobody at the table who worked in either the theatre or the movies, although two of the men had from time to time invested in plays of his. Bertie Folsom had been there as usual. Since his wife died, Bertie Folsom was at every dinner party. Talking about the stock market. At length. Folsom was a few years older than Craig, a short, sharp-faced, balding, insignificant-looking, meticulously tailored man with a neat, round paunch who headed a big brokerage concern on Wall Street. The farther he went downtown, Craig thought, the more Bertie Folsom must gain in significance. He occasionally gave advice to Craig on stocks. Occasionally, Craig took it. Sometimes the advice was valuable. Since being widowed, he was invited to all dinners at the Craig house. Often he called at six in the evening and asked what they were doing that night. When they weren't doing anything in particular, the Craigs asked him to join them for quiet family dinners. Folsom remembered everybody's birthday, brought gifts for Anne and Marcia. Penelope felt sorry for him, she said. Craig figured that Folsom could not be worth less than two million dollars. Perhaps it was evidence of Penelope's warmth of character that she could find time to be sorry for a man who was worth two million dollars. When they had a party like the one tonight, Penelope invited various ladies for Folsom. They were the sort of ladies, usually divorced, who were always free to come to anybody's house for dinner. When Craig was out of town or working, Folsom escorted Penelope to the theatre and to parties. Somebody had once said Folsom was a useful man, one should always have a widower among one's circle of friends.

The conversation during the evening had been, aside from Bertie Folsom's dissertations on the stock market, about servants, the disastrous quality of the plays on Broadway that season, sports cars, Ferraris, Porsches, and Maseratis, the shortcomings of the young, speculation about the amours, legitimate and covert, of friends who were not present that night, the impossibility of finding a decent place anymore in the Caribbean to spend a holiday, and the comparative virtues of various ski resorts. Somehow, everybody there skied each winter. Except Craig. Penelope spent a month a year in Sun Valley and Aspen. Alone. Sitting at the head of his table in the house on the East Side of New York City, Craig felt that he had become an expert on snow. He had nothing against skiing—he wished he had had the time to take it up when he was a young man—but he believed people should ski, not talk about it. No one that evening had mentioned his last picture, or any of his pictures, except the Paines, who had come early so as to have a chance to talk to him alone for a few minutes over drinks before the rest of the guests had arrived. The Paines had liked his last picture, although Alice Paine had been bothered by the violence of a scene in a Parisian nightclub in which the hero got involved in a brawl. "Alice," Robert Paine had said affectionately about his wife, "hasn't learned yet how to stop being a psychiatrist when she enters a movie house."

There had been one interlude in the evening during which Craig had listened with some interest. The subject of Women's Liberation had come up, and Penelope, who ordinarily spoke little in company, had been eloquently vehement on the subject. She was for Women's Liberation. Craig had agreed with her. So had the other women at the table. If they had not all been so busy with fittings and arranging dinner parties and observing the schedules of hairdressers and traveling to the Caribbean and Sun Valley, they undoubtedly would have made a considerable impression on the movement.

Craig did not bother with the guest lists for parties. For one thing, he was too occupied with other matters to take the time. Occasionally, he met someone who interested him enough to suggest his or her name to Penelope, but more often than not Penelope would find some reason, usually perfectly valid, why the man or woman or couple would not fit in with the particular evening she was planning.

He sighed, not actually knowing why he did so. He heaved himself out of the chair and walked in his stockinged feet across the thick pale carpet to the sideboard where the bottles were ranged and poured himself a whisky. Penelope came in from the kitchen, glanced at the glass in his hand. When she did that, he always felt guilty. He picked up the bottle and added another ounce to his drink, splashed some soda into it, and went back to the easy chair. He watched Penelope move about the big, comfortable room in the subdued lamplight that shone in soft creamy pools on the polished wood of end tables, the brocade of chairs, the brass pots full of flowers. Penelope could not stand strong light. It was always difficult in any house she inhabited, even houses they rented for a summer, to find a place where it was possible to read.

She was dressed in a long, loose red velvet robe that swung gracefully around her slender, still youthful figure as she touched a bunch of flowers, put a magazine back in the rack, closed the cover of a silver cigarette box. Her taste was sure. Things looked better after she had touched them. There was nothing ornate or showy about her house, but, Craig thought, it was a wonderful place to live in, and he loved it. With the glass of whisky in his hand, he watched his wife move around the warm, welcoming room, and he forgot the dull departed guests. At that moment, admiring her in the midnight silence, he knew he loved her and felt completely married. He knew her faults. She was a liar, extravagant, cunning, often pretentious; she filled his house with second-rate people because she feared the competition of wit, beauty, intelligence; she had been unfaithful to him and at the same time made him suffer from the blackmail of her jealousy; when things went wrong, she invariably found a way to pass the blame onto other shoulders, usually his; often she bored him. Still, he loved her. No marriage was all of one piece. Each partner paid some price. He had no illusions about his own perfection. He was sure that in her secret heart Penelope's list of his failings was much longer than the account of his own judgments on her.

He put his glass down, stood up, went over to her, kissed the back of her neck. She stiffened as though the gesture had caught her by surprise.

"Let's go to bed," he said.

She pulled away. "You go to bed," she said. "I still have things to do down here."

"I want to go to bed with you," he said.

She walked quickly across the room, put a chair between them as though for defense. "I thought that was just about over," she said.

"Well, it isn't."

"It is for me," she said.

"What did you say?"

"I said it's over for me. Permanently. I don't want to go to bed with you or with anybody." Her voice was low, even, without emotion.

"What brought *that* on?" He tried to keep his anger from showing.

"You," she said. "Everything. Leave me alone."

He went over and got his glass and took a long drink.

"When you sober up in the morning," she said, "you'll find your passion has been neatly filed away in the back of the vault. Along with a lot of other things."

"I'm not drunk," he said.

"Every night," she said.

"Do you mean what you just said?"

"Yes."

"All of a sudden like that?"

"It isn't so sudden," she said, still behind the barrier of the chair. "You've been bored with me for years. And you've shown it. Tonight you did everything but yawn in the face of all my friends."

"You must admit, Penny," he said, "that it was a drab collection tonight."

"I don't admit anything."

"That Bertie Folsom, for God's sake . . ."

"A lot of people think he's a most intelligent, attractive man."

"A lot of people thought Hitler was an intelligent, attractive man." He took a step toward her. He could see her knuckles whiten as she gripped the back of the chair, and he stopped.

"Come on, Penny," he said gently. "Don't let a passing mood make you say things you'll be sorry for later."

"It isn't any passing mood." Her mouth pulled down severely. Even in the soft light she now looked her full age. "I've been thinking about this for a long time."

He finished his drink, sat down, looked searchingly at her. She returned his glance unflinchingly, the enmity plain in her eyes.

"Well," he said, "I suppose this calls for a divorce. And a drink." He stood up and carried his glass to the sideboard.

"There's no need for a divorce," she said. "You don't want to get married again, do you?"

He laughed shortly and poured himself a stiff drink.

"I don't want to get married, either," she went on.

"What do we do—live together just as though nothing had happened?" he demanded.

"Yes. If only for Marcia and Anne. Anyway, it shouldn't be any great hardship. Nothing very much has happened between us for years now. Every once in a while, when you're not bombed to extinction, or you've got a case of insomnia or one of your other girls isn't available, you remember you have a wife, and you come crawling around."

"That's a word I'm going to remember, Penny," he said. "Crawling."

She ignored his warning. "Four or five nights a year," she said, "there won't be any games at home. That's all. I think we both can stand it."

"I'm forty-four years old, Penny," he said. "I don't see myself remaining celibate for the rest of my life."

"Celibate!" She laughed harshly. "There's another word for you. You can do whatever you want. Just the way you always have."

"I think," he said quietly, "tomorrow will be just

the day for me to go on a nice long trip. Europe might be just the thing."

"The girls're coming home for Christmas," she said. "The least you owe them is to be here when they come. Don't take it out on them."

"All right," he said. "Europe can wait until after Christmas."

He heard a telephone ringing. Still dislocated in time, he almost called out, "Penny, will you take that, please?" Then he shook himself, looked around, realized where he was, at an ornate, fake antique desk in a hotel room facing the sea, and reached over and picked up the phone. "Craig speaking," he said.

There was a faraway howling over the wires, American voices jumbled and speaking too low to be understood, then, weirdly, a few notes of a piano, then a click and silence. He frowned, put the phone down, looked at his watch. It was past midnight, between three and six in the afternoon on the continent of America. He waited, but the phone did not ring again.

He stood up and poured himself a drink. He felt a wetness on his cheek. He looked disbelievingly at himself in the mirror. He had been weeping. He brushed the tears roughly away with the back of his hand, drank half the whisky, glared at the telephone. Who had tried to reach him, what message had been baffled in its course to him in midocean?

Perhaps it had been the one voice that could have made everything clear—tell him where he stood, what were his assets, what were his debts, what he owed, what was owed him. On what side of the ledger he might enter his marriage, his daughters, his career. Let him know once and for all if he was morally bankrupt or ethically solvent, announce whether his loving had been a defensible expense, answer the question of whether or not, in an age of wars and endless horror, his preoccupation with fictions and shadows had been a callous waste of honor.

The telephone did not ring. There was no message from America. He finished his drink.

When he had been away from her, Penelope had had the habit of calling him almost every night just before she went to bed. "I don't sleep happily," she had said, "unless I hear your voice and know that you're all right."

The telephone bills had been enormous.

Sometimes he had been irritated by her calls, at other times moved by husbandly tenderness at the sound of the low, familiar, musical voice from a distant city, the other shore of a continent. He had been irritated when he thought that she had been checking on him, testing his fidelity, even though after what had happened between them he felt that he owed her no fidelity, or at least not *that* form of fidelity. He had been unfaithful to her occasionally. Without a sense of guilt, he told himself. Nor did he underestimate the continuing pleasure his indulgence made possible. But he had never allowed himself to become seriously involved with another woman. To that extent, he had felt he had protected his marriage. For the same reason he had refrained from inquiring into his wife's relations with other men. He had never checked on her. She had secretly rifled through all his papers, he knew, hunting for women's names, but he had never picked up a letter addressed to her or questioned her about whom she had seen or where she had gone. Again, without examining this facet of his behavior closely, he had felt that it would have been demeaning to him, a belittling blow to his pride. He had recognized the female cunning in Penelope's late-night telephone calls but for the most part had tolerated them, even been fondly amused by them, flattered by them. Now he knew he had been wrong. He and his wife had avoided candor, and they had drained their marriage.

He had been angry that morning when he had received her letter and had made out the monthly check, and he had reflected on her rapacity and meanness of spirit. But now, after midnight, alone, the memories that had been aroused by passing the house on the Cap d'Antibes that afternoon working within him and the frustrating sounds of the indecipherable voices on the wires still echoing in his ears, he couldn't help but remember better times, gentler encounters.

For Craig, at least, the marriage worked best at times of stress—when late at night, after long hours in the theatre, he would return from the chaos of rehearsals, the savage clash of wills and temperaments whose tensions it was his job as producer to absorb and accommodate, and find Penelope waiting up for him, ready to make a drink for him in the beautifully ordered living room of their house and listen to him pour out his recapitulation of the day's work, the day's problems, the small tragedies, the day's insane comedies, the fears for the morrow, the disputes that remained to be solved. She was sympathetic, cool, understanding. Her intuition and intelligence could be relied on. Invariably, she was helpful, the most reliable of partners, the most useful of advisers, steadfastly faithful to his interests. Out of all the memories of his marriage, all the good times, the summer in Antibes, the deeply satisfying moments with his daughters, even the long-shared pleasure of their lovemaking, it was those countless quiet midnight conversations in which they shared the best of themselves with each other that in retrospect were the real texture of their marriage, the most painful to have to forget.

Well, he had plenty of problems tonight, he could use advice. Despite everything, he knew he longed for the sound of her voice. When he had written her to tell her he was taking steps for a divorce, she had written him a long letter pleading with him not to break up their marriage, with all the reasons, passionate and sensible and homely, for keeping it alive. He had barely glanced at it, afraid, perhaps, that it would sway him, and coldly sent her a note telling her to find a lawyer.

Then, as was almost inevitable, she had become a lawyer's creation, striking for gain, advantage, revenge. Now he regretted not having read her letter more carefully.

On an impulse, he picked up the phone, gave the operator the number of the house in New York. Then, after he had put the instrument down, he remembered from his daughter's letter that Penelope was in Geneva.

Foolish woman, he thought, as he got the operator back and canceled the call, this is one night she should have been at home.

• EIGHT •

HE poured himself a fresh drink, paced the room holding the glass in his hand, angry with himself for submitting himself to the past, torturing himself with the past. Whatever he had come to Cannes for, it had not been for that. Gail McKinnon had a lot to answer for. Well, he had come so far, he thought, he might as well go all the way. Go over all the mistakes, all the wrong turnings, all the betrayals. If masochism was to be the order of the day, enjoy it. Listen to the ghosts, remember the weather of other seasons . . .

He sipped at his drink, sat hunched over at the desk, allowed the past to invade him.

He was in his office, back from three months in Europe. The trip had been neither good nor bad for him. He felt suspended in time, not unpleasantly, postponing all decisions.

There was a pile of scripts on his desk. He leafed through them without interest. Before the breakup with Penelope, or the semibreakup, or whatever it was, it had been his custom to do most of his reading in the small studio he had fixed for himself at the top of his house where he had no telephone and could not be interrupted. But since he had come back from Europe, he had taken a room at a hotel near his office and only occasionally visited the house or slept there. He hadn't moved his clothes or any of his books, and when his daughters were at home, which was rarely, he was there. He did not know how much they knew about the breach between him and their mother, and there were no indications that they had noticed any change. They were so concerned with the problems of their adolescence—dates, school, diets,—that Craig doubted that they would have paid much attention even if their parents had staged Macbeth before their eyes in the living room, complete with bare dagger and real blood. On the surface, he thought, Penelope and he behaved much as they had always done, perhaps a shade more politely than formerly. There had been no further scenes or arguments. They asked each other no questions about their comings and goings. It was a period in which he felt strangely peaceful, like an invalid who is very slowly recovering from a long illness and knows that no great efforts can be demanded of him.

Occasionally, they went out together. Penelope gave him a present on his forty-fourth birthday. They went down to Maryland to see a school play in which Marcia acted a small part. They slept in the same room in a hotel in the town.

None of the play scripts he was offered seemed worth doing, although there were one or two that he was sure would succeed. When they were done by other men and were hits, he felt no sense of loss or opportunity wasted.

He had given up reading the dramatic pages of the newspapers and had canceled his subscriptions to the trade papers. He avoided restaurants like Sardi's and Downey's, which had been favorite places of his and which were always filled with theatrical and movie people, most of whom he would know.

He had not been in Hollywood since the week of the preview in Pasadena. Every once in a while Bryan Murphy would call him and tell him he was sending him a script or a book that might interest him. When they arrived, he read them dutifully, then called Murphy and said he was not interested. After

about a year, Murphy only called to find out how he
was. He always said that he was fine.

There was a knock on the door, and Belinda
came in carrying a playscript with a sealed envelope
clipped to the cover. She had a peculiar, wary expression on her face. "This just came in," she said. "By
hand." She put the script on his desk. "It's Eddie
Brenner's new play."

"Who brought it in?" He kept his voice noncommittal.

"Mrs. Brenner," Belinda said.

"Why didn't she come in and say hello?"

"I asked her to. She said she preferred not to."

"Thanks," he said, and slit the envelope. Belinda
closed the door softly behind her.

The letter was from Susan Brenner. He had liked
her and was sorry events had made it impossible for
him to see her anymore.

He read the letter. "Dear Jesse," Susan Brenner had
written, "Ed doesn't know I'm showing you his play,
and if he finds out, I'm going to be in for a rough
half hour with him. But no matter. Whatever happened between you and him must be ancient history
by now, and all I'm interested in is getting the play
on in the best way possible. He's been mixed up
with mediocre people in recent years, and they've
hurt him and his work, and I have to try to keep him
out of their hands this time.

"I think this is the best thing Ed has written since
The Foot Soldier. It has some of the same feeling, as
you will see when you read it. The only time any of
Ed's plays has received the production it deserved
was that once when he worked with you and Frank
Baranis, and I'm hoping that the three of you can
get together again. Maybe the time has come when
you all need each other again.

"I have faith in your talent and integrity and your
desire to do things in the theater that are worthwhile.

I am sure that you're too reasonable and honorable a man to allow a painful memory to interfere with your devotion to excellence.

"When you've read the play, please call me. Call me in the morning around ten o'clock. Ed rents a little office nearby where he works, and he's out of the house by then. As ever, Sue."

Loyal, innocent, optimistic wife, he thought. As ever. Too bad she hadn't been around that summer in Antibes. He stared at the script on his desk. It had not been typed or bound professionally. Probably Susan Brenner had faithfully typed it herself. Brenner, he knew, could hardly afford hiring a service to do it for him. A painful memory, Susan Brenner had written. It wasn't even that anymore. It was buried under so many other memories, painful and otherwise, that it was like an anecdote told about a stranger in whom he was only remotely interested.

He stood up and opened the door. Belinda was at her desk reading a novel. "Belinda," he said, "no calls until I ask for them." She nodded. Actually, the telephone rang very seldom these days in the office. He had spoken out of old habit.

He sat down at his desk and read the unevenly typed script. It took him less than an hour. He had wanted to like it, but when he put it down, he knew that he didn't want to do it. The play, like Brenner's first one, was about the war but not about combat. It was about troops of a division that had fought in Africa and was now in England preparing for the invasion of Europe. It seemed to Craig that it attempted too much and accomplished too little. There were the veterans, hardened or pushed near the breaking point by the fighting they had already seen, contrasted with the green replacements being whipped into shape, in awe of the older men, uncertain of their courage, ignorant of what to expect when their time came to go under fire. Along with that, and the conflicts engendered by the clash of the two groups, there were scenes with the local English, the girls, British soldiers, families, in which Brenner tried to analyze the difference between the two societies thrown together for a few months by the hazards of war. In style, Brenner varied from tragedy to melodrama to wild farce. His first play had been simple, all of one piece, fiercely realistic, driving in one straight line toward an inevitable bloody conclusion. The new play wandered, moralized, jumped from place to place, emotion to emotion, almost haphazardly. Brenner's maturity, Craig thought, if that was what it was, had deprived him of his useful early simplicity. The telephone conversation with Susan Brenner was not going to be a pleasant one. He reached for the phone, then stopped. He decided to reread the play the next day after he had thought about it for twenty-four hours.

But when he read it the next day, he liked it no better. There was no sense putting off the telephone call.

"Susan," he said when he heard her voice. "I'm afraid I can't do it. Do you want to hear my reasons?"

"No," she said. "Just leave it with your secretary. I'll pass by and pick it up."

"Come in and say hello."

"No," she said, "I don't think I want to do that."

"I'm terribly sorry, Sue," he said.

"So am I," she said. "I thought you were a better man."

He put the telephone down slowly. He started to read another script, but it made no sense to him. On an impulse he picked up the phone again and asked Belinda to get Bryan Murphy for him on the Coast.

After the greetings were over and Craig had learned that Murphy was in splendid health and was going to Palm Springs for the weekend, Murphy said, "To what do I owe the honor?"

"I'm calling about Ed Brenner, Murph. Can you

get him a job out there? He's not in good shape."

"Since when have you been so palsy with Ed Brenner?"

"I'm not," Craig said. "In fact, I don't want him to know that I called you. Just get him a job."

"I heard he was finishing a play," Murphy said.

"He's still not in good shape."

"Have you read it?"

Craig hesitated. "No," he said finally.

"That means you've read it and you don't like it," Murphy said.

"Keep your voice down, Murph, please. And don't say anything to anybody. Will you do something for him?"

"I'll try," Murphy said. "But I don't promise anything. The place is reeling. Do you want me to do something for you?"

"No."

"Good. It was a rhetorical question, anyway," Murphy said. "Give my love to Penny."

"I'll do that," Craig said.

"I have to tell you something, Jesse," Murphy said.

"What?"

"I love to get telephone calls from you. You're the only client who doesn't call collect."

"I'm a wasteful man," Craig said. As he hung up, he knew that the odds were a hundred to one against Murphy's finding anything for Ed Brenner on the Coast.

He didn't go to the opening of the Brenner play, although he had bought a ticket, because the morning of the day of the opening he received a telephone call from Boston. A director friend of his, Jack Lawton, was trying out a musical comedy there and over the phone had said that the show was in trouble and asked him to come up to Boston and look at it and see if he had any ideas as to how it would be helped.

Craig gave his ticket for the opening to Belinda and

took the plane that afternoon to Boston. He avoided seeing Lawton or anybody connected with the show before the evening performance because he wanted to be able to judge it with a fresh eye. He didn't want to go into the theatre burdened with the complaints of the producers against the director, the director's criticisms of the producers and the stars, the star's recriminations about everybody, the usual cannibalistic rites out of town when a show was doing badly.

He watched the performance with pity. Pity for the writers, the composer, the singers and dancers, the principals, the backers, the musicians, the audience. The play had cost three hundred and fifty thousand dollars to put on, talented men in every field had worked for years to bring it on the stage, the dancers performed miracles of agility in the big numbers, the stars, who had been acclaimed again and again in other plays, sang their hearts out. And nothing happened. Ingenious sets flew in and out, the music swelled in an orgy of sound, actors grinned bravely and hopelessly as they uttered jokes at which no one laughed, the producers prowled despairingly in the back of the house, Lawton sat in the last row dictating notes in an exhausted hoarse voice to a secretary who scribbled on a clipboard with a pencil equipped with a small light. And still nothing happened.

Craig writhed in his seat, breathing the air of failure, wishing he could get up and leave, dreading the moment later on in the hotel suite when people would turn to him and say, "Well, what do you think?"

The thin desultory applause of the audience as the curtain came down was a slap in the face to everyone in his profession, and the fixed smiles of the actors as they took their bows were the grimaces of men and women under torture.

He did not go backstage but went directly to the

hotel, had two drinks to restore himself before he went upstairs to the papery chicken sandwiches, the table with whisky bottles, the bitter, pasty faces of men who had not been out in the open air for three months.

He did not say what he really thought while the producers, the author, composer, and scene designer were in the room. He had no loyalty to them, no responsibility. His friend Lawton had asked him to come, not they, and he would wait until they left before he told Lawton his honest opinion. He contented himself with a few anodyne suggestions—cutting a dance here, restaging a song number slightly, lighting a love scene differently. The other men understood that he was not there to say anything valuable to them and left early.

The last to go were the producers, two small, bitter men, jumpy with false nervous energy, rude with Lawton, almost openly scornful with Craig because he, too, had so clearly failed them.

"Probably," Lawton said as the door closed behind the two men who had come to Boston with high hopes and glittering visions of success, "probably they're going to sit down now and call a dozen other directors to come up here and replace me." Lawton was a tall, harassed man with thick glasses who suffered horribly from ulcers every time he staged a play, whether it went well or badly. He sipped from a glass of milk continually and swigged every few minutes at a bottle of Maalox. "Talk up, Jesse."

"I say, close," Craig said.

"It's as bad as that?"

"It's as bad as that."

"We still have time to make changes," Lawton said defensively.

"They won't help, Jack. You're flogging a dead horse."

"God," Lawton said, "you're always surprised at how many things can go wrong at once." He wasn't young, he had directed over thirty plays, he had been highly praised, he was married to an enormously wealthy woman, but he sat there, bent over his ulcer pain, shaking his head like a general who had thrown in his last reserves and lost them all in one evening. "Christ," he said, "if only my gut would let up."

"Jack," Craig said, "Why don't you just quit?"

"You mean on this show?"

"On the whole thing. You're driving yourself into the hospital. You don't *have* to go through all this."

"No," Lawton said, "I suppose I don't." He sounded surprised at his own admission.

"Then?"

"What would I do? Sit in the sun in Arizona with the other old folks?" His face twisted, and he put his hand on his stomach as a new pang gripped him. "This is the only thing I know how to do. The only thing I *want* to do. Even a shitty, dead piece of nothing like this silly show tonight."

"You asked me what I thought," Craig said.

"And you told me," said Lawton. "Thanks."

Craig stood up. "I'm going to bed," he said. "And I advise you to do the same."

"I will, I will," Lawton said almost petulantly. "There're just one or two notes I want to put down while they're still fresh in my mind. I've called a rehearsal for eleven."

He was working on the script even before Craig left the room, jabbing furiously at the pages open before him as though each stroke of his pen was going to transform everything tomorrow by the eleven o'clock rehearsal, make the jokes funny, the music clever, the dances ecstatic, the applause thunderous, as though by his efforts, in his pain, even Boston would be a different city tomorrow night.

When Craig got to his office the next morning, Belinda had the reviews of Brenner's play on his desk.

He didn't have to read them. He could tell by the expression on her face that things had gone badly the night before. When he read the reviews, he knew there was no hope, that the play would close by Saturday night. Even Boston had been preferable.

He was in the theatre Saturday night for the last performance. The theatre was only half-full, most of it, he knew, paper. Brenner, he noted with relief, was not in the audience.

When the curtain came up and the first lines were uttered, he had an odd sensation. He had the feeling that something beautiful was about to happen. The actors were intent and fervent and performed with a contagious belief in the value, the importance, of the words that Brenner had written for them to speak. There was no sign that any of them was affected by the knowledge that the play had been discourteously dismissed as boring or confused by the critics only three days before and that when the curtain came down that night that would be the end of it, the sets dismantled, the theatre dark, and they themselves out on the street looking for other jobs. There was a gallantry about their devotion to their profession that brought tears to Craig's eyes even though, as he watched, he saw the faults in casting, direction, and interpretation that had obscured the subtle, multiple intentions of the play and brought down the critics' wrath on Brenner's head.

As he sat in the darkened theatre, with gaping rows of empty seats behind him, watching what he recognized was a flawed and inadequate production, Craig realized that somehow he had been in error in his judgment of Brenner's script. For the first time in a long while his attention was fully awakened in a theatre. Almost automatically, a list of things that could be done to make the play work, bring out its virtues, eliminate its flaws, began to form in his mind.

When the play was over, there was only a thin

scattering of applause from the audience, but Craig hurried backstage, moved and excited, hoping to find Brenner, praise him, reassure him.

The old man at the stage door recognized Craig and said mournfully, "Isn't it all a shame, Mr. Craig?" as they shook hands. Brenner, the old man said, was on the stage saying good-by to the company and thanking them, and Craig waited unseen in the wings until Brenner had made his little speech and the actors began to troop off to their dressing rooms, defiantly noisy beneath the drab work light.

For a moment Craig did not move but watched Brenner standing alone in the empty set that was supposed to be the corner of a temporary shabby barracks in wartime England. Brenner's face was in deep shadow, and Craig could not see its expression. Brenner was much thinner than when Craig had seen him last and was dressed in a baggy tweed jacket with a long wool scarf thrown around his neck. He looked like a fragile old man who had to think about every step he took for fear of falling. Brenner's hair was thinning, Craig noted. A bald spot gleamed.

The curtain slowly went up, and Brenner raised his head and stared out at the dark, empty theatre. There was a rustle beside Craig, and Susan Brenner went past him. Susan Brenner came up to her husband, took his hand, and raised it and kissed it. He put his arm around her. They were standing like that, silently, when Craig finally walked out of the wings.

"Hello," he said.

The man and the woman looked at him without speaking.

"I saw the play tonight," Craig said, "and I want to tell you I was wrong when I read it."

Still neither of the others spoke.

"It's a beautiful play," Craig went on. "It's the best thing you've done."

Brenner chuckled. It sounded as though he was strangling.

"Susan," Craig said, "you were right. I should have done it, and Baranis should have directed it."

"Thanks for the memory," Susan said. She was wearing no makeup and looked pale and gaunt, depleted in the bare light.

"Listen to me, please," Craig went on earnestly. "You got the wrong production for it, and it came between the play and the audience. That doesn't mean that's the end of it. Wait for a year, work on it, cast it correctly—you never had a chance with all those fancy, overblown sets, with that man in the lead—he's too old, too sophisticated. A year from now we can put it on downtown, off-Broadway—it doesn't belong on Broadway, anyhow—recast it, do it with lights, a structural bare set, use music, it cries for music, get tapes of speeches by politicians, generals, radio announcers, to play between the scenes, frame them in time—" He stopped, conscious that he was rushing too fast, saying more than Brenner could possibly assimilate at this moment. "Do you see what I mean?" he asked lamely.

The Brenners stared blankly at him. Then Brenner chuckled again, the same choking sound. "A year from now," he said ironically.

Craig understood what was going through Brenner's mind. "I'll give you an advance. Enough to live on. I'll . . ."

"Does Ed get another chance to sleep with your wife, Mr. Craig?" Susan said. "Is that included in the advance?"

"Keep quiet, Sue," Brenner said wearily. "I think you're right, Jesse. I think we made a lot of mistakes in the production, a good many of them mine. I agree it should have been done off-Broadway. I think Baranis would know what I was driving at. I think we could make a go of it . . ." He took a deep breath. "And I also think you ought to get out of here, Jesse. Get out of my life. Come on, Sue." He took his wife's hand. "I left a briefcase in the dressing room," he said. "We won't be coming back, and we'd better get it now."

Side by side the Brenners went off the stage. There was a long run in one of Susan Brenner's stockings that Craig hadn't noticed before.

Alice Paine was waiting in the almost-empty bar for him. He had been surprised when she had called him and said she was in the neighborhood and wondered if he had the time to have a drink with her. He had never seen her without her husband except occasionally, by accident. He had also never seen her take more than one drink an evening, and she was not the sort of woman you'd expect to find in a bar at three o'clock in the afternoon.

She was finishing a martini as he came to the table at which she was sitting. He leaned over and kissed her cheek. She smiled up at him, a little nervously, he thought. He signaled to a waiter as he sat down on the banquette beside her. "I'll have a Scotch and soda, please," he said to the waiter. "Alice?"

"I think I'd like another martini," she said.

For a moment Craig wondered if Alice Paine had been hiding something all these years from him and all of her other friends. She fiddled with her gloves, her strong hands, with no polish on the fingernails, uneasy on the table. "I hope I haven't interrupted something important," she said.

"No," he said. "Nothing much is happening in the office at the moment."

She put her hands in her lap under the table. "I haven't had a drink in the middle of the day since my wedding," she said.

"I wish I could say the same."

"Are you drinking too much these days, Jesse?" She glanced quickly at him.

"No more than usual," he said. "Too much."

"Don't let anyone tell you you're an alcoholic," she said. She was speaking more quickly than ordinarily, her voice a little higher in tone.

"Why?" he asked. "Have you heard anyone saying I was an alcoholic?"

"Not really," she said. "Oh, well, Penelope. Sometimes she seems to infer . . ."

"Wives," Craig said.

The waiter came over and placed the drinks before them. They raised their glasses, and Craig said, "Cheers."

Alice made a face as she sipped her martini. "I suppose I'll never find out what people see in these things," she said.

"Courage," he said. "Nepenthe." By now he knew that Alice had not called him merely because she happened to be in the neighborhood that afternoon. "What is it, Alice?" he said.

"Oh, dear," she said, fiddling with her glass. "It's so hard to know where to begin."

He was sure that Alice Paine hadn't said, "Oh, dear," since her wedding day, either. She was not that sort of woman. She was also not the sort of woman who didn't know where to begin.

"Begin in the middle," he said, "and we'll work it around." Her nervousness made him uncomfortable.

"You believe that we're your friends?" she said. "I mean Robert and myself."

"Of course."

"I mean, that's important," she said. "I wouldn't like you to think that I'm a meddlesome woman, or malicious, or anything like that."

"You couldn't be meddlesome or malicious if you tried." By now he was sorry he had been in the office when she had called.

"We had dinner at your house last night," she said abruptly. "Robert and I."

"I hope you had a good meal."

"It was perfect. As usual," she said. "Except that you weren't there."

"I'm not home very much these days."

"So I gathered," Alice said.

"How was the guest list?"

"Unbrilliant."

"As usual," Craig said.

"Bertie Folsom was there."

"As usual," Craig said.

She glanced quickly at him again. "People are beginning to talk, Jesse."

"People are always beginning to talk," he said.

"I don't know what sort of arrangement you and Penelope have," Alice said, "but they're seen together everywhere."

"I don't know what sort of arrangement we have, either," he said. "I guess you could call it a large, loose nonarrangement. Is that what you came to tell me—that Penelope and Bertie have been seen together?"

"No," she said. "Not really. First, I want to tell you that Robert and I aren't coming to your house anymore."

"That's too bad," he said. "Why?"

"It goes a long way back. Four years, to be exact."

"Four years?" He frowned. "What happened four years ago?"

"Do you think I could ask for another martini?" she said. She sounded like a little girl asking for a second ice cream cone.

"Of course." He waved to the waiter and ordered two more drinks.

"You were out of town somewhere," Alice said. "We were giving a little dinner party. We invited Penelope. Then, to round out the table, we had to find an extra man. Somehow, it always turns out that the extra man is Bertie Folsom."

"What else is new?" Craig said lightly.

"The trouble with tall men like you," Alice said severely, "is that they never take small men seriously."

"It's true," Craig said, "he's a very small man. So— he sat next to Penelope at dinner."

"He took her home."

"Zounds! He took her home."

"You think I'm a silly, gossipy woman . . ."

"Not really, Alice," he said gently. "It's just that . . ."

"Sssh," she said, and gestured toward the waiter, who was approaching with their drinks.

They sat in silence until the waiter had gone back to the bar.

"All right," Alice said. "This is what happened. The next morning I received a dozen red roses. Anonymously. No card."

"That could mean anything," Craig said, although by now he knew it couldn't mean anything.

"Every year, on the same date," Alice said, "October fifth, I get a dozen red roses. Anonymously. Of course he knows I know who sends them. He *wants* me to know. It's so vulgar. I feel tainted—like an accomplice—every time I go to your house and see him there eating your food, drinking your liquor. And I've felt like such a coward, not saying anything to him, not telling you. And last night, seeing him there sitting at the head of the table pouring the wine, acting the host, staying on after everybody had left—I talked it over with Robert, and he agreed with me, I couldn't keep quiet anymore."

"Thanks for today," Craig said. He leaned over and kissed her cheek.

"I don't know what kind of code we all go by," Alice said. "I know we're not supposed to take adultery seriously anymore, that we laugh when we hear about our friends playing around—I've heard some stories about you, too."

"I'm sure you have," he said. "Most of them no doubt true. My marriage has hardly been a model of felicity for a long time."

"But this particular thing I can't take," Alice said. There was a catch in her voice. "You're an admirable man. A decent friend. And I can't stand that awful little man. And to tell the truth, I've come to dislike Penelope. There's something false and hard about her with all her charming hostessy tricks. If I *do* have a code, I suppose it's that I think that certain people don't deserve what they have to endure, and if they're my friends, I finally have to do something about it. Are you sorry I've told you all this, Jesse?"

"I don't know yet," he said slowly. "Well, anyway, I'll see to it that you're not bothered by any more roses."

The next day he sent a letter to his wife telling her he was seeing a lawyer about a divorce.

Another bar. In Paris now. In the Hotel Crillon, just across from the Embassy. He had fallen into the habit of meeting Constance there when she got through working. It gave a fixed point to his day. The rest of the time he spent wandering around the city, going into galleries, strolling through open-air markets and among the young people of the Latin Quarter, practicing his French in shops, sitting at café tables reading the newspapers, occasionally having lunch with one or two of the men who had been with him on the movie he had made in France and who were sensitive enough not to ask him what he was working on these days.

He liked the room, with its knots of English and American newspapermen arguing at the bar and its shifting population of polite, well-dressed, elderly Americans with New England accents who had been coming to the hotel since before the war. He liked, too, the looks of admiration on the faces of the other drinkers when Constance came hurrying into the bar.

He stood up to greet her, kissed her cheek. Although she had spent a whole day in a stuffy office chain-smoking cigarettes, she always smelled as though she had just come from a long walk in a forest.

She had a glass of champagne, to get the taste of youth out of her mouth, she said. "I'm always surprised," she said, sipping her champagne, "to find you sitting here when I come in."

"I told you I'd be here."

"I know. Still, I'm surprised. Every time I leave you in the morning, I have the feeling that *this* is going to be the day you're going to meet someone irresistibly attractive or hear about an actor or actress in London or Zagreb or Athens you must have to see perform that night."

"There's nobody in London or Zagreb or Athens I want to have anything to do with, and the only irresistibly attractive woman I've seen all day," he said, "is you."

"Aren't you a nice man." She beamed. She had a childish love of compliments.

"Now tell me what you did all day," she said.

"I made love three times to the wife of a Peruvian tin tycoon ..."

"Yeah, yeah." She grinned. She enjoyed being teased. But not too much.

"I had my hair cut. I ate in a small Italian restaurant on the rue de Grenelle, I read *Le Monde*, I went into three galleries and nearly bought three paintings, I had a glass of beer at the Flore, I went back to my hotel, and ..." He stopped. He was conscious that she wasn't listening to him. She was staring at a young American couple that was passing the table, going toward the back of the room. The man was tall, with a pleasant, open face, as though he had never known doubt or deprivation and that it was inconceivable to him that anybody anywhere could be his enemy or wish him harm. The girl was a pale, tall beauty with dead black hair, wide, dark eyes, something Irish or Spanish in her background, moving with deliberate grace, a dark sable coat rippling about her, smiling at something her husband had just said, touching his arm as they walked between the bar and the tables alongside the windows. They did not seem to see anyone else in the room. It was not discourteous. It was merely that they were so absorbed in themselves that even a careless haphazard glance, the necessity to see or possibly recognize another face, would be a waste, a loss of a precious moment of contact with each other.

Constance kept watching them until they had disappeared in the restaurant section in the rear. She turned back to Craig. "Forgive me," she said. "I'm afraid I wasn't listening. They're people I once knew."

"They're a handsome couple."

"They are that," Constance said.

"How old is that girl?"

"Twenty-four," Constance said. "She was responsible for the death of a friend of mine."

"What?" It was not the sort of thing you expected to hear in the bar of the Crillon.

"Don't look so alarmed," Constance said. "People are responsible for the death of other people all the time."

"She hardly looks like your average murderess."

Constance laughed. "Oh, it wasn't anything like that. A man I knew was in love with her, and he read in the newspapers that she had just been married, and three days later he died."

"What an old-fashioned story," Craig said.

"He was an old-fashioned man," Constance said. "And he was eighty-two years old."

"How did you happen to know an eighty-two-year-old man?" Craig asked. "I know you like older men, of course, but wasn't that pushing it a bit?"

"The old man's name was Jarvis," Constance said. "Kenneth Jarvis."

"Railroads."

"Railroads." She nodded. "Among other things. Many other things. I had a beau who worked with

Jarvis's grandson. Don't glower, dear. It was before your time, long before your time. The old man liked to have young people around him. He had a great big house in Normandy. At one time he owned a racing stable. He gave big weekend parties, twenty, thirty people at a time. The usual thing, tennis, swimming, sailing, drinking, flirting, whatever you call it. They were always fun. Except for the old man. When I first met him, he was already senile. He'd drop food all over himself when he ate, he'd forget to button his fly, he'd fall asleep at table and snore, he'd tell the same story three times in ten minutes."

"You paid for your fun," Craig said.

"People who'd known him when he was younger didn't seem to mind," Constance said. "He'd been a charming, generous, cultivated man. A great collector of books, paintings, pretty women. His wife had died when they were both young, and he'd never remarried. The man I used to go to his place with said that you had to repay some of the pleasure a man like that had distributed all through his life, and watching him dribble a little on his necktie or listening to the same story over and over again was a small price to pay. Especially since the house and the food and drink and entertainment were exactly as they'd always been. Anyway, only stupid people laughed at him behind his back."

"God spare me," Craig said, "from reaching eighty."

"Listen to the rest of the story. One weekend an old mistress of Jarvis's came down. With her daughter. The girl you just saw pass with her husband."

"God spare me," Craig said, "from reaching seventy."

"He fell in love with her," Constance said. "Real old-fashioned love. Letters every day, flowers, invitations to mother and daughter for cruises, the whole thing."

"What was in it for the mother? Or the daughter?" Craig asked. "Money?"

"Not really," Constance said. "They were comfortably enough off. I suppose they got to know a lot of people they otherwise would never have met— that sort of thing. The mother had kept the girl on a tight rein. Her only prize. When I first met the girl, she was nineteen, but she acted fifteen. You half-expected her to curtsy when anybody was introduced to her. Jarvis made her grow up. And then it was flattering. To be the hostess at grand dinner parties, to be the center of attention, to escape her mother. To be adored by a man who in his time had known everybody, had anecdotes about everybody, had ordered the lives of thousands of people, had had affairs with all the famous beauties. She liked the old man, loved him in her own way, maybe, was delighted by her power over him. And overnight, he'd changed completely, he'd become young, vital. He never forgot anything he'd said, he walked erectly, where he used to shuffle, his voice sounded robust, where it used to be a wheeze, he dressed impeccably, he'd stay up all night and be spruce and full of energy in the morning.

"Of course, some people snickered. The sight of an eighty-two-year-old man doting over a nineteen-year-old girl as though it was his first love and he was taking her out to her first ball ... But I saw him once in a while, and I was touched. It was as though a miracle had made time reverse for him. He'd gone back. Not all the way, of course, not to twenty or thirty, but to fifty-five, sixty—"

"He died, you said," Craig said.

"Yes. She met that young man you just saw her with and stopped seeing Jarvis. And he found out that they'd been married only when he saw it in the newspapers. He dropped the paper to the floor and took to his bed and turned his face to the wall, and three days later he was dead."

"It's a nice sensible story," Craig said.

"I think so," she said. "At his funeral a friend of

his said, 'Isn't it wonderful? In this day and age to be able to die for love at the age of eighty-two?' "

"In this day and age."

"He couldn't have wanted anything better, could he, the old man?" Constance said. "He'd had a glorious, foolish, lively eight months or so and a noble exit. No oxygen tent, no doctors hovering around, no pipes and kidney machines and transfusions, just love. Nobody blamed the girl, of course. Just envied her husband. And the old man. Both. You have a funny light in your eye."

"I'm thinking."

"What about?"

"If somebody came to me with a play or a movie script based on the old man's story," he said, "I think I'd be tempted to try to do it. Only nobody has."

Constance finished her glass of champagne. "Why don't you take a shot at writing it yourself?" she said.

It was the first time that she had tried to push him in any direction whatever, the first time that he realized that she knew that he couldn't keep going on the way he had been.

"I'll think about it," he said, and ordered two more drinks.

He walked along the sea front of Saint Sebastian in the morning. The rain had stopped. The wind was blustery, the air washed, the big rock far out in the bay a beleaguered fortress, the waves pounding. When he crossed the bridge, the tide in the river was fierce, foaming water, the clash between ocean and land at the land's gates. Half-remembering where he was from other visits, he walked in the direction of the big bullring. Empty now, out of season, immense, it looked like a deserted temple to a forgotten bloody religion. A door was open. He heard the sound of workmen hammering somewhere, the noise reverberating hollowly in the dark caverns under the stands.

He went up through a passageway, leaned against the *barrera*. The circle of sand was not golden, as in other rings, but ash-colored, the color of death. He remembered the matador's words—"It is the only thing that still amuses me. It is my only playground." Too old for the bulls, his friend, sword in hand, blood on his suit of lights, a fixed, rapt smile on his handsome, scarred young-old face, would be facing the horns later that day hundreds of miles to the south. He would have to send a telegram. "Many ears. *Abrazo*."

Opening-night telegrams. Different formulas for different cultures.

He should send a telegram to Jack Lawton, ulcer-ridden, in Boston, to Edward Brenner, his arm around his wife on the dark stage in New York, to Kenneth Jarvis, buying flowers for a nineteen-year-old-girl, all in their arenas, all facing their particular horns, all faithful to their only playgrounds.

A caretaker, dressed in a kind of imitation uniform, appeared on the other side of the ring, waved at him threateningly, shook his fist, shouted with thin authority as though he suspected Craig of being ready to leap into the ring, a crazed, middle-aged *spontaneo* planning to interrupt a ghostly faena, cite a bull who would not appear for another two months.

Craig gestured courteously to him, a lover of the *fiesta brava*, observing its rules, visiting its holy places, and turned and went down under the stands and out into the ragged sunlight.

By the time he had walked back to his hotel he had made a decision.

He drove back to France slowly, carefully, not stopping at the spot where he had nearly been killed the night before. When he reached Saint-Jean-de-Lux, quiet in the preseason lull, he registered in a small hotel, went out and bought a ream of paper. I am now armed, he thought, as he carried the paper back to the hotel, I am re-entering my playground. By a different entrance.

He stayed in Saint-Jean-de-Luz two months, working slowly and painfully, trying to shape the story of Kenneth Jarvis, who had died at the age of eighty-two, three days after he had read in a newspaper that the girl of nineteen whom he loved had married another man. He had started it as a play, but bit by bit it had slid into another form, and he had gone back to the beginning and started it all over again as a film script. He had worked since his first days in the theatre with writers, suggesting changes, whole scenes, the addition of new themes, but it was one thing to work on the basis of another man's ideas and quite another to have a blank page in front of you and only yourself to try to bring it to life.

Aside from two weekend visits from Constance, he kept to himself, spending long hours at the desk in the hotel room, taking solitary walks along the beach and around the harbor, eating alone in the hotel dining room.

He told Constance what he was doing. She voiced neither approval nor disapproval. He didn't show her what he had written. Even after two months' work there would have been very little to show anyone—just a disconnected jumble of scenes, bald ideas, sketches of possible sequences, notes for characters.

By the end of the two months he realized that simply telling the story of the old man and the young girl was not enough. It wasn't enough because it didn't leave room for him, Jesse Craig, in it. Not the actual Jesse Craig, not the recital of the history that lay behind the man who sat day after day at the desk in the quiet hotel room, but his beliefs, his temperament, his hopes, his judgment on the time through which he had lived. Without all that, he came to realize, whatever he finally accomplished would be fragmentary, useless.

So he invented other characters, other pairs of lovers, to people the great house he had imagined on the north shore of Long Island for the summer in which he hoped to concentrate all the action of the film. He had transposed the locale of the story from Normandy. He didn't know enough about Normandy to write about it, and he knew about Long Island. He brought in a grandson, aged nineteen, in the first raptures of passion, taken with a promiscuous girl three or four years older than he. And drawing on more recent experience, he involved a comfortably adulterous couple of forty.

Using everything he had learned from his reading, his working on other men's plays and films, on his own observation of his friends, enemies, acquaintances, he tried to intertwine his characters naturally and dramatically so that in the end, without ever speaking in his own voice or in using anything but his characters' words and actions, the final result might be Jesse Craig's statement of what, in the second half of the twentieth century in America, it was like to love as a young man or woman, a middle-aged man or woman, and an old man on the brink of death, with all the interplay, the compromising, the wounding, of money, moral stances, power, position, class, beauty and the lack of it, honor and the lack of it, illusion and the lack of it.

After two months the town began to fill up, and he decided it was time to pack and move on. On the long drive north toward Paris, thinking about how he had spent the two months, he knew that he would be lucky if he could get the script written in a year. Maybe lucky if he could ever get it written at all.

It took him the full twelve months. He had written bits and pieces of it in Paris, in New York, on Long Island. Whenever he had come to a point in the script where he couldn't see his way ahead, he had packed and restlessly moved on. But he hadn't once fallen asleep at the wheel on any of his trips.

Even when he had finished it, he showed it to no one. He, who had passed judgment on the work of hundreds of other men, couldn't bear thinking of strangers' eyes reading the words he had written. And any reader, he felt, was a stranger. When he sent it off to be typed, he put no author's name under the title. Merely the legend, Property of Jesse Craig. Jesse Craig, once the boy wonder of Broadway and Hollywood, once known as a keen judge of the dramatic and cinematic art. Jesse Craig, who had no notion whether or not a year of his work was worth anybody's attention for two hours and dreaded to hear either a yes or a no.

When he put the six copies of the script into the valise the day he took the plane to Cannes, there was still no author's name under the title *The Three Horizons*.

The telephone rang. He shook his head dazedly, like a man being suddenly awakened from a deep sleep. Once more he had to remind himself where he was, where the telephone was. I am in my room in the Carlton, he thought, the telephone is on the table on the other side of the big chair. The telephone rang again. He looked at his watch. It was one-thirty-five. He hesitated, almost decided not to answer. He didn't want to hear any more incoherent messages from America. Finally, he picked up the phone.

"Craig speaking," he said.

"Jess." It was Murphy. "I hope I didn't wake you."

"You didn't wake me."

"I just finished reading your script."

"Yes?"

"That kid Harte can write," Murphy said, "but he's been seeing too many old French movies. Nobody's interested in an eighty-two-year-old man, for Christ's sake. You'll never get off the ground with it, Jess. Forget it. I wouldn't even show it around. It'll do you more harm than good, believe me. Drop the option and forget it. Let me work on the Greek thing for you, and we'll keep our eyes peeled for something good for later on."

"Thanks, Murph," Craig said, "for reading it. I'll talk to you tomorrow." He hung up, stared at the phone for a long time. Then he went back to the desk at which he had been sitting. He looked down at the typed list of questions Gail McKinnon had given him, read once more the first question. "Why are you in Cannes?"

He chuckled dryly to himself, picked up the pile of papers and tore them into small bits, dropped them into the wastebasket.

Then he took off his sweater, put on a jacket, and went out. He took a taxi to the casino where he knew the bar would be open all night. He bought some chips, sat down at a chemin de fer table, ordered a double whisky, and played and drank until six in the morning. He won thirty thousand francs, nearly six thousand dollars, mostly from two of the Englishmen who had been in the restaurant with Picasso that evening. It was unfortunate for Ian Wadleigh that he wasn't patrolling the Croisette as Craig walked, almost steadily, through the growing dawn toward his hotel. At that hour Wadleigh would have gotten his five thousand for Madrid.

• NINE •

POLICEMEN with flashlights were guiding the cars toward an open field where many cars were already parked. The air was heavy and cold. When Craig turned off the ignition and stepped out, his shoes squished on the wet grass. He walked up the path toward the big, chateaulike house from which came the sound of an orchestra. The house was on a hill beyond Mougins, and it dominated the land around it like a small fortress.

He was sorry that Anne had not yet arrived. She would have enjoyed going into a house like that on her father's arm, to the sound of a French song, attended by policemen who were diligently engaged in lighting the way for you under dark old trees rather than lobbing tear-gas bombs in front of the Administration Building. He had Anne's cable in his pocket. Surprisingly, she had decided to visit her mother in Geneva and would be coming down to Cannes the next day.

Walter Klein, the host, was standing in the hallway greeting his guests. He had rented the house for a month, choosing it because it was large enough for parties. Klein was a small, powerfully built, youngish man with a deceptively easygoing manner. In the turbulent breaking up and realignments of agencies that had been taking place in the last few years, he had walked away from a decaying organization, taking with him a list of stars and directors, and while other agencies and movie companies were collapsing, he had accommodated himself to the new conditions of the industry so shrewdly that a good proportion of the movies being prepared or shot in America or England at any given moment had one or more clients of his in some key spot or were indebted to him in some way for financing or distribution. Where others cried havoc, he smiled and said, "Kids, we've never had it so good." Unlike Murphy, who had grown to affluence in an easier time, and who scornfully kept aloof from the soul-like atmosphere of Cannes during these two weeks, Klein could be seen at all hours talking earnestly in corners with producers, distributors, money men, directors, actors, wheeling and dealing, promising, signing. For his lieutenants he chose soft-spoken and personable young men who had never known the fat, easy old days, who matched him in avidity and ambition, and who, like their boss, hid their honed-down sharpness under a careful display of charm.

When Klein had met Craig in New York some time before, he had said lightly, "Jess, when are you going to leave that old dinosaur Murphy and come to my office?"

"Never, I guess, Walt," Craig had said. "Murph and I have sworn our bond in blood."

Klein had laughed. "Your loyalty does you credit, Jess," he said. "But I miss your name on the old silver screen. If you ever decide you want to come where the action is, give me a call."

Now Klein was standing in the marble front hallway of the mansion talking to some other people who had just arrived. He was dressed in a black velvet jacket, a ruffled shirt, and a bright red bow tie. Beside him was an anxious-looking woman who ran public relations for his firm. It was she who had sent out the invitations for the evening, and she looked pained when she saw Craig standing there in slacks and a blue blazer. Most, but not all, of the other guests were in evening clothes, and Craig could tell by the look on the woman's face that she sensed a small betrayal in his choice of clothing.

Klein shook his hand warmly, smiling. "Ah," he said, "the great man. I was afraid you wouldn't come." He didn't explain why he was afraid Craig would not come but introduced him to the people whom he had been talking to. "You know Tonio Corelli, of course, Jess," he said.

"By sight." Corelli was the beautiful young Italian actor from the Hotel du Cap swimming pool, now resplendent in a jet black, Roman-tailored dinner jacket. They shook hands.

"And if you will introduce the ladies, *carino*," Klein said. "I didn't quite catch your names, dears," he added apologetically.

"This is Nicole," Corelli said, "and this is Irene."

Nicole and Irene smiled dutifully. They were as pretty and tan and well-shaped as the girls who had been with Corelli at the pool, but they were not the same girls.

He goes in for matched pairs, Craig thought, he must run them in and out on a schedule. Craig recognized envy as easily in himself as in the next man.

"Honey," Klein said to the public relations woman, "take them in and get them a drink. If you want to dance," he said to the girls, "be careful you don't catch pneumonia. The band's outside. I couldn't make a deal on the weather, and winter came up. The merry month of May."

The trio, led by the public relations woman, drifted beautifully away.

"The only thing to be," Klein said, "is Italian."

"I know what you mean," Craig said. "Though you don't seem to be doing so badly." He made a gesture to take in the luxury of his surroundings. He had heard that Klein was paying five thousand dollars for the month he had rented the house.

"I'm not complaining. I go with the flow," Klein

said, grinning. He took an honest pleasure in his
wealth. "It's not an uncomfortable little pad. Well,
Jesse, it's good seeing you again. How're things going?"

"Fine," Craig said. "Just fine."

"I invited Murphy and his frau," Klein said, "but
they declined with thanks. They don't mingle with
the lower orders."

"They're here for a rest," Craig said, lying for his
friend. "They're going to bed early this week, they
told me."

"He was a great man, Murphy," Klein said. "In his
day. You're still with him, of course?"

"Of course."

"As I once told you," said Klein, "your loyalty does
you credit. Is he working on something for you?"
He threw away the line carelessly, turning his head
as he spoke to survey his guests through the archway
that gave into the great living room.

"Not that I know of," Craig said.

"You have anything on the fire yourself?" Klein
turned back toward him.

Craig hesitated. "Maybe," he said. He had told no
one but Constance and Murphy that he was considering doing a picture again. And Murphy had made
his position clear. More than clear. Craig dropped
his hint deliberately now. Of all the men gathered
for the Festival, Klein, with his energy and his laby-
rinthine network of contacts, could be the most useful. "I'm playing with an idea."

"That's great news." The enthusiasm in Klein's
voice was almost genuine. "You've been away too
long, Jess. If you need any help, you know where to
come, don't you?" Klein put an affectionate hand on
his sleeve. "Anything for a friend. We put combinations together these days that make even *my* mind
whirl."

"So I've been told. Maybe I'll give you a call one

of these days and we can talk some more." Murphy would be hurt if he heard. He was a man proud of his acumen, and he took it ill if clients and friends didn't follow his advice. Murphy was contemptuous of Klein. "That punk little hustler" was Murphy's description of Klein. "In three years he won't even be a memory." But Murphy these days did not come up with combinations that made the mind whirl.

"There's a swimming pool out in the garden," Klein said. "Come any time you like. You don't have to call in advance. This is one house in which you're always welcome." There was a last affectionate little pat on the arm, and Klein turned to meet a new group that was arriving as Craig went into the salon.

The room was crowded because it was too cold to go outside where the band was playing, and on his way to the bar Craig had to say, "Excuse me," several times to get past guests clustered around easy chairs and small sofas. He asked for a glass of champagne. He had to drive back to Cannes, and if he drank whisky all night, the trip over the winding dark hillside roads would be a tricky one.

Corelli was at the bar with his two girls. "We should have gone to the French party," one of the girls was saying. She had a British accent. "This one is for the dodoes. I bet the average age here is forty-five."

Corelli smiled, offering the room the glory of his teeth.

Craig turned his back on the bar and looked at the room. Natalie Sorel was seated at a far corner, deep in conversation with a man who was lounging on the arm of her chair. Craig knew that she was so near-sighted that she could never recognize him at that distance. His own eyes were good enough to see that no matter what the English girl said, Natalie Sorel was no dodo.

"I used to hear about the parties in Cannes," the

English girl said. "Wild. Everybody smashing glasses and dancing naked on the tables and orgies in the swimming pools. The fall of the Roman Empire."

"That was in the old days, *cara,*" Corelli said. He had a heavy accent. Craig had seen him in some English films, and now he realized that Corelli's voice had been dubbed. Probably, Craig thought, his teeth aren't his own, either. The thought comforted him.

"This is about as wild as tea at the vicarage," the girl said. "Why don't we just curtsy and say good night and leave?"

"It is not polite, *carissima,*" Corelli said. "And besides, it is full of important people here who are not to be offended by young actors."

"You're a drag, darling," the girl said.

Craig surveyed the room looking for friends, enemies, and neutrals. Aside from Natalie there was a French actress by the name of Lucienne Dullin, seated, as though by some unfailing instinct, in the exact center of the room, attended by a shifting honor guard of young men. She was one of the most beautiful women Craig had ever seen, in a simple, bareshouldered white dress, with her hair pulled back severely so that the feline bone structure of her face and the long elegance of her throat descending to the perfect shoulders could best be appreciated. She was not a bad actress, but if you looked like that, it was unfair if you weren't Garbo. Craig had never met her, and he didn't want to meet her, but looking at her gave him enormous pleasure. . .

There was a huge, fat Englishman, well under forty, accompanied, like Corelli, by two young women. They were laughing hysterically at some joke he had just made. He had been pointed out to Craig on the beach. He was a banker, and the anecdote about him was that the month before in the bank in the city of London over which he presided, he had personally handed over a check for three and a half million dollars to Walt Klein. Craig understood why the two girls flanked the banker and why they laughed at his jokes.

Near the fireplace Bruce Thomas was standing talking to a hulking bald man by the name of Hennessy whom Craig recognized as the director of a film that was to be shown at the Festival later in the week. Thomas had a picture that had already played six months in New York and was still running, and Hennessy's picture, his first hit, was doing record-breaking business in an art house on Third Avenue. It was already being touted for a prize at the Festival.

Ian Wadleigh, not in Madrid, a glass in his hand, was standing talking to Eliot Steinhardt and a third man, portly in a dark suit, the face, bronzed by the sun, under a shock of iron-gray hair. The third man looked familiar to Craig, but he couldn't exactly place him. Wadleigh bulged out of his dinner jacket, which had obviously been bought in better and thinner days. He was not yet drunk but was flushed and talking fast. Eliot Steinhardt listened amiably, a slight smile on his face. He was a small twinkly man of about sixty-five, his face sharp and foxlike and slyly malicious. He had made a score of the biggest hits in the business, going all the way back to the middle 1930s, and although the new critics now sneered at him as old-fashioned, he calmly continued to turn out one hit after another as though success had made him immune to defamation or mortality. Craig liked and admired him. If Wadleigh hadn't been talking to him, he would have gone over to say hello. Later, when he's alone, Craig thought.

Murray Sloan, the critic for one of the trade papers, whose tastes were surprisingly avant-garde and whose most intense emotions seemed to be experienced in darkened projection rooms, was seated on a big couch talking to a man Craig didn't recognize. Sloan was a round, mahogany-tanned, smiling man whose devotion to his profession was so great that he had confided one evening to Craig that he had

stopped sleeping with a girl he had picked up at the
Venice Festival because she didn't appreciate Buñuel
sufficiently.

Well, Craig thought, looking over the room, whether Corelli's English beauty is intelligent or not, she's
right in saying it certainly isn't the fall of the Roman
Empire. It was rich and decorous and pleasant, but
whatever cross-currents were flowing through the
room and whatever corruption lay beneath the fine
clothes, it all was well hidden, the loved and the
unloved, the moneyed and the moneyless observing
an evening truce, ambition and desolation politely
side by side.

It was very different from the old parties in Hollywood when people who made five thousand dollars
a week would not invite people who made less to
their homes. A new society, Craig thought, out of the
ashes of the old. The movement of the proletariat
toward Möet and Chandon and the caviar pot.

He saw the man who was talking to Wadleigh and
Eliot Steinhardt look in his direction, smile and wave,
and start toward him. He smiled tentatively in return,
knowing that he had seen the man somewhere and
should remember his name.

"Hi, Jess," the man said, putting out his hand.

"Hello, David," Craig said, shaking hands. "Believe
it or not, I didn't recognize you."

The man chuckled. "It's the hair," he said. "I get it
all the time."

"You can't blame people," Craig said. David Teichman was one of the first men he had met when he
first went to Hollywood, and even then there hadn't
been a hair on his head.

"It's a wig," the man said, touching the top of his
bush complacently. "It takes twenty years off my age.
I'm even having a second run with the girls. That
reminds me—I had dinner with your girl in Paris.
She told me you were down here, and I told her I'd
look you up. I just got down here this morning, and

I've been playing gin all day. That's some girl you got there. Congratulations."

"Thanks," Craig said. "Do you mind if people ask you why you suddenly blossomed out with a mane?"

"Not at all, not at all. I had a little operation on my dome, and the doc left a couple of foxholes in my skull to remember him by. Not a very happy cosmetic effect, you might say. No sense in an old man going around frightening small children and virgin daughters. The studio hairdressing department fixed me up with the best damn hairpiece in the business. It's the only good thing that goddamn studio has turned out in five years." Teichman's false teeth clamped fiercely in his mouth as he spoke about the studio. He had been forced out of control more than a year ago, but he still spoke of it as though it were his personal domain. He had run it tyrannically for twenty-five years, and the habit of possession was hard to break. Bald, he had been a formidable-looking man, his head suggesting a siege weapon, his features fleshy and harsh, half-Roman emperor, half-merchant skipper, the skin deeply weathered all year round as though he had been in the field with his troops or on deck in storms with his crew. His voice had matched his appearance, brutal and commanding. In his palmy days many of the movies that had come out of his studio had been tender and wistfully comic, one more surprise in a surprising town. With the new wig he looked a different man, gentle and harmless, and his voice, too, as if to accommodate to the new arrangement, was soft and reflective.

Now he put his hand affectionately on Craig's sleeve and said as he looked around him, "Oy, Jess, I am not happy in this room. A flock of vultures feeding off the bones of giants. That's what the movie business has become, Jess. Great old bones with little patches of flesh still left on it that the birds of prey are tearing off bit by bit. And what are they turning out in their search for the Almighty Dollar? Peep shows. Pornography and bloodshed. Why don't they all go to Denmark and be done with it? And the theatre's no better. Carrion. What's Broadway today? Pimps, whores, drug pushers, muggers. I don't blame you for running away from it all."

"You're exaggerating as usual, David," Craig said. He had worked at Teichman's studio in the fifties and had caught on early that the old man was addicted to flights of rhetoric, usually to put over a shrewd and well-taken point. "There're some damn good pictures being made today, and there's a whole rash of young playwrights on and off Broadway."

"Name them," Teichman said. "Name one. One good picture."

"I'll do better than that. I'll name two. Three," Craig said, enjoying the debate. "And made by men right in this room tonight. Steinhardt's last picture and Thomas's and that new fellow talking to Thomas over there, Hennessy."

"Steinhardt doesn't count," Teichman said. "He's a leftover from the old days. A rock that was left standing when the glacier receded. The other two guys—" Teichman made a contemptuous sound. "Flashes in the pan. One-shot geniuses. Sure, every once in a while somebody shows up with a winner. Accidents still happen. They don't know what they're doing, they just wake up and find out they've fallen into a pot of gold. I'm talking about careers, boy, careers. No accidents. Chaplin, Ford, Stevens, Wyler, Capra, Hawkes, Wilder, yourself, if you want to include yourself. Although you were a little too special, maybe, and all over the place, if you don't mind my saying so."

"I don't mind," Craig said. "I've heard worse about myself."

"So have we all," Teichman said, "so have we all. We're living targets. But okay, so I made a lot of junk. I'm not too proud to admit it. Four hundred, five hundred pictures a year. Masterpieces don't come in gross lots, and I'm not saying they do. Junk, okay, mass production, okay, but it served its purpose. It created the machinery the great guys found ready to their hand, the actors, the grips, the scene designers, the audience. And it served another purpose, too. It won the world for America. I can see by the look on your face you think I'm batty. No matter what the fancy intellectual critics said, in their dreams the whole world loved us, we were their mistresses, their heroes. Do you think I'm ashamed of having been in on that? Not for a minute. I'll tell you what I *am* ashamed of. I'm ashamed that we pissed it all away. And if you want, I'll tell you the moment we did it. Even if you don't want." He poked a strong finger into Craig's shoulder. "The day we gave in to the yokels in Congress, the day we said, 'Yes, sir, Mr. Congressman, Mr. FBI man, I will kiss your ass, you don't like this writer's politics or that actress's morals or the subject of my next ten pictures, yes, sir, by all means, sir, they're out. I will slit my best friend's throat if you lift your pinky.' Before that we were the lucky, beautiful people of the twentieth century, we made jokes the whole world laughed at, we made love the way the whole world wished they could, we gave parties the whole world wanted to come to. After that we were just a bunch of sniveling Jews hoping the guy next door would get killed in the pogrom instead of us. People turned to television, and I don't blame them. In television they come right out and tell you they're trying to sell you a bill of goods."

"David," Craig said, "You're getting red in the face."

"You bet I am," Teichman said. "Calm me down, Jess, calm me down, my doctor would appreciate it. I'm sorry I came to this party. No, I'm not. I'm glad I got a chance to talk to you. I'm not finished yet, no matter how I sound. I'm in the process of putting something together—something big." Teichman winked conspiratorially. "Some men of talent. With

old-fashioned values. Discipline. Captains, not cor-
porals. A man like you, for example. Connie told me
you had something cooking, I should speak to you.
Am I talking out of school?"

"Not really," Craig said. "I have something in
mind."

"It's about time. Call me in the morning. We'll talk.
Money is no object. David Teichman is not a maker
of B pictures. I have to get out of here now, excuse
me, Jess. I find it hard to breathe these days when I
get angry. My doctor warns me against it constantly.
Remember what I said. In the morning. I'm at the
Carlton." Rubbing his excellent gray wig, he marched
off, defying ruin.

Craig watched the stiff, erect figure, patriot of de-
feated causes, historian of decay, shouldering toward
the door and shook his head. Still, he decided, he
would call Teichman in the morning.

Craig saw the man who was talking to Natalie Sorel
get up and take Natalie's glass and start toward the
bar, threading his way through the crowd. Craig
moved away from the bar in Natalie's direction. But
before he had covered half the distance, the door from
the patio opened and Gail McKinnon came in with a
small sallow man whose face was vaguely familiar. He
was about thirty-five, with scruffy receding hair and
unhealthy, grape-colored puffs under his eyes. He was
wearing a dinner jacket. Gail McKinnon was wearing a cheap print dress, the skirt above her knees. The
dress didn't look cheap on her. She smiled at Craig,
and there was no avoiding her. For some reason that
he could not explain, he didn't want her to observe
him in conversation with Natalie Sorel. He hadn't
seen her since the lunch with the Murphys, but then
he had stayed in his room most of the time nursing his
cold.

"Good evening, Mr. Craig," Gail McKinnon said. "I
see we make the same stops."

"It looks that way, doesn't it?" he said.

"May I introduce . . . ?" she started to say, turning to her companion.

"We've met," the man said. His tone was unfriendly. "A long time ago. In Hollywood."

"I'm afraid my memory isn't as good as it should be," Craig said.

"My name is Reynolds," the man said.

"Oh, yes," Craig said. He recognized the name, although he didn't remember ever having met the man. Reynolds had written movie reviews for a Los Angeles newspaper. "Of course." He extended his hand. Reynolds seemed to have to make up his mind to shake it.

"Come on, Gail," Reynolds said. "I want a drink."

"You go have a drink, Joe," Gail McKinnon said. "I want to talk for a minute with Mr. Craig."

Reynolds grunted, pushed his way toward the bar.

"What's the matter with him?" Craig asked, puzzled by the man's open antagonism.

"He's had a couple too many to drink," Gail McKinnon said.

"On all our tombstones," Craig said. He took a sip from the champagne glass he was carrying. "What's he doing so far from Los Angeles?"

"He's been in Europe for a wire service for two years," the girl said. "He's been most helpful." For some reason she seemed to be defending him. Craig wondered briefly if she was having an affair with him. Reynolds was an unprepossessing, sour-looking man, but in a place like Cannes you never could tell what a girl would turn up with. Now he remembered why the man's face had seemed familiar to him. Reynolds had been the man who had sat down at the table with Gail McKinnon on the Carlton terrace the other morning.

"He's a nut on movies," Gail McKinnon went on. "He remembers every picture that's ever been made. He's a treasure for me. He's seen all your pictures . . ."

"Maybe that's why he's so rude," Craig said.

"Oh, no," she said. "He likes them. Some of them."

Craig laughed. "Sometimes," he said, "you sound as young as you look."

"That lady over there is waving at you," the girl said.

Craig looked at the corner where Natalie Sorel was seated. She was beckoning him to come over. He had come within myopia range. He waved back. "An old friend," he said, "if you'll excuse me . . ."

"Did you get those questions I left at your hotel?"

"Yes."

"Well?"

"I tore them up," Craig said.

"Oh, that's mean," the girl said. "That's the meanest thing I ever heard. I've heard a lot of bad things about you, but nobody said you were mean."

"I change from day to day," he said. "Sometimes from moment to moment."

"Joe Reynolds warned me about you," she said. "I wasn't going to tell you, but now I don't care. You've got enemies, Mr. Craig, and you might as well know about it. You know why Joe Reynolds was rude to you?"

"I haven't the faintest idea. I never saw the man before the other morning," Craig said.

"Maybe not. Although he says you did. But you once said something about him."

"What?"

"He'd written a very good review of a picture of yours, and you said, 'That man writes so badly, I get angry at him even when he gives me a rave.'"

"When did I say that?" Craig asked.

"Eight years ago."

Craig laughed. "There's no animal more thin-skinned than a critic, is there?"

"You don't exactly go out of your way to be lovable, you know," she said. "You'd better leave now. That pretty lady is practically breaking her arm waving to you." Brusquely, she made her way through the crowd toward the bar where Reynolds, Craig saw, was waiting and watching.

How easy it was to make someone hate you for life. With one sentence.

He turned toward Natalie, dismissing Reynolds from his thoughts. Natalie stood up as he approached her, fair-haired, blue-eyed, luxuriously shaped, with dainty legs and feet, all like a lovingly made doll, too pink, white, and curvy to have any true semblance of reality. Despite her appearance and the soft, bell-like tone of her voice, he knew her as a woman of courage, determination, and lust.

"Take me into another room, Jesse," she was saying, stretching her hand out in greeting. "The biggest bore in the world will be back with a drink for me any minute now." She spoke English so well that anybody hearing her without knowing that she had been born in Hungary would only get a little echo of an unidentifiable accent. She spoke German, French, and Italian equally well. She looked no older than when he had seen her last. They had parted more or less by accident, without recriminations. She had had two pictures to do in England. He had had to go back to America. He hadn't seen either of the pictures she had made in England. He heard that she had taken up with a Spanish count. As far as he knew, he and Natalie had never given each other anything but pleasure. Perhaps that was why they had parted so easily. She had never said she loved him. It was another aspect of her character he admired.

She held his hand as they wove through the other guests toward the library. She had a large diamond ring on her finger. When he had known her, she was pawning jewelry, and he had loaned her money.

"As usual," he said, "you're shining tonight."

"If I had known that Lucienne Dullin was going to be here," she said, "I would never have come. Anyone who looks like that should be forced to wear a sack over her head when she comes to parties with older women."

"Never fear," he said. "You're defending yourself very well."

They sat down side by side on a leather couch. They were the only ones in the room, and the noise of the party, the music and the conversation, was pleasantly subdued here.

"Give me a sip of your champagne," she said.

He handed her his glass, and she drank all of the wine. She had avid appetites, he remembered.

She put the glass down. "You didn't answer my call," she said reproachfully.

"I got in late."

"I wanted to talk to you," she said. "And the other night there were too many people around. How are you?"

"Alive," he said.

"There's no news of you. I have asked."

"I've been vegetating."

"That isn't like the Jesse Craig I knew."

"Everybody's too active. If we'd just stand still six months a year, we'd all be much better off. I stepped off the merry-go-round for a while. That's all."

"When I think of you," she said, "I worry for you."

"Do you think of me often?"

"No." She laughed. She had small, very white teeth and a little pink tongue. "Only at obscene moments." In bed, he remembered, just before she came, she often said, "Fock me, fock me." He had found the mispronunciation endearing. She squeezed his hand affectionately. "How long has it been—five years?"

"More like six or seven."

"Ach," she said, "don't remind me. Are you still as bad as ever?"

"What do you mean by that?"

"I saw you talking to that beautiful young girl. Hanging all over you."

"She's a reporter."

"A woman isn't safe anymore," Natalie said. "Even reporters now look like that."

"It would be unseemly," he said. Natalie's teasing made him uncomfortable. "She's young enough to be my daughter. How about you? Where's your husband?"

"He's not my husband yet. I'm still struggling to land him."

"The other night you told me you were getting married."

"I will believe it when he puts the ring on my finger," Natalie said. "Then no more getting up at five in the morning to get my hair done and my face made up. No more being treated like a beast by temperamental directors. No more having to be nice to producers."

"I was a producer," he said, "and you were nice to me."

"Not because you were a producer, darling." She squeezed his hand again.

"Anyway, where is the husband-designate? If I were going to marry you, I wouldn't let you roam loose in a place like this just before the wedding."

"Only you weren't going to marry me, were you?" For the first time her tone was serious.

"I guess not," he said.

"Like a lot of other people," she said. She sighed. "Oh, well, little Natalie has had her fun. Now it's the time for proper behavior. Or should we be wicked and slip off and find out if they still have that room over the sea in Beaulieu?"

"I've never been to Beaulieu," Craig said, straight-faced.

"What a coincidence," she said. "Neither have I. Anyway, it would hardly be worth it. He's arriving tomorrow."

"Who's arriving tomorrow?"

"The husband-designate," she said. "Philip. He was

supposed to come with me, but at the last minute he had to stay in New York."

"Oh, he's American."

"People tell me they make the best husbands."

"I wouldn't know," Craig said. "What does he do?"

"He makes money. Isn't that charming?"

"Charming. How does he make money?"

"He manufactures things."

"How old is he?"

She hesitated, and the tip of her tongue showed between her lips. He recognized the signs. "Don't lie," he said.

She laughed. "Clever man. As always. Let's say he's older than you."

"How much older?"

"Considerably older." She spoke in a low voice. "He doesn't know anything about you."

"I should hope not. We didn't exactly publish advertisements in the papers." They had had to be discreet. She had had an official lover at the time who was paying some of her bills, and he was still trying to avoid scenes of jealousy with his wife. "And what if he *did* know about me?" he asked. "He doesn't think he's marrying a virgin, does he?"

"No, not exactly." Her smile was a little sad. "But he doesn't know the full extent." She made a wry, childish little grimace. "Not by half. Not by a quarter."

"Who does know the full extent?"

"I hope nobody," she said.

"Just for the record," Craig said, "in the next room there—how many?"

Natalie made a small grimace. "Would you settle for five?"

He grinned and shook his head.

"Six, then," she said. "What do you expect—your little Natalie's been around a long time. And being in the movies is a little like being on an island with the same group of castaways for years and years. A lady is liable to go to and fro—to and fro. A gentleman, too, my friend." She touched Craig's lips lightly with the tip of her finger.

"*Nolo contendere,*" Craig said.

Natalie laughed, little white teeth. "Isn't it nice," she said, "I hardly ever had to lie to you."

"And to your husband-to-be?"

She laughed again. "I hardly ever have to tell him the truth." She grew serious. "He's a solid citizen. Very conservative. A Baptist from Texas. He's so puritanical he hasn't even slept with me yet."

"God," Craig said.

"That's it," she said. "God. When he gets here, I'll have to pretend I barely know you. If we meet, don't be surprised if I call you Mr. Craig. If he heard that I was the sort of lady who was known to go off on weekends with married men, there's no telling what he'd do."

"What's the worst he could do?"

"He could not marry me. You will be careful, won't you, Jesse?" There was a pleading note in her voice that he had never heard before. It occurred to him that she was actually past forty.

"If he hears anything," Craig said, "it won't be from me. But I advise you to get him out of Cannes as quickly as possible."

"He's only going to stay a few days," she said. "Then we're flying to Venice."

"Haven't you and I ever been to Venice together?"

"Don't you remember?"

"No."

"Then we haven't been to Venice," she said. She looked up and smiled. The man she had been talking to in the salon was standing at the door of the library, two glasses in his hands.

"Oh, there you are," the man said. "I've been looking all over for you."

Craig stood up, and Natalie mumbled both their names. Craig didn't recognize the man's name. He

had a small, anxious, easily forgettable face. Arbi-
trarily, Craig decided that he worked on the distribution end for one of the major companies. The man
gave Natalie her glass and shook Craig's hand gravely.

"Well," Craig said, "I'll leave you two kids alone.
You've reminded me I'm thirsty." He touched Natalie's shoulder reassuringly and went out of the library and back to the bar, avoiding Ian Wadleigh en
route.

In the dining room, where a buffet had been set
up, Craig glimpsed Gail McKinnon and Reynolds
waiting to be served.

Murray Sloan was standing at the bar, chubby and
dapper, staring out at the guests. He was smiling
pleasantly, but his eyes were like small, dark com-
puters. "Hi, Jesse," he said. "Join the working press
in a free drink."

"Hello, Murray," Craig said, and asked for a glass
of champagne.

"This isn't your scene anymore, is it, Jesse?" Sloan
said. He was munching contentedly on a small cu-
cumber sandwich that he had lifted from a tray of
hors d'oeuvres.

"It's hard to know just what scene this is," Craig
said. "The Tower of Babel, the entrance to the Ark,
a Mafia meeting, or a prom at a girl's school."

"I'll tell you what the scene is," Sloan said. "It's
the ball at Versailles at the court of Louis the Sixteenth, July thirteenth, 1789, the night before the
storming of the Bastille."

Craig chuckled.

"You can laugh," Sloan said. "But mark my words.
Did you see that picture *Ice* they showed in the Director's Quinzaine?"

"Yes," Craig said. The picture had been made by a
group of young revolutionaries and was a deadly
serious work about the beginning of armed revolt in
New York City in the immediate future. It had some
chilling scenes of castrations, murders of public of-

ficials, street fighting, and bombings, all portrayed in a flat *cinéma vérité* style that made it very disturbing.

"What did you think of it?" Sloan asked, challengingly.

"It's hard for a man like me to know if it has any validity or not," Craig said. "I don't know kids like that. It might just be a put-on."

"It's no put-on," Sloan said. "It's what's going to happen in America. Soon." He waved his arm to indicate the crowd of his fellow guests. "And all these fat cats are going to be in the tumbrels."

"And where will you be, Murray?" Craig asked.

"In the tumbrels with them," Sloan said gloomily. "Those kids aren't going to make any fine distinctions."

Walter Klein wandered over to the bar. "Hi, boys," he said. "Having a good time?"

Craig allowed Sloan to answer the question. "Loving every minute of it, Walt," Sloan said, observing the ritual.

"How about you, Jesse?" Klein asked.

"Every minute," Craig said.

"It's not a bad little do," Klein said complacently. "A nice mixture of beauty, talent, and larceny." He laughed. "Look at those two over there." He indicated Hennessy and Thomas, who were talking earnestly near the fireplace. "Bathing in it. On the crest of the wave," he said. "Nice work if you can get it. They're both clients."

"Naturally," Craig said. He took another glass of champagne from the waiter behind the bar.

"Come on over and say a word to the two geniuses," Klein said. It was his abiding rule to introduce everybody to everybody else. As he told his lieutenants, you never know where the lightning will strike. "You, too, Murray."

"I'll keep the duty here at the bar," Sloan said.

"Don't you want to meet them?" Klein asked, surprised.

"No," Sloan said. "I'm going to pan their pictures, and I don't want to be swayed by any false feeling of friendship."

"Have you *seen* their pictures?" Klein asked.

"No," Sloan said. "But I know their work."

"Lo and behold," Klein said mockingly, "an honest man. Come on, Jess." He took Craig's arm and led him toward the fireplace.

Craig shook Hennessy's hand and apologized to Thomas for not having called him back. Thomas was a slim, gentle-looking man who had a reputation for being unbendingly stubborn on the set.

"What're you two doing?" Klein demanded. "Comparing your grosses?"

"We're crying in our beer," Hennessy said.

"What about?" Klein asked.

"The corruption of the lower classes," Hennessy said. "And how difficult it is to remain pure in an impure world."

"Hennessy's new to the game," Thomas said.

"He can't get over the fact that he had to bribe a sheriff and his deputy when he was shooting in a town in Texas."

"I don't mind a bit of reaming per se," Hennessy said. "But I like it to be a little subtle. At least pay lip service to the notion that the bribery of public officials is somewhat distasteful. But these guys just sat there in my motel room drinking my whisky and saying, 'It's three thousand for each of us or don't bother to take the cover off your camera.'" He shook his head mournfully. "And no nonsense like don't you think a big rich company like yours could make a little contribution to the Policemen's Benevolent Fund, or anything like that. Just put the money on the bed, mister. It's tough on a boy who used to be first in his class at Sunday school to shell out six thousand dollars in cash to a couple of cops in a motel room and put it into the budget as incidental expenses."

"You got off cheap," Klein said. He was a practical,

empirical man. "Don't complain."

"Then, after that," Hennessy said, "they had the nerve to bust the leading man for smoking pot, and there went another two thousand to get him off. What this country needs, like the vice-president says, is law and order."

"You're in France now," Klein said. "Remember?"

"I'm in the movie business," Hennessy said, "wherever I am. And the thing that drives me crazy in the goddamn business is all the dough that flows out that you never see on the screen."

"Easy come, easy go," Klein said. A man who had recently received a check for three and a half million dollars could talk like that.

"I'm teaching a seminar at UCLA next year in the art of the cinema," Hennessy said. He drawled out *cinema* mockingly. "All this will be in my first lecture. Hey, Craig, how'd you like to be my guest one or two hours and tell the kids how it is in the glamorous world of celluloid?"

"I might discourage them for life," Craig said.

"Great," Hennessy said. "Anything to keep the competition down. I mean it, though. Seriously. You could really tell them a thing or two."

"If I'm not busy," Craig said carefully, "and I happen to be in the States, maybe . . ."

"Where can I reach you?" Hennessy said.

"Through me," Klein said quickly. "Jess and I've been talking about the possibility of his getting back into production one of these days, and I'll know where I can get hold of him."

Klein wasn't exactly lying, Craig thought. He was just shaping the truth to his and perhaps Craig's benefit.

The two directors had glanced sharply at Craig as Klein spoke. Now Thomas said, "What's the property, Jesse? Or don't you want to say?"

"It'd rather not say for the moment. It's still all in the dreaming stage." Murphy's dreams, he thought.

There was a small commotion at the doorway, and Frank Garland came in with his wife and another couple. Garland was an actor who had starred in one of Craig's early movies. He was several years older than Craig but looked no more than thirty-five, dark-haired, athletically tall, strong-jawed, and handsome. He was a very good actor and an imaginative businessman and had his own company that produced not only his own films but the films of others. He was a bouncingly healthy, jovial, extroverted man with a pretty wife to whom he had been married for more than twenty years. He had been superb in Craig's picture, and they were good friends, but tonight Craig didn't want to be exposed to that glorious health, that sensible intelligence, that flawless luck, that unfaked and all-embracing cordiality.

"See you boys later," he said to Klein and the two directors. "I need a breath of air." He went out to the patio and down the wet grass of the garden toward the illuminated swimming pool. The band was playing, "On a Clear Day You Can See Forever."

Craig looked down at the bright water. The pool was heated, and a slight mist was rising from the surface. Orgies in the swimming pools, he remembered. Not tonight, Nicole.

"Hi, Jesse," a voice said.

Craig looked up. A man was advancing from the shadows of the shrubbery near the end of the pool. As he came closer, Craig recognized him. It was Sidney Green. The thought occurred to Craig that Green had been driven into the solitude of the cold, wet garden for some of the same reasons as himself. Losers outside, please. Ian Wadleigh would soon appear.

"Hello, Sid," Craig said. "What are you doing out here?"

"It got too rich for my blood in there." Green had a mournful, soft voice, the voice of a man who expects to be treated badly at all times. "I came out and pissed on the expensive green grass of Walter

Klein. A man takes what satisfactions he can find in this world." He laughed apologetically, breathily. "You won't tell Walt, will you? I don't want to seem ungrateful. It was nice of him to invite me. With all those people in that room. There's a lot of power in that room tonight, a lot of clout." Green shook his head slowly to emphasize his respect for the potency of the company assembled by Walt Klein that night. "I tell you, Jesse," he went on, "there are men in there who could get a ten-million-dollar production started tomorrow morning just by crooking a finger. They look like me, maybe even worse than me, they're wearing the same kind of tuxedo, maybe we even had our suits made by the same tailor, but God, what a difference. How about you, Jesse? People've been talking about you, wondering what you're doing here. The guess is you've got a picture ready to go and you're here to make a deal."

"There's nothing definite so far," Craig said. Murphy had been definite enough, but there was nothing to be gained by telling Green about that.

"I saw you talking to David Teichman," Green said. "He was something in his day, wasn't he?"

"He certainly was."

"Finished," Green said.

Craig didn't like the bite of the word. "I wouldn't be too sure," he said.

"He'll never make another picture." Green's judgment was final.

"Maybe he's got some plans he hasn't let you in on, Sid."

"If you're thinking of going into business with him, forget it," Green said. "He's going to be dead before the year's out."

"What're you talking about?" Craig asked sharply.

"I thought everybody knew," Green said. "He's got a tumor of the brain. My cousin operated on him in The Cedars. It's just a wonder he's still walking around."

"Poor old man," Craig said. The wig had taken twenty years off his life, Teichman had said.

"Oh. I wouldn't waste too much pity on him," Green said. "He had it good for a long, long time. I'd settle for his life *and* his tumor at his age. At least his worries're just about over. How about you, Jesse?" The dead and dying had had their moment in Walter Klein's rented garden. "Are you coming back?"

"The possibility exists."

"Well, if you do decide to move, remember me, will you, Jesse?"

"I will indeed."

"I'm underrated as a director, I'm enormously underrated," Green said earnestly. "And that's not only my opinion. There's a guy in there from *Cahiers du Cinéma,* and he made a point of being introduced to me and telling me that in his opinion my last picture, the one I did for Columbia, was a masterpiece. Did you happen to see it?"

"I'm afraid not," Craig said. "I don't go to the movies much anymore."

"Fanfare for Drums," Green said. "That's what it was called. You sure you didn't see it?"

"Absolutely."

"If you want, I'll introduce you to the guy," Green said. "I mean the *Cahiers du Cinéma* guy. He's real smart. He has nothing but scorn for most of the people in there tonight. Scorn."

"Some other time, maybe, Sid. I'm going to make an early night of it."

"Just give me the word," Green said. "I have his address. Boy," he said sadly, "I thought this was going to be my big year in Cannes. I had a two-picture deal with options with Apex and Eastern. That's one of those big conglomerates. Three months ago they looked as though they had all the money in the world. I thought I was all set. I took a new apartment in the sixteenth, they're still putting in *boiserie* that cost fifteen thousand bucks that I haven't paid for yet. And my wife and I decided we could afford another kid, and she's going to have it in December. Then everything went kaput. Apex and Eastern is in receivership, and I can't afford orange juice in the morning anymore. If I don't get something down here these two weeks, you can say farewell to Sid Green."

"Something'll turn up," Craig said.

"It better," Green said. "It just better."

Craig left him standing at the side of the pool, his head bent, staring despondently at the mist rising from the heated green water. At least, Craig thought, as he went inside, I don't owe fifteen thousand dollars for *boiserie,* and my wife isn't pregnant.

He spent the rest of the evening drinking. He talked to a lot of people, but by the time he felt he ought to go back to the hotel, all he could remember was that he had looked for Natalie Sorel to take her home with him and not found her and that he had told Walt Klein that he would show him his script and Klein had said that he'd send one of his boys over to the hotel in the morning to pick it up.

He was standing at the bar having one last drink when he saw Gail McKinnon come hurrying in, a raincoat thrown over her shoulders. He hadn't seen her leave. She stopped for a moment at the doorway, scanning the room, then saw him and came over to him. "I'd hoped you'd still be here," she said.

"Have a nightcap," he said. The evening's drinking had made him mellow.

"I need somebody to drive me and Joe Reynolds home," she said. "He hurt himself. Also he's drunk. He knocked himself out falling down the stairs outside."

"It couldn't happen to a nicer fellow," Craig said, cheered by the news. "Have a drink."

"The policeman out there won't let him get into the car," Gail said.

"Astute," Craig said. "The astute French police.

Bloodhounds of the law. Have a drink to the noble gendarmerie of the Alpes Maritimes."

"Are you drunk, too?" she asked sharply.

"Not really," he said. "Are you? Why don't you drive the critic home?"

"I don't have a license."

"Un-American. Don't tell any congressman who happens to ask you. Have a drink," he said.

"Come on, Jesse," she said pleadingly. It was the first time, he noticed, that she had called him by his first name. "It's late, and I can't handle the pain in the ass myself, and he's howling and threatening the policeman and bleeding all over the place, and he'll wind up in jail if we don't get him out of here fast. I know you think I'm a pest, but this is an act of charity." She looked around the room. It was almost empty. "The party's over. Take us back to Cannes, please."

Craig drained his glass, smiled. "I will deposit the body safely," he said. He took her arm formally and made her say good night with him to Walter Klein before going out into the drizzly night.

Reynolds had stopped yelling at the policeman. He was sitting on the bottom step of the flagstone staircase down which he had fallen, a nasty gash on his forehead, an eye beginning to swell. He was holding a bloodstained handkerchief to his nose. He looked up blearily as Gail McKinnon and Craig approached him. "Goddamn Frog cops," he said thickly. "Walter Klein and his thugs."

"It's all right, monsieur," Craig said in French to the policeman who was standing politely next to Reynolds. "I'm his friend. I'll drive him home."

"He is in no state to drive," the policeman said. "That is evident to the naked eye. No matter what the gentleman says."

"I absolutely agree," Craig said. He was careful to keep his distance from the policeman. He didn't want to chance the man's smelling *his* breath. "Upsy-daisy, Joe," he said to Reynolds, grabbing him under the armpit and hauling him up. Reynolds let the handkerchief fall from his nose, and a fresh gush of blood spattered Craig's trousers. Reynolds smelled as though he had been steeped, with all his clothes, in whisky for days.

With Gail helping on the other side, they got Reynolds to Craig's car and pushed him into the back seat where he promptly went to sleep. Craig drove out of the parking lot under the dripping trees with exaggerated care, for the watching policeman's benefit.

Except for the sound of Reynold's wet and bubbling snoring in the back of the car, they drove in silence to Cannes. Craig concentrated at the wheel, driving slowly, conscious that the road seemed to have a tendency to blur somewhat in the beam of the headlights on the curves. He was ashamed of the amount of liquor he had drunk that night and promised himself that in the future he would abstain completely when he knew he had to drive a car after an evening out.

When they reached the outskirts of Cannes, the girl told Craig the name of Reynolds' hotel. It was about six blocks away from the Carlton, inland, behind the railroad tracks. When they got there, Reynolds, now awake, said thickly, "Thank you, everybody. Don't bother to go in with me. Perfectly all right. Good night."

They watched him walk stiffly and self-consciously into the darkened hotel.

"He doesn't need any more to drink," Craig said, "but I do."

"So do I," said Gail McKinnon.

"Don't you live in that hotel, too?" Craig asked.

"No."

He felt a foolish sense of relief.

All the bars they passed were closed. He hadn't realized how late it was. Anyway, stained as they were from Reynolds' blood, they would have been a disturbing sight for any late-drinking patrons. Craig stopped the car in front of the Carlton but left the motor running. "I have a bottle," he said. "Do you want to come up?"

"Yes, please," she said.

He parked the car, and they went into the hotel. Luckily, there was nobody there. The concierge, from whom Craig got the key to his apartment, had been trained since boyhood not to change his expression at anything he saw in the lobby of any hotel.

In the apartment Gail McKinnon took off her coat and went into the bathroom while Craig poured the whiskies and soda. There was the pleasant domestic sound of running water from the bathroom, sign of another presence, a barrier against loneliness.

When she came back, he saw that she had combed her hair. She looked fresh and clean, as though nothing had happened to her that night. They raised their glasses to each other and drank. The hotel was quiet around them, the city sleeping.

They sat facing each other on large brocaded armchairs.

"Lesson for the day," Craig said. "Don't go out with drunks. If he hadn't had the good sense to fall down those steps, you'd have probably wound up wrapped around a tree."

"Probably." She shrugged. "The hazards of the machine age."

"You could have asked me to drive you home before the fall," Craig said, forgetting that he had been perhaps just as drunk as Reynolds.

"I had decided never to ask you anything again," she said.

"I see."

"He was raving against you when he made his swan dive. Reynolds." The girl giggled.

"Just for one little nasty crack eight years ago?" Craig shook his head, marveling at the persistence of vanity.

"That and a lot of other things."

"What other things?"

"You once took a girl away from him in Hollywood."

"Did I? Well, if I did, I didn't know about it."

"That makes it even worse for somebody like Joe Reynolds. He hit her, and out of spite she told him how all-round marvelous you were and what other women had told her about you and about how intelligent and sensitive and funny you were. What do you expect him to feel about you? And you were such a big shot out there when he was a pimply-faced boy just breaking in."

"Well, he must feel better about me now," Craig said.

"A little," the girl said. "But not enough. He's given me a lot of the information that's in the stuff I've written so far about you. And he's suggested a title for the piece."

"What is it?" Craig asked, curious.

"The Once and Future Has Been," the girl said flatly.

Craig nodded. "It's vulgar," he said, "but catchy. You going to use it?"

"I don't know yet," she said.

"What does it depend on?"

"You. What you seem like to me finally when I get really to know you. If I ever get to know you. How much guts I think you still have. Or will. Or talent. It would help if you let me read the script you're giving to Walt Klein tomorrow."

"How do you know about that?"

"Sam Boyd is a friend of mine." Sam Boyd was one of Klein's bright young men. "He told me he was coming over here in the morning to pick up a script you owned. We're having breakfast together."

"Tell him to come for the script *after* breakfast," Craig said.

"I'll tell him." She held out her glass. "It's empty," she said.

He got up and carried both glasses over to the table where the bottle was. He made the two drinks and carried them back. "Thanks," she said, looking up at him soberly as she accepted the glass. He leaned over and kissed her gently. Her lips were soft, welcoming. Then she averted her head. He stepped back as she stood up.

"That's enough of that," she said. "I'm going home."

He put out his hand to touch her arm.

"Leave me alone!" she said sharply. She put down her glass, seized her coat, and ran toward the door.

"Gail . . ." he said, taking a step after her.

"Miserable old man," she said as she pulled open the door. The door slammed after her.

He finished his drink slowly, then put out the lights and went to bed. Lying naked on the sheets in the warm darkness, he listened to the occasional rubber swish of a car on the Croisette and the tumble of the Mediterranean on the shore. He couldn't sleep. It had been a full night. The liquor he had drunk drummed at his temples. Bits and pieces of the evening formed and reformed kaleidoscopically in his brain—Klein, in his velvet jacket, introducing everybody to everybody, Corelli and his two girls, Green pissing forlornly on the expensive green grass, Reynolds' blood . . .

Add to the mixture . . . The game (was it a game?) of Gail McKinnon. Her flickering young-old sensuality. Invitation and rejection. Remember and regret the lushness of Natalie Sorel, try to forget David Teichman, death under the studio wig.

Craig moved uneasily in the bed. It had been like a gigantic Christmas office party. Except that in other businesses they weren't held twice a week.

Then there was the soft, half-expected knock on the door. He got up, put on a robe, and opened the door.

Gail McKinnon was standing in the dim corridor.

"Come in," he said.

• TEN •

He was aware that it was light, that he was not yet awake, that there was soft breathing somewhere beside him, that the phone was ringing.

Without sitting up or opening his eyes, postponing the day, he groped for the phone on the bedside table. A faraway voice, through a curtain of mechanical buzzing, said, "Good morning, darling."

"Who's this?" he said. His eyes were still closed.

"How many people call you darling?" the thin, distant voice said.

"I'm sorry, Constance," he said. "You sound a million miles away." He opened his eyes, turned his head. The long brown hair was on the pillow beside him. Gail stared at him, the blue-flecked eyes fixed gravely on him. He was half-out from the sheet that covered her, and he had an enormous erection. He didn't remember ever having seen his cock that size. He had to suppress a ludicrous impulse to grab at the sheet and cover himself.

"You're still in bed," Constance was saying. Distant electronic accusation across six hundred miles of inaccurate cable. "It's past ten o'clock."

"Is it?" he said idiotically. His cock swelled malevolently. He was conscious of the level glance from the next pillow, the shape of the body under the sheet, the neatly turned-down second bed in the room, still unslept in. He regretted having spoken Constance's name, any name. "This is a late town," he said. "How're things in Paris?"

"Deteriorating. How're things with you?"

He hesitated. "Nothing new," he said.

Gail did not smile or change her expression. The weight of her glance was almost palpable on the insanely stalwart penis towering into the golden morning air like a permanent and shameless feature of the landscape. Gail reached over slowly, deliberately, and ran one experimental finger from its base to its flaming crown. A convulsion racked him as though he had been touched by a high-tension wire.

"Holy man," she whispered.

"First of all," the wavery, mechanical, almost unrecognizable voice was saying in the telephone, "I want to apologize . . ."

"I can hardly hear you," he said, making an agonizing effort to speak calmly. "Maybe we'd better hang up and call the operator again and . . ."

"Is this better? Can you hear me now?" Suddenly the voice was clear and strong, as if Constance were in another room of the hotel or around the corner.

"Yes," he said reluctantly. Desperately, he tried to think of something to say to Constance that would hold her off, give him time to put on some clothes and go into the living room and wait there for her to call back. But for the moment he didn't trust himself with anything more ambitious than a monosyllable.

"I said I wanted to apologize," Constance said, "for being so bitchy the other day. You know how I am."

"Yes," he said. Nothing had changed below.

"And thanks for the picture of the lion. It was a nice thought."

"Yes," he said.

"I have some good news," Constance said. "At least I hope you'll think it's good news."

"What's that?" Slyly, surreptitiously, he had managed to cover himself almost entirely from the waist down with the sheet. The sheet still stuck up, though, like a circus tent.

"I may have to be in your part of the world tomorrow or the day after. Marseilles," she said.

"Marseilles?" he asked. For the moment he couldn't quite remember where Marseilles was. "Why Marseilles?"

"I can't say over the phone." Her suspicion of the French telephone system was as strong as ever. "But if things work out up here, I'll be there."

"That's fine," Craig said, his mind on other things.

"What's fine?" Now Constance was beginning to sound irritated.

"I mean maybe we can see each other . . ."

"What do you mean *maybe?*" The tone was becoming ominous.

He felt the shift in the bed beside him. Gail stood up, walked slowly, naked, slender-waisted, pearly-hipped, gently swelling tanned calves, into the bathroom, without a backward glance. "Well, there is a complication . . ."

"This is another damned unsatisfactory conversation, lad," Constance said.

"My daughter Anne is arriving here today," Craig said, grateful that Gail was no longer in the room. The erection went down suddenly, and he was grateful for that, too. "I sent her a cable inviting her."

"Everybody's at the mercy of the goddamn young," Constance said. "Bring her along to Marseilles. Every virgin ought to see Marseilles."

"Let me work it out with her." He withheld comment on the "virgin." "When you know definitely what your plans are, call me. Maybe you could come to Cannes," he added insincerely.

He heard the water of the shower being turned on in the bathroom. He wondered if Constance could hear the shower in Paris.

"I hate Cannes," Constance said. "I decided to divorce my first husband there. Christ, if it's too much trouble for you to get in a car and drive a couple of hours to see a girl you're supposed to be in love with . . ."

"Don't work yourself up into one of your rages, Constance," Craig said. "You don't even know if you're going to be in Marseilles or not yet . . ."

"I want you to be eager," she said. "You haven't seen me for a week now. The least you could be is eager."

"I *am* eager," he said.

"Prove it."

"I will meet you anywhere you want anytime you want," he said loudly.

"I suppose that'll have to do, lad," she said. She chuckled. "Christ, it's like pulling teeth. Are you drunk?"

"Hung over."

"Have you been debauching?"

"I suppose you could say that." One stone, at least, in the arch of truth.

"I never liked a sober man," she said. "All right, I'll wire you as soon as I know anything. How old is your daughter?"

"Twenty."

"You'd think a girl twenty years old would have something better to do than hang around with her old man."

"We're a close-knit family," Craig said.

"I've noticed that. Have fun, darling. I miss you. And the little lion *was* a sweet idea." She hung up.

Ignoble, ignobly comic, he thought resentfully as he swung out of bed and began hurriedly to dress. He had on a shirt and a pair of pants by the time Gail came out of the bathroom, still naked, slender and superb, her brown skin glistening with the last drops of the shower that she had neglected to dry off.

She stood with her legs wide apart, her hands on her hips, in a caricature of a model's pose, and grinned at him. "My," she said, "we're a busy little fellow, aren't we." Then she came over to him and pulled his head down a little toward her and kissed his forehead. But when he put his arms around her and tried to kiss her in return, she pulled away abruptly and said, "I'm dying for breakfast. Which bell do you ring?"

He was early when he got to the airport at Nice. The plane from Geneva wasn't due for almost another half hour. His feeling about arrivals and departures had been developed in his marriage. His wife had been a woman who had never been able to get anywhere on time, and his memory of the years with her was composed of a succession of infuriating scenes, his shouting at her to hurry, her tears and neurotic slamming of doors to punish him for his reproaches, and the recurring small agony of apologizing to friends for keeping them waiting, waiting for dinner, planes, trains, theatres, weddings, funerals, football games. Because of that, now that he was rid of her, he allowed himself the satisfaction of getting everywhere with time to spare, his nerves serene. "Leaving your mother," he had once told Anne, who understood what he was talking about because she had developed into a monster of punctuality as a result of her mother's vice, "has added ten years to my life."

He went upstairs and sat on the airport balcony overlooking the runway and the sea. He sat at a little iron table and ordered a whisky and soda. Although it was early in the afternoon, a brisk wind made the air cool and whipped up small curls of whitecaps on the blue water.

Consciously, sipping his drink, he tried to compose himself to greet his daughter. But his hand trembled minutely as he picked up the glass. He felt tense and weary, and when he tried to focus on a plane that was coming in to land but was still about a mile away from the end of the runway in the bright sky, his eyes blurred momentarily behind his sunglasses. He hadn't slept well. And for the wrong reason. Gail McKinnon had come to his room and shared his bed, but she had not permitted him to make love to her. She had offered no explanations. She had merely said, "No," and had gone to sleep in his arms, calm, silken, fragrant, perverse, and sure of herself, abundant and tantalizing in her youth and beauty.

Now, thinking of it while waiting for his child to come down out of the afternoon sky, he was shamed by the absurdity of the night. A man his age allowing himself to be trapped in a silly adolescent game like that! And by a girl young enough to be his daughter. He should have turned on the light, ordered her out of the room, taken a pill, and gone to sleep. Or at least put on a pair of pajamas and gotten into the next bed and slept alone and told the girl he never wanted to see her again when she awoke in the morning. Instead, he had held her close, drowned in melancholy tenderness, wracked by desire, sleepless, caressing the nape of her neck, sniffing the perfume of her hair, listening to her steady, healthy breathing as the light of dawn outlined the shutters of the windows.

And over breakfast, annoyed by the leer, real or imagined, of the waiter, he had told her he'd meet her for drinks that afternoon. And because of her he had offended Constance, lied or half-lied on the phone, risked compromising what he had thought until last night was his faithful love for a grown competent woman who played no games with him, who made him happy, a beautiful, intelligent, useful woman who met him on equal terms, whose affection (why not call it by its proper name?), whose passion for him had helped him in the last two years to get through some of the darkest moments of his life. He had always prided himself on being a man who in good times and bad was in reasonable control of his actions, his fate. And here, in a few drunken hours, he had shown that he was as capable of mindless choice and self-destructive drifting as any romantically brainwashed idiot.

Drunken. He was lying to himself. He had drunk—but not that much. He knew that even if he hadn't touched a drop all night, he would have behaved no differently.

Cannes was to blame, he told himself defensively. It was a city made for the indulgence of the senses, all ease and sunshine and provocative flesh. And in the darkened auditoriums of the town he had delivered himself over to the dense, troubling sensuality of film after film, glorious couplings, the delicious odor of vice, emotion everywhere, the denial of reason, the rites of youth, too heady a mixture for an aging man unanchored and voyaging without a compass across a troubled year.

And now, to make things worse, his daughter was entering the picture. What the hell could have possessed him to have sent that cable! He groaned, then looked around to see if anybody had noticed, pretending that it had not been a groan but a cough. He brought his handkerchief falsely to his lips, ordered another whisky.

He had come to Cannes looking for answers. What he had done in a few short days was multiply the questions. Maybe, he thought, the thing to do is go down to the ticket counter and buy a seat for Paris or New York or London or Vienna. Northern man, at home in a more stringent climate, the white, pagan cities of the south were not for him. If he were wiser, he would leave the complicated, sinister temptations of the Mediterranean once and for all. The idea was a sensible one. But he didn't move. He knew he was not buying any tickets for anywhere. Not yet.

Klein's assistant, Boyd, had telephoned from the lobby during breakfast, and Craig had sent a copy of

the script of *The Three Horizons* down with a bell-
boy. If Klein's reaction was a negative one, he thought,
he would get out of Cannes. His decision soothed him.
It gave him a fixed point to look forward to, a choice
that was mechanical, out of his hands. He felt better.
When he lifted his glass, he noticed that his hand was
no longer trembling.

The plane came to a halt on the tarmac. The passengers came streaming out, dressed for holiday,
dresses blowing in the sea wind. He picked out Anne,
bright blonde hair whipping around her head, walking quickly and eagerly, looking up at the terrace,
searching for him. He waved. She waved back, moved
more quickly. She was carrying a bulging khaki bag
made out of canvas that looked as though she had
picked it up in an Army and Navy store. He noted
that she still walked clumsily, in a kind of uncollect-
ed slouch, as though she hesitated to pretend to womanly grace. He wondered if he might suggest lessons
in posture. She was wearing a wrinkled blue raincoat
and drab brown slacks. Except for her hair, she looked
dun, self-consciously sober and inconspicuous in her
dark clothes among the summery dresses and the pat-
terned shirts and madras jackets of the other passengers. What is she pretending to be *now*, he thought.
Irrationally, he was annoyed with the way she was
dressed. Back in the time when the money was rolling
in, he had set up trust funds for her and her sister.
The income from them wasn't extravagant, but it
certainly was enough to buy some clothes. He would
have to persuade her, tactfully, to shop for some new
things. At least, he comforted himself, she was clean
and was wearing shoes and didn't look like a Co-
manche squaw stoned on pot. Be grateful for small
favors.

He paid for his drinks and went down to greet her.

As she came out, following a porter trundling her
two valises, he arranged his face to welcome her.

Childishly, she threw herself into his arms and kissed him, rather inaccurately, somewhere in the region of the throat. "Oh, Daddy," she cried, muffled against him.

He patted the shoulder of the wrinkled blue raincoat. Inevitably, as she pressed against him, he remembered the other young body in his arms that morning, the other kiss. "Let me look at you," he said. She pulled away a little so that he could take stock of her. She wore no makeup and didn't need any. She had a California look about her, clear-eyed, tanned, and blooming, her hair bleached in streaks by days in the sun, a light sanding of freckles across the bridge of her strong, straight nose. He knew from her marks that she was an excellent student, but from her appearance it was hard to believe that she ever bothered to open a book or did anything but spend her time on beaches, surfboards, and tennis courts. If he were twenty years old and was a girl who looked like that, he would not slouch.

He hadn't seen her in six months, and he noticed that she had filled out since their last meeting, that her breasts, free under a dark green sweater, were considerably heavier than before. Her face was fined down, almost triangular, with faint hollows under the prominent cheekbones. She had always been a healthy child, and she was growing into a robust woman.

"Like what you see?" she asked, smiling. It was an old private formula between them that she had hit on when she was still a little girl.

"More or less," he said, teasing. It was impossible to phrase the pleasure, the tenderness, that overwhelmed him, the irrational, warm sense of self-satisfaction she gave him, fruit of his loins, evidence of his vitality and parental wisdom. He took her hand and pressed it, wondering how, just a few minutes before, he could have been dismayed at the thought of her arrival.

Hand in hand, they followed the porter out of the terminal. He helped the porter throw her luggage into the back of the car. The khaki canvas bag was heavy, stuffed with books. One book fell out as he lifted the bag. He picked it up. *Education Sentimentale,* in French. He couldn't help smiling as he pushed the book back into the bag. Careful traveler, his daughter, preparing for a previous century.

They started back toward Cannes, driving slowly in the heavy traffic. Occasionally, Anne leaned over and patted his cheek as he drove, as if to assure herself by the fleeting touch of fingers that she was really there, side by side with her father.

"The blue Mediterranean," she said, looking across him at the sea. "I tell you, it's the wildest invitation I ever got in my whole life." She chuckled at some private thought. "Your wife says you are buying my affection," she said.

"What do you think?" he asked.

"If that's what you're doing," she said, "keep buying."

"How was your visit?" he asked carefully.

"Average gruesome," Anne said.

"What's she doing in Geneva?"

"Consulting private bankers. Her friend is with her, helping her to consult." A sudden hardness came into Anne's voice. "She's become a demon investor now that you're giving her all that money. The American economy doesn't look strong enough for her, she says, she intends to go into German and Japanese companies. She told me to tell you you ought to do the same. It's ridiculous, she says, for you to get only five per cent on your money. You never had a head for business, she says, and she's thinking of your best interests." She made a little grimace. "In your best interests, she says, you also ought to give up your lady friend in Paris."

"She told you about that?" He tried to keep the anger out of his voice.

"She told me about a lot of things," Anne said.

"What does she know about the lady in Paris, anyway?"

"I don't know what she knows," Anne said. "I only know what she told me. She says that the lady is ridiculously young for you and looks like a manicurist and is out for your money."

Craig laughed. "Manicurist. Obviously, she's never seen the lady."

"Oh, yes she has. She's even had a scene with her."

"Where?"

"Paris."

"She was in Paris?" he asked incredulously.

"You bet she was. In your best interests. She told the lady what she thought of adventuring ladies who took advantage of foolish old men and broke up happy homes."

Craig shook his head wonderingly. "Constance never said a word about it."

"I guess it's not the sort of thing a lady likes to talk about," Anne said. "Am I going to meet Constance?"

"Of course," Craig said uncomfortably. This was not the conversation he had imagined he was going to have with his daughter when he took her in his arms at the airport.

"I tell you," Anne said, "Geneva was just pure fun all the way. I got to have dinner at the Richemonde with Mummy and her friend, along with all the other goodies."

Craig drove silently. He didn't want to discuss his wife's lover with his daughter.

"Little pompous show off," Anne said. "Ugh. Sitting there ordering caviar and yelling at the waiter about the wine and being gallant for five minutes with Mummy and five minutes with me. I suddenly knew why I've hated Mummy ever since I was twelve."

"You don't hate her," Craig said gently. Whatever he was responsible for, he didn't want to be responsible for alienating his daughters from their mother.

"Oh, yes I do," Anne said. "I do, I do. Why did you tolerate that miserable, boring man around the house pretending to be your friend all those years, why did you let them get away with it for so long?"

"Betrayal begins at home," Craig said. "I was no angel, either. You're a big girl now, Anne, and I imagine you've realized quite a while ago that your mother and I have been going our separate ways for years—"

"Separate ways!" Anne said impatiently. "Okay, separate ways. I can understand that. But I can't understand how you ever married that bitch—"

"Anne!" he said sharply. "You can't talk like that—"

"And what I can't understand most of all is how you can let her threaten to sue you for adultery and take all your money like that. And the house! Why don't you put a detective on her for two days and then see how she behaves?"

"I can't do that."

"Why not? She put a detective on you."

Craig shrugged. "Don't argue like a lawyer," he said. "I just can't."

"You're too old-fashioned," Anne said. "That's your trouble."

"Let's not talk about it, please," he said. "Just remember that if I hadn't married your mother, I wouldn't have you and your sister, and maybe I think because I do have you two, everything else is worth it, and no matter what your mother does or says I am still grateful to her for that. Will you remember?"

"I'll try." Anne's voice was trembling, and he was afraid she was going to cry. She had never been an easy crier, even as a child. "One thing, though," she said bitterly, "I don't want to see the woman again. Not in Switzerland, not in New York, not in California. No place. Never."

"You'll change your mind," he said gently.

"Wanna bet?"

Oh, Christ, he thought. Families. "There's one fact

I have to make absolutely clear to you and Marcia," he said. "Constance had nothing to do with my leaving your mother. I left because I was bored to the point of suicide. Because the marriage was meaningless and I didn't want to lead a meaningless life anymore. I'm not blaming your mother any more than I'm blaming myself. But whoever's fault it was, there was no point in trying to continue. Constance was just a coincidence."

"Okay," Anne said. "I'll buy that."

Anne didn't speak for several moments, and he drove past the Cannes racecourse, grateful for the silence. The horses of the south. Simple victories, unqualified defeats. The sprinklers were on, myriad arched fountains over the green infield.

"Now," Anne said finally, her voice brisk, "how about you? Are you having fun?"

"I suppose you can call it that," he said.

"I've been worried about you," Anne said.

"Worried about me?" He couldn't help sounding surprised. "I thought it was modern doctrine that nowadays no child ever worried about any parent."

"I'm not as modern as all that," Anne said.

"Why're you worried about me?"

"Your letters."

"What did I say in my letters?"

"Nothing I can pin down," she said. "Nothing overt. But underneath—I don't know—I had the feeling you were dissatisfied with yourself, that you weren't sure about yourself or what you were doing. Even your handwriting . . ." she said.

"Handwriting?"

"It just looked different," Anne said. "Not as firm, somehow. As though you'd lost confidence in how to make an 'e' or a capital 'G.' "

"Maybe I ought to begin typing my letters," Craig said, trying to make a joke out of it.

"It's not as easy as that," she said earnestly. "There's a professor in the psychology department who's a handwriting expert, and I showed him two of your letters. One that I got from you four years ago and . . ."

"You keep old letters of mine?" Extraordinary child. He had never kept any of his parents' letters.

"Of course, I do. Well, anyway, this professor was saying one day that very often, long before anything shows or there are any symptoms or anything like that or before a person feels anything at all, his handwriting sort of—well—*predicts* changes . . . disease, death even."

He was shaken by what she had said but tried not to show it. Anne had always been a blunt, candid child, blurting out everything that crossed her mind. He had been proud and a little amused by her unsparing honesty, finding it evidence of an admirable strength of character. He was not so amused now, now that it was he who was not being spared. He tried to pass it off lightly. "And what did that smart man have to say about your father's letters?" he asked ironically.

"You can laugh," she said. "He said you'd changed. And would change more."

"For the better, I hope," Craig said.

"No," she said. "Not for the better."

"God Almighty," Craig said. "You send your children to a big fancy college for a scientific education and they come out with their heads stuffed with all kinds of medieval superstitions. Does your psychology professor read palms, too?"

"Superstitions or not," Anne said, "I promised myself I was going to tell you, and I told you. And when I saw you today, I was shocked."

"By what?"

"You don't look well. Not at all well."

"Oh, don't be silly, Anne," Craig said, although he was sure she was right. "I've had a couple of rough nights, that's all."

"It's more than that," she persisted. "It's not just a rough night or two. It's something fundamental. I don't know whether you've realized it or not, but I've been studying you ever since I was a little girl. No matter how you tried to disguise things, I always knew when you were angry or worried or sick or scared ..."

"And what about now?" He challenged her.

"Now—" She ran her hand nervously through her hair. "You have a funny look. You look—uncared for —I guess that's the best description. You look like a man who spends his life moving from one hotel room to another."

"I *have* been living in hotel rooms. Some of the best hotels in the world."

"You know what I mean," she said.

He did know what she meant, but he did not admit it. Except to himself.

"I made up my mind when I got your cable that I was going to deliver a speech," Anne said, "and now I'm going to deliver it."

"Look at the scenery, Anne," he said. "You can make speeches any time."

She ignored what he had said. "What I want to do," she said, "is live with you. Take care of you. In Paris, if that's where you want to be. Or New York, or wherever. I don't want you to turn into a solitary old man eating dinner alone night after night. Like . . . like an old bull who's been turned out from the herd."

He laughed despite himself at her comparison. "I don't want to sound boastful," he said, "but I don't lack for company, Anne. Anyway, you have another year to go in college and . . ."

"I'm through with education," she said. "And education is through with me. At least *that* sort of education. I'm not going back, no matter what."

"We'll discuss that some other time," he said. Actually, after the years of wandering, the thought of living in an ordered household with Anne suddenly seemed attractive. And he recognized that he still suffered from the old, unworthy, and by now unmentionable belief that education was not terribly important for women.

"Another thing," Anne said. "You ought to go back to work. It's ridiculous, a man like you not doing anything for five years."

"It's not as easy as all that," he said. "Nobody's clamoring to give me a job."

"You!" she cried incredulously. "I don't believe it."

"Believe it," he said. "Murphy is down here. Talk to him about the movie business."

"People're still making pictures."

"People," he said. "Not your father."

"I can't bear it," she said. "You talking like a failure. If you'd only make up your mind to *try* instead of being so damn proud and remote. I've talked it over with Marcia, and she agrees with me—it's sheer, dumb, shameful waste." She sounded close to hysteria, and he put his hand out and patted her soothingly.

"Actually," he said, "the same idea has occurred to me. I've been working for the last twelve months."

"There," she said triumphantly. "You see! With whom?"

"With nobody," he said. "With myself. I've written a script. I've just finished it. Somebody's reading it right now."

"What does Mr. Murphy say?"

"It stinks, Mr. Murphy says. Throw it away."

"Stupid old man," Anne said. "I wouldn't listen to a word he says."

"He's far from stupid."

"You're not listening to him, though, are you?"

"I haven't thrown it away yet."

"Can I read it?"

"If you want."

"Of course, I want. Can I tell you exactly what I think of it?"

"Naturally."

"Even if Mr. Murphy is right," Anne said, "and it turns out that what you've done isn't good enough or commercial enough or whatever it is they want these days, you could do something else. I mean, the movies aren't the only thing in the world, are they? In fact, if you want to know the truth, I think you'd be a lot happier if you forgot them altogether. You have to deal with such awful people. And it's all so cruel and capricious—one minute you're a kind of Culture Hero and the next minute everybody's forgotten you. And the people you have to pander to, the Great American Audience—good God, Daddy, go into a movie house, any movie house, on a Saturday night and see what they're laughing at, what they're crying over . . . I remember how hard you used to work, how you'd be half dead by the time you finished a picture . . . And for whom? For a hundred million goons!"

He recognized the echo of some of his own thoughts in Anne's tirade, but he wasn't pleased by what she had said. Especially by the word she had used—pander. It was one thing for a man his age who had worked and won and lost in that harsh arena to have his doubts in moments of depression about the value of his efforts. It was another to hear such a sweeping condemnation from the lips of an untried and pampered child. "Anne," he said, "don't be so hard on your fellow Americans."

"Anybody who wants my fellow Americans," she said bitterly, "can have them."

Another item on the agenda, he thought. Find out what happened to my daughter in her native land in the last six months. At our next meeting.

He changed the subject. "Since you've been doing so much thinking about my career," he said with mild irony, "perhaps you have a suggestion about what I should do."

"A million things," she said. "You could teach, you could get a job as an editor for a publisher. After all, that's what you've been doing practically all your life, editing other people's scripts. You could even become a publisher yourself. Or you could move to a peaceful small town and run a little theatre somewhere. Or you could write your memoirs."

"Anne," he said half-reprovingly, "I know I'm old, but I'm not *that* old."

"A million things," she repeated stubbornly. "You're the smartest man I've ever known, it'd be a crime if you just let yourself be thrown into the discard just because the people in the movie business or in the theatre are so stupid. You're not *married* to the movie business. Moses never came down from Sinai saying, 'Thou Shalt Entertain,' for Christ's sake."

He laughed. "Anne, darling," he said, "you're making a mixed salad out of two great religions."

"I know what I'm talking about."

"Maybe you do," he admitted. "Maybe there's some truth in what you say. But maybe you're wrong, too. One of the reasons I came to Cannes this year at all was to make up my mind about it, to see if it was worth it."

"Well," she said defiantly, "what have you seen, what have you learned?"

What had he seen, what had he learned? He had seen all kinds of movies, good and bad, mostly bad. He had been plunged into a carnival, a delirium of film. In the halls, on the terraces, on the beach, at the parties, the art or industry or whatever it deserved to be called in these few days was exposed in its essence. The whole thing was there—the artists and pseudo-artists, the businessmen, the con men, the buyers and sellers, the peddlers, the whores, the pornographers, critics, hangers-on, the year's heroes, the year's failures. And then the distillation of what it was all about, a film of Bergman's and one of Buñuel's, pure and devastating.

"Well," Anne repeated, "what have you learned?"

"I'm afraid I learned that I'm hooked," he said. "When I was a little boy, my father used to take me to the theatre, the Broadway theatre. I used to sit in my seat, not budging, waiting for the theatre to go dark and the footlights go on, afraid that something would happen and the darkness would never come and the stage lights never come on. And then it would happen. I would clench my fists with happiness and worry for the people I was going to see on the stage when the curtain went up. The only time I ever remember being rude to my father was at a moment like that. He said something to me, I don't know what, and it was destroying that great moment for me, and I said, 'Pop, please keep quiet.' I think he understood because he never said a word again once they began to dim the house lights. Well, I don't have that feeling anymore in the Broadway theatre. But I have it each time I buy a ticket and walk into a darkened movie house. That's not a bad thing, you know —for a forty-eight-year-old man to have one repetitive thing in his life that makes him feel like a boy again. Maybe it's because of that that I make up all sorts of excuses for movies, that I rationalize away the hateful aspects, the cheapness, the thousand times I've walked out disgusted, and try to convince myself that one good picture makes up for a hundred bad ones. That the game is worth the candle."

He didn't say it, but he knew now, had really always known, that the good ones weren't made for the people in the audience on Saturday night. They were made for the necessity of making them, for the need of the people who made them, just like any other work of art. He knew that the agony and what Anne called the cruelty and capriciousness involved in the process, the maneuvering, the wooing, the money, the criticizing and wounding, the injustice, the exhaustion of nerve, was part of the pleasure, the profound pleasure of that particular act of creation. And even if you only played a small part in it, a subordinate, modest part, you shared in that pleasure. He knew now that he had punished himself for five years in denying himself that pleasure.

They were approaching Antibes now, and he turned down toward the road along the sea. "Hooked," he said, "that's the diagnosis. And that's enough about me. Let me say that I'm pleased to see there's another adult in the family." He looked across at her and saw that she was flushing at the compliment. "Now," he said, "what about you? Aside from being sufficiently educated and taking care of me. What are your plans?"

She shrugged. "I'm trying to figure out how to survive as an adult. Your word," she said. "Aside from that, the only thing I'm sure of is that I'm not going to get married."

"Well," he said, "that seems like a promising start for a career."

"Don't make fun of me," she said sharply. "You always tease me."

"People only tease the ones they love," he said, "but if you don't like it, I'll try to stop it."

"I don't like it," she said. "I'm not secure enough to take it."

There was a rebuke there, he realized. If a girl of twenty was not secure, who but her father was to blame? He had learned a great deal about his daughter between Nice and Antibes, and he wasn't certain that it was reassuring.

They were going along the outside road of the peninsula and approaching the house he had rented for the summer of 1949, the house in which Anne had been conceived. She had never been here before, but he wondered if some prenatal memory would make her look up and notice the tall white building in the garden above the road.

She did not look up.

I hope, he thought as they passed the house, that at least once she has three months like the three months her mother and I had that summer.

• ELEVEN •

GAIL MCKINNON was just coming out of the hotel as they drove up, and there was no avoiding introducing her. "Welcome to Cannes," she said to Anne. She stepped back a pace and examined Anne coolly. Insolently, Craig thought. "The family is getting handsomer as it goes along," she said.

To stop any further discussion of the progression toward perfection of the Craig family, he said, "What's new with Reynolds? Is he all right?"

"I imagine he's alive," Gail said carelessly.

"Didn't you go to see him?"

She shrugged. "What for? If he needed help, somebody would call. See you around," she said to Anne. "Don't walk alone at night. See if you can't convince your father to take us to dinner sometime." She hardly looked at Craig and went striding off, her bag swinging from her shoulder.

"What a peculiar, beautiful girl," Anne said as they went into the hotel. "Do you know her well?"

"I just met her a few days ago," Craig said. The truth, as far as it went.

"Is she an actress?"

"Some kind of newspaperwoman. Give me your passport. You have to leave it at the desk."

He registered Anne and went over to the concierge's desk for his key. There was a telegram for him. It was from Constance. "ARRIVING MARSEILLES TO-MORROW MORNING STAYING HOTEL SPLENDIDE STOP DEPENDING UPON YOU

MAKE GLORIOUS ARRANGEMENTS STOP
LOVE C."

"Is it important?" Anne asked.

"No." He stuffed the telegram in his pocket and followed the clerk who was going to show Anne her
room. The manager had not been able to free the
room connecting with Craig's apartment, and Anne
would be on the floor above him. Just as well, he
thought, as they got into the elevator.

The short man with the paunch he had seen once
before in the elevator with the pretty young girl
went in with them. The man with the paunch
was wearing a bright green shirt today. "It'll never
go in Spain," he was saying as the elevator started. He
looked appraisingly at Anne, then across at Craig.
Was there a kind of conspiratorial smile at the corner of his lips? In a simpler world Craig would have
punched him in the nose. Instead, he said to the
clerk, "I'll stop at my floor first. You take my daughter
to her room, please. Anne, come down as soon as
you're settled."

The man in the green shirt dropped his eyes. He
had been holding the pretty girl's elbow. Now he
took his hand away. Craig smiled meanly as the elevator came to a halt and he went out.

In the living room he looked at the schedule of
movies that were being shown that day. At three
o'clock there was an Italian film he wanted to see. He
picked up the phone and asked for Anne's room.
"Anne," he said when she answered, "there's an interesting movie this afternoon. Would you like to see
it with me?"

"Oh, Daddy," she said, "I'm just putting on a
bathing suit. The water looks so marvelous . . ."

"That's all right," he said. "Have a good swim. I'll
be back a little after five."

When he had put the phone down, he reread Constance's telegram. He shook his head. He couldn't refuse to meet her in Marseilles. And he couldn't take

Anne with him. There were limits to the frontiers of the permissive society. But leaving his daughter alone in Cannes immediately after she had flown five thousand miles to be with him could hardly add to her sense of security. He would have to work something out with Constance so that at most he would be gone only a day or two. Glorious *arrangements*.

Dissatisfied with himself, he went over to the mantelpiece and stared at his reflection in the mirror hanging there. Anne had said that he didn't look well. It was true there were unaccustomed deep lines under his eyes, and his forehead seemed fixed in a permanent frown. His complexion now seemed pale, almost pasty, to him, and there was a slight film of sweat above his mouth. It's a hot day, he thought, summer is coming on, that's all.

The psychologist in California had said that there were secret predictions buried in the way your hand shaped a word on paper. Change, Anne had said, disease, death even ...

His throat felt dry, he remembered that he sometimes felt slightly dizzy these days when he got up from a chair, that he had little appetite for his food ... "Fuck it," he said aloud. He had never talked to himself before. What sort of sign was that?

He turned away from the mirror. *He has a certain dry elegance,* Gail had written about him. She had not consulted Anne's professor.

He went into the bedroom, stared down at the bed, now neatly made, which he had shared, if you could call it that, with the girl the night before. Would she share it again tonight? Would he be fool enough to open the door for her once more? He remembered the silken feel of her skin, the fragrance of her hair, the clean swell of her hip as she lay beside him. He would open the door if she knocked. "Idiot," he said aloud. It might be a symptom of some obscure aberration, a warning of eventual senescence, but the sound of his own voice in the empty room somehow relieved him. "Goddamn idiot," he said, looking down at the bed.

He bathed his face with cold water, changed his shirt, which was damp with sweat, and went to see the Italian movie.

The movie was disappointing, plodding, and serious and dull. It was about a group of immigrant anarchists in London, led by a Sicilian revolutionary, in the beginning of the century. It was probably as authentic as the writer and director had been able to make it, and it was plain that the people who were responsible for the film had a laudable hatred for poverty and injustice, but Craig found the violence, the shooting, the deaths, melodramatic and distasteful. So many of the other films he had seen since he arrived in Cannes had dealt with revolution of one kind or another, millions of dollars handed over by the most Republican of bankers to be invested in the praise of violence and the overthrow of society. What motivated those neat, prosperous men in the white shirts and narrow suits behind the wide, bare desks? If there was a dollar to be made in a riot, in the bombing of a courthouse, in the burning of a ghetto, did they feel that they, honorable accruers, owed it to their stockholders to offer the fortunes from their vaults, regardless of the consequences? Or were they more cynical than that? Wiser than lesser men, with their hands on the levers of power, did they know that no movie had ever brought about public upheaval, that no matter what was said in a theatre, no matter how long the lines were in front of the ticket offices for the most incendiary of films, nothing would change, no shot would be fired? Did they laugh in their clubs at the grown-up children who played their shadowy celluloid games and whom they indulged with the final toy—money? He himself had never gone raging out into the streets after any film. Was he any different from the others?

Was it a sign of age that he was unconvinced, that

he believed these reckless calls to action could only lead to worse abuses than the ones they sought to correct?

If he were twenty, like Anne, or twenty-two, like Gail, would he be encouraged to revolt, would he not glory in plotting the destruction of cities?

He remembered Murray Sloan's tumbrels, Versailles the night before the fall of the Bastille. Whose side would he be on the day the tumbrels rolled down his street? Where would Anne be riding? Constance? Gail McKinnon? His wife?

The Italian film was a bad one for a man to see just after he had told his daughter he was hooked on making films. It was stillborn from the beginning, worthless or evil as art, finally boring. It didn't even have the true tragic advantage of reducing his own predicament to scale, of making his own small, private concerns, his entanglements with women, his professional drifting, seem picayune or comfortingly inconsequential.

He left before the end, and as he went out of the theatre to restore himself, he tried to remember, frame by frame, the films of Buñuel and Bergman he had seen that week.

The sun was still high over the horizon, and on the chance that Anne hadn't gone in yet, he went down the steps to the Carlton beach to look for her. She was at a table near the bar in the briefest of bikinis, broad-shouldered and opulently shaped. A father, he would have preferred a less revealing costume. Seated next to her was Ian Wadleigh in swimming trunks. Across the table from the two of them was Gail McKinnon, wearing the scant, pink, two-piece bathing suit she had worn at the Murphys' cabana. Craig felt guilty for allowing Anne to go off on her own, not providing her with other company.

Wadleigh had obviously not been wasting his time seeing too many films. He was as brown as the two girls. In his ill-fitting clothes he had seemed un-gracefully shaped, almost tumescent, but stripped for the beach as he was now, his flesh was solid, and he looked powerful and dominating. He was laughing and gesturing with a glass he held in his hand. None of the three noticed Craig for the moment, and he half-resolved to turn and walk away. There was some-thing too reminiscent in the group for him, it was too much like the Italian actor on the beach showing his teeth in a smile, the two girls listening to him.

But he fought down the impulse as bad-tempered and childish and went up to the table. Gail was fid-dling with her tape recorder, and for a second Craig was seized by the uneasy thought that she had been in-terviewing Anne. He had neglected to warn Anne to keep her mouth shut. But as he came up to the table, he heard Gail saying, "Thanks, Ian. I'm sure they'll like it back in the States. I'm not so sure that you'll ever be allowed back in Cannes again, though."

"Down with double talk," Ian said. "Screw *polites-se*. Name the whores and their works, that's my motto."

Oh, Christ, Craig thought, he's still on that kick. "Good evening, folks," he said.

"Hi, Jess," Ian boomed out, his voice as imperial as his bronze body. With an audience of two pretty girls, he was transformed. "I was just instructing these charming young women on the inner workings of film festivals," Wadleigh said. "Who sells what, who buys whom, in what sweat and slime Golden Palms are traded across secret counters. Sit down, Father. What'll you have? Waiter. *Garçon!*"

"Nothing, thank you," Craig said. Wadleigh's "Fa-ther" had a derisive ring to it. He sat down next to Gail, facing Anne. "What are you drinking?" he asked Anne.

"Gin and tonic," she said.

He had never seen her drink before. When he had offered her wine at meals, she had refused, saying she didn't like the taste. Gin, perhaps, was more suitable to youthful palates.

"It's awfully good of you, Father," Wadleigh said, "to import admirers, at great personal expense, across continents and oceans."

"What're you talking about?" Craig asked.

"I read his novels," Anne said. "They were assigned in a Modern Lit course."

"Hear that," Wadleigh said, "I am a fixture in Modern Literature. Nubile scholars from coast to coast burn the midnight oil in honor of Ian Wadleigh. Imagine, on the bleak and desperate shingle of Cannes, I have found a reader."

"I've read a couple of them, too," Gail said.

"Praise them, dear, praise them," Wadleigh said.

"They're okay," Gail said.

"My poor girl," Wadleigh said jovially, "I'm afraid you've flunked the course."

Wadleigh was being obnoxious, but Craig couldn't help being offended by Gail's offhand dismissal of a man's life's work. "I think perhaps you ought to re-read his books, Gail," Craig said. "When you grow up." For once he could take advantage of the difference in their ages. "Perhaps you'll make a more enthusiastic judgment."

"Thanks," Wadleigh said. "A man needs all the protection he can get from the young."

Gail smiled. "I didn't know you were such close friends, you two," she said. "Now, Jesse, there're a couple or so more questions I have to put to the maestro, and then you can have him all to yourself . . ."

"I'm sorry," Craig said, standing. "I didn't mean to interrupt. I just came down looking for Anne. You ought to go in now," he said to Anne. "It's beginning to get cold."

"I'd like to listen to the end," Anne said. "I'm not cold."

"You stay, too, Jess," Wadleigh said. "I'm at my

most eloquent before my peers."

Unwilling, for no sensible reason, to leave Anne there with Gail McKinnon, Craig said, "Thanks for the invitation," and sat down again. "As long as I'm here," he said, "I'll take a whisky."

"Two more," Wadleigh said, holding up his glass to a passing waiter. Then to Gail McKinnon, "Shoot."

Gail turned her machine on. "Mr. Wadleigh," she said, "earlier in this interview you said that the position of the writer for films is being steadily eroded. Would you care to enlarge on that?"

Craig was conscious of Anne's close, admiring attention to Gail as she worked. He had to admit that her manner was professional, her voice pleasant and unaffected.

"Well," Wadleigh was saying, "in one way, the writer for films is more powerful than ever. I'm speaking of the writer who directs his own stuff and because of that controls the final result, the man who gets the critical attention and reaps the financial rewards. On the other side of the coin, however, the writer who is only a writer is lost in the shuffle." He was speaking seriously now, not trying to amuse or play the great man before the two girls. "For example—at this Festival—there are rewards for actors, directors, composers, cameramen, etc., but not one for writers. This is a recent development, and it's been brought about largely by the critical acceptance of the *auteurist* theory of film making."

Now Craig was sure Wadleigh had written all this before, probably for an article that had been turned down by a dozen magazines.

Gail flicked off the machine. "Remember, Ian," she said, "this is for American listeners. You'd better explain, don't you think?"

"Yeah, you're right," Wadleigh said. He took a gulp of the fresh whisky the waiter had put down in front of him.

"I'll ask you the question," Gail said. She started

the machine again. "Would you like to describe that theory for us, Mr. Wadleigh?"

"The *auteurist* theory of film making," he said, "is very simple. It rests on the conviction that a film is the work of one man—the director. That in the final analysis the man behind the camera is the real author of the work, that the film, in essence, is written with the camera."

"Do you agree with that theory?"

It's like a charade, Craig thought, little girl wearing Mummy's dress, or in this case, Mummy's bikini, and going down to Daddy's office and sitting at his desk and talking into the intercom.

"No," Wadleigh said. "Of course, there are directors who are in fact the authors of their films, but all that means is that as well as being directors, they are also writers. If they deserve a prize for their work, they deserve two prizes—one for the script and one for the direction. But the truth is that in America, at any rate, there are only five or six men who are really both. Of course, directors being the self-deluding beasts they are, there are plenty of them who *think* they are writers and impose their written efforts on the audience."

The same old whine, Craig thought.

"We are fortunate enough," Gail said calmly into the microphone, "to have Mr. Jesse Craig, the eminent film producer with us here on the beach in Cannes. I wonder if I could ask you, Mr. Craig, if you agree with Mr. Wadleigh. Or if you disagree, why?"

Craig's hand tightened on his glass. "Cut out the jokes, Gail," he said.

"Oh, Daddy," Anne said, "go ahead. You were talking to me for half an hour about the movies in the car. Don't be sticky."

"Shut the damn machine off, Gail," Craig said.

Gail didn't move. "There's no harm done. I splice together what I want later and throw out the junk. Maybe," she said, smiling agreeably, "if I can't have you, I'll put Anne on the air. The confidences of the daughter of the abdicated king, the Life and Loves of the one after the last Tycoon, as seen through the clear young eyes of his nearest and dearest."

"Any time you say," Anne said.

"I'm sure your listeners in Peoria," Craig said, making an effort to keep his temper and sound offhand at the same time, "are waiting with bated breath for just that program." I'm going to wipe that dancing smile off your face, lady, he thought. For the first time in his life he understood those writers who regarded the penis as an instrument of revenge.

"We'll just keep it in mind, Anne," Gail said. "Won't we? And now Mr. Wadleigh—" She resumed her professional voice. "In a conversation with Mr. Craig some days ago on the same subject, when I asked him why he had not directed any of the films he had produced, he replied that he didn't think he was good enough, that there were perhaps fifty men in Hollywood who were better at the job than he thought he could be. Similarly," she went on, staring coolly at Craig as she spoke so that it was evident to him, if not to the others, that she was maliciously playing with him, using their presence to ensure that he suffered in silence, "similarly, is it an equally admirable modesty on your part that prevents you from working behind the camera?"

"Shit," Craig said. "Shit, shit. Send *that* out to the homes of America."

"Daddy!" Anne said, shocked. "What's the matter with you?"

"Nothing. I don't like to be trapped, that's all. When I want to give an interview, I'll give it. Not before." He remembered the title Gail had said she was going to use on the piece about him, "The Once and Future Has Been," but he couldn't tell that to Anne. He also couldn't tell Anne that he had slept with that cool, smiling girl in the pink bathing suit the night before and that if he could, he would sleep with her in the night to come.

"If you recall my question, Mr. Wadleigh," Gail said, "has it been due to modesty, as in the case of Mr. Craig, that you have not directed any of the scripts you have written for films?"

"Hell, no," Wadleigh said. "If I couldn't do better than ninety-nine per cent of those bums out there, I'd shoot myself. It's just that the bastards in the front offices won't hire me."

"I think that brings us to the end of this program," Gail said into the microphone. "Thank you very much, Mr. Wadleigh, for your frank and enlightening discussion of the problems of the writer for the motion pictures. I am sorry that Mr. Craig was unexpectedly called away so that we were denied the benefits of his long experience in the field. Perhaps we shall be lucky enough in the near future to have Mr. Craig, who is an extremely busy man, with us at greater length. This is Gail McKinnon, broadcasting from the Cannes Film Festival."

She flipped off the machine, smiled brightly and innocently. "Another day, another dollar." She started to pack away the machine. "Isn't Daddy the *funny* one?" she said to Anne.

"I don't understand you, Daddy," Anne said. "I thought you and she were friends."

There's a description, Craig thought.

"I don't see what harm it would do to say a few words," Anne persisted.

"What you don't say can't hurt you," Craig said. "You'll find that out eventually, too. Ian, what the hell good do you think you did yourself just now? Can you figure out why you did it?"

"Sure," Ian said. "Vanity. A trait not to be taken lightly. Of course, I know you're above such human failings."

"I'm not above anything," Craig said. He wasn't

arguing for himself but for Anne, for Anne's education. He didn't want her to be taken in by the American craze for publicity, for self-congratulation, for flattery, for the random, glib chatter on television whose real, dead serious purpose was to sell automobiles, deodorants, detergents, politicians, remedies for indigestion and insomnia. "Ian," he said, "I know why Gail goes through all this nonsense—"

"Careful, careful," Gail said mockingly.

"She makes her living out of it, and maybe it's no more discreditable than the way you and I make our living . . ."

"Blessings on you, Daddy," Gail said.

I'm going to lock the door tonight, Craig thought, and stuff cotton in my ears. With a wrench he made himself look away from the lovely, teasing face and talk to Wadleigh. "What possible good did babbling away here this afternoon do you? I'm serious. I want to know. Maybe you can convince me."

"Well," Ian said, "first of all, before you came, good old Gail plugged my books. Gallant little liar, she had a good word to say for all of them. Maybe her program'll get one person to go into a bookstore to buy one of them or two or all of them. Or since they're out of print, maybe it'll get a publisher to bring out my collected works in paperback. Don't be holy, Jess. When you make a picture, you want people to see it, don't you?"

"Yes," Craig admitted.

"Well, how does that make you different from me?"

"Do you want me to use the machine, Jesse?" Gail said. "It'll only take a minute. We can start the interview right now."

"I'm not selling any pictures at the moment," Craig said. "Leave the machine alone."

"Or some producer or director might happen to tune in on the program," Wadleigh continued, "and say, 'Hey, I thought that guy was dead. If he isn't dead, he might be just the guy to write my next picture.' We all depend on luck, you, I, Gail, even this beautiful young girl who has turned out to be your daughter. A switch of the dial on the radio might mean the difference in life or death for somebody like me."

"Do you really believe that?" Craig asked.

"What do you think I believe in?" Wadleigh said bitterly. "Merit? Don't make me laugh."

"I'm remembering all this," Gail said. "I'm sure it's going to be useful for something. For the piece I'm doing about you, Jesse, for example. The public figure who refuses the public role. Is it for real, I'll ask my readers, or is it a clever play to titillate, to invite while seeming to reject? Is the veil more revealing than the face behind it?"

"Mr. Wadleigh is right," Anne broke in. "He's written these wonderful books, and he's being neglected. And I listened to the whole interview. He said a lot of things that people ought to hear."

"I've told Anne," Gail said, "that you're being difficult about cooperating."

"You two girls seem to have managed to cover a lot of ground in two hours," Craig said sourly.

"There was an instant bond of sympathy," Gail said. "We bridged the generation gap between twenty and twenty-two in a flash."

"People your age, Daddy," Anne said, "are constantly complaining the young don't understand you. Well, here you have a perfect chance to get whatever it is you want to say to *hordes* of people of all ages, and you turn the chance down."

"My medium is film," Craig said, "not indecent public exposure."

"Sometimes, Mr. Craig," Gail said with a straight face, "I get the feeling that you don't approve of me."

Craig stood up. "I'm going in," he said. He pulled

some bills out of his pocket. "How many drinks did you have, Anne?"

"Forget it." Wadleigh waved grandly. "I have it."

"Thanks," Craig said. On my three hundred dollars for Spain, he thought. "Coming, Anne?"

"I'm going to have one last swim."

"Me, too," Gail said. "It's been hot work this afternoon."

"I'll join you girls," Wadleigh said. "You can save me from drowning. Oh, by the way, Jesse," he said as he finished his whisky and stood up, "I suggested we all have dinner tonight. Shall we say eight o'clock at the bar?"

Craig saw Anne looking appealingly at him. Anything, he thought, rather than have dinner alone with Dad. "Don't you have to see the picture tonight for your article?" he asked Wadleigh.

"I read the synopsis," Wadleigh said. "It's something about raising hawks in Hungary. I think I can skip it. My fairies in London aren't mad about Hungarian hawks. If it's any good, I can quote from *Le Monde*. See you at eight?"

"I'll see what my schedule is," Craig said.

"We'll be there," Anne said. "Come on, let's hit the water."

He watched the two girls, one tall, one short, both swift and young, silhouetted against the evening light, run down the beach and dive into the water. He was surprised that Wadleigh could run so fast as he followed and plunged into the sea in a huge splash of foam.

He climbed up from the beach slowly. As he stepped off the curb of the Croisette, a car nearly ran him down. There was a squeal of brakes, and a policeman shouted at him. He smiled politely at the policeman, apologizing for almost having been killed.

In the lobby, when he picked up his key, he asked for messages. There were none. Klein hadn't called. Of course, he told himself, it's too early. In the old days when Jesse Craig sent anybody a script, there was a call within three hours.

Going toward the elevator, he met Reynolds. Reynolds had a big fresh bandage on his forehead, a huge lump, yellow and green, over one eye, and his cheek had jagged scabs on it as though he had been dragged through broken glass.

"I'm looking for Gail," Reynolds said without saying hello. "Have you seen her?"

"She's swimming in the direction of Tunis," Craig said. "How do you feel?"

"About the way I look," Reynolds said.

"You can't be too careful in the movie business," Craig said, and went into the elevator.

• TWELVE •

In every group, however small, there is one person who is its center of gravity, its reason for existence as an entity and not merely a collection of unconnected egos. For this night, Craig thought, it was Gail McKinnon. Anne was clearly fascinated by her, reacting openly to every word she spoke, addressing herself more often to Gail than to any of the others, and even when talking to Craig or Wadleigh, looking for approval or criticism in Gail's direction. On the way over from the hotel to the restaurant Craig had been half-amused, half-irritated when he noticed that Anne was subtly imitating, consciously or unconsciously, Gail's striding, brusque manner of walking. Still, it was an improvement on Anne's habitual, over-modest, childish slouch.

For Wadleigh, Gail represented an audience. In recent years he had had no surfeit of audiences, and he was making the most of it.

As for Craig, he would not have been there tonight had it not been for Gail. It was as simple as that. Watching her across the table, he knew that the movies were not the only thing he was hooked on. I am here, he thought, to unhook.

He let the others talk most of the time. When Gail spoke, he listened secretly for a hint, a signal from her, a guarded promise for the night, a tacit refusal. He found neither.

I will forget her tomorrow, he told himself, in Constance's arms.

Wadleigh insisted on acting the host, ordering the wine and suggesting what dishes the girls should choose. They were in the restaurant on the old port in which Craig had seen Picasso at dinner. If Wadleigh was going to pay the bill tonight, Craig thought, he'd be lucky to get as far as Toulon, let alone Madrid.

Wadleigh was drinking too much but up to now wasn't showing it. For once he was dressed well, in a gray suit and oxford shirt with a collar that was buttoned neatly below the heavy throat and a new striped tie.

Gail was wearing rose-colored, tight-fitting shantung slacks and a soft silk blouse. She had swept her hair up for the evening, and it made her head seem charmingly and incongruously mature over the slender youthful column of her neck.

Anne, poor girl, was wearing a disastrous billowing yellow organdy dress, too short for her long legs, making her look gawky, like a high school junior dressed for her first prom.

The restaurant was not yet full, but Craig could see by the little signs on the vacant tables that the room would be crowded before long. He hoped, for Anne's sake, that one of the tables was being kept for Picasso.

Two young men, one with a lion cub, the other with a Polaroid camera, whom Craig recognized as one of the teams that worked the Croisette and the cafés, came into the restaurant. As they approached the table, Craig tried to wave them away. "At these prices," he said, "we ought to be protected from lions."

But Wadleigh took the cub from the man who was holding him and put him on the table between Gail and Anne. "I want a picture of them with the king of the beasts," he said. "I've always had a weakness for lady lion-tamers. One of my fantasies is making love to a woman in tights and spangles, with a chair, inside a cage."

Depend on Wadleigh, Craig thought, to make you uncomfortable with your daughter.

The photographer, using a flash, which made the cub snarl, snapped one picture after another. Gail laughed at the show of infant ferocity, stroked the animal. "Come around when you've grown up, Sonny," she said.

"I heard someplace," Craig said, "that most of them die in a month or so. They can't stand the handling."

"Who can?" Wadleigh asked.

"Oh, Daddy," Anne said, "don't spoil the fun."

"I'm devoted to ecology," Craig said. "I want to keep the population of lions in France in balance. So many lions eating so many Frenchmen a season."

The cameraman developed the photographs swiftly. They were in color. Anne's bright hair and Gail's dark pile made an effective composition with the tawny cub snarling among the wineglasses. On the shiny print, except for the blonde hair, Anne looked disturbingly like her mother.

The cameraman's helper picked up the lion, and Wadleigh paid, extravagantly. He gave one of the photographs to Gail, the other to Anne. "When I am old and gray and full of sleep," he said, "and having a bad day, I will summon one or the other of you to my rocking chair and order you to produce this picture. To remind me of a happy night when I was young. Did you ask for the wine, Father?"

Wadleigh was pouring when Craig saw Natalie Sorel come through the door of the restaurant with a tall, beautifully dressed man with silvery hair. Fifty-five, sixty, Craig thought, with everything that a barber and a masseur and the best tailors could do to make it seem like less. Natalie, in a dress that was designed to show off her slender waist, her graceful hips, looked fragile and dependent beside him.

The woman who owned the restaurant was leading

the couple toward the rear, and they would have to pass Craig's table. Craig saw Natalie glance at him quickly, look away, hesitate for a moment as though she meant to go by without stopping, then decide differently.

"Jesse," she said, halting at the table and putting her hand on her escort's arm. "How nice to see you."

Craig stood up, and Wadleigh followed. "This is my fiancé, Philip Robinson," Natalie said. Only Craig, he hoped, heard the warning clarity of the word "fiancé." "Mr. Jesse Craig."

Craig shook hands with the man and introduced the others. Anne stood up. Gail remained seated. Craig wished Anne were wearing another dress. The man's hand was dry and smooth. He had a slow, warm, Texas smile, an outdoor complexion. He didn't look like a man who manufactured things, as Natalie had described him.

"It seems as though Natalie knows everybody in this town," Robinson said, touching Natalie's arm affectionately. "I'm having trouble keeping all the names straight. I've seen your pictures, haven't I, Mr. Craig?"

"I hope you have," Craig said.

"*Two Steps to Home,*" Natalie said quickly. "That was his last one." She was protecting everybody.

"Of course," Robinson said. He had a deep, self-assured voice. "I liked it very much."

"Thank you," Craig said.

"And did I hear correctly?" Robinson said to Wadleigh. "You're the writer?"

"Once upon a time," Wadleigh said.

"I really admired your book, sir," Robinson said. "Immensely."

"Which one?" Wadleigh asked.

Robinson looked a little flustered. "Well," he said, "the one about the boy growing up in the Midwest and . . ."

"My first one." Wadleigh sat down. "I wrote it in 1953."

"Please sit down," Natalie said hurriedly. "Everyone."

Anne sat down, but Craig remained standing. "Are you having a good time in Cannes, Mr. Robinson?" he asked, steering the conversation away from the dangers of literature to the safer banalities of tourism.

"Well, I've been here before, of course," the man said. "But this is the first time I've seen it from the inside, so to speak. Thanks to Natalie. It's a whole new experience." He patted her arm, a fatherly pat.

You don't know how much on the inside you are, Brother, Craig thought, smiling socially.

"We'd better sit down, dear," Natalie said. "The lady's waiting for us."

"I hope I see your fine folks again real soon," Robinson said. "You and your pretty daughter, Mr. Craig, and you, Mr. Wadleigh, and your . . ."

"I'm not anybody's daughter," Gail said, chewing on a piece of celery.

"She defies description," Wadleigh said. His tone was hostile. Robinson obviously was no fool, and his face hardened. "Enjoy your meal," he said, and allowed Natalie to lead him to the table that the owner was pulling out for them.

Craig watched Natalie as she passed, in the light-footed, slightly swaying dancer's walk he would always remember, between the rows of tables. Frail and elegant and carefully prepared to please men's eyes, rouse men's desires, courageous, and full of guile.

In a place like this you had to expect bits and pieces of your past to float by, to exert the power of nostalgia, to become again, for a little while at least, part of the present. Staring at Natalie Sorel, lovely and memorable, walking away from him on another man's arm to the rear of the restaurant, he wondered what perversity of chance had ruled that the part of his past embodied in Ian Wadleigh was claiming him tonight instead of Natalie Sorel.

As he sat down, he was conscious of Gail's looking at him quizzically, knowingly.

"Did I hear correctly?" Wadleigh was saying, mimicking Robinson's slight Texas drawl. "Are you the writer?"

"Keep it low," Craig said. "This is a small restaurant."

"I really admired your book, sir," Wadleigh said. Then, bitterly, "I've been writing for twenty years, and I've got eight books to show for it, and he liked my book."

"Calm down, Ian," Craig said.

But the wine was beginning to work. "And it's always the first one. The one I did when I hardly knew how to spell my own name. I'm getting so tired of that book I think I'm going to burn it in the public square on my next birthday." He poured himself a full glass of wine, spilling some on the tablecloth.

"If it'll make you feel any better," Anne said, "my English professor said he thought your second book was the best one you've written."

"Screw your English professor," Wadleigh said. "What the hell does he know?"

"A lot," Anne said defiantly. Craig was glad to see that his daughter had that most difficult of virtues, courage among the teacups. "I'll tell you another thing he said . . ."

"Do, do!" Wadleigh said. "I can't wait to hear."

"He said that the books you've written since you've moved abroad are comparative failures," Anne said. Craig recognized the way she lifted her chin, a habit she had developed as a child when she decided to be stubborn and willful. "That you're not really exploring your talents to their utmost, that you ought to come back to America . . ."

"Did he say that?"

"Yes, he did."

"And you agree with him?" Wadleigh asked, icy and calm.

"I do," Anne said.

"Screw you and your English teacher both," Wadleigh said.

"If you're going to talk like that," Craig said, "Anne and I will be going home." He knew that the drink had made Wadleigh reckless, that he was ripe for torture, and that he had been touched on his sorest point, but he didn't want to expose Anne to Wadleigh's agonized thrashing about.

"Cut it, Ian," Gail said crisply. "We can't all be loved by the whole world every minute of our lives. Be a big grown man, for God's sake. Be a writer, a *professional* writer, or go do something else for a living."

If Craig had said that, he knew there would have been an explosion. But Wadleigh blinked, shook his head as though emerging from a wave, grinned at Gail. "Out of the mouths of babes," he said. "Forgive me, folks, I hope you're having a good time in Cannes. I want some more fish. Waiter . . ." He waved, but politely, to the waiter who was hurrying past him with a tureen of steaming soup. "Should we order a soufflé for dessert?" Wadleigh said, the perfect host. "I understand they do them very well here. Grand Marnier or chocolate?"

Craig saw Murphy come rolling through the door, looking, as usual when he entered a room, like a bouncer hurrying to break up a fight. Behind him was Sonia Murphy and Lucienne Dullin and Walter Klein. The tribes are on the move, Craig thought, the princes are meeting at the summit. He had lived in Hollywood too long to be surprised at seeing men who at other times denounced each other in the bitterest terms dining cordially together. In that tight, competitive world the lines of communication had to be left open at all times. He was sure that Murphy would not tell Klein that he had read *The Three Horizons* and that Klein would not tell Murphy that the script was on his desk. The princes were discreet and made their dispositions under cover of night.

Even so, he was relieved to see that the owner was seating the group near the entrance, well away from their own table. A long time ago, when Wadleigh was in fashion, Murphy had been his agent. When Wadleigh's bad years began, Murphy had dropped him, and Wadleigh, as might be expected, bore him no great love as a consequence. If the two men were to be seated near each other, with Wadleigh as far gone in drink as he was, the atmosphere would be less than friendly.

But Murphy, who scanned each room he entered like a ship's radar, spotted Craig, and while the others settled themselves at the table near the door, came rolling down the central aisle of the restaurant to greet him. "Good evening, everybody," he said, smiling at the girls and somehow excluding Wadleigh from the greeting. "I called you five times today, Jess. I wanted to invite you to dinner tonight."

Translated, that meant that Murphy had called once, had heard the phone ring twice, had nothing of importance to say to him, and had hung up, too impatient to get the operator back to leave a message. Or it might even mean that Murphy hadn't called at all.

"I had to go to Nice," Craig said, "to pick up Anne."

"God," Murphy said, "this is Anne! I wondered where you'd found the beauty. Turn your back for a minute on a scrawny little freckled kid and look what happens."

"Hello, Mr. Murphy," Anne said gravely.

"Sonia'd love to see you, Anne," Murphy said. "I

tell you what. Why don't you and Miss McKinnon and your father come over to Antibes for dinner with us tomorrow night?"

"I won't be here tomorrow," Craig said. "I'm leaving Cannes." He saw Anne's questioning look. "Just for a couple of days. We'll do it when I get back."

"I'm not leaving Cannes, Murph," Wadleigh said. "I'm free for dinner tomorrow night."

"Isn't that interesting?" Murphy said flatly. "See you later, Jess." He turned and went toward his table.

"The gracious benefactor of the rich," Wadleigh said. "Bryan Murphy, the walking Who's Who. Gee, Jesse," he said with mock innocence, "I sure am glad you're still in there in the current issue." He was going to continue but stopped because Murphy was coming back.

"Jesse," Murphy said, "I forgot something. Did you see the *Tribune* today?"

"No," Craig said. "Why?"

"Edward Brenner died yesterday. A heart attack, the story said. It was short, the obit, I mean, but not too rough. The usual— After an early success, he faded away from the theatrical scene, etc. They mentioned you."

"What did they say about me?"

"Just that you did his first play. Pick up a copy of the paper and read it yourself. Do you have his address? I'd like to send a cable to his family."

"I have an old address," Craig said. "I'll give it to you in the morning."

"Okay," Murphy said. He went back to his table.

"Was he a friend of yours, Daddy?" Anne asked. "Edward Brenner?"

"Not recently." He was conscious of Gail's eyes fixed on him, searching his face.

"Wipe away a tear," Wadleigh said. "Another writer gone. Waiter," he called, *"encore une bouteille.* Let's drink to the poor bastard."

An old friend, an old enemy, now just a name in an obsolete address book, was dead across the ocean, and some ritual, some grave marking of the moment, was in order, but Craig contented himself merely with bringing the wine glass to his lips when Wadleigh raised his glass and said flippantly, "To dead writers everywhere."

Observing himself as though from outside himself, Craig noted that he ate his meal with relish and enjoyed the soufflé when it came. Brenner, he thought, would have been more demonstrative if it had been Craig's name in the obituary column.

He wondered if some months before he died, Edward Brenner's handwriting had changed.

By the end of the meal Wadleigh was very drunk. He had opened his collar, complaining that the restaurant was too hot, and had added up the check slowly, three times, and fumbled with the crumpled hundred-franc notes he pulled out of his pocket to pay the bill. As he stood up, he knocked over his chair.

"Get him out into the open air quick," Craig whispered to Gail. "Anne and I have to stop and say hello to Sonia Murphy."

But when they came to the Murphy table, even though Gail kept tugging at Wadleigh's sleeve to get him to move, he planted himself behind Murphy's chair as Sonia greeted Craig and Anne and Klein introduced Miss Dullin, who said, with a lilting French accent, that she had long wanted to meet *Monsieur* Craig. While Sonia Murphy was telling Anne how happy she was to see her again after all these years and to make sure to come over and use their cabana at the Hotel du Cap any time, Wadleigh, rocking gently back and forth on the balls of his feet behind Murphy's chair, began to hum loudly, "Hail to the Chief."

Klein, diplomatically, pretended to be amused. "I

didn't know you were so musical, Ian," he said.

"Among my many talents," Wadleigh said. "Mr. Murphy is going to book me into La Scala next season, isn't he, Mr. Murphy?"

Murphy ignored him. "Give me a ring in the morning, Jess," he said, and turned back to his dinner.

"Come on, Ian," Craig said.

But Wadleigh refused to budge. "Mr. Murphy is a great little old booker, isn't he, Mr. Murphy? All you have to do is have a number-one best seller for a year and a picture that has just grossed forty million dollars and Mr. Murphy is almost a sure thing to get you a job writing a Lassie picture or a television commercial for aspirin. Don't you wish you were as successful a flesh-peddler as Mr. Murphy, Mr. Klein?"

"Indeed I do, Ian," Klein said soothingly. "And you can call me Walter."

"Cut it out, Ian," Craig said sharply. Wadleigh was talking loudly, and the people at the surrounding tables had all stopped eating and were watching him.

"I'll give you a hint, Mr. Klein," Wadleigh went on, still rocking gently and dangerously back and forth behind Murphy's chair. "I'll tell you the secret of Mr. Murphys' great success. You, too, can be rich and famous and invite girls to your cabana any time. It's not whom you represent that counts, it's whom you drop. You have to learn how to drop the deadwood, Mr. Klein, and drop them fast, before anyone else even knows they're droppable. One bad review and you drop. You'll never get as expert at it as Mr. Murphy, Mr. Klein, because he's got it in his blood, he's the genius of the age for dropping, he lets nothing stand in the way of his craft, not friendship or loyalty or talent, he's like the war-horse in the Bible, he sniffs failure from afar. The telephone rings, and he's not in. See, that's the secret. When the telephone rings and you know it's me, you're not in. The fact that you made thousands and thousands of dollars on me doesn't make any difference. You're not in, see.

Remember that simple rule, Mr. Klein, and you'll go far, very far. Won't he, Mr. Murphy?"

"Take him away, Jesse," Murphy said.

"Come on, Ian." Craig tried to lead Wadleigh away. "Everybody gets the point."

But Wadleigh pushed away his hand. "I can't get to talk to Mr. Murphy on the telephone," he said, "so I talk to him in restaurants. I like to talk to Mr. Murphy about his profession—about all the jobs he could have suggested me for that he didn't suggest me for . . ."

Finally, Murphy turned around. "Don't make me laugh, Wadleigh," he said calmly. "With the way you've been going for the last ten years, I couldn't sell you for dog meat."

Wadleigh stopped rocking. His lips twitched. The entire restaurant was silent. Sonia Murphy was sitting with her head bowed, staring down at her plate. Lucienne Dullin was smiling slightly, as though she were being amused. The chances were that she couldn't follow Wadleigh's drunken English and probably thought it was a friendly, if rather boisterous, conversation. Klein was playing with his glass, not looking at anybody. Anne was the only one who moved. With a gasp, she bolted out the door. Wadleigh took a step as though to follow her, then suddenly turned and hit Murphy. The blow was aimed at Murphy's head but slid off and landed on Murphy's shoulder. Murphy didn't move as Craig threw his arms around Wadleigh and pinned his arms.

"Get that bum out of here, Jesse," Murphy said, "before I kill him."

"I'm going home," Wadleigh said thickly, Cautiously, Craig released him. Wadleigh walked stiffly out the door.

"I'll get a taxi," Gail said, "and take him to his hotel." She hurried after Wadleigh.

"I do like your friends," Murphy said to Craig.

"He's drunk," Craig said inanely.

"So I gathered," Murphy said.

"I'm sorry for everything," Craig said to the others.

"It's not your fault," Sonia said. "It's just too bad. He used to be such a nice man."

The noise in the restaurant was rising to its normal pitch as Craig went out into the street.

• THIRTEEN •

WADLEIGH was on the quay puking into the harbor.
Gail was standing near him, ready to grab him if he
started to teeter toward the black water. Anne was a
few yards away from Gail, making a point of not
looking at Wadleigh. Drunk as he was, Wadleigh,
Craig was sure, was not vomiting because of the wine
he had downed.

Watching Wadleigh bent over the harbor edge, his
shoulders heaving convulsively, Craig felt his anger
cool. He put his arm around Anne to comfort her. He
felt her shiver minutely. "I'm sorry, Anne," he said,
"to have let you in for something like that. I
think that's the last dinner we'll have with Mr. Wadleigh for some time."

"The poor, poor, desperate man," Anne said. "Everybody is so hard on him."

"He asks for it," Craig said.

"I know," she said. "But even so."

Wadleigh stood straight, turned around, dabbing
with a handkerchief at his mouth. He tried to smile.
"There goes a hundred-franc meal," he said. "Well,
it's been a nice party. Worth every penny of it. All
right, Jesse, say what's on your mind."

"Nothing's on my mind," Craig said.

Gail hailed a taxi that was making a U turn in
front of the restaurant. "I'll take you to your hotel,
Ian," she said gently.

Docilely, Wadleigh allowed himself to be led to the
taxi. The door closed behind him, and Gail and the

taxi spurted off. No hints, no signals.

"Well," Craig said, "that's that."

Then Anne began to cry, hard, wracking sobs. "There, there," he said helplessly. "Just try to forget it. He'll probably forget the whole thing by morning."

"He won't forget it," Anne said between sobs. "Not for his whole life. How can people be so ugly to each other?"

"They manage it," Craig said dryly. He didn't want to show too much sympathy for fear of further tears. "Don't take it so hard, darling. Wadleigh's survived a lot worse things than tonight."

"You never imagine a man would behave like that," Anne said wonderingly as the sobs subsided. "A man like that who can write so beautifully, who seems so sure of himself in his books . . ."

"A book is one thing," Craig said. "The man who writes it is another. More often than not a book is a disguise, not a description."

"When the telephone rings, and you know it's me, you're not in," Anne said. The tears had stopped, and she rubbed her eyes with the back of her hand like a little forlorn girl. "What a terrible thing to know about yourself. I hate the movie business, Daddy," she said fiercely. "I just hate it."

Craig dropped his arm from her shoulders. "It's no different from any other business," he said. "It's just a little more concentrated."

"Can't anybody do anything for him? Mr. Murphy? You?"

Craig was surprised into laughing. "After tonight . . ." he began.

"*Because* of tonight," Anne insisted. "On the beach today he told me what good friends you'd been, what great times you'd had together, how marvelous he thought you were . . ."

"That was a long time ago," Craig said. "The good

times we had together. People wear away from each other. As for his thinking how marvelous I am—that comes as news to me. If you want to know the truth, I'm afraid it's something of an inaccurate statement about your father."

"Don't *you* run yourself down, too," Anne said. "Why should it only be people like Mr. Murphy who are sure of themselves?"

"Okay," he said. He took her elbow, and they started to walk slowly along the quay. "If there's anything I can do for him, I'll try to do it."

"You drink too much, too, you know," Anne said, walking beside him.

"I suppose I do," he said.

"Why do people over thirty try so deliberately to ruin themselves?"

"Because they're over thirty."

"Don't make jokes," she said sharply.

"If you don't have the answer to a question, Anne," he said, "you're liable to make a joke."

"Well, then, don't make them in front of me," she said.

They walked in silence, her rebuke between them. "God," she said, "I thought I was going to have such a wonderful time here. The Mediterranean, this great city, all these famous, talented people . . . Being with you." She shook her head sadly. "I guess you shouldn't expect *anything* in advance."

"It's only one night, Anne," he said. "It's bound to get better."

"You're leaving tomorrow," she said. "You didn't tell me."

"It came up suddenly," he said.

"Can I come with you?"

"I'm afraid not."

"I won't ask why," she said.

"It's only for a day or two," he said uncomfortably.

They walked in silence, listening to the lapping of

the harbor water against the boats tied up along the quay.

"Wouldn't it be nice," Anne said, "to get on one of these boats and just sail off?"

"What have *you* got to run away from?"

"Plenty," she said quietly.

"Do you want to talk about it?"

"When you come back," she said.

Women, at all ages, he thought, have the knack of making you feel you are deserting them even when you are only going down to the corner for ten minutes for a pack of cigarettes. "Anne," he said, "I have an idea. While I'm gone, why don't you move over to Cap d'Antibes? The swimming's better, and you can use the Murphys' cabana and . . ."

"I don't need any chaperone," Anne said harshly.

"I wasn't thinking of chaperones," Craig said, although he realized now that she had used the word that was exactly what had been at the back of his mind. "It was just that I thought you'd enjoy it more there, you'd have someone to talk to . . ."

"I'll find somebody to talk to right here," she said. "Anyway, I want to see a lot of movies. It's funny, I love to see movies. I just hate what it does to the people who make them."

A car with two women in it came up alongside the quay and slowed down. The woman nearest them smiled invitingly. Craig ignored her, and the car moved off.

"They're prostitutes," Anne said, "aren't they?"

"Yes."

"In the temples of ancient Greece," Anne said, "they prostituted themselves to strangers before the altars."

"The altars have changed since then," Craig said. Don't walk alone at night, Gail had told Anne when they had met on the steps of the hotel. Don't walk with your father, either, she should have added. Even whores, he thought angrily, should observe *some* rules.

"Have you ever gone with one of them?" Anne asked.

"No," he lied.

"If I were a man," Anne said, "I think I'd be tempted to try."

"Why?"

"Just once, to see what it was like," she said. Craig remembered a book he had read when he was young, *Jurgen*, by James Branch Cabell. He had read it because it was supposed to be dirty. The hero kept saying, "My name is Jurgen, and I will taste any drink once." Poor Cabell, who had been sure of his fame ("Tell the rabble/My name is Cabell," he had announced from what he had considered his enduring and disdainful eminence), poor Cabell, dead, discounted, forgotten even before his death, might now find consolation in the fact that a whole generation so many years later was living by his hero's disastrous slogan, was tasting any drink once, trying any drug once, any political position, any man or woman, once.

"Maybe," Anne said with a gesture of her head for the disappearing red lights of the whores' car, "maybe it would help define things."

"What things?"

"Love, maybe."

"Do you think that needs definition?"

"Of course," Anne said. "Don't you?"

"Not really."

"You're lucky," she said. "If you really believe that. Do you think they're having an affair?"

"Who?" Craig asked, although he knew whom she meant.

"Gail and Ian Wadleigh."

"Why do you ask?"

"I don't know," she said. "The way they behave together. As though there's something between them."

"No," he said. "I don't think so."

Actually, he thought, I refuse to think so.

"She's a cool girl, isn't she, Gail?" Anne said.

"I don't know what people mean by cool anymore," he said.

"She goes her own way," Anne said, "she doesn't depend on anyone. And she's beautiful, and she doesn't make anything of it. Of course, I only met her today, and I may be way off base, but she gives you the feeling that she makes people live up to the way she wants them to be."

"Do you think she wanted Wadleigh to end up the night puking his guts out because he behaved like a fool?"

"Probably," Anne said. "Indirectly. She cares for him, and she wanted him to see for himself what a dead end he'd reached."

"I think you're giving her more credit than she deserves," he said.

"Maybe," Anne admitted. "Still, I wish I could be like her. Cool, above things, knowing what she wants. And getting it. And getting it on her own terms." She paused for a moment. "Are you having an affair with her?"

"No," he said. "Why would you think so?"

"I just asked," Anne said offhandedly. She shivered a little. "It's getting cold, I'd like to go back to the hotel and go to bed. I've had a long day."

But when they got back to the hotel, she decided it was too early to go to bed and came up to his apartment with him for a nightcap. She also wanted to get a copy of his script, she said.

If Gail knocked on the door while Anne was there, Craig thought ironically as he poured the whiskies and soda, they could have a nice little family get-together. He could start the evening off on the right foot by saying, "Gail, Anne has some interesting questions she'd like to ask you." Gail would probably answer them, too. In detail.

Anne was staring at the title page of the script

when he brought her her drink. "Who's Malcolm Harte?" she asked.

"A man I knew during the war," Craig said. "He's dead."

"I thought you said you wrote the script yourself."

"I did." He was sorry that he had been so careless on the trip back from the airport and had told her he had done the writing himself. Now he would be forced to explain.

"Then what's another man's name doing on it?"

"I guess you could call it my *nom de plume,*" he said.

"What do you need a *nom de plume* for?"

"Business reasons," he said.

She made a face. "Are you ashamed of it?" She tapped the script.

"I don't know. Yet," he said.

"I don't like it," she said. "There's something shady about it."

"I think you're being a little too fine." He was embarrassed by the turn the conversation had taken. "It's in an old and honorable tradition. After all, a pretty good writer by the name of Samuel Clemens signed his books Mark Twain." He saw by the set of her lips that this had not convinced her. "I'll tell you the truth," he said. "It comes from uncertainty. Put it more bluntly. From fear. I've never written anything before, and I haven't the faintest notion of how good or bad it is. Until I get some opinions on it, I feel safer hiding behind another man's name. You can understand that, can't you?"

"I can understand it," she said. "But it still strikes me as wrong."

"Let me be a judge of what's right and what's wrong, Anne," he said with a firmness he didn't feel. At this stage of his life he was not prepared to live up to the dictates of his twenty-year-old daughter's stainless-steel conscience.

"Okay," Anne said, hurt, "if you don't want me to

say what I think, I'll shut up." She put the script down on the desk.

"Anne, darling," he said gently, "of course I want you to say what you think. And I want to say what *I* think. Fair enough?"

She smiled. "You think I'm a brat, don't you?"

"Sometimes."

"I guess I am," she said. She kissed his cheek. "Sometimes." She raised her glass. "Cheers."

"Cheers," he said.

She took a long swallow of her whisky. "Mmmm," she said appreciatively. He remembered watching her drink her milk before bedtime when she was a little girl. She looked around at the large room. "Isn't this awfully expensive?"

"Awfully," he said.

"Mummy says you're going to wind up a pauper."

"Mummy is probably right."

"She says you're wildly extravagant."

"She should know," he said.

"She keeps asking me if I take drugs." Anne was obviously waiting for him to ask the same question.

"I take it for granted, from all I see and hear," he said, "that every student in every college in America has smoked pot at one time or another. I imagine that includes you."

"I imagine it does," Anne said.

"I also imagine that you're too smart to fool around with anything else. And that takes care of that," he said. "And now let's call a moratorium on Mummy, shall we?"

"You know what I was thinking all through dinner, looking at you?" Anne said. "I was thinking what a handsome man you are. With all your hair and not fat and those lines of wear and tear in your face. Like a retired gladiator, a little delicate now from old wounds."

He laughed.

"*Noble* wear and tear," she said quickly. "As

though you'd learned a lot and that's why the lines were there. You're the best-looking man I've seen since I came here—"

"You've only been here a few hours," he said. But he couldn't help sounding pleased. Fatuously pleased, he told himself. "Give yourself a couple of days."

"And I wasn't the only one," she said. "Every lady in that restaurant looked at you in that certain way ladies have—that little butterball, Miss Sorel, that fabulous French actress, even Sonia Murphy, even Gail McKinnon."

"I must say, I didn't notice it." He was being honest. He had had other problems to think about during and after dinner.

"That's one of the great things about you," Anne said earnestly. "You don't notice it. I love coming into a room with you and everybody is looking at you like that and you not noticing it. I have a confession to make—" she said, sinking back luxuriously in an easy chair. "I never thought I'd grow up enough to be able to talk to you the way I've done today and tonight. Are you glad I came?"

For an answer he went over and leaned down and kissed the top of her hair.

She grinned, looking suddenly boyish. "Someday," she said, "you're going to make some girl a good father."

The telephone rang. He looked at his watch. It was nearly midnight. He didn't move. The telephone rang again.

"Aren't you going to answer it?" Anne asked.

"I'll probably be happier if I don't," he said. But he went over and picked up the instrument. It was the concierge. He wanted to know if Miss Craig was with him, there was a call for her from the United States.

"It's for you, Anne," he said. "From the United States." He saw Anne's face become sullen. "Do you want to take it here or in the bedroom?"

Anne hesitated, then stood up and placed her drink carefully on the table beside her chair. "In the bedroom, please."

"Put it on the other phone, please," Craig told the concierge.

Anne went into the bedroom, closing the door behind her. A moment later he heard the phone ring there and then the muffled sound of her voice.

Holding his glass, he went to the window, opened it, and stepped out onto the balcony to make sure he didn't overhear Anne's conversation. The Croisette was still full of people and cars, but it was too cold for anybody to be sitting on the terrace. There was a long swell coming in, and the sea was breaking heavily on the beach, the white of the foam ghostly in the reflected lights of the city. *Sophocles, long ago,/Heard it on the Aegean,* he recited to himself, *and it brought,/Into his mind the turbid ebb and flow of human misery.* What ebbing and flowing and turbidity would Sophocles be reminded of listening to the sea in Cannes tonight? Who was ebbing, who flowing? Was Sophocles his real name? Or did he, too, use a *nom de plume? Oedipus at Colonus,* by Malcolm Harte, now dead.

He wondered if Penelope had also read the *Tribune* that day and what she had felt, if she had felt anything at all, when she had come across the name of Edward Brenner, another dead writer.

He heard the living-room door open and went in from the balcony. Anne's face was still sullen. Without a word she picked up her drink and finished it with one swig. Maybe, he thought, I am not the only one in the family who drinks too much.

"Anything serious?" he asked.

"Not really," she said, but the expression on her face didn't match her words. "It's just a boy I know in school." She poured herself another drink. With very little soda, he noted. "Ah, Christ," she said. "Nobody leaves you alone."

"You want to talk about it?"

"He thinks he's in love with me. He wants to marry me." She plumped herself down despondently in the easy chair, cradling her drink, her long brown legs stretched out in front of her. "Prepare for visitors," she said. "He said he's coming over. Air fares're ridiculously cheap these days, that's the trouble. Anybody can follow anybody. One of the reasons I asked you to let me come here was to get away from him. You don't mind, do you?"

"It's as good a reason as any," Craig said noncommitally.

"I thought I was in love with him, too," she said. "For a hot month. I liked going to bed with him, maybe I still like going to bed with him. But marriage, for God's sake!"

"I know I'm being old-fashioned," Craig said, "but what's so awful about a boy wanting to marry a girl he's in love with?"

"Everything. You don't see Gail McKinnon rushing off and getting married to any half-baked jock college boy, do you? You don't see *her* sitting at home and popping television dinners into the oven, waiting for dear little hubby to come home from the office on the five-thirty commuters' train, do you?"

"No, you don't," he said.

"I'm going to be my own woman first," Anne said. "Like her. And then if I want to get married, my husband'll know what the rules are."

"Can't you be your own woman, married?"

"Not with that stupid jock," she said. "He's not even a good jock. He got a scholarship to play football, he was all-state in high school, or all-idiot, or something like that, and the first week in practice with the varsity team, he tore his knee to bits, and he can't even play football anymore. That's the kind of fellow he is. Ah, maybe I *would* marry him if he was smart or ambitious, if I thought he was going to amount to something. His father owns a grain and

feed business in San Bernardino, and all he wants is
to go into the grain and feed business in San Bernardino. San Bernardino, for God's sake! Bury me
not on the lone prairie. He says he's not against
women working. Until they have children, of course.
In this day and age! With all the things happening in
the world, wars, revolutions, crazy men with hydrogen
bombs, Blacks being gunned down, women finally
standing up and asking to be treated like human beings. I know I sound adolescent and naïve, and I
don't know what the hell I expect I can do about any
of it, but I know I don't want to wind up teaching
kids the multiplication table in San Bernardino just
because some big California lunk has got a fix on me.
I tell you, Daddy, sex is the biggest goddamn trap ever
invented, and I'm not having any of it. The worst
thing is, when I heard his voice on the telephone saying, 'Anne, I can't bear it,' I felt as though all my in-
sides were melting into one big stupid syrupy lump.
Ah, shit! I wouldn't care if he didn't have a penny, if
he walked around barefooted, if he only wanted to *do*
something, join a commune and bake organic bread
or run for Congress or be a nuclear physicist or an ex-
plorer or anything. I'm not all that freaked out myself,
but I'm not all that square, either." She stopped, stared
at Craig. "Am I? Do you think so?"

"No," Craig said. "I don't think so."

"I just don't want to live in the nineteenth century. Ah, what a day," she said bitterly. "He had to
come over and sit next to me in the library. Limping
from his goddamn knee. With long hair and a blond
beard. You can't tell what people are like from the
way they look anymore. And now he's coming over
here to moon away at me with his big baby blue eyes,
flexing his goddamn biceps and walking around the
beach looking as though he ought to be on a marble
pedestal somewhere in Thrace. What do you think I
ought to do—run away?"

"That's up to you," Craig said. "Isn't it?" So that's

what had happened to her in the last six months.

She put her glass down roughly. Some of the drink spilled over on the table. She stood up. "Don't be surprised if I'm not here when you get back from wherever you're going," she said.

"Just leave word where I can reach you," he said.

"Have you got any pills?" she said. "I'm all jangled. I'll never get any sleep tonight."

Modern father, after having plied his daughter with drink during the evening and having listened without comment or demur to her description of her carnal relations with a young man she scorned to marry, he went into the bathroom and returned with two Seconals to assure her night's rest. When he was twenty, he remembered, he had slept undrugged, even under bombing and occasional shellfire. He had also been a virgin. Insomnia began with liberty. "Here," he said, handing her the pills. "Sleep well."

"Thanks, Daddy," she said, taking the pills and throwing them into her bag. She picked up a script. "Wake me in the morning before you leave and I'll come down and have breakfast with you."

"That would be nice," he said. He did not mention the possibility that there might be other company present for the same meal. Or that she might expect the waiter to look at her oddly. He took her to the door, kissed her good night, and watched her go down the corridor toward the elevator with her pills and her problems. Even now, he noticed, she was imitating, just a little, Gail McKinnon's way of walking.

He didn't feel like sleeping. He fixed himself a fresh drink, looked at it thoughtfully before taking the first sip. Was it possible that he did drink too much, as Anne had said. The censorious young.

He picked up a copy of *The Three Horizons* and began to read. He read thirty pages. They didn't make much sense to him. I've reread it too often, he thought, it's gone dead on me. He couldn't tell wheth-

·er he should be ashamed of it or not. At that same moment, perhaps, Walter Klein in his castle and Anne upstairs in her single room were reading the same thirty pages. He was being judged. The thought made him uneasy. He noticed that he had finished his drink as he read. He looked at his watch. It was nearly one o'clock. He still wasn't sleepy.

He went onto the balcony and looked out. The sea was higher than before, the noise of the waves greater. The traffic on the Croisette had diminished. American voices floated up, women's laughter. Women should be forbidden to laugh outside your window after midnight, he thought, when you are alone.

Then he saw Anne coming out from under the porte-cochère. She was wearing her raincoat over the yellow organdy dress. He watched as she crossed the street. Two or three men who were passing by glanced at her, he saw, but kept on walking. Anne went down the steps to the beach. He saw her shadowy form moving close to the water's edge, outlined against the luminous gleam of the breakers. She walked slowly, disappeared into the darkness.

He checked an impulse to hurry after her. If she had wanted to be with him, she would have let him know. There was a certain point at which you no longer could hope to protect your child.

The young spoke candidly, endlessly, shockingly, about themselves to you, but in the long run you didn't really know any more about them than your father in his time had known about you.

He went back into the room, had his hand on the whisky bottle, when the knock came at the door.

When he awoke the next morning in the tumbled bed, he was alone. There was a note for him in Gail's handwriting on the desk in the living room. "Am I a better lay than my mother?" she had written.

He called her hotel, but the operator said Miss Mc-

Kinnon had gone out.

All those big masculine writers were wrong, Craig thought, it was actually the vagina that was the instrument of revenge.

He picked up the phone again and called Anne's room and told her to come down for breakfast. When she came down, in her bathrobe, he didn't tell her he had seen her leave the hotel the night before.

When the waiter came in with the two breakfasts, he looked at Anne the way Craig had known he would look. He didn't tip the man.

• FOURTEEN •

On a curve, a Peugeot loaded with children and going ninety miles an hour nearly hit him head on. He swerved, just avoiding the ditch alongside the road. He drove slowly and carefully after that, wary of all Frenchmen on wheels and not enjoying the views of the vineyards and olive groves through which the road ran or the occasional glimpses of the sea off to his left.

He was in no hurry to get to Marseilles. He had not yet decided what to say to Constance. If he was going to say anything. He wasn't sure that he was a good enough actor to be able to pretend successfully that nothing had happened. He wasn't certain that he wished to pretend that nothing had happened.

The night had shaken him. This time there had been no coquetry or refusal. Wordlessly, in the dark, with the sound of the sea outside the window, Gail had accepted him, gently, gravely. Her hands were soft, her mouth sweet, her touch delicate and slow. He had forgotten the skin of young girls. He had expected avidity, or if not that, brusqueness, or even resentment. Instead, she had been . . . Well, he thought, the best word he could find was welcoming, profoundly welcoming. At the back of his mind a thought flickered at the edge of consciousness—*This is better than anything I've had in my whole life.* He recognized the danger. But some time during the night he had said, "I love you."

He had felt tears on her cheek.

And then in the morning there had been that harsh

joke, the note on the desk. Who the hell could her mother have been?

As he approached Marseilles, he drove even more slowly.

When he got to the hotel, there was a note from Constance. She would be back some time after five, she had reserved a room adjoining hers for him, she loved him. And there was a message at the concierge's desk. Mr. Klein had called and would like him to call back.

He followed the clerk up to his room. The door between his room and Constance's was standing open. When the clerk had left and the porter had put down his bag, he went into Constance's room. Her familiar comb and brush were on the bureau, and a linen dress that he recognized was hanging outside a closet door to shake out the wrinkles. The rooms themselves were dark and hot and heavily furnished. There was a great deal of noise coming in from the street, even though the windows were closed.

He went back into his own room and sat on the bed, his hand on the telephone. When he picked it up, he started to give the number of Gail's hotel to the operator, then corrected himself and asked for Klein's number.

Klein answered himself. He was a man who was never more than five feet from a telephone. "How's the great man?" Klein asked. "And what is he doing in Marseilles?"

"It's the heroin center of the world," Craig said. "Haven't you heard?"

"Listen, Jesse," Klein said, "hold on a minute. I have to go to another phone. There're a lot of people in here with me and . . ."

"I'll hold," Craig said. There were always a lot of people in there with Klein.

A moment later he heard the click as Klein picked up the other phone. "Now we can talk," Klein said. "You're coming back to Cannes, aren't you?"

"Yes."

"When?"

"In a couple of days or so."

"You'll get back before everybody breaks camp, won't you?"

"If necessary," Craig said.

"I think it'll be useful," Klein said. "Look, I read that Harte script you sent me. I like it. I think I may be able to put something together. Right here. This week. Are you interested?"

"It all depends."

"It all depends on what?"

"On what you mean by putting something together."

"I think I may have a lead," Klein said. "With a director. I won't tell you his name because he hasn't said yes or no yet. But he's read it. And nobody's said a word so far about money. And there's many a slip et cetera . . . You understand."

"Yes," Craig said. "I understand."

"What I mean," Klein said, "is that I think it'd be worth your while to get back here as soon as possible. But there're no promises. You understand that, too, don't you?"

"Yes."

"Another thing," Klein went on. "I think the script needs work."

"I never heard of a script that didn't," Craig said. "If Shakespeare showed up with the manuscript of Hamlet, the first man he showed it to would say, 'I think this script needs work.'"

"I don't know who this fellow Harte is, but he's no Shakespeare," Klein said. "And I have the feeling he's shot his load on this draft. I mean, I think whatever director agrees to do it would want to bring in another writer for a second version. Before I talk to the director, I have to know what you think about that."

Craig hesitated. Maybe, he thought, this was the moment to announce that there was nobody named

Malcolm Harte. But he said, "I'd have to talk it over with whoever was finally going to do it. See what his ideas are."

"Fair enough," Klein said. "One more thing. Do you want me to tell Murphy I'm handling this, or will you? He's bound to hear. And soon."

"I'll tell him," Craig said.

"Good," Klein said. "It's going to be a rough ten minutes."

"Let me worry about it."

"Okay. Worry. Can I reach you at the Marseilles number if something comes up?"

"If I move," Craig said, "I'll let you know."

"I don't know what's so great about Marseilles, for Christ's sake," Klein said. "We're having a ball here."

"I bet."

"Keep your fingers crossed, kid," Klein said, and hung up. Craig looked at the telephone. He who lives by the telephone, he thought irrelevantly, dies by the telephone. He supposed he should have been elated by Klein's reaction to the script. Not wildly elated but cautiously, quietly elated. Even if nothing ever came of it in the end, here was some proof that he hadn't been wasting his time entirely.

He picked up the phone again and asked for the Carlton. Anne must have read the script by now, and it might help to know what she thought of it. Also, good father, having left her with the problem of the young man arriving from California, perhaps he could offer some useful advice. If she asked him for any.

While he was waiting for the operator to reach the Carlton, he shaved and took a shower. He should look and smell his best for Constance. It was the least he could do.

He had to climb out of the shower when he heard the telephone ring. As he stood dripping, waiting for the operator at the Carlton to connect him with Anne's room, he looked at his wet, high-arched footprints on the worn carpet. At least I'm not flatfooted, he thought. A man could be vain about the most idiotic things.

There was no answer from Anne's room. If she needed advice, she was getting it elsewhere. From Gail, most likely. He wondered what Gail would have to say to his daughter, how much she would tell her. What if she told her everything? And what, exactly, was everything? Cross that bridge when you come to it.

He went back into the bathroom and stood under the cold water rinsing the soap off. He dried himself and dressed quickly. He needed a drink, he told himself. He hadn't brought a bottle along, and he would have to go to the bar. There was a certain amount of cowardice involved there, he acknowledged to himself. He didn't want to greet Constance in their rooms. Where she might expect him to get into bed with her immediately. Immediately was not for today.

The bar was dark red, blood-colored. There were two small Japanese men in identical dark suits looking over a thick bundle of mimeographed sheets of paper and speaking Japanese earnestly, in voices just above a whisper. Were they planning to bomb the harbor of Marseilles? He wondered how he could have hated small neat polite men like that as much as he had when he was a young man. *Banzai*.

He was on his second Scotch when Constance came into the bar. Red was not her color. He rose and kissed her. Her hair was a little damp from the heat. He should not have noticed. "You look beautiful," he said. Everything else could wait.

"Welcome, welcome," she said.

The word had an echo, he would have preferred not to hear.

"I need a Tom Collins," she said. "He knows how to make them." She gestured toward the barman. She had been there before. With whom? Had there been tears on her cheek recently?

He ordered the Tom Collins and another Scotch for

himself. "How many does that make?" she asked lightly.

"Only three," he said. Anne was not the only one who was concerned about his drinking. Next month he would go on the wagon. Just wine.

"I knew I would find you in the bar," she said. "I didn't even bother to ask the concierge."

"I have no mystery left for you," he said. "It's a bad sign."

"You have plenty of mystery," she said. "Never fear."

They were uneasy with each other. She picked up her bag and put it down, her fingers fiddling with the clasp.

"What're you doing in Marseilles, anyway?" he asked. Klein had asked him the same question. Was it possible that all the million inhabitants of the city asked each other every morning, "What are you doing in Marseilles?"

"One of my darling Youths is in trouble," she said. Verbally, she always capitalized Youth. The police picked him up in the Vieux Port with two pounds of hash in his rucksack. I pulled some wires, and they told me in Paris that if I came down and flung my charms around liberally, I might be able to get the idiot out of the French pokey some time before the end of the century. I've been flinging my charms around liberally for the whole afternoon. The Youth's father has also promised to cable an interesting selection of money for the support of the French narcotic squad from St. Louis. We'll see. I'll have to hang around at least two days. God, I need a drink. And God, I'm glad to see you." She reached out and took his hand, squeezed it. She had strong fingers, smooth palms. Delicately made, she was a strong, smooth woman. Damp hair and all. Bold, intelligent, inquisitive features, direct, humorous green eyes, dark now in the red light of the bar. Much sought after by men. He had been told that by friends. Also by her. Active in the service. She had a bad temper, a sunny smile, was easily hurt, quick to hurt in return. Always something for a man to think about. Take nothing for granted. How many men had she abandoned? He would have to ask some day. Not in Marseilles.

They touched glasses before they drank. "I needed that," she said after the first long draft. "Now tell me everything."

"I can't," he said. "We are surrounded by Japanese spies." Postpone with a joke.

She grinned. "Glad you came?" she asked.

"All my life," he said, "I have dreamt of meeting a girl in Marseilles. Now that I've done it, let's go someplace else. If you've got to hang around a day or two, anyway, there's no sense in staying here. If the money comes from St. Louis, they can call you."

"I suppose so," she said doubtfully.

"This hotel is death," he said. "And there's so much noise outside, we won't sleep all night."

"I didn't know you'd come here to sleep," she said.

"You know what I mean."

She smiled. "Where can we go? No Cannes."

"Forget Cannes. There's a place I've heard of," he said, "in a village called Meyrague. Somebody told me about it. It's a converted chateau on a hill. We can get there in under two hours."

"Have you ever been there with anybody else?"

"No," he said truthfully.

"On to Meyrague," she said.

They packed hurriedly, no time for love. It would be dark before they got to Meyrague as it was. He was afraid the telephone would ring before they got out of the room. The telephone didn't ring. The clerk at the cashier's desk was sullen but resigned. He was used to guests leaving his hotel suddenly. "You understand," he said in French, "I am obliged to charge you for the full night."

"I understand," Craig said. He paid both bills. The least he could do for an American Youth in the hands of the French police.

The traffic was bad as they started out, and Craig had to pay attention to the driving, and there was no chance for talking until they were outside the city limits, going north in the direction of Aix-en-Provence.

He sorted out the subjects in his head as they drove. Fidelity, parenthood, career, his wife, his daughter, Klein, Gail McKinnon. The mother of Gail Mc-Kinnon. Not necessarily in that order.

Constance sat beside him, her short hair blowing in the wind of their passage, a small contented smile on her lips, the tips of her fingers on his leg.

"I love going on trips with you," she said. They had been to the Loire Valley together, to Normandy and to London. Small, delightful voyages. Simpler than this one. He wondered if he was glad or sorry she had refused to come to Cannes with him.

"Did you talk to David Teichman?"

"Yes," Craig said.

"Isn't he a nice man?"

"Very." He didn't tell her what he had heard about the old man. Keep death out of the conversation on the road from Marseilles. "I said I'd be in touch. His plans're vague." He hurried past the subject of David Teichman. "Actually, somebody else may be interested in the script. I'll probably know when I get back to Cannes." He was preparing for departure. Constance took her fingers away from his leg.

"I see," she said. "What else? How's your daughter?"

"It would take all night to tell you," he said. "She's after me to quit the movie business. Altogether. She says it's cruel and capricious and the people're awful."

"Did she convince you?"

"Not quite. Although I more or less agree with her. It *is* cruel and capricious, and most of the people *are* awful. Only it's no worse and probably better than most other businesses. You get more bootlicking and lying in one day in any army, for example, than in a year in every studio in Hollywood combined. And there's more throat-cutting and double-dealing in politics, say, or selling frozen foods than there ever possibly could be on a movie set. And the end product, no matter how bad it is, can't do any more harm than generals and senators and TV dinners.

"I take it you told her you'd hang in there."

"More or less. If they let me."

"Was she happy about it?"

"At her age I think that she believes the idea of being happy is a betrayal of her generation."

Constance laughed ruefully. "God, I have it all ahead of me with my kids."

"So you do," he said. "Another thing my daughter told me—she's been to see her mother." He could feel Constance tense slightly beside him. "Her mother told her she'd been to see you."

"Oh dear," Constance said. "You don't have a bottle stashed away in the car somewhere, do you?"

"No."

"Should we stop somewhere for a drink?"

"I'd rather not," he said.

Constance moved a little toward her side of the car. "I hadn't planned to tell you," she said.

"Why not?"

"I thought it might disturb you."

"It does," he said.

"She's an attractive woman," Constance said. "Your wife."

"She did a very unattractive thing."

"I suppose you could say that. The Youths in the office got an earful." Constance shrugged. "I don't know what I would do if I'd been married to a man for over twenty years and he left me for another woman."

"I didn't leave her for another woman," Craig said. "I left her for her."

"It's hard for a woman to believe that," Constance

said. "When you reach her age, in a situation like that, you're not likely to be completely reasonable. She wants you back, and she'll do everything she can to get you back."

"She's not going to get me back. Did she insult you?"

"Naturally. Can't we talk about something else? This is holiday time."

"My lawyer says she's threatening to name you in the suit for divorce," Craig said. "In the end she probably won't because I'll pay her off not to do it. But I thought you'd better know."

"Don't pay her off on my account," Constance said. "My reputation will survive."

He chuckled dryly.

"Isn't it dreary to think of—a poor little French detective standing outside my window all night while we tossed and turned in the steamy raptures of middle-aged passion?" Her tone was mocking and bitter. His wife, Craig realized, had accomplished at least part of her mission in the scene with Constance.

"You're not middle-aged," he said.

"I don't feel middle-aged," she said. "Tonight." They were passing a roadside sign. "Aix-en-Provence," she said. "Minstrels at the court singing to the sound of lutes. Tournaments of Love."

"I'll tell you if anything happens," he said.

"Do," she said. "Keep me posted."

Unreasonably, he felt, she was blaming him. No. Reasonably. After all, it was his wife. He had had more than twenty years to train her to behave politely to his mistresses.

A car came in from a side road, and he had to jam on the brakes. Constance put out her hand to brace herself against the glove compartment. "Would you like me to drive?" she said. "You've been driving all day, and you must be tired."

"I'm not tired," he said shortly. He stepped on the accelerator, although he knew he was driving too fast. For a while in the car, it was not holiday time.

The hotel was a chateau on top of a wooded hill, and it was warm enough to eat outdoors, by the light of candles, on a flagstone terrace overlooking the valley. The food was very good, and they had two bottles of wine and finished off the meal with champagne. It was the kind of place and the kind of dinner that made you understand why, for some part of your life, it was imperative to live in France.

After dinner they wandered down the road through the little forest, through patches of moonlight, into the village and had coffee in a tiny café where the proprietor had the week's football scores chalked up on a slate.

"Even the coffee is good," Craig said.

"Even everything," Constance said. She was wearing the blue linen dress because she knew he liked her in blue. "Happy you're here?" she asked.

"Uhuh."

"With me?"

"Well," he said slowly, as though he was considering the question very carefully, "I suppose if you have to be in a place like this with a girl, you're as good a choice as any."

"Why, that's the nicest thing anybody has said to me all day," she said.

They both laughed.

"Spell Meyrague," he said.

"J-e-s-s-e C-r-a-i-g."

They laughed again. She looked at the slate with the scores on it. "Isn't it wonderful that Monaco won?" she said.

"It makes my week," he said.

"We've both had too much to drink," she said. "Wouldn't you say?"

"I would say." He gestured to the proprietor behind the bar. "*Deux cognacs, s'il vous plaît.*"

"Aside from everything else," she said, "it speaks French."

"Among its many accomplishments," he said.

"Tonight," she said, "you look twenty years old."

"Next year," he said, "I'm going to vote."

"For whom?"

"Muhammad Ali."

"I'll drink to that," she said.

They drank to Muhammad Ali.

"Whom are you going to vote for?" he asked.

"Cassius Clay."

"I'll drink to that," he said.

They drank to Cassius Clay. She giggled. "Aren't we being foolish?" she said.

"I'll drink to that," he said. He gestured toward the bar. *"Encore deux cognacs, s'il vous plaît."*

"Eloquent, eloquent," she said. "In several Romantic languages."

He stared across the table at her. Her face became grave, and she reached across to grasp his hand as if for reassurance. He was on the verge of saying, Let's stay here all week, all month. And after that we'll take a year to cross the roads of France in the sunshine. But he didn't say anything, just gripped her hand a little more tightly.

"Did I spell Meyrague correctly?" she said.

"It's never been spelled better," he said.

On the way up the hill he said, "Walk in front of me for a while."

"Why?"

"I want to admire your glorious legs," he said.

She walked ahead of him through the woods. "Admire," she said.

The bed was huge. The moonlight came in through the open windows and the smell of the pine forest. He lay on his back in the silvery darkness listening to

Constance moving around in the bathroom. She never undressed in front of him. It was a good thing, he thought, that Gail was not one of those girls who raked a man with her nails in the act of love. He had been marked in his time. Then he was displeased with himself for thinking of it. The treachery of memory, eroding the body's pleasure. He was determined not to feel guilty. Tonight's choice was not last night's choice. Each night to its own innocence. He had never sworn fidelity to Constance or she to him.

She glided across the room, a pale shadow, slipped into the bed beside him. Her body was precious to him, generous and familiar. "Home again," he whispered to her, erasing other memories.

But later on, lying still, side by side, she said, "You didn't really want me to come to Cannes."

He hesitated. "No," he said.

"It wasn't only because of your daughter."

"No." He had been marked. Somehow.

"There's somebody else there."

"Yes."

She was silent for a moment. "A serious somebody else or an accidental somebody else?"

"I would say accidental," he said. "But I'm not sure. Anyway, it *happened* accidentally. That is, I didn't go to Cannes to meet her. I didn't know she was alive until a few days ago." Now that she had broached the subject, he was relieved that he could talk about it. She was too dear to him for lying. "I don't really know how it happened," he said. "It just happened."

"I didn't stay home alone in Paris every night since you were gone," she said.

"I won't ask you what you mean by that," he said.

"It means what it means."

"Okay."

"We're not bound to each other," she said, "by anything else but what we feel for each other at any given moment."

"All right."

"Do you mind if I smoke a cigarette?"

"I always mind if anybody smokes a cigarette."

"I promise not to come down with cancer tonight." She got out of bed, put on a robe, and went to the dresser. He saw the flare of the match. She came back to the bed and sat on its edge, her face from time to time lit by the glow of the cigarette tip when she inhaled. "I have some news for you tonight, too," she said. "I was going to save it for another time, but I'm in a chatty mood."

He laughed.

"What're you laughing at?" she asked.

"Nothing," he said. "Just laughing. What's the news?"

"I'm leaving Paris," she said.

Unreasonably, he felt that this was a blow aimed at him. "Why?"

"We're setting up a branch in San Francisco. There's been a big movement of the Youth back and forth to and from the East. Exchange scholarships—stuff like that. We've been negotiating with an organization in California for months, and it finally came through, and I'm elected. I'm going to be our private Window on the Awakening Orient."

"Paris won't be the same place without you."

"I won't be the same lady without Paris," she said.

"How do you feel about it?"

"About living in San Francisco? Curious. It's a pretty city, and I hear it's seething with cultural aspiration." Her tone was mocking. "It'll probably be good for my kids. Improve their English. A mother has to think about improving her children's English from time to time, doesn't she?"

"I suppose so," he said. "When are you going to make the move?"

"Sometime this summer. A month or two."

"I have lost another home," he said. "I will wipe Paris off my itinerary."

"That's loyal," she said. "Will you add San Francisco? They tell me there are some good restaurants."

"So I hear," he said. "I'll be there. From time to time."

"From time to time," she said. "A girl can't ask for everything, can she?"

He didn't answer her. "Foundations keep shifting," he said.

Then, much later, she said, "I don't pretend I'm wildly pleased by what you told me tonight. But I'm no child, and neither are you. You didn't expect me to make a scene, or throw myself out the window, or anything like that, did you?"

"No, of course not."

"As I said, I'm not wildly pleased," she said. "But I *am* wildly pleased about a lot of other things about us. Will you do me a favor?"

"Of course."

"Say, I love you."

"I love you," he said.

She stubbed out the cigarette, took off the robe, dropping it onto the floor, and got into the bed beside him, her head on his chest. "And that's enough talk for tonight. I'm not in a chatty mood anymore."

"I love you," he whispered into her tumbled hair.

They slept late and woke to sunlight and birds singing. Constance called Marseilles, but the money from St. Louis hadn't arrived yet for her Youth, and the narcotics man would not be in until tomorrow. They decided to stay in Meyrague another day, and he didn't call Cannes to let anyone know where he was. The day was going to be only theirs.

Then, the next morning, the money still hadn't come, and it was too nice to leave, and they stayed another twenty-four hours.

When he left her at the hotel in Marseilles the next morning, he told her he would take her to lunch in Paris on Monday. It looked, she said, as if she had a good chance to spring the Youth by nightfall. If she failed, she'd go back to Paris, anyway, and leave him to his fate. She had spent enough time in the south, she said. She was a working woman.

• FIFTEEN •

"DAMN it, Jesse," Klein was saying loudly over the phone, "I tried to get you ten times. Where are you now?"

"Cassis," Craig said. He had stopped off for lunch on the way back from Marseilles. He was calling from a restaurant on the harbor. The harbor was blue and toylike. The season hadn't begun yet, and there was a sleepy, tranced look about it, the boats all closed up under their winter canvas and everybody away for lunch.

"Cassis," Klein said. "Just when you need people, they're in Cassis. Where the hell is Cassis?"

"In between," Craig said. "What did you want to talk to me about?"

"I think I have a deal for you. That's what I want to talk to you about. When can you get here?"

"Three, four hours."

"I'll be here," Klein said. "I won't move all afternoon."

"Will you do me a favor?" Craig said.

"What?"

"Will you call Murphy for me and ask him to be at your place at five o'clock, too?" He could sense Klein's hesitation at the other end of the line, an intake of breath, an almost-cough.

"What do you want Murphy here for?" Klein asked.

"I want to spare his feelings as much as possible," Craig said.

"That's a new one, a client wanting to spare an agent's feelings," Klein said. "I wish I had some like that."

"I'm not sparing an agent's feelings," Craig said. "I'm sparing a friend's feelings."

"Murphy's read the script, of course," Klein said.

"Of course."

"And he said he didn't want to handle it."

"Yes."

"Well," Klein said reluctantly, "if you insist."

"I think it would be better all round," Craig said. "But if you don't want to do business with someone looking over your shoulder . . ."

"Hell," Klein said, "I'll do business with the Pope looking over my shoulder. I'll call Murphy."

"That's a good fellow."

"That's me," Klein said. "Despite all rumors to the contrary."

"I'll be there at five," Craig said. He hung up. While it was a fact that he was asking for Murphy out of affection for his old friend, he also wanted him in on the beginning of the talks about the deal. He knew that he himself was a poor dealer for himself, loath to press for advantage, and Murphy had always protected him in all the contracts he had signed. And this contract promised to be a complicated one. It was true that he had written *The Three Horizons* for other reasons than the money he might eventually make out of it, but he had been around the movies long enough to know that the more money you were paid, the easier it was to get your way in other matters. While the old formula, Money versus Art, often held, he had found that in the movie business, in his case, the formula, Money multiplies Art, was likely to be the more valid one.

Craig went out and sat at a table overlooking the harbor. He was the only customer. It was restful, being the only customer, looking out at the sunny little blue body of water, thinking of lunch and Klein not moving for an entire afternoon. He ordered a *pastis* in honor of the fishermen and vintners of Cassis and leisurely examined the menu.

He ordered a dorade and a bottle of white wine and sipped at his *pastis*. The liquorice taste made the Mediterranean richer for him, brought back the memory of a hundred lazy afternoons. The time with Constance had been good for him. He thought of her fondly. He knew that if he ever used the word in her presence, she would be enraged. No matter. It was a fair enough word. People were not fond enough of each other. They said they loved each other, but what they meant was that they wanted to use each other, patrol each other, dominate each other, devour each other, destroy each other, weep for each other. Constance and he enjoyed each other, at least most of the time, and fond was as good a word as any for that. He postponed thinking of San Francisco.

He had said, "I love you," to Constance, and he had said, "I love you," to Gail McKinnon, and he had meant it both times, and perhaps he meant it simultaneously. In the sunlight, alone over a milky cold southern drink, it seemed easily possible.

He also did not deny to himself that it was pleasant to sit idly by the side of a deserted harbor and know that a man as involved in important affairs as Walter Klein had called him ten times the day before and was even now waiting impatiently for his arrival. He had thought that he had given all that up, but he realized now, with some satisfaction, that he was not immune to the joys of power.

Well, he thought, with everything that has happened, it wasn't a bad idea coming down to Cannes after all. He hoped that when he arrived in Cannes that evening he would discover that Gail McKinnon had left town.

When he reached Klein's house just a little after

five, he saw a car with a chauffeur parked in the courtyard and knew that Murphy was already there. Murphy didn't like to drive himself. He had been in three accidents and had, as he put it, gotten the message.

Murphy and Klein were sitting by the side of the heated swimming pool, Murphy drinking. The last time Craig had been there, the night of the party, it had been Sidney Green, the director who had been hailed by *Cahiers du Cinéma* and who couldn't get a job, who had come out of the bushes to greet him after pissing on the expensive green grass of Walter Klein. For losers only, Craig remembered thinking. Today he didn't feel like a winner, but he didn't feel like a loser, either.

"Hi, boys," Craig said as he came up to the side of the pool. "I hope I haven't kept you waiting." He sat down quickly so that they wouldn't have to decide whether or not to stand up to greet him.

"I just got here," Murphy said. "A half ounce of Scotch ago."

"I explained a little of the situation over the phone to Murph," Klein said.

"Well," Murphy said gruffly, "if there's somebody damn fool enough to put up a million bucks for that script on today's market, more power to him."

"Where did you get that amount?" Craig asked. "A million dollars?"

"That's what I figure it'll cost to make," Murphy said. "Minimum."

"I haven't discussed money yet with anyone," Klein said. "It's all according how you want to make it and with whom."

"You told me a director had read it," Craig said to Klein. "Which director?"

"Bruce Thomas," Klein said. He looked quickly from one to the other of the two men, enjoying his moment of triumph.

"If Bruce Thomas wants to make it," Murphy said, "you can get all the money you need." He shook his head. "I would never have guessed Thomas. Why he would want to do something like this. He's never done anything like this before."

"That's exactly why," Klein said. "That's what he told me. Now," Klein said to Craig, "Thomas agrees with me, the script needs a lot of rewriting. What do you think, Murph?"

"Yeah. A lot," Murphy said.

"And Thomas would like to bring in another writer," Klein said. "To work on it alone, preferably, or if there's a hitch, to work with this fellow Harte. Just what sort of deal do you have with Harte, Jesse?"

Craig hesitated. "No deal," he said.

Murphy made a startled noise. "What do you mean by no deal?" Klein asked. "Do you own the script or don't you?"

"I own it, all right," Craig said.

"So?" Klein asked.

"I wrote it," Craig said, "with my own little old fountain pen. There is no Malcolm Harte. I just picked a name at random and put it on the script."

"What the hell did you do that for?" Murphy said angrily.

"It's too complicated to go into now. Anyway, there we are," Craig said. "Let's move on from there."

"Thomas is going to be surprised when he hears," Klein said.

"If he likes the script with the name Malcolm Harte on it," Murphy said, "he's going to like it with the name Craig on it."

"I suppose so," Klein said doubtfully. "But it's bound to change his thinking somewhat."

"How?" Murphy asked.

"I don't know how, but somehow," Klein said.

"Where is Thomas?" Craig asked. "Why don't we call him up and have him come over?"

"He had to leave for New York this morning," Klein said. "That's why I was calling you so frantically. God, I hate it when people drop out of sight."

"You're lucky, Murphy said. "You only lost him for one day. I sometimes lose him for three months at a time."

"Well," Klein said, "I might as well give you the whole thing. First, as I said, he wants another writer. Now, hold your hats, boys. The man he wants is Ian Wadleigh."

"Oh, shit," Murphy said.

Craig laughed.

"You laugh," Murphy said angrily. "Do you see yourself working with Ian Wadleigh?"

"Maybe," Craig said. "Probably not. What made Thomas pick on Wadleigh, of all people?"

"I asked him that myself," Klein said. "He just happened to see Wadleigh around, you know how it is down here. He talked to the guy by accident once or twice, and Wadleigh gave him a copy of his last book. I guess he couldn't sleep one night, and he picked it up and looked through it, and something caught him."

"Wadleigh's last book!" Murphy snorted. "It got the worst reviews since Hiawatha."

"You know Thomas," Klein said. "He doesn't read reviews. Not even his own."

"The perfect reader," Craig murmured.

"What did you say?" Klein asked.

"Nothing."

"Well, anyway," Klein said, "Thomas thinks Wadleigh's just the man to bring out the feeling he's looking for in the script. Whatever that means. Don't blame *me*, Jesse. I had nothing to do with it. It wouldn't occur to me in a million years to read a book by Ian Wadleigh. You know my position—my client wants him—I try to get him. How the hell was I to know that you're Malcolm Harte?"

"I understand," Craig said. "I don't blame you."

"The question is, What am I going to tell Thomas? Will you talk to Wadleigh at least? Let him read the script and see what his ideas are?"

"Sure," Craig said. "I have no objections to talking to him." While Klein had been talking, the idea of collaboration with Wadleigh had begun to seem attractive. The uncertainty that had made him put a *nom de plume* on the title page of the script had not been dispelled by Thomas's approval. The thought of sharing final responsibility was not unwelcome. And Wadleigh's talent, however tarnished, was a real one. Finally, he knew, there almost never was a screenplay that was completely the work of one pair of hands. "I don't promise anything," Craig said, "but I'll talk to him."

"There's another thing," Klein said. Now he looked embarrassed. "There's no sense in not putting it all on the table right from the beginning. You know, Thomas has produced his last two pictures himself. He doesn't need another producer and . . ."

"If he wants to do this picture," Craig said crisply, "he needs another producer. And that producer is me."

"Murph . . ." Klein looked appealingly to Murphy.

"You heard what the man said," Murphy said.

"Okay," Klein said. "There's nothing I can do about it, one way or another. I think the best thing we all can do is get on a plane to New York and talk it out with Thomas. And take Ian Wadleigh along with us and see if we can fit all the pieces together."

Murphy shook his head. "I'm due in Rome next week and London the week after that. Tell Thomas to wait."

"You know Thomas," Klein said. "He won't wait. He's got another commitment starting in January, and everybody'll have to work day and night to get this one in the can before then. One of the things he likes about your script, Jesse, is that it's easy to do and he can fit it in."

"Jess?" Murphy said. "You're really the one who has to do the talking. I can come in later."

"I don't know," Craig said. "I'll have to think about it."

"I'm going to call Thomas tonight," Klein said. "What should I tell him?"

"Tell him I'm thinking about it," Craig said.

"He'll love that," Klein said sourly. He stood up. "Anybody want a drink?"

"No, thanks." Craig stood up, too. "I have to get back to Cannes. I appreciate what you've done so far, Walt."

"Just out to turn an honest dollar for me and my friends," Klein said. "I don't know why the fuck you didn't use your own name."

"I'll tell you some day," Craig said. "Murph, why don't you drive with me to Cannes? Tell your chauffeur to pick you up at the Carlton."

"Yeah." Murphy looked strangely subdued.

Klein walked out with them to the courtyard. They all shook hands ceremonially, and then there was the ringing of the telephone from inside the house, and Klein hurried in as Craig and Murphy drove off, the chauffeur following in Murphy's Mercedes.

Murphy was silent for a long time, staring out at the wild green countryside, the trees throwing long shadows in the evening light. Craig didn't speak, either. He knew that Murphy was troubled and was preparing himself for the conversation that had to take place.

"Jess," Murphy said finally, his voice low. "I want to apologize."

"There's nothing to apologize for."

"I'm a horse's ass," Murphy said. "An old horse's ass."

"Cut that," Craig said.

"I've lost my touch. I'm just no good any more."

"Oh, come on, Murph. Everybody makes mistakes. I could tell you about some of mine." He thought of Edward Brenner in the empty theatre on the night after the final performance of Brenner's last and best play.

Murphy shook his head sadly. "I had that script in my hand, and I told you to forget it, and that little punk Klein got you the hottest director in the business for it with one telephone call. What the hell do you need me for?"

"I need you," Craig said. "Is that clear enough? I should have told you I wrote it myself."

"That makes no difference," Murphy said. "Even though it was a crappy thing to do to me. After all these years."

"I have my own problems," Craig said. "You know some of them."

"Yeah," Murphy said. "There's one big problem I could have helped you with—should have helped you with—a long time ago . . . And I didn't."

"What's that?"

"Your goddamn wife."

"What could you have done?"

"I could have warned you. I knew what was happening."

"So did I," Craig said. "In general. And late in the game. But I knew."

"Did you ever figure out why she did it?" Murphy asked. "I mean, she wasn't a nymphomaniac or anything like that. It wasn't as though she couldn't control herself. She isn't one of those women who throw themselves in bed with the boy who delivers the groceries, for Christ's sake."

"No, she isn't."

"Has it ever occurred to you how she made her choices?"

"Not really."

"If this is painful to you, Jess, I'll shut up."

"It's painful," Craig said, "and don't shut up."

"She always picked your friends," Murphy said, "people who admired you, people you worked with, people *you* admired."

"I can't say that I'm wild with admiration for her last choice," Craig said.

"Even him," Murphy insisted. "He's a successful man, successful at something that you're lousy at, that you're ashamed you're lousy at. You went to him for advice. You trusted him with your money. Do you see what I mean?"

"In a way," Craig said, "yes."

"And all these people always wanted to see you, listen to you, you were the center of attraction. She was always in the background. There was one way she could stop being in the background. And she took it."

"And she took it." Craig nodded.

"I saw it a long time ago," Murphy said. "So did Sonia. And while there was still time to do something about it, I kept my mouth shut, I left you with your problem. And how do I make up for it?" He shook his head mournfully again. "I become another one of your problems." He looked tired, somehow diminished, sitting in the small car, his bulk slack in the flimsy bucket seat, his voice weary, his face sorrowful in the moving shadows from the trees that lined the road.

"You're not a problem," Craig said sharply. "You're my friend and my partner, and you've done wonders for me in the past, and I expect you to do wonders for me in the future. I wouldn't know what to do without you."

"Being an agent is a joke," Murphy said. "I'm a sixty-year-old joke."

"Nobody thinks you're a joke," Craig said. "Not me

and certainly not anyone who has to do business
with you. Snap out of it." He hated to see Murphy,
whose style, whose reason for living, even, was to be
robust, assured, overriding, in a mood like this.

"If you want, Jess," Murphy said, "I'll cancel Rome
and London and fly to New York with you."

"Unnecessary," Craig said. "You'll come on stronger when they know they have to wait for you."

"Don't make any concessions before I get there."
Murphy's voice was stronger now. "Don't give a fucking inch. Let me think about it overnight, and tomorrow you tell me exactly what you want and we'll figure out just how much of it you can get and how
you can get it."

"That's more like it," Craig said. "That's why I
told Klein to ask you to be there when I saw him."

"Christ," Murphy said loudly, "how I hate to have
to split a commission with that little punk."

Craig laughed. Then Murphy laughed, too, sitting
up straighter in the bucket seat, his laughter resound-
ing in the little car.

But when they reached the Carlton, he said, "Jess,
do you have an extra copy of the script? I'd like to
read it again, just to see how stupid I can be."

"I'll have it for you tomorrow," Craig said. "Give
my love to Sonia."

When Murphy got out of the Simca and walked
over to his own car, he was striding imperiously,
huge and dangerous, a terrible man to cross. Craig
couldn't help grinning as he saw his friend hurl himself into the big black Mercedes.

The lobby of the hotel was crowded. There were
already people in dinner jackets and evening gowns,
dressed for the showing in the Festival Hall that
night. Automatically, as he made his way to the concierge's desk, Craig looked around the lobby to see if
Gail was there. There were many familiar faces, Joe

Reynolds' among them, but no Gail. Reynolds' bruises had turned a streaky yellow. It didn't help his looks. He was talking earnestly to Eliot Steinhardt. A large young man with a blond beard was standing near the elevator, and Craig felt him staring at him. While Craig was collecting his mail and his key, the young man with the beard came up to him. "Mr. Craig?" he said.

"Yes."

"I'm Bayard Patty," the young man said.

"Yes?"

"I mean I'm Anne's friend. From California."

"Oh, how do you do?" Craig extended his hand, and Patty shook it. He had an enormous, crushing hand.

"I'm very pleased to meet you, sir," Patty said. He sounded mournful.

"Where is Anne?" Craig said. "Let's get her and have a drink."

"That's what I've been waiting to talk to you about, Mr. Craig," Patty said. "Anne's not here. She's gone away."

"What do you mean, she's gone away?" Craig said sharply.

"She's gone away, that's all," Patty said. "This morning. She left me a note."

Craig turned back to the concierge. "Has my daughter checked out?" he asked.

"Yes, *monsieur*," the concierge said. "This morning."

Craig looked through his mail and messages. There was nothing there from Anne. "Did she leave a forwarding address?" he asked the concierge.

"No, *monsieur*."

"Patty," Craig said, "did she tell you where she was going?"

"No, sir," Patty said. "And please call me Bayard. She just vanished."

"Wait here for me, Bayard," Craig said. "Maybe there's a note from her in my room."

But there was nothing from Anne in his apartment. He went downstairs again. Patty was waiting near the desk like a huge, faithful, shaggy Newfoundland.

"Was there anything?" Patty asked.

Craig shook his head.

"She's a peculiar girl," Patty said. "I just got here yesterday. I flew over the Pole."

"I think we both could use a drink," Craig said. He felt very small walking beside the enormous young man along the corridor toward the bar. Patty was dressed in blue jeans and skivvy shirt and a light brown windbreaker. He limped a little, too, which made him even more conspicuous among the dinner jackets and jewelry.

"I see you're still limping," Craig said.

"Oh, you know about that." Patty sounded surprised.

"Anne told me about it."

"What else did she tell you about me?" There was a childish bitterness in the way Patty asked the question that was incongruous in a man his size.

"Nothing much else," Craig said diplomatically. He was certainly not going to repeat Anne's judgment on the bearded boy from San Bernardino.

"Did she tell you I wanted to marry her?"

"I believe she did."

"You don't think there's anything so all-out horrible or depraved about a man wanting to marry the girl he loves, do you?"

"No."

"It cost me a fortune to fly over the Pole," Patty said. "I see her for a few hours—she wouldn't even let me stay in the same hotel—and then, bang, there's a note saying she's leaving and good-by. Do you think she'll be coming back here?"

"I have no idea."

All the tables were full, and they had to stand at the crowded bar. More familiar faces. "I tell you," a young man was saying, "the British film industry has signed its death warrant."

"Maybe I should have put on a suit," Patty said, looking around uneasily. "I *own* a suit. In a fancy place like this."

"Not necessary," Craig said. "Nobody notices how anybody dresses anymore. For two weeks here you have a really open society."

"You can say that again," Patty said sourly. He ordered a martini. "That's one good thing about my leg," he said. "I can drink martinis."

"What's that?"

"I mean I don't have to worry about keeping in shape and all that crap. I'll tell you something, Mr. Craig, when I heard my knee go, I was relieved, mightily relieved. You want to know why I was relieved?"

"If you want to tell me." Craig sipped his whisky and watched Patty knock off half his martini in one gulp.

"I knew I didn't have to play football anymore. It's a game for beasts. And being my size, I didn't have the guts to quit. And another thing—when I heard it snap, I thought, 'There goes Vietnam.' Do you think that's unpatriotic?"

"Not really," Craig said.

"When I got out of the hospital," Patty went on, wiping the martini-damp beard with the back of his hand, "I decided I could finally ask Anne to marry me. There was nothing hanging over us anymore. Only her," he added bitterly. "What the hell has she got against San Bernardino, Mr. Craig? Did she ever say?"

"Not that I remember," Craig said.

"She's given me proof that she loves me," Patty said

belligerently. "The most convincing proof a girl can give. As recently as yesterday afternoon."

"Yes, she mentioned something about that," Craig said, although the yesterday afternoon surprised him. Unpleasantly. Most convincing proof. What proof had *he* given yesterday afternoon in Meyrague? The boy's vocabulary had not yet emerged from the Victorian era. It was somehow touching. Anne had not been circumspect in her choice of words when she had spoken on the subject.

"I've *got* to go back to San Bernardino," Patty said. "I'm the only son. I've got four sisters. *Younger* sisters. My father worked for a lifetime to build up his business. He's one of the most respected men in the town. What am I supposed to say to my father—'You did it all for nothing'?"

"I find your attitude refreshing," Craig said.

"Anne doesn't," Patty said dolefully. He finished his drink, and Craig motioned for two more. He wondered how he was going to get rid of the boy. If music was the food of love, Patty was a high school band playing the school anthem between halves of a football game. He couldn't help grinning slightly at the thought.

"You think I'm foolish, don't you, Mr. Craig?" Patty asked. He had noticed the twitch of Craig's lips.

"Not at all, Bayard," Craig said. "It's just that you and Anne seem to have two different sets of values."

"Do you think she'll change?"

"Everybody changes," Craig said. "But I don't know if she'll change in your direction."

"Yeah." Patty hung his head, his beard down on his chest. "I don't like to say this to any girl's father," he said, "but the truth is I'm a shy man, and I don't make advances to anybody. Your daughter led me on."

"That's quite possible," Craig said. "You're a handsome young man and, as far as I can tell, a very nice one . . ."

"Yeah," Patty said without conviction.

To cheer him, Craig said, "She even told me that when you walked on the beach, you looked as though you belonged on a marble pedestal in Thrace."

"What does that mean?" Patty asked suspiciously.

"It's very flattering." Craig handed him his second martini.

"It doesn't sound so damned flattering to me," Patty said, taking a gulp from his drink. "Actions speak louder than words, I always say. And your daughter's actions are mystifying, to say the least. Ah, what the hell—I know how she's been brought up . . ."

"How do you think she's been brought up, Bayard?" Craig honestly wanted to know.

"Fancy school in Lausanne. Speaking French. Famous father. All the money in the world. Talking to high-flying people all her life. I must look like a big Mr. Nobody to her. I suppose I ought to have more sense. Only when I think about her, I don't have any sense at all. You must have *some* idea, Mr. Craig —do you think she'll come back here or not?"

"I really don't know," Craig said.

"I have to be back in California in a week," Patty said. "They're operating on my knee again. They promise me I'll be able to walk okay in three months. So it's not as though she'd be marrying a cripple or anything like that. One year ago, if anybody'd told me that me, Bayard Patty, would fly six thousand miles across the Pole to come to France to see a girl for one week, I'd have told them they were crazy. I tell you, Mr. Craig, I don't think I can live without her." There were tears in the bright, clear blue eyes. "I sound dramatic, don't I?" he said, pushing an enormous hand at his eyelids.

"A little."

"I mean every word I say," Patty said. "She's got to get in touch with you, doesn't she?"

"Eventually."

"Will you tell her that she's got to phone me?"

"I'll pass on the word."

"What do you think of me, Mr. Craig? Honestly. You've lived through a lot. You've seen people come and go. Am I so bad?"

"I'm sure not."

"I'm not the smartest guy in the world. But I'm not the dumbest, either. It's not as though I'd be dragging her down. I'd respect her tastes. I'd be happy to respect her tastes. You've been married, Mr. Craig. You know. It isn't as though marriage has to be a prison, for God's sake. That's what she said, Anne, prison."

"I'm afraid my marriage hasn't given my daughters a very encouraging example," Craig said.

"I know you're separated," Patty said, "and I know you and your wife aren't on very good terms . . ."

"That's one way of putting it," Craig said.

"But that doesn't mean *every* marriage has to break up," Patty said doggedly. "Hell, my father and mother have had some pretty rough times. Still have. You should hear some of the arguments around my house. But that hasn't scared me off. Even having four sisters hasn't scared me off . . ."

"You're a brave man, Bayard."

"I'm not in the mood for jokes, sir," Patty said.

"I wasn't really joking," Craig said soothingly. It occurred to him that if Patty ever got angry, he'd be a ferocious man to deal with.

"Anyway," Patty said, partially placated, "if you'd put in a good word for me with Anne when you hear from her, I'd deeply appreciate it."

"I'll put in a word," Craig said. "Whether it will be good or not only time will tell."

"It helps me to talk to you, Mr. Craig," Patty said. "It's a, well—a kind of connection with Anne. I don't like to impose, but I'd be honored if you'd allow me to take you to dinner tonight."

"Thank you, Bayard," Craig said. He felt he had to repay some devious family debt. "That'd be very nice."

There was a tap on his shoulder. He turned. Gail was standing there in the same print dress she had worn at Klein's party. They stared at each other for a moment in silence. "Buy me a drink," she said.

"Do you know Bayard Patty?" Craig said. "Gail McKin—"

"Yes, we've met," Gail said. The man who was sitting next to Craig got up from his stool, and Gail swung up and sat down, putting her bag on the bar.

"Good evening, Miss McKinnon," Patty said. "Anne introduced us," he explained to Craig.

"I see." Craig wished that Patty would disappear. "What are you drinking?" he asked Gail.

"Champagne, please," she said. She looked fresh, demure, as though she had never drunk a glass of champagne in her life or was ever capable of asking a man if she was as good a lay as her mother.

Craig ordered the champagne. "Bayard tells me that Anne left this morning. Do you happen to know anything about it?"

Gail looked at him queerly. She didn't speak for a moment but shifted her bag on the bar. "No," she said finally. "Nothing. Did you have a good time in Marseilles?"

"How did you know I was in Marseilles?"

"All movements are charted," she said. "Walt Klein was spastic because he couldn't reach you."

"It's a charming town, Marseilles. I recommend it to you," Craig said. "Yes, I had a good time."

Gail sipped at her champagne. "Are you staying on here in Cannes, Mr. Patty?"

"Call me Bayard, please. I'm not sure. I'm not sure of anything."

"We're having dinner together, Bayard and I," Craig said. "Would you like to join us?"

"Sorry," she said. "I'm waiting for Larry Hennessy. They're showing his picture tonight, and he's too nervous to sit through it. I promised I'd have dinner with him and hold his hand. Some other night, perhaps?" Her tone was flat, deliberately provocative.

"Perhaps," Craig said.

"There's going to be a party in his rooms after the showing," Gail said. "I'm sure he'd be delighted if you two gentlemen came along."

"We'll see how we feel," Craig said.

"I'm doing a piece on him," Gail said. "The other piece I was doing seems to have fallen through. He's a sweet man. And wonderfully cooperative." She sipped her champagne. "With other people it's so uphill. Ah, there he is." She waved toward the door. "Oh, dear, he's being waylaid by bores. I'd better go and rescue him. Thanks for the wine." She slipped off her stool and strode toward the door where Hennessy was talking volubly to two women and not seeming bored at all.

"I don't like to say this, Mr. Craig," Patty said, "and I only met her yesterday, but I have the feeling that girl isn't a good influence on Anne."

"They hardly know each other," Craig said shortly. "Look, I have to go up and shower and change. I'll meet you in the lobby in half an hour."

"Do you think I ought to put on my suit for dinner?" Patty asked.

"Yes," Craig said. Let him suffer, too, that evening, with a tie around that bull neck. Craig paid for all the drinks and went out through the terrace entrance so that he wouldn't have to pass the door where Hennessy stood talking jovially, his arm around Gail McKinnon's shoulders.

It was almost an hour later that he went down to the lobby. Before starting to get dressed, he had picked up a copy of *The Three Horizons* and had glanced through it. Knowing that other people had read it, had liked it well enough to start the whole intricate and exhausting process of bringing it to life on the screen, made him review his work with fresh eyes. Despite himself, he felt the old excitement run through him as he read the pages. They were not dead to him anymore. Ideas for casting, for changes in the writing, for using the camera, for the kind of music for specific scenes, flooded through his mind. He had to wrench himself away from the script to shave and take his shower and dress. He couldn't leave poor Bayard Patty standing in the lobby all night, bereft and pitiful in his suit, waiting for him.

He was annoyed with Anne's behavior but not much more than that. He wasn't really worried about her. She was a grown girl and could take care of herself. She had been cruel to Patty, and not being cruel himself, he disapproved. When he saw her, he would make that clear. Going to bed with the boy and then disappearing the next morning was a monstrous thing to do, but she was not the first girl to waver, then run away from a problem. Nor the first man, either. Nor the first member of the Craig family, if it came to that.

He called Klein and got Bruce Thomas's address in New York. Pleased with his own impatience, he told Klein that he would take the plane the next day.

"That's what I like to hear," Klein said. "Get the wheels moving. This Festival has run out of gas, anyway. You're not missing anything." There was the babble of many voices over the telephone. Klein was giving a cocktail party. He was getting his money's worth out of his five-thousand-dollars-a-month rent. Craig felt benevolent and unwontedly friendly toward the man. The world was full of useful people, and Klein was one of them. He would have to get Murphy to stop calling him that little punk.

He wrote out a cable to Thomas telling him he

was arriving in New York and would call as soon as he landed. He thought of sending a telegram to Constance canceling their lunch date on Monday, then decided against it. He would call her in the morning and explain. He knew she'd understand. And approve. And New York was closer to San Francisco.

In the lobby, with Bayard Patty standing next to him in a dark blue suit and necktie, he gave the cable to Bruce Thomas to the concierge and asked him to reserve a seat on a plane the next day from Nice to New York.

Patty looked forlorn as he listened to Craig's conversation with the concierge. "You're leaving so soon?" he said. "What if Anne comes back?"

"You'll have to take care of her," Craig said.

"Yeah," Patty said without conviction.

They got into the car, and Craig drove to Golfe Juan where they ate in a seafood restaurant built right on the beach. The sea was rough and growled at the pilings on which the restaurant was built. Patty drank more wine than was good for him and was garrulous. By the end of the meal Craig knew all about his family, his politics, his ideas of love and student revolt. ("I'm not a typical jock, Mr. Craig, I'll tell you that. Most of the things the kids are complaining about, they're right. But I don't go along with taking over buildings and bombing banks and crazy stuff like that. At least that's one thing Anne and I agree about. My father thinks I'm a wild-eyed Red, but I'm not. And there's one thing about my father—you can stand up to him like a man and he listens to you and tries to see your point of view. When you get out to California, you've got to meet him. I'll tell you something, Mr. Craig, I'm a lucky man to have a father like that.") At no point did he say that Anne was a lucky girl to have a father like Craig. He had seen two of Craig' movies and was polite about them. He was a polite young man. By the end of the meal Craig was certain that, politics or no politics, it would be disastrous for Bayard Patty if his daughter married him, but he didn't think he had to tell the boy that.

By the time they had had their coffee, it was still too early to go to the Hennessy party, which wouldn't begin until around midnight. And Craig wasn't sure that he wanted to go to the party or that Patty would be at ease there.

"How old are you?" he asked as they went out of the restaurant toward the car. (Patty had insisted on paying for the dinner.) "Over twenty-one?"

"Just," Patty said. "Why?"

"Have you got your passport with you?"

"What do you want me to do?" Patty asked in a flare of belligerence. "Prove it to you?"

Craig laughed. "Of course not. I thought we might take in the casino. You ought to see some of the sights, anyway, as long as you're here. And you need your passport to get in." At the gambling tables he would be spared the boy's dejected confidences for an hour or two.

"Oh, I'm sorry," Patty said. "Sure. I have it in my pocket."

"Would you like to go?"

"What have I got to lose?"

"Money," Craig said. "That's all."

In the casino, Craig explained briefly about roulette and put Patty next to a croupier to help him out. He himself sat down at a chemin de fer table. He had only played the one time since coming to Cannes, the night he had loaned Wadleigh the three hundred dollars, the night Murphy had told him to forget the idea of putting on *The Three Horizons*. He chuckled to himself, remembering Murphy on the phone. As he sat down at the table, he thought comfortably, I'm thirty thousand francs ahead, I can afford to fool around.

From time to time, when they were making up a

new shoe at his table, Craig went over to where Patty was playing. There was a sizable pile of chips in front of Patty and an intent and fascinated glint in his eyes. I have introduced him to a new vice, Craig thought. But at least, putting his money on the numbers and on the red or black, he wasn't mooning about Anne.

A place fell vacant at his table opposite his, and a woman sat down at it. She was a buxom woman in a bare-shouldered white silk dress that left a good deal of craftily engineered bosom showing. Her hair was marvelously set, and there was a considerable amount of heavy eye shadow. Thin, incongruous lips in the round, lacquered face were filled out dramatically in gleaming red. The deeply tanned skin of shoulders and bosom shone as though it had been oiled. Her fingers, armed with long curved crimson nails, were heavy with diamonds, which Craig, who was not expert at such matters, took for authentic. She had carried a pile of big chips from another table and placed them geometrically in front of her, tapping possessively on them with the long painted fingertips. She looked across at him and smiled cunningly, without warmth.

Now he recognized her. It was the plump woman who had been sunning herself when he and Murphy had passed on the way to the bar at the Hotel du Cap. He remembered the sweaty makeup, the naked, spoiled expression, the marks on the ill-tempered, self-loving face, he had thought, of grossness, devouring lust. The other side of the sensual coin. He was sorry she had come to the table.

He was sure she would win. She did. After a few hands he got up from the table, carrying his winnings. The pile of chips in front of Patty had grown somewhat, and Patty was hunched over the table in deep concentration on the spinning wheel.

"I've had it, Bayard," Craig said. "I'm cashing in. How about you?"

Patty seemed to come back from a long distance as he turned at the sound of Craig's voice. "Yeah, yeah," he said. "I might as well quit while I'm ahead."

At the cashier's desk Craig saw that Patty had won a little over a thousand francs. "How much is that in dollars?" Patty asked.

"About two hundred and fifty."

"What do you know," Patty said wonderingly. "As easy as that. Well, like they say, lucky in love . . ."

"Oh, come on now, Bayard," Craig said.

"Anyway," the boy said, "it helps pay for the trip." He folded the bills neatly and put them into an ostrich-skin wallet with gold corners. He stared mournfully at the wallet. "Anne gave this to me," he said. "In better days. It has my initials on it."

They walked back to the hotel. They were solicited several times by whores. "Disgusting," Patty said. "Open like that." He said he didn't want to go to the Hennessy party. "You know as well I do, Mr. Craig," he said, "parties like that aren't for me." He went into the lobby of the hotel with Craig just in case there was a message from Anne. There was no message.

"If I hear anything before I leave, I'll let you know," Craig said. He felt uneasy in the boy's presence, as though he were deserting him.

"You're a friend," Patty said. "I regard you as a real friend, Mr. Craig."

Craig watched the enormous form of his daughter's lover limp forlornly out into the night through the lobby doors.

I have done my duty as a father, Craig thought, as the boy disappeared. Or part of my duty.

The door to Hennessy's apartment was open, and the noise of the party could be heard all the way down the hall. It was the unmistakable noise of success. Hennessy's movie must have been very well received that evening. There was also the equally unmistakable smell of marijuana floating out through the open door.

In my day, Craig thought, we just got drunk. Was there what the professors of sociology called a value judgment there?

The room was crowded as Craig pushed in. Murray Sloan, the critic from the trade paper, was standing next to a big table ranged with bottles. He was not smoking marijuana. Faithful to an older tradition, he was loading up on free whisky. On a big couch against the wall on the other side of the room Gail was sitting next to the hero of the evening. Hennessy was in his shirt sleeves, in suspenders, beaming and rosy and sweating. He was sharing a joint with Gail, who looked remote and cool, beyond the noise and celebration.

"How did it go tonight, Murray?" Craig asked Sloan.

"As you can see." Sloan waved his glass at the chattering guests. "They slobbered over it."

"Is that what you're going to write?"

"No. I'm going to write that it was full of genial, rough American humor and that the audience reaction was all that the producers could hope for. It is a candidate for the highest honors." Sloan teetered a little, decorously, and Craig could see that he had done his drinking diligently. "Another thing that I am not going to write is that the money spent on hash tonight would have financed a small-budget pornographic film. Another thing I am not going to write is that if it wasn't for the free liquor, I would never go to another festival. And how are you, my friend? Is there any news of you I ought to put on the telex?"

"No," Craig said. "Have you seen Ian Wadleigh around?"

"No," Sloan said. "Old drinking companion. Notable by his absence. I heard about his big night with Murphy in the restaurant. He's probably crawled into a hole in the basement and pulled it in after him."

"Who told you about that?" Craig asked sharply.

"The wind speaks," Sloan said, teetering and smiling. "The Mistral mutters."

"Have you written anything about it?" Craig asked.

"I am not a gossip columnist," Sloan said with dignity. "Although others are."

"Has there been anything in any of the columns?"

"Not that I know of," Sloan said. "But I don't read the columns."

"Thanks, Murray." Craig moved away from the critic. He hadn't come to the party to spend his time with Murray Sloan. He made his way across the room toward Gail and Hennessy. Corelli, the Italian actor, was there, sitting boyishly on the floor, showing his teeth, with his inevitable two girls. Craig couldn't remember whether he had seen these particular two girls before or not. Corelli was sharing his cigarette with the girls. One of them said, "Pure Marrakesh heaven," as she exhaled. Corelli smiled sweetly up at Craig as Craig nearly stumbled over his outstretched foot.

"Join us, Mr. Craig," Corelli said. "Please do join us. You have a *simpatico* face. Doesn't Mr. Craig have a *simpatico* face, girls?"

"*Molto simpatico,*" one of the girls said.

"Excuse me," Craig said, being careful not to step on anyone as he made his way to Hennessy and Gail McKinnon. "Congratulations, Hennessy," he said. "I heard you killed them in there tonight."

Hennessy beamed up at him, tried to stand, fell back. "I am immortal tonight," he said. "Move over for the new Cecil B. DeMille. Isn't this a nice party? Booze, hash, and fame, with the compliments of the management."

"Hello, Gail," Craig said.

"Why, Malcolm Harte, as I live and breathe," Gail said. Craig couldn't tell whether she was drunk or drugged.

"What's that, what's that?" Hennessy said querulously. "Did I invite anybody else?"

"It's a private joke," Craig said, "between Gail and myself."

"Great girl, this kid," Hennessy said, patting Gail's arm. "Drank me drink for drink all night long while my fate was being decided on the Côte d'Azur. Interested in my early life. Up from slavery. Amateur boxer, truck driver, stunt man, pool hustler, bartender, publicity man . . . What else was I, dear?"

"Garage mechanic, farmhand . . ."

"That's it." Hennessy beamed at her. "She's got me down pat. Perfect American banality. I'm famous, and she's going to make me famous, aren't you, dear?" He passed his cigarette to Gail, and she drew in a long draft, closing her eyes as she did so.

This isn't any party for me, Craig thought. "Good night," he said as Gail opened her eyes and slowly let out the sweetish smoke. "I just wanted to tell you I'm leaving for New York tomorrow."

"Traveling man," Gail said, giving the cigarette back to Hennessy. "Good night, traveling man."

He was awakened by the ringing of the telephone. It seemed to him that he had never been asleep, that he was in the middle of one of those dreams in which you feel you are really awake but are dreaming that you are asleep. He fumbled for the telephone in the darkness.

"I knocked and knocked," Gail said, "but nothing happened." Her voice sounded as if she, too, were in his dream.

"What time is it?"

"Three A.M.," she said, "and all's well. I'm coming up."

"No, you're not," he said.

"I'm floating, floating," Gail said. "And I'm horny. Beautifully horny for the touch of my true love's lips."

"You're stoned," he said.

She giggled. "Beautifully stoned. Beautifully horny. Leave the door open."

"Go home and go to bed," he said.

"I have a joint with me. The most beautiful Moroccan kif. Leave the door open for me. We'll drift away together into the most beautiful Moroccan heaven."

He hesitated. He was fully awake now. The familiar dreamy caressing voice troubled him, traveled insinuatingly along the electric circuits of his nerves.

Gail giggled again. "You're crumbling," she said. "My true love is crumbling. I'm on my way up." There was the click of the telephone.

He thought for a moment, remembering what it had been like to make love to her. Young girl's skin. The soft, bold hands. It would be the first and last time he would ever know what the rest of the world seemed to know about drugs. Whatever else Gail was at the moment, she was certainly happy. If he was to share that secret and delicious happiness for an hour or two, who would be the loser? He was going to be on another continent in twenty hours. He would never see her again. Another ordered life was to begin for him tomorrow. He had one last night to enjoy the pleasures of chaos. He knew that if he kept the door closed, there would be no sleep for him that night. He got out of bed and went to the door, unlatched it. He was naked, and he stretched out on top of the bed sheets and waited.

He heard the door open, close, heard her come into the room. "Sssh, sssh, my true love," she whispered.

He lay still, heard her undress in the darkness, saw

her face briefly in the flare of the match as she lit up. She came over to the bed, got in beside him without touching him, moved a pillow, sat up cross-legged, propped against it, the pinpoint of light glowing and getting larger as she pulled at the beautiful Moroccan kif. She handed him the cigarette. "Keep it down as long as you can," she said in her dreamy, remote voice.

He had given up smoking, from one day to the next, more than ten years ago, but he remembered how to inhale.

"Beautiful," she whispered. "Beautiful boy."

"What was your mother's name?" he asked. He had to ask quickly before the smoke began to take effect. Even the first lungful was already at work.

She giggled. "Full fathom five my mother lies," she said. She reached for the cigarette, touched his hand. He felt as though his body was being swept by a soft, warm wind. It was too late for questions.

They finished the joint slowly, alternating it from hand to hand. The room was misty with smoke. The sound from the sea outside was musical, a rhythmic, soothing resonance, an organ in a cathedral. She slid down beside him, touched him. They made love timelessly, tracklessly. She was all the girls, all the women of that southern coast, the plump, lustful woman stretched out on her belly in the sun with her legs apart, the blonde young mother at the pool, all of Corelli's bread-brown, bread-warm girls, Natalie Sorel, white-bosomed and dancing, Constance spelling Meyrague.

After, they did not sleep. Nor talk. They lay side by side in what seemed like an endless, perfect trance. But when the first light of dawn slanted in through the shutters, Gail stirred. "I must go now," she said. Her voice was almost normal. If he had had to speak, his voice would come from miles away. It made no difference to him whether she went or stayed, whether anyone went or stayed. Through a haze he watched her dress. Her party dress.

She leaned over him, kissed him. "Sleep," she said. "Sleep, my true love."

And she was gone. He knew he had a question to ask her, but he didn't know what the question was.

• SIXTEEN •

HE was almost finished with his packing. He moved with a minimum of luggage, and he could pack for anywhere in a quarter of an hour. He had a call in for Paris, but the operator had reported that all lines were busy. He had told her to keep trying.

When the phone rang, he picked it up without enthusiasm. He didn't relish having to explain to Constance that he wasn't going to take her to lunch on Monday, after all. But it wasn't Constance. It was Bayard Patty speaking in a voice that sounded as though someone had him by the throat. "I'm in the lobby, Mr. Craig," Patty said. "And I have to see you."

"I'm in the middle of packing and . . ."

"I tell you I have to see you," Patty said in that strangling voice. "I've heard from Anne."

"Come on up," Craig said, and told him the number of his apartment.

When Patty came into the room, he looked wild, his hair and beard disheveled, his eyes red-rimmed as though he hadn't slept in days. "Your daughter," he said accusingly. "Do you know what she's done? She's run off with that fat old drunken writer, Ian Wadleigh."

"Wait a minute," Craig said. He sat down. It was an automatic reaction, an attempt to preserve at least the appearance of reasonableness and convention. "It can't be. It's impossible."

"You say it's impossible." Patty stood over him, his hands working convulsively. "You didn't talk to her."

"Where did she call from?"

"I asked her. She wouldn't tell me. All she said was she was through with me, for me to forget her, she was with another man. That fat old drunken . . ."

"Hold on a second." Craig stood up and went over to the phone.

"Who're you phoning?"

Craig asked the operator for Wadleigh's hotel. "Calm down, Bayard," he said while waiting for the call to be put through.

"Calm down, you say. You're her father. Are *you* calm?" Patty strode over and stood close to him as though he didn't trust any message that Craig might give or receive and wanted to hear everything that was said with his own ear.

When the operator at Wadleigh's hotel answered, Craig said, *Monsieur* Wadleigh, *s'il vous plaît.*"

"*Monsieur* Wadleigh *n'est pas là,*" the operator said.

"What's she saying?" Patty asked loudly.

Craig waved to him to be quiet. "*Vous êtes sûre, madame?*"

"*Oui, oui,*" the operator said impatiently, "*il est parti.*"

"*Parti ou sorti,* madame?"

"*Parti, parti,*" the operator said, her voice rising. "*Il est parti hier matin.*"

"*A-t-il laissé une adresse?*"

"*Non, monsieur, non! Rien! Rien!*" by now the woman was shouting. The Festival was abrasive for hotel operators' nerves. The line went dead.

"What was all that about?" Patty demanded.

Craig took a deep breath. "Wadleigh checked out yesterday morning. He didn't leave any forwarding address. There's your French lesson for the day."

"Now, what are you going to do?" Patty demanded. He looked as though he was going to hit something. Probably me, Craig thought.

"I'm going to finish packing my bags," he said,

"and I'm going to pay my bill, and I'm going to drive to the airport, and I'm going to take a plane for New York."

"You're not going to look for her?" Patty asked incredulously.

"No."

"What kind of father are you, anyway?"

"I guess I'm the kind of father it's necessary to be these days," Craig said.

"If I was her father, I'd track him down and kill the bastard with my bare hands," Patty said.

"I guess we have different notions about fatherhood, Bayard," Craig said.

"It's your fault, Mr. Craig," Patty said bitterly. "You corrupted her. The life you live. Throwing money around as though it grew on trees. Running after young girls—don't think I don't know about that Gail McKinnon chick—"

"That's enough of that, Bayard," Craig said. "I know I can't throw you out of here personally, but I can get the police to do it for me. And even a very small French policeman can make things very uncomfortable for a very large young American."

"You don't have to threaten me, Mr. Craig, I'm going. Don't worry about that. I'm disgusted. With you and your daughter." He started to leave, then wheeled around. "I just want to ask you one question. Are you *happy* she's gone off with that old fart?"

"No," Craig said, "I'm not happy. Not at all happy." At the moment he didn't think it was necessary to remind Patty that Ian Wadleigh was quite a few years younger than Jesse Craig. "And I'm sorry for you, Bayard. I really am. And I think the best thing for you to do is take Anne's advice and forget about her."

"Forget about her." Patty shook his head sorrowfully. "That's easy to say. Forget about her. I'm not going to be able to do it, Mr. Craig. I know myself. I just won't be able. I don't know if I'll be able to *live* without her." His face contorted, and he was shaken by an enormous sob. "How do you like that," he said in a small voice. "I'm crying." He almost ran out of the room, slamming the door behind him.

Craig passed his hand wearily over his eyes. He had looked at himself closely while shaving, and he knew that he didn't look much better than Patty this morning. "The son of a bitch," he said aloud. "The miserable son of a bitch." He was not speaking of Bayard Patty.

He went into the bedroom and resumed his packing.

His plane would be an hour late in leaving, the man at the check-in counter told him. The man said it graciously, as though he were bestowing a gift on Craig. Sixty minutes extra of the civilization of France. Craig went over to the telegraph desk and sent an apologetic telegram to Constance. He was writing out a cable to his secretary in New York telling her to meet him at Kennedy and get him a hotel reservation when he heard Gail's voice saying, "Good morning."

He turned. She was standing beside him. She was wearing the blue polo shirt, the white, hip-hugging jeans. Her face was hidden behind dark green sunglasses, uselessly large, like the ones she had worn the first morning and then thrown out of the car on the way back from Antibes. Perhaps she bought them by the dozen.

"What are you doing here?" he asked.

"Seeing a friend off," she said, smiling. She took off the sunglasses, twirled them carelessly. She was fresh and clear-eyed. She might just have come from a dip in the sea. She was a perfect advertisement for the benefits of marijuana. "The concierge told me when your plane was leaving," she said. "You don't have much time."

"The concierge was wrong. The plane's an hour late," Craig said.

"One precious hour." Her tone was mocking. "Good old Air France," she said. 'Always time for farewell. Do we get a drink?"

"If you want," he said. Leaving was going to be more difficult than he had expected. He fought down the impulse to go over to the check-in counter and reclaim his luggage and tell the man there he had changed his mind about traveling. He gave the cable to the man behind the desk and paid. Carrying a leather envelope with the script of *The Three Horizons* in it and with a raincoat over his arm, he started toward the staircase up to the bar. He was sorry Gail had come. Seeing her there after the scene with Patty eroded the memory of their night together. He walked swiftly, but Gail kept up with him easily.

"You look funny," Gail said.

"I had an unusual night."

"I don't mean that. It's just that I've never seen you with a hat on before."

"I only wear a hat when I travel," he said. "It always seems to be raining everywhere when I get off a plane."

'I don't like it," she said. "'It adds other facets to your character. Disturbing facets. It makes you look more like everybody else."

He stopped walking. "I think we said good-by last night better than we can possibly do this morning," he said.

"I agree," she said calmly. "Ordinarily, I hate fraying away from people in waiting rooms and on train platforms. It's like old tired rubber bands stretching and stretching. But this is a special occasion. Wouldn't you say so?"

"I would say so." They started walking again.

They went out to the balcony overlooking the field and sat at a small table. He ordered a bottle of champagne. Just a few days before he had sat on the same balcony waiting for his daughter to arrive. She had arrived. He remembered the copy of *Educa-*

tion Sentimentale falling out of the canvas bag. He remembered being annoyed at the unattractive way she was dressed. He sighed. Gail, sitting across from him, did not ask him why he sighed.

When the waiter came with the champagne, Gail said, "That should do us for an hour."

"I thought you didn't drink until nightfall," he said.

"It looks pretty dark out there to me," she said.

They drank in silence, looking across the concrete to the blue sea at the field's edge. A ketch, heeling over in the wind, all sails taut, foamed through its bow wave on its way toward Italy.

"Holiday country," Gail said. "Will you sail away with me?"

"Maybe some other time," he said.

She nodded. "Some other time."

"Before I go—" He poured himself some more champagne—"you have to answer one question. What was all that about your mother?"

"Ah, my mother," Gail said. "I guess you have a right to ask. My mother is a woman of many interests." She twirled the stem of her glass absently and stared out at the white sails beyond the landing strip. "She went to art school for a while, she dabbled in pottery, she directed plays for a little theatre group, she studied Russian for a year, she took a Yugoslav ballet dancer as a lover for six months. One of the things that she *wasn't* interested in was my father. He had a merchant's soul, she told him, whatever that is. Another thing she wasn't interested in, it turned out, was me."

"She sounds like hundreds of women I've met in the course of my life," Craig said. "What did she have to do with *me*? I was never a Yugoslav ballet dancer."

"May I have some more wine, please?" Gail offered her glass. He filled it. The smooth muscles of her throat moved almost imperceptibly as she lifted her chin. He remembered kissing her throat. "She worked for you once. A long time ago. If I know my mother, you went to bed with her."

"Even if I did," he said angrily, "don't make it sound like incest."

"Oh, I didn't think of it that way at all," Gail said calmly. "I thought it was just a private joke. Between me and me. Don't worry, dear, I'm not your daughter."

"It never occurred to me that you were," he said. On the tarmac below a group of mechanics were working omniously on the undercarriage of the plane that was to fly him to New York. Perhaps he would never leave French soil. Or die on it. Gail sat across from him, lounging, aggravatingly at ease. "All right," he said, "what was her name, and when did she work for me?"

"Her name was Gloria. Gloria Talbot. Does that mean anything to you?"

He thought hard, then shook his head. "No."

"I suppose not. She only worked for you for a month or two. When your first play went on. She was just out of college, and she was hanging around the theatre, and she got a job in your office doing the scrapbooks, pasting up reviews and publicity stories about you and the people in the play."

"Good God, Gail," Craig said, "I must have hired and fired five hundred women since then."

"I'm sure," she said calmly. "But you seem to have had a special effect on dear old Mums. She just happened never to stop the good work. I don't imagine any of the other five hundred ladies got married and then continued to keep a scrapbook with every word written about you and every picture ever printed of you from 1946 to 1964. *'Jesse Craig to present new play by Edward Brenner this season. Jesse Craig signs one-picture deal with Metro. Jesse Craig to be married tomorrow. Photograph of Jesse Craig and wife leaving for Europe. Jesse Craig to . . .'*"

"Enough," he said. "I get the idea." He shook his

head wonderingly. "What would she want to do that for?"

"I never got a chance to ask her. Her loyalties were tangled, perhaps. I only came across all the clippings after she'd run off. When I was sixteen. With an archaeologist. I get postcards from Turkey, Mexico. Places like that. Twenty-two volumes bound in leather. In the attic. She was in such a hurry, she only packed an overnight bag. My father was only away for two days, and she had to move fast. I was cleaning out the attic—my father decided he didn't like the house anymore, and we were moving—when I came across them. Many's the happy hour I spent after that rummaging through the history of Jesse Craig." Gail smiled crookedly.

"That's how you knew so much about me."

"That's how. Do you want to know where you spent the summer of 1951? Do you want to know what *The New York Times* said about you on December 11, 1959? Ask me. I'll tell you."

"I'd rather not know," Craig said. "So you took it for granted that I'd had an affair with your mother because of all that?"

"If you knew my mother," Gail said, "you'd know it would be natural to take it for granted. Especially for a romantic sixteen-year-old girl sitting in an attic with her mother off in the wilderness someplace with an archaeologist. If you want, I can send you a picture of her to refresh your memory. People say I look like her when she was my age."

"I don't need any picture," Craig said. "I don't know what sort of life you think I led as a young man . . ."

"You led an enviable life. I've seen the expression on your face in the photographs."

"Perhaps. But one of the enviable things about me at that time was that I was in love with the woman I later married, and I believed she was in love with me, and I never looked at anybody else all that time. And no matter what it may seem like to you after this week, I've never been a promiscuous man, and I certainly remember the names of all the ladies I've ever . . ."

"Will you remember mine in twenty years?" Gail asked, smiling.

"I promise."

"Good. Now you know why I was so keen on seeing you when I found out you were in Cannes. I'd grown up with you. In a manner of speaking."

"In a manner of speaking."

"It was a sentimental reunion. You were a part of my family. Also in a manner of speaking." She reached over and poured some champagne for herself. "Even if you never touched my mother and never even knew her name, you had some sort of weird permanent effect on her. She was obviously fascinated with your life. And just as obviously dissatisfied with her own. And in some foolish way one thing was connected to the other. You can't really blame me if I began to look on you with some disfavor. And curiosity. Finally, I knew I had to meet you. Somehow. Remember I was only sixteen."

"You're not sixteen now."

"No, I'm not. I'll tell you the truth—I was *offended* by you. You were too successful. Everything turned out too well for you. You were always in the right places. You were always surrounded by the right people. You lived in a bath of praise. You never seemed to say the wrong thing. As you got older, you never even got fat in your pictures . . ."

"Newspaper handouts, for God's sake!" He gestured impatiently. "What could that possibly have to do with reality?"

"That's all I knew about you, remember," she said, "until I walked into your room. It was all such an awful contrast with my foolish mother, with her pottery and her Yugoslav and my father, scraping away at a miserable living in a dingy office in Philadelphia. First, I wanted to see what you were like. Then I wanted to do you as much harm as I could. I made a pretty good start, didn't I?"

"Yes, you did. And now . . . ?"

There was the silvery tinkle of the public address system and a woman's voice announcing that passengers were to board immediately for the flight to New York. Miraculously, the group of mechanics around the plane had disappeared. Gail reached over and touched the back of his hand lightly. "And now I think you'd better go down and get on your plane."

He paid, and they walked past the bar and down the steps to the main hall. He stopped as they came up to the passport control booth. "Am I going to see you again?" he asked.

"If you come to London. There will be complications, of course."

He nodded. "Of course." He tried to smile. "Next time you write to your mother," he said, "give her my regards."

"I'll do that," she said. She dug in her bag. "I have something for you." She pulled out a thick envelope. "The concierge gave it to me when I said I was going to see you off. It came just after you left."

He took the envelope. He recognized Anne's handwriting. The letter bore a Nice postmark. He looked up at Gail as he stuffed the envelope in his pocket. "You know about Anne?"

"Yes," she said. "We had a long discussion."

"Did you try to stop her?"

"No."

"Why not, for Christ's sake?"

"I was hardly in the position to."

"I suppose you're right." He put his hands on her arms, pulled her toward him, kissed her briefly. "Good-by," he said.

"Good-by, my true love," she said.

He watched her stride brusquely toward the exit of the terminal, her bag swinging from her shoulder, her long hair streaming brightly behind her and every man she passed looking hard at her. He saw that she took out the sunglasses and put them on as she approached the door. He felt bruised and old. They were announcing the departure of his plane as he went through the passport gate. He touched the bulk of Anne's letter in his pocket. Reading matter for the Atlantic.

A decorously dressed tall African with tribal scars and his pretty buxom wife, swathed in gorgeously colored silks, were the only other passengers in first class with him. Craig always felt guilty about paying for first class on airplanes and always paid. The African and his wife were speaking in a language he couldn't understand. He hoped they spoke no English or French. He didn't want to talk to anyone before he reached New York. The man smiled politely at him. He half-smiled in return, a rigidity of the lips, and looked out the window. It was not beyond the bounds of possibility, he thought, that twenty years from now they would meet again, perhaps in the final confrontation between the races, and the man, or his son or daughter, would say, "I remember you. You were the white traveler who refused the smile of friendship offered in the plane at Nice. You are a racist colonial, and I condemn you to die."

You were the helpless addition of the accidental and unconsidered moments of your history. Unknowing, you impinged upon the population of your past. Carelessly, you made a joke about a man you had never met—oblivious of his existence, you took his mistress to dinner—for the rest of his life he did what he could to harm you. A silly, stage-struck girl wandered into your office and was hired by your secretary and was a vague, nameless presence in the background for a month or two when you were a young man. More than twenty years later you suffered

—profited from?—the consequences of the acts, or the nonacts, of your early manhood. Nothing was lost, nothing forgotten. The man who had devised the first computer had merely organized the principle of inexorable memory into a circuit of wires and electrical impulses. Unnoticed passers-by noted your orbits, punched their private indestructible cards. For better or worse you were on file, the information was stored for eventual use. There was no escape. The process was perpetual. What would Sidney Green say about him among the unpaid-for *boiserie* in the Sixteenth Arrondissement? What would David Teichman's final instructions be concerning Jesse Craig before he died? How would Natalie Sorel refer to him in the mansions of Texas? What would be the reaction of Gail McKinnon's daughter upon hearing his name when she was twenty?

He looked hopefully toward the tall African across the aisle, but the man's face was averted. The engines started up, the demonic howl luxuriously muted by the sound-proofed hull. He took two Miltowns before the plane started to taxi. If he was going to crash, he was going to crash tranquilly.

He waited until after lunch was served before he opened Anne's letter. He knew that whatever she had to say would not improve his appetite.

There was no date on the letter and no address. Just "Dear Daddy . . ."

Dear Daddy put on his glasses. Anne's handwriting was difficult to decipher, and this was worse than ever. It looked as though it had been written while she was running down a steep hill.

"Dear Daddy," she wrote, "I'm a coward. I knew you'd disapprove and argue, and I was afraid you'd try to convince me and afraid you *would* convince me, so I'm taking the coward's way out. Just forgive me. Just love and forgive me. I'm with Ian. I thought a long time about it . . ."

How long was it, he thought. Three days, five? Well, perhaps when you're twenty years old, five days are a long time to figure out how to waste your life. He didn't remember.

"I won't go into the details," she wrote. "I'll just tell you that that night in the restaurant when Ian was treated so horribly by Mr. Murphy, I felt something that I'd never felt for anybody else in my life before. Call it love. I don't care what it's called. I felt it. Don't think it's just hero worship for a writer whose books I admire. And it's no schoolgirl crush. No matter what you may think, I'm past stuff like that. And I'm not looking for a father figure, which I'm sure you would have said if I had stayed to tell you. I have a perfectly good father. Anyway, Ian's only forty, and look at you and Gail McKinnon."

I am served, he thought, and well served. He asked the stewardess for a whisky and soda. It was a letter that needed alcohol. He looked out the window. The valley of the Rhone was hidden by cloud. The clouds looked so solid that you were tempted to believe that you could jump out and swim through them. He sipped at his whisky when the stewardess gave it to him and went back to the letter.

"Don't think for a minute," he read, "that I'm against anything you've done with Gail. I'm absolutely pro. After what you've gone through with Mummy, I wouldn't blame you if you took up with the bearded lady in the circus. And, good God, Gail is one of the best people I've ever met in my whole life. What's more, she told me she was in love with you. I said, of course, everybody's in love with him. And that's almost true. What you're going to do with the lady in Paris is your own business. Just like Ian is my own business.

"I know the arguments, I know the arguments. He's too old for me, he's a drunk, he's poor, he's out of fashion, he's not the handsomest man in the world, he's been married three times." Craig grinned sourly at the accurate description of the man his daughter was in love with.

"It's not as though I haven't taken these things into consideration," Anne wrote. "I've had long serious discussions with him about it all."

When? Craig wondered. The night he saw her leave the hotel and walk down the beach? On getting out of bed after having offered her convincing proof to Bayard Patty? He felt a pain at the back of his head, thought of aspirin.

"Before I told him I'd go away with him," Craig read on without aspirin, "I laid down conditions. I'm young, but I'm not an idiot. I've made him promise to quit drinking, first off. And I made him promise to come back to America. And he's going to keep his promises. He needs someone like me. He needs *me*. He needs to be esteemed. He's a proud man, and he can't go through life being derided, deriding himself, the way he's been doing. How many scenes like that one in the restaurant can a man go through in one lifetime?"

Oh, my poor daughter, Craig thought, how many women through the ages have ruined themselves under the illusion that they, and only they, can save a writer, a musician, a painter? The dread hold of art on the imaginations of the female sex.

"You're different," Anne wrote. "You don't need anyone's esteem. You're twenty times stronger than Ian, and I'm asking you to be charitable toward him. In the end, knowing you, I'm sure you will be.

"Sex is a big tangle, anyway, and you should be the first one to admit it." Craig nodded as he read this. But it was one thing to be forty-eight and come out with a truism like that, another to be twenty. "I know that I was mean to poor old Bayard, and I suppose he's got to you by now and has been crying on your shoulder. But that was just flesh . . ."

Craig squinted at the word, stopped on it. Flesh. It was a strange word for Anne to use. He wondered for a moment if Wadleigh had helped her write the letter.

"And flesh isn't enough." The scrawl dashed on. "If you've talked to Bayard, you must know that was impossible. Anyway, I never asked him to come to Cannes. If I'd married him, as he kept asking me to do (I nearly screamed, he was so insistent), in the long run I'd have been his victim. And I don't want to be anybody's victim."

Some day, Craig thought, I am going to make up a list for her. One thousand easy ways to be a victim.

"Don't be down on poor Ian for our sliding out the way we did. He wanted to stay and tell you what we were doing. I had the hardest time convincing him not to. Not for his sake but mine. He's in something of a daze for the time being. A happy daze, he says. He thinks I'm something extra-special, and he says he fell in love with me that first day on the beach. He says I'm so absolutely different from all the other women he's known. And he says he never dreamed I'd even look at him. He hasn't touched a drink in two days. Even before we left Cannes. He says it's a world record for him. And I read the part of the book he's working on that he has finished, and it's just wonderful, and if he doesn't drink, it'll be the best thing he's ever done. I'm convinced. And don't worry about money. I'm going to get a job, and with the money from the trust fund we can get along all right until the book is finished."

Craig groaned. The African with the tribal scars looked over at him politely. Craig smiled at the man, to reassure him.

"I'm sorry if I'm causing you any pain," Anne went on, "but later on I'm sure you'll be happy for me. I'm happy for myself. And you have Gail. Although it's more complicated with Gail than you think."

That's what *you* think, Craig almost talked back aloud to the page.

"There's a long story about her mother," Anne wrote, "that she told me but I haven't the time to go into now. Anyway, she told me that she was going to explain everything to you. Whatever it is, I'm sure it can't do you any discredit, no matter how it looks on the surface. I really am sure, Daddy.

"I'm still cowardly enough, even now with Ian at my side, not to tell you where we're going. Just for the moment I couldn't bear the thought of seeing you and having you disapprove of me in that reasonable, austere way you have. But as soon as we're settled in the States, I'll get in touch with you, and you can come and visit us and see for yourself that all is well. Please love me, Daddy, as I love you, Anne.

"P.S. Ian sends his best regards."

Best regards. Out of consideration for the African couple Craig refrained from groaning again. He folded the letter neatly and put it in his pocket. It would bear rereading.

He thought of Ian Wadleigh in bed with his daughter. "Miss," he said to the stewardess who was walking down the aisle, "do you have any aspirin?"

SEVENTEEN

BELINDA EWEN, his secretary, was waiting for him when he came through customs. He saw that she had not lost her disastrous taste for loud colors in her clothes since he had seen her last. She had been working for him twenty-three years, and it seemed to him that she had always been the same age. He kissed her on the cheek. She seemed happy to see him. He felt guilty because he hadn't answered her last two letters. If a woman has spent twenty-three years of her life working for you, how do you avoid feeling guilty when you see her?

"I have a limousine waiting for us," she said. She knew better than anyone that the money wasn't coming in as it had done for so long but would have been shocked if he suggested that a taxi would have done just as well. She had a fierce sense of their joint status. She screamed over the phone at agents when she discovered that scripts they had sent to the office had first been offered elsewhere.

It was a muggy, oppressive day, and it began to drizzle as they waited for the limousine to be brought around. He touched his hat grimly. The voices of the travelers piling into cars and taxis seemed harsh and angry to him. A child's screaming grated on his nerves. He felt tired, and the aspirin hadn't helped much.

Belinda peered at him anxiously, scrutinizing him. "You don't look well, Jesse," she said. He had been so young when he hired her that it had been impossible to ask her to call him Mr. Craig. "At least I thought you'd have a tan."

"I didn't go to Cannes to lie on the beach," he said. The limousine drove up, and he sank gratefully onto the back seat. Standing had been an effort. He was sweating, and he had to mop his face with a handkerchief. "Has it been as warm as this all along?" he asked.

"It's not so warm," Belinda said. "Now will you tell me why in the name of heaven you asked me to put you into the Manhattan Hotel? On Eighth Avenue, of all places!" He usually stayed at a quiet, expensive hotel on the East Side, and he could tell that in Belinda's eyes the change represented a demeaning attempt at economy. "I thought it would be more convenient," he said, "to be closer to the office."

"You're lucky if you're not mugged every time you go out the front door," Belinda said. "You don't know what Eighth Avenue is like these days." She had a sharp, aggressive voice. She had always had a sharp, aggressive voice, and for a while he had toyed with the idea of suggesting to her that she might go to a speech teacher. He had never quite had the courage. Now, of course, it was too late. He didn't tell her he had decided to go to the Manhattan only at the last moment, as he was writing out the cable to her in the Nice airport. The Manhattan was a brassy commercial hotel that he would ordinarily avoid, but he had suddenly remembered that he had lived there while he was putting on Edward Brenner's first play. With Edward Brenner. Now no longer writing plays. It had been called the Hotel Lincoln then. Presidents everywhere were being downgraded. He had been lucky at the Hotel Lincoln. He wished he could remember the number of the room. But he couldn't tell any of that to Belinda. She was too sensible a woman to pamper her employer's superstitions.

"You certainly didn't give me much warning," she said, aggrieved. "I just got your cable three hours ago."

"Something came up suddenly," he said. "I'm sorry."

"Anyway—" she smiled forgivingly. She had sharp little teeth, like a puppy's. "—anyway, I'm glad to have you back. The office has been like a morgue. I've been going mad with boredom. I even have taken to keeping a bottle of rum in my desk. I nip at it in the afternoons to keep sane. Don't tell me you've finally condescended to go to work again."

"In a way," he said.

"Hallelujah," she said. "What do you mean, in a way?"

"Bruce Thomas wants to do a script I own."

"Bruce Thomas," she said, impressed. "Oo, la, la." This was the year when everybody spoke the name of Bruce Thomas in a certain tone of voice, he noticed. He didn't know whether he was pleased or jealous.

"What script?" Belinda asked suspiciously. "I haven't sent you anything in three months."

"It's something I found in Europe," he said. "In fact, I wrote it myself."

"It's about time," she said. "It's got to be better than the junk we've been getting. You might have let me know," she said. She was hurt. "You might even have sent me a copy."

"Forgive me," he said. He reached over and patted her hand.

"Your hand is icy cold," she said. "Are you all right?"

"Of course," he said shortly.

"When do we start?" she asked.

"I'll know better after I see Thomas," he said. "There's no deal yet." He looked out the window of the car at the heavy clouds weighing on the flat landscape. "Oh," he said, "I wanted to ask you something.

Do you remember a woman by the name of Gloria
Talbot? I think she worked for us."

"Just in the beginning, for a couple of months,"
Belinda said. She remembered everything. "Absolutely incompetent."

"Was she pretty?"

"I suppose men thought she was pretty. My God,
it was nearly twenty-five years ago. What made you
think of her?"

"She sent me a message," Craig said. "Indirectly."

"She's probably on her fifth marriage," Belinda
said primly. "I spotted the type right off. What did
she want?"

"It was hard to say. I imagine she just wanted to
communicate," he said. Talking, somehow, was a
great effort. "If you don't mind, Belinda," he said,
"I'm going to try to nap a little. I'm absolutely
bushed."

"You travel too much," she said. "You're not a
baby anymore."

"I guess you might say that." He closed his eyes
and leaned his head back against the cushions.

His room was on the twenty-sixth floor. It was
misty outside, and drops of rain slid down the win-
dowpanes. The towers of the city were glints of glass,
dim tiers of light in the wispy late-afternoon grayness.
The room was hygienic and impersonal and had not
been furnished for Russian nobility. He could hear
horns from the Hudson River a few blocks away.
There was nothing in the room to remind him of the
lucky time with Brenner's play. It occurred to him
that he ought to find out where Brenner was buried
and lay a flower on the grave. Unpacking was an effort. The light clothes he had worn in Cannes seemed
incongruous in the rainy city. There were many
people whom he would call, but he decided to put it
off to another day. Still, there was one call he had to
make, to Bruce Thomas, who was expecting him.

He gave Thomas's number to the operator. The brisk, cheerful American voice of the operator was welcome after the shrill, harassed voices of the *standardistes* of Cannes. Thomas was cordial when he came to the phone. "Well, now," he said, "that was a surprise, your writing a script like that. A pleasant surprise." Klein had spoken to him. "I don't know exactly what we can work out, but we'll work out something. Are you busy now? Do you want to come over?"

Thomas lived on East Seventieth Street. The thought of trying to traverse the city was fatiguing. "Let's do it tomorrow, if you don't mind," Craig said. "The jet lag's got me."

"Sure," Thomas said. "How about ten in the morning?"

"I'll be there," Craig said. "By the way, do you happen to have Ian Wadleigh's telephone number in London?"

He could sense Thomas hesitating. "You know," Thomas said, "I suggested Wadleigh before I knew you'd written the script."

"I know," Craig said. "Have you talked to him yet?"

"No," Thomas said. "Naturally, I wanted to find out what you thought about it. But after Klein told me you didn't mind discussing it, I tried to get in touch with him. He's not in Cannes, and there's no answer at his London address. I've sent him a cable asking him to call me here. Wait a minute, I'll give you his number."

When he came back to the phone and gave Craig the number, Thomas said, "If you do find him, will you tell him I've been trying to reach him? And would you mind if I sent him a script? I've had some copies Xeroxed. There's no sense in his coming over here if for some reason or another he doesn't want to work on it."

"I think I heard somewhere that he's planning to

come back to the States to live, anyway," Craig said. Somewhere. Flying over France, heading toward the English Channel, the brave New World. *Dear Daddy*.

"That's interesting," Thomas said. "Good for him. See you in the morning. Have a good night." He was a nice man, Thomas, polite, thoughtful, with delicate manners.

Craig asked the operator for the London number and lay down on the bed to wait for the call. When he moved his head on the pillow, he felt dizzy, and the room seemed to shift slowly around him. "You travel too much," Belinda had said. Wise woman. Twenty-three years in the service. He was terribly thirsty, but he couldn't make himself get up and go into the bathroom for a glass of water.

The phone rang, and he sat up, having to move slowly to keep the room from spinning around him. The operator said that there was no answer at the London number and asked him if he wanted her to try again in an hour. "No," he said, "cancel the call."

He sat on the edge of the bed until the room steadied, then went into the bathroom and drank two glasses of water. But he was still thirsty. He was cold now, too, from the air conditioning. He tried to open a window, but it was nailed shut. He looked at his watch. It was six-thirty. Twelve-thirty tomorrow morning in Cannes. He had been up a long time, journeyed a great distance. He didn't remember ever having been so thirsty. An ice-cold glass of beer would do wonders for him. Maybe two. The next time he crossed the ocean, he decided, he would go by boat. America should be approached cautiously, in slow stages.

He went downstairs to the grill room, which was decorated with posters from plays. I am in a familiar arena, he thought. He remembered horns, the color of the sand in Saint Sebastian. He sat at the bar and ordered a bottle of beer, drank half the first glass in one gulp. The ache at the back of his throat subsided. He knew he should eat something, but all he wanted was more beer. He ordered another bottle, treasuring it, drinking slowly. By the end of the second bottle he felt pleasantly lightheaded. The grill room was filling up now, and he balanced the possibility of running into someone he knew and having to talk to him against the joy of one more bottle of beer. He decided to take the risk and ordered a third bottle.

It was nearly eight o'clock by the time he got back to his room. He hadn't had to talk to anybody. It was his lucky hotel. He undressed, put on pajamas, got into bed, and turned out the light. He lay there listening to the muted hum of the city far below him. A siren screaming past reminded him that he was in his native city. Ah, he thought regretfully as he slipped off to sleep, there will be no knock on my door tonight.

He awoke in pain. His stomach was contracting spasmodically. The bed was soaked in sweat. The pains came and went, sharp and stabbing. Christ, he thought, this must be something like what women go through in childbirth. He had to go to the bathroom. He put on the light, swung his legs carefully over the side of the bed, walked slowly into the bathroom, sat on the toilet. He could feel what seemed like gallons of hot liquid gushing out of him. The pain went down, but he wasn't sure he would be strong enough to get back to bed. When he finally stood up, he had to hold onto the shelf over the basin for support. The liquid in the toilet bowl was black. He pulled the chain. He felt a hot wetness dripping down the inside of his legs. It was blood, blackish red. There was no way in which he could control it. He wrinkled his nose in disgust. He knew he should be afraid, but all he felt was disgust at his body's betrayal. He got a towel and stuffed it up between his legs. Leaving his stained pajama bottoms on the bathroom floor, he made his way back to the bed and dropped on it. He felt weak, but there was no pain. For a moment he thought that he had dreamt it all. He looked at his watch. It was four-thirty in the morning. New York time, he remembered. Zone of blood. It was no hour to wake anyone. If he was still bleeding by eight o'clock, he would call a doctor. Then he realized that he didn't know the names of any doctors in New York. The penalty of health. He would figure it out in the morning. He put out the light and closed his eyes and tried to sleep. *If I die before I wake, I pray the Lord my soul* ... Childhood formulas.

Anne's psychology professor had seen something in his handwriting. Had he seen this night in New York?

Then he fell asleep. He slept without dreaming.

He was bone-tired when he awoke, marrow-tired. But there was no more bleeding. It was almost nine o'clock. There was pale, smog-diluted sunlight outside the window. The city shimmered in a haze of heat.

He took the towel out from between his legs. He had obviously bled for a while during his sleep, but by now the blood was caked and dry on the towel. Old, unsolved, interior murders. He moved with care, showered for a long time but did not have the courage to turn the water cold. As he dressed, his body felt broken, as though he had fallen from a great distance.

He went downstairs and had breakfast among the tourists and traveling salesmen in the coffee shop. The factory taste of frozen orange juice. No Mediterranean outside the window, no daughter, no mistress across the table, no leer from the waitress. The coffee of his homeland was like dishwater. He made himself eat two pieces of toast for strength. No croissants, no brioches. Had he come to the wrong country?

He read *The New York Times*. The casualty count was down in Vietnam. The vice-president had made a provocative, alliterative speech. A plane had fallen. He was not the only one who traveled too much. A critic he had never heard of scolded a novelist he had never read. Teams that had not been created when he still went to baseball games had won and lost. A pitcher who was nearly as old as he still made a living throwing the knuckle ball. The men and women who had died the day before were people he had not known. Informed now, he faced the day.

He went from the world of air conditioning out into the climate of New York. He winced on the sidewalk. Remembering his secretary's warning, he was wary of muggers. If he announced, I have bled this night, would a boy scout find him a taxi? He had no quarter for the doorman, so he gave him a dollar bill. He remembered when doormen were grateful for dimes.

Getting into the taxi was like climbing a cliff. He gave the address on East Seventieth Street. The taxi driver was an old man with a greenish complexion who looked as though he were dying. From the permit on the back of the driver's seat, Craig saw that the man had a Russian name. Did the driver regret that he, or his father before him, had left Odessa?

The taxi inched, spurted, braked, missed other cars by inches on its way across town. Near death, the driver had nothing to lose. Forty-fourth Street, going East, was his Indianapolis. He was high in the year's standings for the Grand Prix. If he survived the season, his fortune would be made.

Bruce Thomas lived in a brownstone with newly painted window frames. There was a little plaque near the front door that announced that the house was protected by a private patrol service. Craig had been there several times before, to big parties. He remembered having enjoyed himself. He had wandered once into Bruce's study on the second floor. The shelves of the study had been laden with statues, plaques, scrolls, that Thomas had won for his movies.

Craig had won some statues, scrolls, and plaques himself, but he didn't know where they were now.

He rang the bell. Thomas opened the door himself, dressed in corduroy slacks and an open-necked polo shirt. He was a neat, graceful, slight man with a warm smile.

"Bruce," Craig said as he went into the hallway, "I think you'd better get me a doctor."

He sat down on a chair in the hall because he couldn't walk any farther.

· EIGHTEEN ·

HE was still alive after three days. He was in a bright room in a good hospital, and Bruce Thomas had found him a soft-voiced old doctor who was soothing and taciturn. The chief surgeon of the hospital, a cheerful round man, kept dropping in as though he just wanted to chat with Craig about the movies and the theatre, but Craig knew that he was watching him closely, looking for symptoms that would mean that an emergency operation might be necessary at any moment. When Craig asked him what the chances were after an operation like that, the surgeon said flatly, without hesitation, "Fifty-fifty." If Craig had had any relatives the doctor could talk to, the doctor would probably have told them instead of the patient, but the only people who had come to his room so far were Thomas and Belinda.

He was under light sedation and suffering from no real pain except for the bruised places on his arms where the needles had been placed for five transfusions and for the varying intravenous feedings of glucose and salt. For some reason the tubes kept clogging, and the needles kept falling out. The veins in his arms had become increasingly difficult to find, and finally the hospital expert, a lovely Scandinavian girl, had been called in to see what she could do. She had cleared the room, even shutting the door on his private day nurse, a tough old ex-captain in the Nursing Corps, a veteran of Korea. "I can't stand an audience," the expert had said. Talent, in a hospital as elsewhere, Craig saw, had its imperious prerogatives. The Scandinavian girl has pushed and prodded, shaking her neat blonde head, and then with one deft stroke had inserted the needle painlessly into a vein on the back of his right hand and adjusted the flow of solution to it. He never saw her again. He was sorry about that. She reminded him of the young Danish mother by the side of the pool in Antibes. Fifty-fifty, he marveled, and that's what a man thinks of.

The worst thing was the headaches that came after the transfusions. That was normal, he was told. Naturally, in a hospital, pain must seem normal to the people who work there.

Thomas had been perfect. He visited the room twice a day, not overdoing his concern. "There's a good chance," he said on the third day, "that you'll be out of here in less than two weeks, and then we can get to work." He had not wasted any time. He had secured an O.K. from United Artists, and they were talking of a budget of a million and a half dollars for the picture. Thomas had already found a great old mansion in Sands Point where they could shoot on location. He took it for granted that Craig would be the co-producer. If he had heard the surgeon's fifty-fifty estimate, he gave no hint of it.

He was in the room on the third day when the door swung open and Murphy strode in. "What the hell is going on, Jesse?" Murphy asked loudly.

"What the hell are you doing here?" Craig said. "I thought you were in Rome."

"I'm not in Rome," Murphy said. "Hi, Bruce. Are you two guys fighting already?"

"Yes," Thomas said, smiling. "Art is long and ulcers fleeting."

Craig was too tired to inquire how Murphy had found out that he was in the hospital. But he was happy to see him there. Murphy would arrange everything. He himself could just drift into his doped and not unpleasant dreams in which night and day blended, pain and pleasure were impersonal abstractions. Knowing that all was now in safe hands, he could concentrate merely on dominating the rebellion of his blood.

"They told me I could only stay five minutes," Murphy said. "I just wanted to see if you were still alive. Do you want me to fly in my guy from Beverly Hills? He's supposed to be the best in the country."

Everything that Murphy touched was the best in the country. "No need, Murph," Craig said. "The men I have here are fine."

"Well, you just don't worry about anything but getting better," Murphy said. "By the time you get out of here, I'll have a contract ready for you to sign that'll have United Artists screaming in anguish. Come on, Bruce. We have things to discuss that are not for invalids' ears." Murphy patted Craig's shoulder roughly. "You mustn't scare your old friends like this," he said very gently. "Sonia sends her love. All right, Nurse, all right, I'm going." The ex-captain in the Nursing Corps was glowering blackly at him and looking dramatically at her watch.

The two men went out. The nurse fussed a little with a pillow. "Business," she said, "kills more men than bullets."

For a man who has begun his working life in the theatre, Craig thought, a hospital room is a fitting place to end it. It is like a stage. The hero is in the center with all the lights upon him. The doctor is the director, although he doubles by playing one of the parts. He watches mostly from the wings, preparing to intervene when necessary, whispering to the other actors that they can go on now, that they must enter smiling, that they are not to prolong their scenes unduly. The nurses, like stagehands, move the props around—hurry on with thermometers, trays, bedpans, syringes, instruments for the taking or infusion of blood.

The hero has a long part to play—the work is constructed around him, he never leaves the stage, he has a run-of-the-play contract. Ungratefully, he sometimes grumbles at his prominence, is quick to criticize the manner in which other actors play their scenes with him, would replace them or cut them if he could.

The first one he would have eliminated, if he could, was Belinda Ewen. By the fourth day in the hospital she had decided that he was going to recover and that his recovery would be speeded by forcing him to stop brooding, as she described it, and occupy himself with the business of everyday life. She reported that she had checked him out of the hotel and packed his things. His suitcases were now thriftily stored in the office. Mail and messages were to be forwarded. People had been notified. She had called the *Times*. When he protested weakly about this, she said, firm in her concept of orderly, civilized behavior, that friends and family and the public had a right to know. He refused to ask her what friends and family she had selected. The telephone in the office rang all day. He'd be surprised how many people were interested in him. With her efficiency it was likely that hundreds of well-wishers would soon be thronging through his room. He pleaded with the doctors for release, plotted escape.

In fact, by now he felt strong enough to see people. They had removed the needles from the battered veins, there were no more transfusions, he could sit up and take liquid nourishment. He had even shaved. His face in the mirror had shocked him. It had the same greenish pallor as the Russian taxi driver's. He resolved that until he left the hospital he would allow Miss Balissano, his military day nurse, who had offered to do so, to shave him.

The mail Belinda brought him included a bill from his wife's lawyer for five thousand dollars. On account. He had agreed to pay her lawyers in the first burst of generosity and relief when he had finally made the decision to get a divorce and realized that, with money, it was possible to obtain one.

A letter from his accountant reminded him that he had to make up his mind about what he wanted to do about the seventy thousand dollars that the Internal Revenue Service was demanding from him. They were becoming menacing, his lawyer wrote.

Belinda had found the copy of *The Three Horizons* in his hotel room and had read it. She was favorably impressed by it and brought over large casting books with the photographs of actors and actresses in Hollywood and New York for him to glance through and think about who might play which part. He fingered through the books languidly to please Belinda.

She had brought over his checkbook. There were bills to be paid. He had no Blue Cross or Health Insurance, and the hospital had asked her discreetly for an advance. She had made out a check for a thousand dollars. Obediently, he signed it. He signed checks for office rent, telephone and telegraph bills, the Diners' Club, the Air-Travel Card. Dead or alive, he must maintain his credit rating. He hoped Anne's psychology professor would never see his signature.

Now that he was back in business, Belinda said, she had brought over the scripts of two plays by prominent authors that had come into the office in the last week. She had read them and hadn't thought much of them, but the prominent authors would expect a personal note from him. She would bring her pad the next day, prepared to take dictation. He promised to read the plays by the prominent authors. She admired the flowers that the Murphys and the Thomases and Walt Klein had sent, all lavish displays from the most expensive florist on Fifth Avenue. She was shocked when he said, "They make me feel as though

I'm on my own bier. Send them down to the children's ward."

She warned him darkly about Miss Balissano. The woman was callous, she said, and at the same time maniacally overprotective. She practically had to fight her way with physical force to get into his room each time she came. Fanatical overprotectiveness was dangerous. It was negative thinking. He promised to indulge in no negative thinking, to consider replacing Miss Balissano.

Miss Balissano came in at this point, and Belinda said, "I see my time is up," her tone suggesting that she had been struck across the face with a weapon. She left, and for the first time since Craig had met Miss Balissano, he was glad to see her.

Miss Balissano took one look at the manuscripts and casting books piled on his bedside table and picked them up and put them on the floor out of sight. She had learned something in Korea.

He was lying in his bed with a thermometer in his mouth when Anne came in. It was a gray day, almost evening, and the room was dark. Anne opened the door tentatively, as though ready to flee at the first word from him. He waved a dumb greeting to her, indicating the tube in his mouth. She smiled uncertainly, came over to the bed, leaned over and gave him a little nervous peck on the forehead. He reached out his hand and held hers. "Oh Daddy," she said. She wept softly.

Miss Balissano came in, turned on the light, took the thermometer, made a notation on his chart. She always refused to tell him what his temperature was.

"This is my daughter, Miss Balissano," Craig said.

"We've met," Miss Balissano said grimly. But then she said everything grimly. She took no notice of the girl's tears. She fussed with his pillows, said, "Good night. Sleep well. Don't be long, miss." She marched out, the sound of guns over the horizon. The night nurse would be in soon. The night nurse was a Puerto Rican young man who was a student at City College. He sat in a corner of the room all night reading textbooks in the glow of a carefully shaded lamp. His only duty was to call the intern on the floor if he thought Craig was dying. So far, he had not called the intern.

"Oh, Daddy," Anne said, her voice trembling. "I hate seeing you like this."

He had to smile a little at the youthful egotism of her first words to him. I, I, I.

"It's not my fault, is it, Daddy?" she said.

"Of course not."

"If it's too much trouble to talk, don't talk."

"I can talk," he said irritably. He was irritated with his illness, not with Anne, but he could see that she thought his temper was directed at her.

"We came as soon as Ian got Mr. Thomas's cable," Anne said. "We were in London."

Craig wondered from whom Wadleigh had borrowed the money for the voyage. But he didn't ask the question. "It was good of you to come," was all he said.

"You're going to be all right, aren't you?" Anne asked anxiously. Her face was pale. Traveling didn't agree with her. He remembered all the times he had had to stop the car on trips when she was young and prone to carsickness.

"Certainly, I'm going to be all right," he said.

"I talked to Dr. Gibson yesterday, I came right to the hospital as soon as we got in, they said I should wait a day to see you, but Dr. Gibson wouldn't say yes or no when I asked him about you. 'Only time will tell,' he said. I hate doctors."

"He's very good," Craig said. He felt a great affection for Dr. Gibson, quiet, efficient, modest, lifesaving man. "He just doesn't like being asked to be a prophet."

"Well," she said childishly, "he might at least try to be a little bit encouraging."

"I guess he doesn't think that's his business," Craig said.

"You mustn't try to be too stoical," Anne said. "Ian says that that's what you are—stoical." She was already quoting her lover, Craig noted. "He says it's an unprofitable attitude in this day and age."

"Will you pour a glass of water for me please, darling," Craig said. He wanted no more quotations from the accumulated wisdom of Ian Wadleigh. He wasn't really thirsty, but Anne seemed embarrassed and uneasy with him, and asking for a small service from her, even one as minute as pouring water out of a thermos, might make a dent in the painful barrier between them. He saw that the "darling" had pleased her. He sipped a little from the glass she offered him.

"You're going to have more visitors," she said. "Mummy's arriving tomorrow and . . ."

"Oh, God," Craig said. "How does she know?"

"I called her," Anne said defensively. "She was terribly upset. You don't mind that I told her, do you?"

"No," he said, lying.

"It's only human," Anne said.

"I agree," Craig said impatiently, "I agree. It's only human."

"Gail is on her way, too," Anne said.

"You called her, too?"

"Yes. I only did what I thought was right, Daddy. You're not angry at me, are you?"

"No." Craig put the water tumbler down and lay back resignedly, closing his eyes, to show Anne that he was tired and wished to be alone.

"I have something to apologize to you about," Anne said. "In my letter I was too much in a hurry to say anything about your script. I don't know whether it means anything to you or not, but I love it, and I should have told you . . ."

"You had other things on your mind," he said.

"I suppose you have a right to be sarcastic with me," Anne said humbly. "But, anyway, I love it. So does Ian. He wanted me to tell you."

"Good."

"He's talked to Mr. Thomas already. He and Mr. Thomas agree on a lot of things about the script. They're both wildly hopeful."

"Good," Craig said again.

"Of course, Mr. Thomas doesn't know anything about me yet," she said. She hesitated. "Ian is afraid that because of me you're going to be against him. About working on the script, I mean." She waited for Craig to speak, but he kept silent. "I told Ian you're too big a man to stand in his way just because . . ." She trailed off.

"I'm not quite as big a man as I was last week," Craig said.

"Ian needs the job badly," Anne said. "It'll get him off the ground, he says. He's been having such a bad time . . . You're not going to say no, are you, Daddy?" She was imploring now.

"No," he said, "I'm not going to say no."

"I knew it," she said. She was his happy little daughter now, being promised a treat, oblivious of the world of hospitals, pain, blood. "Ian's downstairs," she said. "He'd love to come up and say hello. He's terribly worried about you. Can I tell him to come up? Just for a minute?"

"Tell Ian to go fuck himself," Craig said.

Anne took in her breath sharply. It was the first time, as far as he could remember, that he had ever said the word in front of her. "Oh, Daddy," she said. "How can you be so unjust!" She turned and ran out of the room.

She's a big girl now, Craig thought as he sank deeper into the pillows. She knows all the words. I'm going to move into a public ward. Where they don't allow visitors.

They operated on him that night. There was no enormous hemorrhage like the night in the hotel, but the tests had shown that he had begun to bleed again, a slow, steady seeping away in his gut whose source they couldn't locate, dangerous and life-sapping.

Before he was given the preoperative shot of morphine, while they were shaving his chest and abdomen, he realized that he wasn't afraid. Fifty-fifty, the doctor had said. A man couldn't ask for fairer odds.

Faces came and went, briefly, silently, seen obscurely, through haze—Murphy, Thomas, Dr. Gibson, noncommittal, no warnings or encouragement, his wife, his daughter Marcia, grotesquely plump and weeping, Gail McKinnon, sea-fresh, Constance, almost unrecognizably stern, Edward Brenner . . . But Edward Brenner was dead. Were they all a dream? He spoke only once. "Marcia," he said, "you're a good size."

He was in great pain, but he kept from groaning. The African with tribal scars in first class would not understand. The White Man's burden. He was stoical and waited for the morphine every four hours without asking for more. Who had said that stoicism was an unprofitable attitude? No friend of his.

The stagehands, in white, brought on the props— the syringes, the blood. The lighting stage center was rearranged. There was the sound of surf in his ears. He woke. He slept. The faces came and went, with their several claims. Where was Ian Wadleigh, that loose, deceitful man? Belinda Ewen, in electric blue? What checks did she have for him to sign?

Other doctors. The best man in the country. Soft medical voices, whisperings offstage. The Scandinavian blonde with the expert hands did not reappear. Alas.

How many days ago had he left Meyrague? What drink had he ordered on the *terrasse* of the little restaurant overlooking the harbor of Cassis? What had that girl said about her mother?

He could sit up in bed and even eat a little, but the fever persisted. In the morning it was around a hundred and one, in the evening it went up to one hundred and three and a half. The plastic bag hung on a stand above his head dripping antibiotics into his veins day and night. Either the fever or the antibiotics, or both, kept him in a heavy-lidded daze, and he began to lose track of time and not remember how long he had been there. Nobody mentioned it, not he nor any of the doctors, but he knew that they were afraid that he had picked up one of those new hospital-bred wild strains of bacteria for which no treatment had yet been found.

Dr. Gibson had forbidden any visitors, and he was grateful for that. Dr. Gibson had told him that when he had been free of fever for three whole days, he would be discharged. In the meanwhile, he sleepily watched the television set that had been wheeled into his room and placed at the foot of his bed. Mostly, he just watched the baseball games. It gave him pleasure to watch young men running swiftly across green grass in the sunshine, clearly winning and distinctly losing. He remembered having read about the condemned murderer in Massachusetts who also had watched the baseball games on television in his cell and whose only regret was that he would never know whether or not the Dodgers had won the pennant.

He wondered if he would know who won the pennant this year.

Finally, Murphy convinced Dr. Gibson that he had to see Craig. Craig had had two good days. The fever had gone down to ninety-nine in the morning and one hundred and two at night. Miss Balissano still refused to tell him what his temperature was, but Dr. Gibson was more lenient.

Murphy's face when he saw Craig told him as accurately as any mirror how bad it was. He hadn't looked in a mirror since the operation.

"I had to see you, Jess," Murphy said. "I have to leave for the Coast tomorrow. Things're piling up, and I just have to be there."

"Sure, Murph," Craig said. His voice sounded thin and old in his ears.

"Three weeks in New York is all I can manage," Murphy said.

"Is that how long I've been here?" Craig asked.

Murphy looked at him queerly. "Yes," he said.

"A long time," Craig said.

"Yes. And the doctors won't give me an estimate about when you'll get out."

"They don't know."

"Gibson tells me you won't be able to work—at anything—for at least six months even if you get out tomorrow."

"I know," Craig said. "He told me."

"Thomas can't wait," Murphy said. "He's got to start shooting in a month if he wants to do it this year. For the weather."

"For the weather," Craig nodded.

"He and Wadleigh have been working eighteen hours a day. Thomas says Wadleigh is really panning out. He says you'll be crazy about the final script."

"I'm sure."

"Do you want me to tell you about who they've got to play it?"

"Not really, Murph."

Again, Murphy looked at him queerly. "Don't worry about the money," he said. "You've got a big chunk up front and five per cent of the profits."

"Tell me some other time," Craig said.

"Thomas has been a real gent about everything."

"I'm sure." Craig closed his eyes. Murphy seemed to be far away, at the other end of a long hall, and it disturbed him.

"You're tired," Murphy said. "I won't bother you

anymore. Just call me if you need anything."

"I'll do just that." Craig didn't open his eyes.

"Sonia sends her love."

"Thanks Murph."

"Take it easy, kid." Murphy went softly out of the room as Miss Balissano came in.

"Turn on the television, please," Craig said.

When he heard the noise of the crowd, Craig opened his eyes. It was sunny in St. Louis.

On the day that his temperature was normal for the first time, Dr. Gibson allowed his wife to visit him. As far as he knew, Dr. Gibson hadn't been told that they were in the process of getting a divorce, so it was natural for him to let her in. Dr. Gibson hadn't warned Craig that his wife was coming to see him. He probably thought it would be a salutary surprise.

Penelope was smiling tremulously as she came into the room. She had had her hair done, and it hung youthfully down to her shoulders. She was wearing a navy blue dress. He had once said that it was the color he liked best on her. A long time ago.

"Hello, Jess," she said. Her voice was soft, shaky, her face drawn. The last time they had met it had been in a lawyer's office. He couldn't remember how many months ago. She bent over and kissed his cheek. The ten thousandth kiss.

"Hello, Penny," he said. "How's the web going?" It was an old joke between them.

"What?" she asked, frowning. "What web?"

"Never mind," he said. She had forgotten.

"How do you feel?"

"Fine," he said. "Can't you tell?" He thought about her lawyers to keep from thinking about her.

He saw her lips set, then soften. He knew she was trying to restrain her anger. "Dr. Gibson says there are encouraging signs. Very encouraging."

"I'm very encouraged," he said.

"You don't change, do you?" she said. Anger had

momentarily gotten the better of her.

"I'm a faithful man," he said. He was fighting against her pity. What she probably would call her love. What might very possibly be her love.

"Dr. Gibson says you will have to rest for a long time after you get out of here," she said. "You'll need someone to look after you. Do you want to come home?"

He thought about the broad brick house on the quiet, tree-lined New York street, the small back garden, now a dusty green, the desk in his study, his books on the shelves. They had agreed to divide the furniture, but they had not yet done so. There was no place he could put it. He couldn't carry his desk from hotel room to hotel room. She waited for his reply, but he said nothing. "Do you want to call off the divorce?" she said. "I do."

"I'll think about it." He wasn't strong enough to struggle with her now.

"What made you do it?" she asked. "Out of a blue sky. Writing me that awful letter asking for a divorce. After all, we were getting along. You were free to come and go. For months at a time I didn't even know whether you were in the country or not. I never asked you about your other—whatever they were. Maybe we weren't love's sweet young dream, but we were getting along."

"Getting along," he said. "We hadn't slept with each other for five years."

"And whose idea was that?" Her voice grew harsher.

"Yours," he said. She had a convenient memory, and he waited for her to deny it and believe her own denial. Surprising him, she said, "What did you expect? You'd been making it plain for years that I bored you. You'd invite anybody in the world to keep from having a meal alone with me."

"Including Bertie Folsom."

She flushed. "Including Bertie Folsom. I suppose

that slut daughter of yours told you about Geneva."

"She did."

"At least he paid attention to me."

"Bully for him," he said. "Bully for you."

"There's another victim you can add to your score," she said, all holds barred now, the hospital room, the plastic bag dripping ineffectual remedies into his vein from its chromium stand, all ignored. "Driving her into that drunkard's arms."

"He's stopped drinking." Too late, he realized how idiotic it sounded.

"He hasn't stopped doing anything else," she said. "Married three times and looking around for more. I'll never talk to that girl again. And your other daughter. Poor Marcia. Flying here all the way from Arizona to comfort her father. And what did you have to say to her? The one sentence that crossed your lips. 'Marcia, you're a good size.' She cried for days. You know what she said? She said, 'Even when he's bleeding to death, he makes fun of me. He hates me.' I tried to get her to come up here with me, and she wouldn't do it."

"I'll make it up to her," he said wearily. "Sometime. I don't hate her."

"You hate *me*."

"I don't hate anybody."

"Even now you have to humiliate me." Coldly, he noticed the old false melodramatic tone that came into her voice when she recounted her trials. "Right now that woman is shamelessly parading herself downstairs, waiting to come up here as soon as you've thrown me out."

"I don't know any 'that woman,' " he said.

"That whore from Paris. You know her all right. And so do I." Penelope paced around the room, obviously trying to regain control of herself. He lay with his eyes closed, his head back on the pillow. "I didn't come up here to argue, Jesse," Penelope said, switching to her reasonable voice. "I came up here to tell you you are welcome to come home. More than welcome."

"I told you I'd think about it," he said.

"Just for my own satisfaction," she said, "I'd like to know once and for all why you thought you had to have a divorce."

Well, he thought, she's asking for it. He opened his eyes so that he could see her reactions. "I met Alice Paine in New York one day," he said.

"What's Alice Paine got to do with it?"

"She told me a peculiar story. Every October fifth she gets a dozen roses. Without a card. Anonymously." He could tell by the sudden rigidity of her face, her shoulders, that she knew what he was talking about. "Any woman," he said, "who has anything to do with a dozen roses on October fifth, year in, year out, is not ever going to get me—alive or dead." He lay back and closed his eyes once more. She had asked for it, and he had given it to her, and he felt a great relief that he had finally gotten it out.

"Good-by, Jesse," she whispered.

"Good-by," he said.

He heard the door closing softly behind her. Then, for the first time, he wept. Not from anger or loss but because he had lived more than twenty years with a woman and had had two children with her and he didn't feel anything when he said good-by, not even rage.

After a while he remembered that Penelope had said that Constance was in the building. "There's a lady downstairs waiting to see me," he said to Miss Balissano. "Will you ask her to come up, please? And let me have the comb and brush and a mirror."

He brushed back his hair. It had grown very long in the three weeks. Vigorous, his hair had rejected his illness. There was no more gray in it than before. His eyes looked enormous and overbright in his thin face. Losing weight had made his face look much younger. He doubted that Constance would appreciate this new simulation of youth.

But when the door opened, it was Belinda who came in. He hid his disappointment. "Belinda," he said heartily, "I *am* glad to see you."

She kissed his cheek. She looked as though she had been crying, the small sharp face made more womanly by her sorrow. She was still in electric blue. It was her costume for deathbeds.

"They're monsters in this hospital," she said. Her voice was softer, too. My illness has improved her, he thought. "I've been here every day this week," she said, "and they wouldn't let me see you."

"I'm sorry about that," he lied.

"I've kept track, though," she said. "I've talked to Mr. Murphy, too. You're not going to work on the picture."

"I'm afraid not."

She pulled on her hands. They were small and harsh. Twenty-three years at the typewriter. Her nails were painted blood-red. She had an unerring eye for the wrong colors. She went to the window, pulled the shade down a little. "Jesse," she said, "I want to quit.'

"I don't believe you."

"Believe me," she said.

"Have you got another job?"

"Of course not." She turned away from the window, her face hurt.

"Then why quit?"

"You're not going to be able to work when you get out of here," she said.

"For a while."

"For a long while. Jesse, let's not kid ourselves. You don't need me or that office. You should have closed the office five years ago. You kept it open just for me."

"That's nonsense," he said, trying to sound sharp. She knew he was lying, but the lie was necessary.

"I've just been going through the motions," she

said quietly. "Thank you and enough. Anyway, I have to get out of New York. I can't stand it anymore. It's a madhouse. Two of my friends have been mugged just this month. In broad daylight. My nephew was stabbed in the chest for a pack of cigarettes, and he nearly died. I don't dare leave my apartment at night. I haven't seen a movie or even a play in a year. I have four different locks on my door. Every time I hear the elevator doors open on my floor, I tremble. Jesse, if they want this city so much, let them have it."

"Where are you going to go?" he asked gently.

"My mother still has our house in Newtown," she said. "She's ailing, and I can help her. And it's a beautiful quiet little town, and you can walk in the streets there."

"Maybe I'll move there, too," he said, only half-joking.

"You could do worse," she said.

"What are you going to do for money?" Finally, you always had to come down to this question.

"I don't need much," she said. "And I've managed to save quite a bit. Thanks to you, Jesse. You're a marvelously generous man, and I want to let you know that I know it."

"You worked."

"I loved working for you. I was lucky. It was better than any marriage I've seen around."

Craig laughed. "That doesn't say very much, does it?"

"It says a lot to me," she said. "The lease for the office is up for renewal this month. Shall I tell them we're not signing?" She waited for his response, pulling at the blood-red fingernails.

"We've had a nice long run, Belinda," he said softly, "haven't we?"

"Yes, we have," she said. "A nice long run."

"Tell them we're not renewing," he said.

"They won't be surprised," she said.

"Belinda," he said, "come here and give me a kiss."

She kissed him, decorously, on the cheek. He couldn't embrace her because of the tube in his arm. "Belinda," he said as she stood up straight again, "who's going to write out the checks for me to sign now?"

"You can write them out yourself," she said. "You're a big, grown man. Just don't write out too many."

"I'll try not to," he said.

"If I stay here one more minute," she said, "I'm going to bawl." She fled from the room.

He lay back in the bed staring at the ceiling. There goes twenty-three years, he thought. Add to that the twenty-one years of his wife. The sentences having been served concurrently.

Not a bad day's work.

He was asleep when Constance came into the room. He dreamt that a woman whom he couldn't quite identify was kissing him. When he opened his eyes, he saw Constance standing near him staring gravely down at him.

"Hello," he said.

"If you want to sleep," she said, "I'll just sit here and watch you."

"I don't want to sleep." She was on his good side, the one without the tube, so he could stretch out his hand and take hers. Her hand was cool and firm. She smiled down at him. "You really ought to leave your hair long," she said. "It's very becoming."

"Another week," he said, "and I'll be able to play at the next Woodstock Festival." He would have to try to maintain the light tone. Constance wasn't his wife or Belinda Ewen. They had to avoid hurting each other or reminding each other of different moments they had spent together.

She drew up a chair and sat next to the bed. She was wearing a black dress. It didn't look funereal on her. She looked serene and beautiful, the hair brushed back from her broad, fine forehead.

"Spell Meyrague," he said. Then he was sorry he had said it. It had just come out automatically.

But she laughed, and it was all right. "Obviously you're getting better."

"Rapidly," he said.

"Rapidly. I was afraid I wasn't going to get the chance to see you. I have to go back to Paris tomorrow," she said.

"Oh."

There was silence for a moment. "What are you going to do when you get out of here?" she asked.

"I have to take it easy for a while," he said.

"I know. It's too bad about the picture."

"Not so bad. It's served its purpose. Or most of its purpose."

"Are you coming back to Paris?"

"When are you leaving Paris?" he asked.

"I'm supposed to leave in two weeks."

"I guess I'm not coming back to Paris."

She was silent for a little bit. "They've rented a house for me in San Francisco," she said. "You can see the bay, they tell me. There's a big room at the top of the house where a man could work. You wouldn't hear the kids yelling. Or hardly."

He smiled.

"Does that sound like a bribe?" She answered herself. "I suppose it does." She laughed, then became serious. "Have you thought about what you're going to do after you get out of here, where you're going to go?"

"Not really."

"Not San Francisco?"

"I think I'm a little old for San Francisco," he said gently. He knew it really wasn't the city he was thinking of, and she knew it, too. "But I'll visit."

"I'll be there," she said. "For a while, anyway." The warning was clear, but there was nothing to do about it. "Sweep the town by storm," he said.

"I'll try to take your advice." She was grave again. "It's too bad," she said. "Our times didn't really coincide. Anyway, when you run out of hotel rooms, think of Constance." She reached out and stroked his forehead. Her touch was pleasant, but there were no sexual stirrings in him. The ailing body devoted all its time to its ailment. Illness was the supreme egotism.

"I've been doing something that I abhor these last few days," she said, taking her hand away. "I've been adding up love. Who loves whom the most. My accounts came out cock-eyed. I love you more than you love me. That's the first time it ever happened to me. Well, I suppose it had to happen once."

"I don't know . . ." he began.

"I know," she said harshly. "I know."

"I haven't added up any accounts," he said.

"You don't have to," she said. "Oh, that reminds me—I met your pretty young friend from Cannes. Dr. Gibson introduced us one night. We became very chummy. We had lunch together several times. She's very bright. And very tough. Enviably tough."

"I don't know her that well," he said. Surprisingly, it was the truth. He didn't know whether Gail was tough or not.

"She knew all about me, of course."

"Not from me," he said.

"No, I'm sure not," Constance said, smiling. "She's going back to London, did you know?"

"No, I haven't seen her."

"Poor Jesse," Constance said ironically, "all the working ladies are running out on him. In the future I suggest you stick to one town and pick on women of leisure."

"I don't like women of leisure," he said.

"Neither do I," Constance said. "Here—" She rummaged in her bag and brought out a slip of paper. He recognized Gail's handwriting. "I promised her I'd give you her telephone number if I saw you before she did. She's in Philadelphia, staying with her father to save money. She's flat broke, she told me."

He took the slip of paper. There was an address, a telephone number. No message. He put the slip of paper on the bedside table.

Constance stood up. "Your nurse told me not to tire you," she said.

"Will I see you again?"

"Not in New York," she said. She began pulling on her gloves. "You can't keep gloves clean more than an hour in this city." She brushed the back of one glove with an annoyed gesture. "I won't pretend I enjoyed New York this trip. A kiss for good-by." She leaned over and kissed him on the mouth. "You're not going to die, darling, are you?" she whispered.

"No," he said. "I don't think so."

"I couldn't bear it if you did," she said. Then stood erect and smiled. "I'll send you a card from the Golden Gate," she said, and was gone.

She was the best girl he had ever known, and she was gone.

He didn't call the Philadelphia number until the next morning. A man who answered the phone and who said he was Miss McKinnon's father asked him who was calling. When Craig gave him his name, Mr. McKinnon's voice grew icy, and he seemed to be delighted to be able to tell Craig that Miss McKinnon had left the day before for London.

Fair enough, Craig thought. He himself would have been no more polite with Ian Wadleigh.

A week later they let him out of the hospital. His temperature had been normal for three days in a row. The evening before he was discharged Dr. Gibson had a long talk with him. Or what passed for a long talk with Dr. Gibson. "You're a lucky man, Mr. Craig," Dr. Gibson had said. He sat there, a spare,

ascetic old man who did a half-hour of exercise every
morning and swallowed ten yeast tablets a day, laying down the law. "A lot of people wouldn't have
pulled through the way you did. Now, you've got to
be careful. Very, very careful. Stick to the diet. And
no alcohol. Not even a sip of wine for a year. Maybe forever." Dr. Gibson was a fanatic teetotaler, and
Craig thought he detected a steely pleasure in Gibson's voice as he said this. "And forget about working
for six months. And you seem to be a man who leads
a complicated life—most complicated, I would say."
It was the first time that Dr. Gibson had suggested
that he had drawn any conclusions from the list of
people who had . come to visit his patient. "If I
were forced to make one single diagnosis of what produced your attack, Mr. Craig," the doctor said, "I
would hazard the guess that it was not a functional
accident or malformation, or some hereditary weakness. You understand what I mean, I'm sure, Mr.
Craig."

"I do."

"Uncomplicate yourself, Mr. Craig," Dr. Gibson
said. "Uncomplicate yourself. And eat yeast."

Eating yeast, Craig thought, as Dr. Gibson stalked
out, eating yeast would be easy.

He shook hands with Miss Balissano at the hospital door and stepped out into the street. He had told
Miss Balissano that he would have somebody pick
up his things. He walked out into the sunshine slowly, blinking, his clothes hanging loose around his
body. It was a clear, warm day. He hadn't let anyone,
not even Belinda, know that today was to be the day.
Superstition. Even as he went out the door, he was
afraid that Miss Balissano would come running after
him and say that a terrible mistake had been made
and that he was to be rushed back into bed and the
tube stuck once more into his arm.

But nobody came after him. He walked aimlessly

on the sunny side of the street. The people he passed seemed beautiful. The girls were lithe and walked with their heads up, half-smiling as though they were remembering innocent but intense pleasures of the night before. The young men, bearded and unbearded, walked with a purpose, looking everyone in the eye. The little children were clean and laughing, dressed in anemone colors, and darted past him with immortal energy. The old men were neat and sprightly, philosophic about death in the sunshine.

He had made no hotel reservation. He was alone, alive, walking, each step stronger than the one before it, alone, with no address, drifting down a street in his native city, and no one in the whole world knew where he was; no friend, enemy, lover, daughter, business associate, lawyer, banker, certified public accountant, knew where he was going, had any claims on him, could reach him or touch him. For this moment, at least, he had made a space for himself.

He passed a shop in which typewriters were on display. He stopped and examined the window. The machines were clean, intricate, useful. He went into the shop. A soft-spoken clerk showed him various models. He thought of his friend the matador making a selection of swords in the shop in Madrid. He told the clerk he would be back and leave his order.

He left the shop, the future, comfortable clatter of the machine he would eventually buy tapping in his ear.

He found himself on Third Avenue. He was in front of a saloon he had once frequented. He looked at his watch. Eleven-thirty. Time for a drink. He went in. The saloon was almost empty. Two men talking at the other end of the bar. Male voices.

The bartender came up. The bartender was powerful, pink and fat in his apron, and had an old fighter's broken nose, scarred eyebrows. The bartender was beautiful. "A Scotch and soda," Craig said. He watched with great interest as the bartender poured the whisky into a jigger, splashed it over ice, opened a bottle of soda. He poured the soda himself, carefully, enjoying the cold feel of the bottle in his hand. He stood looking thoughtfully at his drink for a full minute. Then he drank, with truant joy.

From the other end of the bar a man's voice said loudly, "Then I told her—you know what I told her—'Fuck off!' I told her."

Craig smiled. Still alive, he took another sip of his drink. He didn't remember when a drink had ever tasted as good.

More great reading from

IRWIN SHAW

author of *Rich Man, Poor Man*

Dell Bestsellers

- ☐ **THE PROMISE** a novel by Danielle Steel based on a screenplay by Garry Michael White $1.95 (17079-6)
- ☐ **PUNISH THE SINNERS** by John Saul $1.95 (17084-2)
- ☐ **FLAMES OF DESIRE** by Vanessa Royall $1.95 (14637-2)
- ☐ **THE HOUSE OF CHRISTINA** by Ben Haas $2.25 (13793-4)
- ☐ **CONVOY** by B.W.L. Norton $1.95 (11298-2)
- ☐ **F.I.S.T.** by Joe Eszterhas $2.25 (12650-9)
- ☐ **HIDDEN FIRES** by Janette Radcliffe $1.95 (10657-5)
- ☐ **SARGASSO** by Edwin Corley $1.95 (17575-5)
- ☐ **CLOSE ENCOUNTERS OF THE THIRD KIND** by Steven Spielberg $1.95 (11433-0)
- ☐ **THE TURNING** by Justin Scott $1.95 (17472-4)
- ☐ **NO RIVER SO WIDE** by Pierre Danton $1.95 (10215-4)
- ☐ **ROOTS** by Alex Haley $2.75 (17464-3)
- ☐ **THE CHOIRBOYS** by Joseph Wambaugh $2.25 (11188-9)
- ☐ **CLOSING TIME** by Lacey Fosburgh $1.95 (11302-4)
- ☐ **THIN AIR** by George E. Simpson and Neal R. Burger $1.95 (18709-5)
- ☐ **PROUD BLOOD** by Joy Carroll $1.95 (11562-0)
- ☐ **NOW AND FOREVER** by Danielle Steel $1.95 (11743-7)
- ☐ **A PLACE TO COME TO** by Robert Penn Warren $2.25 (15999-7)
- ☐ **STAR FIRE** by Ingo Swann $1.95 (18219-0)

At your local bookstore or use this handy coupon for ordering:

Dell **DELL BOOKS**
P.O. BOX 1000, PINEBROOK, N.J. 07058

Please send me the books I have checked above. I am enclosing $_____
(please add 35¢ per copy to cover postage and handling). Send check or money
order—no cash or C.O.D.'s. Please allow up to 8 weeks for shipment.

Mr/Mrs/Miss_____

Address_____

City_____ State/Zip_____

REMEMBER IT DOESN'T GROW ON TREES

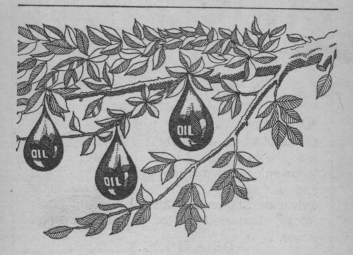

ENERGY CONSERVATION -
IT'S YOUR CHANCE TO SAVE, AMERICA

Department of Energy, Washington, D.C.

A PUBLIC SERVICE MESSAGE FROM DELL PUBLISHING CO., INC.